# MANHATTAN ROULETTE

## A NOVEL
## BY
## WALT CODY

*To Brandon /*
*Hope you find this a*
*good read.*
*Best wishes,*
*Walt Cody*

**Cheshire House Books**
**New York**

Design and production: Bernard Chase

ISBN: 978-09675073-92

Library of Congress Catalog Card Number
2015949788

*My mama done tol' me*
*When I was in knee pants*
*My mama done tol' me,*
*Son.*
*A woman'll sweet talk*
*And give you the Big Eye*
*But when the sweet-talkin's*
  *done*
*A woman's a two-face*
*A worrisome thing*
*Who'll leave you to sing*
*The Blues...*
*In the night.*

*My mama done tol' me*
*When I was in pigtails*
*My mama done tol' me,*
*Hon.*
*A man's gonna sweet talk*
*And give you the Big Eye*
*But when the sweet-talkin's*
  *done*
*A man is a two-face*
*A worrisome thing*
*Who'll leave you to sing*
*The Blues...*
*In the night.*

"Blues in the Night"
Johnny Mercer, Harold Arlen,© 1941

*With thanks to
Audrey Silk and Adam Wright of the N.Y.P.D.
for their technical advice
and to Henry Morrison
for his unwavering faith*

1

It was 4:30 on December 31st and Guy was exhausted. He clicked the scissors he held in his hand and
drank some coffee from a china cup embossed with the
single initial G. He put down the cup, grabbed himself a handful of crystalized ginger and, clicking the
scissors, continued to pace. He paced to the windowed
wall in his office and peered through the back of a one-
way mirror and into the oval waiting room beyond—
a room designed to look like an indoor gazebo, with
its white wicker tables and its white wicker chairs and
the green-and-white trellis paper on the wall and the
actual ferns and the one-two-three-four-five—sweet
Jesus, *five! Five* women still waiting to be done. Five
more heads to be magically transformed into Crown-
ing Glories in time for the boredom of New Year's Eve.
*Depressing* boredom. Who in the hell ever liked New
Year's Eve? It was worse than a birthday. It *was* a birthday. Everybody turning an entire year older on exactly
the same lousy day.

Guy shook his head now and looked at the women,
a typical group of G clientele. He loved them, hated
them, pitied them, envied them, but most of all, Guy
Laval understood them, knew what was going on in their
minds. Jesus, who knew better than he what it was like
to love unrequited, to wait by the phone for a man who
won't call, when all you want to do is to hold him again;
hold him; shake him; make him respond. Respond and
*commit.* He sipped some more coffee and clicked his
scissors. He could feel the anger rise in him now. He

5

would not think. Tonight he would absolutely not think of Him. It was too depressing, too outrageous, too disgusting, too unfair. Clicking his scissors, he walked through the door.

In the waiting room, he smiled at one of the women, beckoned with his finger, and she tilted her head. Said, "Wish me luck," to the rest of the group and, rising, followed him in through the arch, into the hum of the Main Salon, with its celadon walls and matching chairs and clicking scissors and glossy heads.

He watched her now as she sat in the chair, meeting his eyes in the light-rimmed mirror. He knew all about her Recent Troubles, but today she was wearing a confident calm. He ran his hands through her shiny hair. So much like His hair. Thick; straight. He caught a lustrous clump in his fingers and, thinking the things he'd vowed not to think, he looked at her said, "So what shall we do?"

And she looked at him slowly and said: "Whack it off."

## 2

*Friday, January 23rd:*

"Well hey there, Gorgeous. What'll it be?"

"Um. I don't know. A Scotch on the rocks?"

"A general Scotch or a particular Scotch?"

"I really don't care. Oh wait a second.— How much is Scotch around here?"

"Depends on what Scotch. A good single malt'll go fourteen to twenty. The usual stuff only sets you back eight."

"Okay. Then I think I'll have an eight on the rocks."

"Coming up.... Is it starting to snow now or what?"

"A little. But it's just plain freezing out there."

"Well, this'll warm you up."

"That's some giant drink."

"I gave you a double. Second half's on the house."

"Well, thanks. I think."

"De nada. I figure it'll keep you here a while. Which'll give me enough time to put a move on you."

"Aw. Gee. I bet you say that to *all* the girls."

"Nope. Only the gorgeous ones."

"Right. You say *that* to all the girls too."

"Okay, okay. Are you new to the nabe? What I mean is, I haven't seen you here before."

"I don't live here, is why. Not that I'd be hanging out in bars if I did, but I'm in for the weekend for my brother's graduation and I'm staying with a friend. And the thing is, I seem to have forgotten her key. I mean I left it in the house and I've been trying to reach her, but her cell doesn't answer. And it's freezing out there so I figured I could wait it out here and have a drink."

"And keep calling her?"

"Yeah. I *think* I know where she's gonna be around eight, but if she's not and if she stays with her boyfriend overnight... I don't know. I don't know. I can't afford a hotel room..."

"Well what about your brother? I mean, can't he help?"

"My brother's in New Jersey."

"What college?"

"No college. Police Academy. Tomorrow afternoon he's officially a cop. My father's one too."

"Well... that's interesting. And what about you?"

"You mean am I a cop?"

7

"No. I was roundabout asking what you do. Model? Actress?"

"Teacher."

"No way! You mean all that beauty wasted on the young?"

"And what about you? All that palaver wasted on the drunk?"

"Hah! You're funny. In fact, I'm an actor."

"Of course you're an actor."

"No really. I am. Ever watch CSI? I did five major episodes. That was last year. Except, hey, in between stuff, I have to pay the rent—. Excuse me. I gotta get some beers for these guys....Sorry. Didn't know it'd take me so long. That tall guy— the baldie? He's a top level agent. So listen. I was thinking. If you can't find your friend and you can't reach your brother and you're really in a jam, right here's my address. I get off here at three. Come back, meet me there, or whatever you want to do. You can stay in my living room. Sleep on the couch."

"Uh-huh. On the couch."

"Well of course you'd have your choice among sleeping accommodations..."

"You know? That's pretty nice. I mean, taking in a stranger. Only, hey.— How do you know I'm not an axe-murderer?"

"Well....How do you know that *I'm* not?"

"I guess you've got a point. Anyway, it's practically eight—"

"You gonna go?"

"I want to try to find my friend."

"Yeah. Well. Right. See you later, though. I hope."

"Yeah. Well. Maybe you'll be lucky. Who knows?"

## 3

*Saturday, January 24th:*

Right in the middle of Brymmer's nightmare, somebody somewhere started to scream. He wondered who it was and exactly where it was, and exactly what Whoever was expecting him to do because he'd have to do something. A cop siren wailed. It was somewhere in his overcoat or somewhere in his head ... or...

He swam into consciousness, blinked and then moaned. The cell phone— where the hell was it?—gave up. The cacophanous atmosphere clicked into view. The walls shrieked in salmon. The rug hollered "Blue!" He shuttered his eyes again and vaguely concluded he'd awakened in hell. His headache pounded; his muscles ached. He lifted his head now, slowly, with care, like a busted egg, and tried to remember what happened last night. Must have been one hell of a night. The other side of the bed had a dent; lipstick on the pillow; a blondish hair. He wondered who she'd been and how much she'd cost, and then wondered idly if he'd had a good time.

Not that it mattered.

He fumbled a cigarette out of a pack, lit it, and looked at the writing on the wall. "No...Smoking," it said on the wall. A card on the night table told him he'd been sleeping at the "Kern's Motor Inn. 11th Avenue." West Forty-Third. The last thing he clearly remembered was the Village. Squinting, he tried to remember the blonde, couldn't, shrugged, knuckled his jaw and limped naked to the vinyl bureau where he glanced at his cell phone (the call was from Ross) and then picked up his wallet (a hundred still left) and then glanced at his wristwatch which told him it was going on eleven after noon.

"Hell of a night." He said it out loud in a voice he'd borrowed from a rubber duck; heard it, laughed, coughed up some junk, and then peered at the mirror. Jesus Christ! Whatever it was, he decided quickly, he'd much rather meet it in a mirror than an alley, but Jesus Christ. He fingered the scars. Stigmata that spread from his cheekbone to his jaw and resembled nothing less than a freaking topographical map of California—its valleys and mountaintops perfectly described. He grinned at the mirror and winked at himself.

Sleeping Beauty was now awake.

In the icy bathroom, he turned on the shower and stood underneath it, soaping himself with a tiny pinkish bar of Camay, feeling the hangover starting to lift. Turning his chin up, he just let the water drum on his head. He soaped his head.

The telephone rang. This time, the actual Motor Inn phone. "Wrong number!" he hollered through the steam. Had to be. Nobody'd know he was here. Even *he* hadn't known. But the rings didn't quit.

15...16...17 rings. Cursing, he bolted and dripped to the phone.

"Brymmer?"

He sat on the bed; wet. "*Ross*? How the hell did you know where I am?"

"I didn't. I called every fleabag in town."

"Wrong."

"Right."

"So how did you know?"

"I know cause I'm the best fuckin cop in the city. I know where you can still buy a twenty-ounce Coke. I know six, seven places you can smoke in New York. And I knew where you were because Dubisky told me."

"Dubisky?"

"Yeah. You were with him last night."

Brymmer squinted at the hair on his bed. "Is Dubisky a blonde?"

"You and Dubisky picked up the blonde but she thought you were cuter so Dubisky went home."

"Goody for me."

"Well, I don't know. Dubisky said she looked like she might have the clap."

"I'm going now, Ross."

"Hey wait a second. Shit. I didn't just give you that build-up for nothing. I'm in need of a favor."

Brymmer rolled his eyes. "What's wrong with your car *now*?"

"Nothing," Ross said, "that a hernia wouldn't fix. It's buried under fifty-thousand acres of snow. Archeologists will find it in ten thousand years. A dented Beetle with a dead battery. They'll think it's a prehistoric bidet."

"Take the subway."

"Forget it. I gotta take the kid to the hospital, see? It's Saturday, Brymmer. You ever try Bellevue on a Saturday, Brymmer? I won't get back till a quarter of four. The streets are like ice. I will break my neck running to the subway. Eight blocks, Brymmer. It's minus twelve. That's sixty below on the Celsius scale. Kathy went to stay with her sister last night and she twisted her ankle and—"

"Right. I'll pick you up at a quarter of—"

"Fine. I'm hanging up now before you change your mind."

Brymmer let the phone drop back to the cradle and sat for a moment, shaking his head. Ross was in one of his manic moods and Brymmer had finally broken the code. Manic One meant things-could-be-worse. Manic Two meant that they were. Brymmer yawned and went to the window, scanning the day: Sky the color of dirty sidewalk; sidewalk the color of dirty snow. Down on the street at the corner of Eleventh, a bar girl was purchasing some chemical respite from a guy who had a street vendor's pass to sell socks. Brymmer padded back through the sick orange room and glanced at the hair and the lipstick on his bed. If this were a crime scene, he suddenly thought, his detectives would be jumping up and down at the find.

Brymmer shivered.

The room was cold.

Dressing hurriedly, he went home to shave.

---
**4**
---

The kitchen clock said 3:31 and Ross stood there, still in his coat, blowing on his red, scratchy hands. Brymmer was due at a quarter of four, which meant there was time to heat up the coffee. Only he didn't want any coffee. What he wanted— not needed, just wanted— was a Scotch. So screw it. Shit. It was cold outside. He'd been running around in the freezing cold. He'd eaten his spinach. He'd done his chores.

He found the bottle in a tidy cabinet over the stove, poured out a shot and toasted himself in a toaster so clean you could see yourself in it. Bogart's voice came in from the hall, over the sound of a gurgling chant. Billy was planted in front of the set. For the hell of it, Ross had lugged the kid in and left him watching *To Have and Have Not* which was sure to make mommy get boiling mad on account of *The Electric Company* was on and she wouldn't admit it was all the same thing.

Poor mommy.

Poor kid.

He finished the shot with a Bogart leer and watched his face distort in the toaster. He liked it that way. Slightly skewed. A truer reflection of the Basic Ross than the clean, almost innocent Golden Boy front that someone had mistakenly slapped on his head.

"Hey, is that you?" It was Kathy's voice, yelled from the echoing tomb of the tub. Ross poured a quick half-shotful of Cutty. "Would you bring me an aspirin? Up by the sink."

He found the aspirin. Up by the sink. Shoving it into his coat pocket, he left the kitchen, leaving his glass. Billy stared through the living room arch, the large, lolling, vacuous head propped against the padded back of his chair. Giving the kid a salacious wink, Ross said, "Hi! How's daddy's little onion?" Billy drooled. Ross hardly ever called the kid Billy, preferring the apter vegetable names— carrot, onion, turnip, beet.

Kathy soaked in a bubbled tub, her russet hair caught up in a knot, tendrils wisping around the ears. Ross filled a bathroom glass with water and handed it to her along with a pill. "If it hurts, you should call a doctor," he said.

"We've got enough *doc*tor bills around here." She swallowed the aspirin, keeping the glass, lifting her ankle out of the tub, the bubbles clinging around its curves. "So— how's Billy?" she asked quickly.

"Fine. For Billy." Ross moved away, leaning his back on the back of the door.

"I mean what did Dr. Rinaldo say?"

"Fine..." He shrugged and reached for a smoke.

13

"Coach says with only a little more practice, the kid'll be playing in the Vegetable Bowl."

She gave him a cool indifferent look. "You realize I hate you when you do this, don't you?"

"I realize you hate me when I *don't* do it, too, so I figure what the hell, I got nothin' to lose."

She continued to give him the baleful eye, then moved in the water, baring her breast. She held out the glass. "Would you *mind*?" and he took it, put it back on the sink. When he turned, she was dramatically shaking her head. "Poor...poor...poor...Steven. Really we do put up*on* you so."

He nodded. "Uh-huh. Anything else?"

"I was thinking what a fine person you are."

"Fine."

"I said that, didn't I? Fine. Fine, upright, noble, good."

"Christ."

"I think that's going too far, but you're certainly upright, noble and good. And handsome too." She tilted her head. "I bet girls actually kill themselves too, just on the chance you'll discover their body."

Ross said, "Stop it," which wouldn't help. It was like telling somebody not to vomit. He watched her, cupping her chin in her hand, leaning her elbow on the edge of the tub. Pensive. Coiled:

"Ever made it with a corpse?"

He lifted his shoulders. "You should know."

She laughed. "Oh well. Forget about me. Do not speak evil of the living dead. But you must be getting it somewhere, eh? I mean, I don't see your balls turning blue."

Ross just stood there, dragging his smoke. It was such an old and ridiculous fight that he didn't know

14

why it held his attention, kept him, as now, glued to the spot. Guilt, Brymmer said. Fascination with guilt. To a Wasp, Brymmer said, it's a new toy. An endlessly virile Erector Set, a chance to construct an actual hell.

Grinning now, he suddenly looked at his watch. "Well," he said brightly, "time to move on. Always nice to stop by for a chat." Turning, he saw her start from the tub, slowly, carefully, holding the sink.

"Come on," he said sharply and held out a hand, and she took it, leaning against his arm, dripping water on the sleeve of his coat; an improbable scene in the bathroom mirror. She saw it too, and stared at the glass: the tired, pale, naked girl and the tall, dressed, holstered cop.

Softly, she said, "I wish...oh God, I wish you'd arrest me. Lock me away. Lock up my mouth." She watched his eyes in the mirror now, and her own were wide, starting to mist.

Turning her gently, he cupped her chin. "I have to go now. It's twenty to four."

She shrugged then, lightly, tossing her head. "It's always twenty to four," she said. "Truly. In the real dark night of the soul it is always, always twenty to four."

"Right," he said quickly. "Whatever you say."

As he walked to the corner of Avenue C, at the ass-end of Peter Cooper Village, he wondered how long they could keep it up, how long they could hack away at each other, how long before something snapped in his head:

POLICEMAN MURDERS ONION AND WIFE

The real killer was, that he still loved her.

"So what do you say?" Brymmer said in the car. "How're things doing at the tragedy mill?"

"Grinding them out," Ross said blithely. "Making the quota for our Five Year Plan." He yawned. "Can I borrow your life for a week?"

"You wouldn't like it."

"And how would *you* know? Christ. You don't even remember the dirty parts."

"Right. And speaking of dirty parts, kiddo, we just caught a case."

"Yeah? What kind?"

"The worst," Brymmer said, and added, "Like Clawson."

"Shit." Ross whistled and then rolled his eyes. "Who caught it first?"

"This one? Matson."

"Great. And the Clawson?"

"Ritter. Downtown."

"So they called in the cavalry."

"Yep. Except one of us didn't have his horse."

"So true. Where we going?"

"Padillo said we ought to fly straight to the scene. East Sixty Second Street. Two-ninety-three."

They were stopped now at Sixtieth, waiting for a light. Ross sat slumped in the corner of his seat, staring at the overhead tramway port that looked like a giant Fisher-Price toy and wondering again if he might still be suited for another line of work.

"I'm gonna meet you there," he said. "Let me off at the corner.— Want coffee?"

Brymmer frowned. "You'll only barf it all up."

"I know." Ross shrugged and then grinned. "It's for after."

# 5

"Um, take three. This is Jamie Rogers, On The Spot News and, as you can see, I'm standing in front of a modest brownstone on East Sixty Second Street in snowy Manhattan which seems to be the scene of another very grizzly and brutal murder. From what we can gather, this — wait a second. Harry? That car that pulled up. Right behind the ambulance? Track me on this one. I'm pretty sure it's—yeah. This is Sergeant Burt Brymmer of the Major Manhattan Homicide Squad. Sergeant, could you tell us—"

"Not now, lady. Kell, could you get this crowd away?"

"Um. Sergeant, could—"

"You really gonna tail me down the street?"

"Is there a law against it?"

"No."

"Okay. Is this related to the Clawson case, Sergeant?"

"Task Force."

"What?"

"You said squad. It's a task force. Manhattan... Major... Homicide...Task Force."

"Right. Is this related to the Clawson case, Sergeant?"

"What makes you think so?"

"You do."

"Me?"

"Well, you're only called if it's a front page murder or a serial killing. Isn't that so?"

"So?"

"This is sounding like the Clawson case, Sergeant. Man in his thirties? Stabbed in his bed?"

17

"And where'd you get *that* from?"

"Woman upstairs."

"That one? The blonde hanging out of her window?"

"Yeah. That's the one."

"Uh-huh. Got it how? Did she holler down the news?"

"No. She pulled up to the building in a cab. The police and the ambulance were already here and they wouldn't let her in. They told her to wait. So while she was waiting—"

"You ambushed her."

"No. I mean yes. It's my job. It was obvious the cops were in Apartment One-A— I mean the window's in the front— so she told me who lived there—"

"And also how he died there?"

"No. Not exactly. She speculated."

"Ah! And you've got it on video?"

"Yeah."

"Don't erase it."

"Sergeant—"

"What's your name?"

"Jamie. Rogers. On The Spot News."

"Yeah.— Well thanks a lot for the interview, Jamie."

"Sergeant—? Oh shit! Kill the camera, Harry. There's nothing I can use."

---

## 6

Ross made a low gutteral grunt.

Brymmer sucked his breath in and entered the bedroom: a typical brownstone eleven by twelve.

Detective Matson was standing by the window, engrossed in the task of unwrapping his gum. He looked up at Brymmer and popped it in his mouth. "Call came in around 3:07. Door was ajar. Guy down the hall discovered the body. Smartass crip. Puked on the rug. Got here myself about half-hour later. Photographers have already been here and gone."

Brymmer said nothing and headed for the bed. Holding his breath in. Tightening his jaw. Most of the time, it didn't really get him. Most of the time, he didn't even blink. He'd long ago learned all the body's secrets: that the vaunted brain was gelatinous goo; the romanticized heart, a mere unpoetic muscle. He wasn't offended by viscera, flesh, evacuated colons, raw bloody bone, in fact, he could find them tremendously touching— brave; miraculous; brilliant; even possible proofs of a God. But this time it gagged him— forced him to whistle as a way to catch his breath. He looked up at Ross who was practicing the color of generic canned peas. "Toldja not to buy that coffee," he said.

Blood had patterned the gray and white sheets like a maniac's Rorschach. Dried clumps of fecal matter squatted on the blood. Focusing, he swallowed what had climbed to his throat and looked at the throat that was gaping, open. His nose prickled; the air was rank. A bedside lamp shade, skewed to the side, angled a harsh light on the body. Body looked about six feet long, which in better days would be six feet tall. Eyes: blue. Hair: black. Crotch: a socket of blackened red.

"You find the penis?" He turned from the bed.

Matson shook his head. "Just like the other one. No sign of robbery, no forced entry, no weapon, and no cock." On that one, he grinned. Brymmer just stood there and eyeballed the man. Starting with the gum

19

wrap he'd dropped on the floor and going up six feet of green polyester to a smug, self-satisfied faceful of jaw and a couple of hardball meaningless eyes. He didn't have to *know* Matson to hate him. He figured he could hate him across a ballpark.

"So—" Matson said, and grinned around his gum, "Gonna wrap it all up in a weekend, Brymmer? Like you did with DiChecco?"

Brymmer said nothing and looked at the corpse, the face getting bloated, the skin turning gray, the left hand, reaching, palm up, on the bed, the right arm dangling. There was blood on the hands but there were no other wounds— no slashes on the forearms, the hands, or the wrists to indicate the victim had battled with the knife. Throat first, Brymmer thought. Then he reaches for his throat. Then......What? He would have bled to death in how many minutes? Before or After?

"What's his name?" Brymmer said.

Matson said, "Starrett. First name, Monty. Age thirty-two. Bartender. Single. Supposedly straight."

Ross said to Brymmer, "Say ten or twelve hours?"

Brymmer said nothing and squinted at his watch. It was 4:27. An hour and a half since the call had come in. He studied the stiff and said, "Yeah. Maybe so." Which would locate the action at about 4 AM. He looked at the toe tag. Body had been clocked in at 3:17 on 1/24 by a uniformed officer (Illegible) McCain. Probably the guy who was stationed at the door.

Brymmer said to Matson, "Was anything moved?"

"Hey. Am I stupid? I told the photographers to not even breathe."

"And they didn't, and they died, I imagine," Ross said.

Brymmer knelt down and looked closely at the

bed. He focused on the blood-speckled opposite pillow, then cocked his head at Ross. "Hey, Blondie," he said. "C'mere. This yours?" He pointed at the pillow.

Ross leaned over and examined the hair. "Nah. It's a little too long to be mine. And besides, I've got an alibi."

"Bag it," Brymmer said, "before it gets lost," and while Ross went fumbling for some tweezers and a bag, Brymmer took a picture of the hair with his phone. It was longish and blonde and he thought about the similarly longish blonde hair on his Motor Inn pillow. Life, with its vagaries, was always a gamble. Sex had become a game of Russian Roulette.

There were loud new voices in the living room now—a second wave of the Crime Scene Unit. Matson playing boss, informing them the bedroom was strict-ly under lock until the body'd been examined but to look around the house. Ross was on the phone, saying "Look, we need bodies. And preferably live." They'd need them for the job of a many-block canvass—look-ing for a witness, looking for a weapon, looking for a raw anatomical part.

Brymmer, now alone with what remained of Monty Starrett, took another long analytic look around the room. Its single side window was locked from inside and it didn't look messed with. The night table surface held nothing but a lamp and a half-glass of water. A seven-drawer dresser stood opposite the bed. In the corner was a chair and a table with a laptop. Nothing was messy here, nothing disarranged. It bothered him. Something was off about the scene. Yes. No clothes. Figure it. Guy enters bedroom with a girl. Or a guy, for that matter. Maybe they'd partied in the living room a while. Had a drink. Had a smoke. Or maybe they'd gotten down directly to the point— exploding on the bedroom in a momentary heat. Only where were his clothes? They were neither on the floor nor the cushion of the chair. Which meant? Take a shot. It was someone he lived with. Or lived with at times. Someone he could open the door to in a towel. Or someone with a key. In which case, it counted as domesticated sex where we fold our clothes carefully and put them all away, brush our teeth, take a leak and then slowly go about it with proprietary calm. Or... Brymmer squinted—or... none of the above.

He moved to the living room as Thompson, with his little black bag, hurried in. "Colder'n a goddam freezer out there."

Brymmer said: "You'll like it in here. It's nice."

The M.E. nodded. "Bedroom, right?"

"Death time. I'm figuring it's just about four, but if I'm wrong about it, tell me. If you find some ejaculate, I'd like to know its age. And the rest of the rundown. What's in his stomach. Drugs in his blood. I'd also like your expert opinion on the weapon."

"Anything else?"

"Yeah," Brymmer added, "Have-a-nice-day."

He walked through the living room, where Sanders and Patterson were scraping up the puke.

"Just for the record," Brymmer said, "that belongs to the neighbor down the hall." He looked around the room— a dark room dully done in glass-leather-chrome. Except for the drying bits of puke on the rug, there were no indications that the room had been used—no dents in the sofa, no glasses, no cups. Ross wandered in with the neatly bagged hair and a dusted wallet. "Mastercard. License. Thirty-five bucks and a paid-up Actor's Equity card." He pulled out a wallet-size photo.

"That's him."

The back of the photo said, *Monty Starrett. Agent: Wells & McLaughlin Inc.* The front showed a slick, square-jawed face.

Brymmer said: "Lady-killer, I bet."

"Yeah. And it looks as though she killed him right back."

"So we'll see if there's some lady-goop drying on the sheets." He tossed that to Patterson who answered with a nod. To Sanders, he said, "There's a laptop in the room. Get me his address book. That, I want fast. Then see if he's been hanging out at Craig's List or something. And you," he said to Ross, "check the lady upstairs. Two-A, I believe. She told that reporter-chick she thinks it's 'like Clawson.'"

Ross raised his eyebrows.

"Also, she's a blonde."

"And you're not coming with me?"

"What's the matter? You're armed."

"Okay. But if I'm not back for supper, call the cops."

Brymmer poked his head through the door to the bedroom. Thompson looked up and said, "Yeah, call it four. —Ish."

"How ish?"

"Call it four, call it six. And the weapon was a razor."

"A razor?"

"You ever seen the play *Sweeney Todd*? Like a barber's razor. Five-inch blade with a handle. Like so." Thompson made a rough illustration with his hand. "Oh. And don't bother asking who heard him scream. His vocal cords—"

"Christ."

"That's a pretty deep cut."

23

"Take a pretty strong hand?"

"I'd say."

"Are you finished?"

"Uh-huh. Just about.— Have patience."

"I'm the absolute soul of it."

"Right."


Brymmer stepped out of the apartment to the hall. It was small, dark, ochre, with a muddy tiled floor. A glass panelled door looked obliquely at the street. It was dark now and snow was falling thickly, like feathers, but the packed crowd of gawkers was continuing to grow. He rubbed at his eyes now and lit a cigarette and then drew in deeply on the harsh, soothing smoke.

He knocked on the door. The uniformed cop standing guard on the doorstep turned around and looked in.

Brymmer cracked the door. "McCain?"

"Sergeant?" A fresh-faced rookie. Twenty-three, Brymmer guessed. Looking paler than the snow.

"So was this your first stiff?"

"No sir. I got an old lady died of stroke. But, Jesus. You know. It was nothing like this."

Brymmer just nodded. Paternal; sympathetic. "When you got here," he said, "did you touch something? move something?"

Rookie shook his head. "Door was part open so I nudged it with my foot. Bedroom door was open, so I didn't touch a thing."

"How about the blanket? I mean, when I saw it, it was bundled to the side, sort of centered on the bed..."

"Oh yeah," McCain said, looking suddenly embarrassed. "I had to move it over when I had to do the tag."

"So it was covering his feet."

"Uh, yes sir."

24

"And how much higher did it go?"

"About only to his shin."

"Shin singular or plural?"

"Both of em."

"Good.— And is Matson aware of that?"

"Uh…"

"It's okay, son. As long as you remembered to report it to me. —Did you talk to the neighbor?"

"The guy in One-B?" McCain jerked his jaw at the only other door on the narrow little hall—opposite Starrett's but buried in the shadow of a gritty flight of stairs. "Just briefly, is all. The detective, though— Matson— he was there quite a while."

"What's his name?"

"Uh, Seigel."

"And his first name?"

"Jerome. "

"Would you do me a favor?"

"Sure."

"See that car? The one behind the ambulance? In the glove box you'll find a pack of Marlboro Reds. Would you get it for me?"

"Sure. Happy to. I guess you want to duck the reporters."

"Good guessing," Brymmer said.

Closing the door again, he stared at the circus. The television news people vulturing around. Waiting for a headline. Waiting for a clue. Waiting for the money shot: Starrett in a bag. The faces, most of them at least, were familiar. Dorgan; Lippman: the network boys. Harris of the *News*. Rorkas of the *Post*. And the red-headed looker in the yellow down coat, a microphone dangling in her leather-gloved hand. She was drinking coffee from a Styrofoam cup and she looked as though

25

she thought she were freezing to death.

She saw him and bravely started moving up the stairs. She moved to the door. Brymmer shook his head. She eyed him from the opposite side of the glass. He folded his arms. She shivered, then smiled. Her hair was the astonishing color of sunset. Tousled and tumbling. Dotted with snow. The eyes that watched him were inquisitive, amused. She tilted her head. He leaned on the wall. The rookie came back with the Marlboro pack, said something to the girl, which Brymmer didn't catch, and the girl said something and the rookie seemed to laugh— the "Ha" coming out of him like smoke in the air.

Brymmer clicked the latch up and yanked at the door, but only just wide enough to stick out his hand.

The girl stuck her foot in.

"Christ," Brymmer said. "I was afraid you'd do that."

"And yet another reason to give up smoking." Her voice had a neat, pleasant little catch.

The rookie looked watchful as he carefully handed in the cigarettes to Brymmer who nodded mechanically and squinted at the floor. "You want to play chicken-out with your foot?"

"You want to just say if it's connected to—"

"No. I don't want to say."

He jiggled the door.

The foot didn't move.

"Pity," he said. "Those are nice boots too."

McCain said, "You want me I should—"

"No. It's okay." And to Jamie Rogers, he explained, in his deliberate and no-kidding cop-voice, "I'm counting to three."

"And you wouldn't even—"

"Two."

"Okay, but I—"

"Three." He bent down suddenly and picked up the foot, removed it from the doorway and then slammed the door.

Turning instantly, he walked down the hall and then leaned on the buzzer of apartment One-B.

## 7

"Aw, man. Already told this to ninety-seven cops. What's the matter? Don't you guys ever talk to each other?"

Brymmer just shrugged and said, "Not if I can help it." He was sitting on a club chair and taking in the man and his small dark apartment: Seigel, on the couch, with what looked like a typewritten manuscript beside him. Turtle-necked. Blue jeaned. Bare-footed. Left foot prosthetic. Strong arms. Strong hands. Smart eyes looking over from a long bony face. The kind of face, Brymmer thought, that had been sculpted by irony and weathered by woe.

"All right," Seigel muttered. "Go on. Do your thing."

"Last night..." Brymmer said.

"I conked out around ten. Took an Ativan. I just hadn't slept the night before. I was watching some news show and zonk, I was out. Woke up around seven. TV was still on."

"And then."

"You want to hear the shower and the shave?"

"I was thinking of the part where Mr. Starrett comes in."

27

"That was later," Seigel said. "When I left in the morning— maybe ten, I'm not sure, Starrett's door was part open—"

"How much?"

"I don't know. Six inches? Little more?"

"Go on."

"Well I didn't really think about it much. Just noticed it. But then I came back around three and the door was still open. I knocked. Rang the bell. No answer. Called in. No answer. *Walked* in."

"Go on."

"No 'on.' I found him. That's it."

"And *then*…?"

"Then I threw up my kishkas on his rug." That last seemed to bother him. He squinted at the floor.

"It's the penis," Brymmer said. "It kinda gets you where you live."

"I dunno. Maybe so. Because I've seen a lot worse. I did a stint in Fallujah where the usual procedure there was 'Off with his head.'"

"It's not the same," Brymmer said. "I mean a head is just a head. You can't play with it or nothin."

For a second, Seigel frowned, then he nodded. "So I guess you do the *good* cop, huh?"

"Moi?" Brymmer said.

"Are we finished?"

"Not quite."

"Then I think I want a beer." Seigel rose and then asked unexpectedly, "You?"

"Yes I would," Brymmer nodded. "But I wouldn't. Go ahead."

He waited while Seigel futzed around in the kitchen, making use of the time to lean forward in his chair, glancing quickly at the manuscript, reading upside down across the table, *Chapter Two*. Jerry Seigel came back with a cold can of Miller's and a large bag of chips which he spiraled to the table, across from which Brymmer sat examining his thumb.

Brymmer reached over and grabbed a hand of chips. "So you're a writer," Brymmer said.

"I try."

"To write what?"

"For a living? Throbbing knobs."

Brymmer waited.

"His excitement now mounted by the second. Crushing her against him, McCallum felt the hard, pointy points of her nipples and the soft, ever-quickening throb of her heart. Eagerly, she guided his erection to her twat. 'Oh babe,' he said, 'Babe, babe, babe.'" Seigel grinned. "Porn. Pays the rent."

"Is that some of it?" Brymmer flicked a thumb at the manuscript.

"*That*," Seigel sighed, "is the sad aborted fetus of the Great American Novel."

"Trouble," Brymmer said.

"You could call it that, yeah. Trouble with *me* is, I write great shit but then I write shitty Great."

Brymmer gave a short but appreciative laugh and then zig-zagged instantly without a missed beat. "So tell me," he invited, "why you didn't like Starrett."

"Who says I didn't like him?"

"You wouldn't, that's all. I mean *I* wouldn't either. And I didn't say you hated him, I said 'didn't like.'"

Jerry Seigel shook his head. "Hardly spoke to him at all. 'Shitty day,' 'Got some ice.' The extent of conversation."

"Did he often borrow ice?"

"On occasion. Now and then."

"Did a lot of entertaining?"

"You could call it that, I guess."

"Lotta screwing?" Brymmer said.

"Hey, look. Like I told you, I didn't really know him."

"Right. I don't know the guy across from me either. But I know how often his bed springs creak."

"Often," Seigel said. "I mean his bedroom's next to mine."

"Same woman?"

"Couldn't say. Except the morning parade coming out of there at breakfast time was interesting and varied."

"Any blondes?"

"I didn't hang around examining his chicks." Seigel paused, sipped his beer, and said, "Jealous as I am."

"Were you?"

He laughed. "Try again, Sergeant Brymmer."

"Any blondes?"

"Chances are."

"Any boys?"

"I wouldn't think. Or at least I never noticed any small-assed poon."

"And the girls," Brymmer said. "Just describe them in general."

"Lookers, that's all. I couldn't get more specific."

"Getting back to what you thought of him..."

"I said I didn't think."

"Hey you *think* about everything, Jerry. That's your thing."

Seigel took a long hard pause and then sighed. "Cocksucker. That's what I thought of him."

"Why?"

"It's a very long story."

"Would you mind if I smoke?"

"Use the can for an ashtray." Seigel put a quick final ending to his beer and passed the can on to Brymmer.

"If I tell you the story, man, you'll think I'm a jerk."

"Unless, of course, I think you're a jerk already."

"Right.— And what the fuck do I care what you think." Seigel said it flatly in a half-friendly tone. "There's a girl," he said slowly. "Kate Marrott was her name. And the point was, I often used to see her with Starrett."

"When?"

"About ten in the morning, I suppose."

"What I meant was how long ago?"

"Oh. June-July."

"Go on."

"It's a Sunday and it's raining like a bitch and I arrive, soaked and cursing, and she's pacing in the hall. It's about seven-thirty. So I ask her what's up and she tells me— and she's also pretty rain-dragged herself— that she's supposed to meet Starrett but it seems he isn't there. So I say to her, Look, leave a note on Starrett's door and come in and have a drink. So she does."

Seigel paused and then propped up his curved metal foot on the table. Brymmer waited.

"So she does. So anyway, I pull out the company Cutty and we really start to talk. I suppose I don't need to reassure you that was all. Anyway, she's...great. Smart. Funny. And absolutely out of her mind about Starrett. Checking her watch every six, seven minutes and pretending that she isn't. Anyway, after an hour or so passes, I really get the feeling that she starts to relax. And she's telling me a bunch of these really wacky tales about the cop show she works on. She's... production or something. I mean she's not an actress. Anyway, by

31

now it's getting on to nine-thirty and I say to her 'You want to order a pizza or something?' and she looks at her watch again, her eyes getting misty and she suddenly discovers that it's really getting late and that she really has to go. And she does." Seigel stopped, looking sheepishly at Brymmer. "And you may have heard a few shorter stories in your life, but I doubt you've heard duller."

Brymmer said nothing but a smoky "Go on."

"Okay, so I've practically gotten to the point. The point is, I walk her through the hall to the door and as we pass Starrett's doorway, she unsticks the note, where she told him she'd be waiting in apartment One-B, and I tell her, 'I could throw that in the garbage if you like' and I take it, but I don't. I mean I don't throw it out. Out of warped curiosity, I stick it back up. Like I want to know when Starrett gets back and what he says." He looked sideways at Brymmer. "That's crazy, I suppose."

"Not very," Brymmer said. "What happened?"

"One-thirty, Starrett's pounding on the door. He's blitzed. He says, 'So— she still waiting?' I say no and then he mutters, 'Dumb cunt,' and then he says to me, 'I thought she might've gotten me a job but she didn't. What the hell. It's as good a way of getting rid of her as any.' So I just thought Cocksucker. Crass son of a bitch. In fact, I had a quick-running movie-hero fantasy of taking out his package with a hard metal heel." He looked back at Brymmer, half-angling his head. "Now what was that essay in answer to?"

"Why was he a cocksucker."

"Right. That's why," Seigel said.

"Was she blonde?"

"Who, Kate? No,no," Seigel said. "A very short-haired brunette."

32

"That's Marrott," Brymmer said. "Two r's, two t's?"

Seigel nodded.

Brymmer wrote it in his notebook and rose. "If you think of something else…" He tossed his card on the table as he divebombed his cigarette into the dead can. "And don't be too terribly surprised if tomorrow, say, you get another call."

"From who?"

"From another damn cop," Brymmer said.

## 8

The body was gone.

So was the press and the remnants of the crowd.

Clark and Dubisky had arrived at the building and were already checking out the other apartments. There were ten in the building— two to each floor.

Matson, whose squad was checking dumpsters for a weapon, had emerged, self-appointed, as the Spokesman To The Press. He had not yet given out the name of the victim, but described his condition as "assorted mutilations."

"*Assorted*," Ross said. "Do you like that? As*sort*ed?"

They were standing in the vestibule where Brymmer'd just arrived from apartment One-B.

"Well *maybe*," Brymmer said, "he meant 'a sordid mutilation.'"

"Nah," Ross decided. "He wouldn't know the word."

"So what else am I missing?"

"I can tell you on the way."

"Way to where?"

"To where Starrett did his bartender shtick. Called McGinty's. On Lex. We can walk it."

Brymmer gestured a dramatic After You.

It was crunchy on the street. The snow, having fallen on the residues of ice, made a crisp and entirely satisfying sound.

"Would you mind?" Brymmer said. "I'd like a small patch of silence. My ear's been talked off."

"Fine with me. When you're ready."

Brymmer listened to the snow. There was no one on the street except a diehard dog-walker walking seven dogs.

They got all the way to Third—a whole blockful of silence. Brymmer nodded. "Okay."

"Okay," Ross offered. "So what do you want first now? The bathroom or the lady?"

"Dealer's choice," Brymmer said.

"Then the bathroom," Ross chose. "Okay, so I checked it out with Patterson and Sanders."

"And?"

"Tub was cleaner than a nun's reputation."

"Clever. But I guess we don't know the same nuns."

"Ah yes. I suppose you mean hookers in wimples."

"You got me."

"A fat can of Comet's on the rim."

"So the cleaning lady did it."

"The sink was clean too. Ex*cept*—" Ross paused until Brymmer cocked his head— "Ex*cept*— we found some little blonde curlies in the drain."

"That's convenient," Brymmer said. "Any blood specks?"

"Maybe. Maybe. Not sure. The damn bleach fucked the test. And meanwhile, there's nothing very urgent in the cabinet. Only prescription was for Valium fives. Half full."

They were turning onto Lexington now and they

both lit a cigarette, knowing there'd be no chance to do it in a bar. You could drink yourself crazy, you could snort in the john, but you couldn't smoke a Marlboro.

"Lady," Brymmer said. "The upstairs neighbor."

"Jennifer Symington. Ad lady. Want to take a guess? Thirty-five. She slept with him."

"She say so?"

"Nope. But she did. She talked about how he was a charmer and a bullshit artist and a creep."

"So of course," Brymmer said, "she slept with him. And?"

"She's a newbie to the building. Only six, seven months and they were friendly for a time. That's all she had to say."

"And she didn't say a word about his dying 'like Clawson'?"

"Nope. Only said he must've picked up a psycho."

"Where was she? At the time."

"She got home around midnight. Buzzed. Went to sleep. Heard nothing. Saw nothing. Woke at seven, hit the gym. Met some lady-friends for lunch. That's it," Ross concluded. "Except of course this. Ta *da!*" He produced a little baggie from his coat. In the street light, it sparkled with some curly blonde hairs. Ross cackled. "Did the old 'Use your bathroom, ma'am?' bit. Where I found, as expected, there's some brushes on the shelf."

"Tsk-tsk." Brymmer grinned. "Of course you know that's illegal."

"Of course," Ross agreed. "But so's murder, last I looked.— Here we go," he said pointing at a blue neon sign.

They stubbed out their cigarettes and moved through the door.

35

# 9

Saturday at six and the place was half empty. It was one of those dark little neighborhood dives, with a curved wooden bar, a few checker-clothed tables holding glass-enclosed candles, and a restaurant in back. Two women and a man they wouldn't give the time of day to were sitting at the bar and a couple of couples had the tables at the side. Brymmer took a slightly-cracked red leather stool at the corner—at the far right corner— of the bar, where it butted on the wall and put his bad side wallward. Ross knew he went for that position when he could and while he vaguely understood it, it amazed him nonetheless. He approved of Brymmer's face. A kind of jigsaw puzzle where the pieces didn't fit but then eternally intrigued. Kathy found him handsome "in a half-assed way," and the women at the bar were looking up at him with quick, cool dartings of appraisal: Green eyes. Straight nose. Good bod. Nice hair.

"Are we drinking?" Ross said, "or we pretending to be cops?"

"He's gonna make us," Brymmer said, as the barman wandered over. A middle-aged, Irish-faced, barrel of a man.

"What's up?" he said, instead of the expected What'll it be?

"I tolja," Brymmer muttered. To the guy, he said, "You happen to've been here last night?"

"Uh-huh. Till seven. So what's this about?"

Ross watched as, redundantly, Brymmer flashed his shield. "It's about Monty Starrett."

"Okay. What'd he do?"

"You a friend of his?"

36

"No. We just work here is all. I get off around seven, he comes on around seven. What's the matter? He got a ticket?"

"He got dead," Brymmer said.

The bartender's eyes grew wider, then froze. He looked at the two of them and slowly shook his head. "That's impossible," he said. "I just saw him last night."

"Here today, gone tomorrow," Ross helpfully explained and then watched as the bartender couldn't stop his head from just wagging back and forth.

Brymmer shot Ross a quick cut-it-out look, but Ross felt entirely beyond the reproach. The one thing that Ross couldn't ever understand was how people couldn't ever understand about life. They imbued the mere fact of three-dimensional existence with delusions of permanence. Your *couch* doesn't simply disappear overnight, so how could your uncle? It didn't compute. That a life was a lightbulb that could simply go *pop* was a concept not easily encompassed by the mind.

Brymmer said, "You saw him last night then at seven."

The bartender nodded.

Brymmer asked his name. It was Alfred O'Shae. "Alfie, they call me. Like the movie. On accounta I was once quite the stud. Wouldn't know it to look at me now but I was. Like Starrett."

"So Starrett was a stud," Brymmer said. "And the bar was his pasture?"

For a moment, Alfie blinked. Then he got it. Then he laughed. "His pasture. That's good. Oh yeah, oh yeah. And he made a lotta hay here. Ya like that? A pun."

"That's funny," Brymmer said. And he actually chuckled. Ross chuckled too but he was chuckling at Brymmer who could, when he wanted to, bullshit a

37

bull. "But the thing I was wondering about was last night and you were off here at seven…"

"I was, I was. Monty came in a little early last night, which for him was like something he didn't ever do, like he's always like five, ten, twenty minutes late, which means *I'm* working late for which I never get paid, so I says to him, to make up for all that I done, I says to him, 'Bartender! Fix me good Irish whiskey on the rocks.'"

"So then," Ross injected, "you *didn't* leave at seven."

"I was here just sittin at the bar until eight. Boss wouldn't mind, though he wasn't here either. I been working for him close now to twenty-five years."

"Uh-huh." Brymmer nodded. "What time's the place close?"

"Three," Alfie said. "So Monty, like he's on here from seven to three."

"And who else is?"

"What."

"Is here until three."

Ross said, "We need to talk to someone who was here. Someone who could tell us if he left with a lady."

"Carmen," Alfie said. "The waitress. She was here. She serves at the tables. Carmen," he added, "works from seven, but tonight she's here early, til three. You want me I should call her?"

"Yep," Brymmer said. "And in the meantime, Bartender, fix me a good Irish whiskey on the rocks."

Alfie made a "You too?" gesture at Ross who nodded, looking over as Alfie poured the booze and yelled "Carmen!" at the air.

The waitress materialized along with the drinks. Carmen turned out to be a definite Carmen. A hot little item with a toss of black hair, a Hello in her eyes, and

38

a fine little *tuchis* wrapped in Latex-to-go. Ross looked her over and she looked him over back.

Carmen reported that Starrett left alone. In fact, he'd appeared rather anxious to get home. As for general action, there hadn't been a lot. "Just the neighborhood people and not a lot of them. All the action here usually starts around ten, only last night it didn't. It's the weather," Carmen said. "Like you just want to kinda stay bundled in your bed, and you either already got something on your mattress, or you don't go out looking."

Brymmer nodded. "So Starrett didn't pitch any girls."

She shrugged. "I don't think so. There wasn't what to pitch." Her eyes traced the ceiling. "Nope. I didn't once see him talking to a girl."

"Except early," Alfie said. He'd been leaning on the bartop and watching from behind. "Early, he was coming on to some little number like he really wants to score. A cutie. He was practically drooling in her drink.— You saw the one, didn't you?" He tossed that to Carmen.

"Yeah," she said. "So? He didn't leave with her, did he? She came, maybe forty-five minutes, and she left."

"I dunno," Alfie said. "They mighta had a late date. I heard what they were saying, or part of it at least." He looked back at Brymmer. "Like I know she was telling him she— yeah, lost her keys. And something how her father and her brother were a cop and she was...nah...I'm not certain I remember any more."

Ross said, "Describe her."

"Pretty thing. Maybe kinda skinny. Couldn't tell. I mean she never took her coat off."

"And what color hair?"

39

Alfie shook his head and then shrugged at them. "She never took her hat off either. Wait! I remember how she comes from out of town."

"What town?" Brymmer said.

"I dunno. Didn't hear."

Carmen said, "I'm pretty sure the coat was dark blue and I really liked the hat. Light blue. Red flowers. It was one of those knitted things that's tight around your head and has flaps around the ears and had some braids coming out of it, falling down to here."

"What *color*—" Brymmer sounded almost testy— "were the braids?"

"They were wool," Ross injected. And when Brymmer looked inquisitive, he added, "How I'm sure of it is Kathy has the hat. There's a street vendor selling it, on Thompson, near the park." He looked up at Carmen now. "You think of something else? Like girls he might've gone for? A blonde would be the thing."

"Like when?" she said.

"Any time."

"Any time? Wow. What I know about Monty is, he'd have them for a week, maybe some of them a month and then pfft! they were gone. Never saw them after that. It would take some remembering."

Ross produced a card. "Call me," he offered, "if you think of something else." He also grabbed a green business card off the countertop. *McGinty's*, it said, with a number and address. Brymmer eyed him knowingly. Ross built a shrug.

## 10

Brymmer walked back to the Starrett apartment while Ross bought some sandwiches to have later on. It would be a long night. Long, and crudded up with irritating scut work.

Back in the bedroom now, Brymmer looked over at the rank empty bed— the corpse and the bedding underneath it gone away, leaving only the dull red stains on the mattress. He imagined it—imagining that Starrett was asleep, or just-enough-asleep to not hear it when it came—that groan of the mattress springs, the quick artful lunge.

He crossed to the closet, looked it over, found the light. Bartender's trousers— black ones, like Alfie's— were hanging from a hook. There were two decent suits, one blazer, six slacks and a fraying pair of jeans.

The laptop was missing from the setup in the corner, taken by the Crime Scene Unit to explore. The table, however, flaunted two sets of drawers: Bank statements; check book. Starrett, unsurprisingly, was living on the edge. Money in, money out. No address book. Or date book. Everything undoubtedly recorded on the Mac. Brymmer wondered idly what the Starrett types would do if their hard drives exploded and their data disappeared, taking with it all the names, dates, and places of their lives, all the memories that had no longer had to be remembered but were simply "on file." Would they ditch their old friendships? forget their own names? The final drawer had offered up a fine mis-cellanea of un-information— a dry cleaning ticket, a bill from Con Ed. But an envelope, opened, still holding an actual handwritten letter with the greeting, "Dear son," was the pillager's reward.

Brymmer walked back to the now-lighted living room where Clark and Dubisky were improving on their notes. "Holy shit!" Dubisky said. "I can write the stuff down and then it's twenty seconds later and I can't read it back." He grunted as he handed off his notebook to Clark. "What does *that* word look like?"

"It looks like it was written by a backward third grader." Clark looked at Brymmer who was standing at the coat closet, frisking the coats.

"De*served*!" Dubisky triumphed. "What it says is de*served*."

"What's deserved?" Brymmer exited the closet with a phone.

"That was Four B's opinion that the victim was a louse. And before you start slavering, she's eighty years old."

"So what else you got?"

"Nothin.— Middle of the night, baby, everyone's asleep. And before that, they're deaf, dumb and didn't see a thing."

"Except Stauzer," Clark said. "Mrs. Stauzer saw him leaving, six-thirty. Alone."

"What apartment?"

"Five A.—So we're finished," Clark said. "The next question's What Now?"

Brymmer handed him the letter. "Next of kin," he said. "Call em."

"Why me?"

"Because you're blessed with that Morgan Freeman voice."

"He means a nigger voice," Dubisky said. "It's steeped in molasses and in centuries of woe."

"Haven't Jews got some woe?"

"Yes we do," Dubisky said, "except we render it

42

in chicken fat. It's greasy."

Brymmer laughed.

Ross, in the doorway, said, "Your food is in the car." He squinted down balefully at Clark and Dubisky. "A meeting of the minds," he said. "And what have they wrought?"

"Sit down," Brymmer said. "And let us reason together." He sat down himself in a creaky leather chair and let his head tip backwards while he briefly closed his eyes. "Friday night," Brymmer said. "He left the bar in a hurry and he left there at three. He'd be home in five minutes. He departed mother earth within the general parameters of four A.M. to six, only somewhere in between, he undressed and, for one of many reasons, went to bed. Does that sound like it's solid?"

No one seemed to disagree.

He looked around briefly and knuckled at his jaw. "Okay. So whoever unhitched him took a shower after which she cleaned the tub. Which would mean that she's exiting from— what? five to seven? And arrived, unless she entered with his key, three to six. By seven, you've already got traffic on the street, so she might go unnoticed." He looked at Dubisky. "So who'd be out witnessing from, say, three to six? On a Saturday morning. On East Sixty-Second."

"The cameras," Clark said.

"And I'm already on it. Or McAllister is. The nearest ones however, are Sixty-Third and Third, or else Sixtieth and Third. And if she didn't go that-a-way, she ain't on the map.—Any other ideas then?"

Clark said, "The kids out delivering the *Times*. They're usually out about—"

"Good," Brymmer said. "And since you thought it, you own it. Any other ideas?"

"Drunks," Dubisky said.

"I was thinking about dog walkers," Brymmer threw in, "*and* drunks, even joggers. The drunks come home at four, and the joggers go out at six. Even five."

"That's incredibly obscene," Dubisky said. "Self-improvers make me sick."

Clark considered it a while. "But do joggers jog on snow?"

"They're ob*sess*ives, man!" Dubisky started working up his wrath. "They jog anywhere, any time. On *nail* beds, they jog. They run around in their little *tee* shirts when it's twenty-six below and drink *water*! Eat *pita*! They're *Nazis*!" he exploded, "and I tell you, man, you watch yourself, they're stomping on the world."

There was silence. Brymmer turned around and squinted up at Clark. "What was *that* about?"

"That's about Dubisky's on a diet. Or supposed to be. Dubisky got the lecture from the doc."

"And in the meanwhile," Ross injected, "there were joggers in the park. This morning. I saw them. So the answer would be yes, which would lead us to the question What the hell is on your mind? You want someone on the sidewalk here to snoop for early joggers and a pack of pissing dogs?"

Brymmer nodded. "More or less."

"Well it better not be me."

"Take it easy, Steve. I'll toss it to the Matson team."

"Fine."

"You can tackle transportation."

"Meaning?"

Brymmer shrugged. "That she was here and then she left. How? By what means? Taxicab? Drivers might remember such a girl and have a record where she went. Figure bus drivers too. Not a heavy crowd of bus riders

44

riding into dawn. And then the subway's up at Lex—"

"And then suppose she had a car. Or that she walked," Dubisky said. "What's to say she didn't walk? Suppose she's living in the neighborhood and—"

"Nothing," Brymmer said. "Nothing says she didn't walk or says she didn't have a car. I'm simply covering the bases. And aside from that, I couldn't even swear that it's a she."

"Aw come on now. It's more than very likely," Ross said. "I mean some of those hairs were like a thousand feet long. And he's naked and in bed and he's a cocksman and he's straight."

"For all we know," Brymmer added.

"Okay. For all we know."

Brymmer yawned, rubbed his shoulderblade and glanced around the room. Less than twenty-four hours ago, the room belonged to Starrett. Now it was a meeting room for alien invaders—like Goldilocks, slinking into Papa Bear's chairs. "Moving on," he said dryly. "Any other ideas?"

There was silence for a time.

"E.R.'s," Dubisky said.

They looked at him.

"Okay, so she's walking. It's a bitch. Very icy on the streets. She slips. Breaks her ankle. Maybe even breaks her head." He looked around for approval. "Not bad. What do you think?"

"As ideas go, it qualifies as desperate," Clark said.

Ross, who'd been pacing back and forth, shook his head. "Or how about she didn't need to travel," Ross said. "Like she's living—" he pointed at the ceiling—"upstairs."

"Did you like her?" Brymmer said. Meaning "like her" as It.

"I didn't, but I liked her enough to steal her hair. But we could check her out further. I could dig a little more..."

"Is that spoken like a man? or a policeman?" Brymmer said.

"Policeman. I swear."

"So we can wait until Forensics gives us more about the hair."

"Maybe days. Maybe years. She was bitchy," Ross said, "and she was strong enough to do it. I was thinking I could check out her mental inclinations. I could start with her druggist. Like to see if she was ever taking psychiatric pills."

"And her druggist would be..?"

"Walgreen's. And no I didn't peek. Her little birth control whatsisthing was lying on the sink."

"You'd need a warrant and you wouldn't ever get it," Brymmer said.

"I have ways..." Ross reminded.

"Don't tell me what they are. And on the day you're suspended—"

"I'll retire to Miami. I'll become a private eye."

"Good luck with that." Brymmer started rising from his chair. "Dubisky—find the other guys and see what you can do. Clark— phone the Starretts."

"And you?" Dubisky said.

"Me? I'm clocking out to eat a sandwich in the car."

## 11

"Can I help you sir?"

"Yeah. Thanks.— I came to get that prescription for Symington. Jennifer," he added. "She phoned it in before."

The white-coated Asian girl smiled, turned around and then rummaged through a basket.

"Pretty cold out," Ross observed.

"I've been hearing that. And everybody's coming down with flu. It's not the cold, you know. It's people huddled up in heated rooms."

"I didn't know that."

"Oh yes." Still rummaging. "Hmmm... I'm not finding it."

"Oh?— Symington. East Sixty-Second Street."

"No. But I can check behind the counter. — Do you know what time she called?"

Ross shrugged. "Didn't say. She just said to pick it up. It was...Lithium, I believe."

"Oh dear." The young woman disappeared behind a wall and went to look in a cubicle. "No," she called out from it. "Nothing. Are you sure? I mean you sure she phoned in? It would have to be a refill if she phoned it in herself."

"Could you check the computer?"

The computer was on the counter, maybe inches from Ross's nose but turned backwards. Young woman hurries back, starts to type. "Symington," she says. "And that's East Sixty-Second Street?"

"Two-ninety-three."

A moment of pained silence.

"Well I found her but...there's nothing about *Lithium* here at all. She took Valproate once but hasn't had it since July."

Ross frowned. "Are you sure?"

"Take a look," the woman said as she pivoted the monitor. Ross checked the listing. Valproate (for manic depression?) in July and only birth control and Levoquin happily ever after.

"Wow," he said. "I guess someone totally messed it up. Because she really needs the Levoquin."

"Sir? You said Lithium."

"Did I?" Ross frowned and then offered a helpless shrug. "Those names," he said, "they all sound the same to me either way. They're just gobbledegook to a layman.— She's got pneumonia," he added.

"Oh. Then it's definitely Levoquin, sir. They probably called her doctor since it wasn't up for renewal. That explains why it isn't here. Although I really can't account for why it isn't in the computer."

"Human error," Ross decided. "Human beings make mistakes.—Not you," he added hastily. "In fact, you've been very kind."

Walking out of the Walgreen's at 67th and Third, Ross huddled in a doorway and fiddled with his phone. Should he or Shouldn't he? Would he, or Not?

He made the first phonecall. And then, after chewing up his lip, made the second.

The phone rang endlessly. He glanced at his watch and saw the time was 10:30.

Kathy came on with a sleep-drunk, "Mmmm."

"Sorry," Ross said, "I didn't think you'd be asleep.— How's the ankle?"

"I don't know. When I was sleeping, it didn't hurt.— What's the matter? Why did you call?"

"I *called*," Ross said, "to find out how you're doing.

I also called to tell you that we just caught a case. If you can rouse yourself at eleven, it'll probably make the news."

"Uh-huh," she said. "You're working overtime, of course."

"Well hey. What do you think? Burt wants me working on a dawn patrol later— a stakeout for pissing pups. I'll explain to you later on."

"How's it going?"

"I pulled a coup."

"Well of course you did. Before the night is over, you'll pull some more. I mean the plural of coup is—"

"Stop it!" Ross commanded. "Just stop it! Turn it off. Is there anything I can bring you?"

"Bring me?"

"From the big, nasty, murderous outside world. Is there anything you desire? Candy? Cigarettes? Peanut butter?"

"Nothing, darling. Not even you."

Ross raised his head and breathed a long whistling sigh which then sat on the frosty air— an objective correlative (the phrase came to mind) of all the wearying and dissipating thoughts that besieged his brain.

"Goodnight," he said. "Darling."

"Goodnight," she said. "Dear."

# 12

It was practically 12:20 when Brymmer, unwinding, lit the second cigarette from the luxury of his desk in the second floor squad room of the 19th precinct where his task force, all six of them, were temporarily housed. The "temporary" nature having lasted for three years, Brymmer took it as being home, although the premises, small and crowded, half belonged to the resident squad. That aside, he had a relatively functioning computer, which was all that a man could ask, and when he'd finally been promoted to a supervisory rank (no run-of-the-mill Sergeant, he was suddenly SDS), a retiring lieutenant had rewarded him with an ashtray— a large yellow diamond with a garishly purple rim that held a standing figure of Bloomberg looking scornfully down at the butts. He inflicted a glowing ash and started thinking about the night.

So far, it had given nothing. The original team of detectives, who'd been canvassing now since four, had found... nothing. Not a witness, not a weapon, and not a part.

Starrett's phone was a disappointment. He'd deleted most of the logs— all the names, numbers, times, dates and messages in and out— which in itself had produced a Why? As in Why the deletions? A morbidly jealous girlfriend? Jealous girlfriends invaded phones. Or, considering Occam's razor (the theory that the simplest explanation is the One), it was simply a new phone. The catalogued address book was similarly spare, having listed only the numbers of Starrett's agent ("The office is closed"), a couple of women ("Please leave a message") and one brother (listed as "Bro").

When Brymmer'd talked to him, Jimmy Starrett, who lived in Nebraska, had already heard so, aside from condolences, Brymmer was spared. Brymmer had asked him if Monty Starrett had ever complained about being stalked, or had mentioned the names of particular women he'd deeply repented of having shtupped (Brymmer used the word "dated") who seemed to be nuts. Or women with husbands who seemed to be nuts. Or with nutsy boyfriends. The answer was "No."

Choosing his words with the utmost caution, Brymmer had asked him if brother Monty had ever had "contact with homosexuals," causing Nebraska to burst into flames. *"You take that back!"* hollered Jimmy Starrett. *"How dare you imply that my brother's a fag?"* Brymmer corrected the misunderstanding. He'd only meant that a good-looking actor in wicked Manhattan could capture the eye of a less than entirely masculine male and could rudely rebuff him, inspiring revenge. This slimy appeasement elicited, "No."

Brymmer had spoken, of course, to Matson, taking a friendly, respectful tone and encouraging Matson to get the idea that an early stakeout could lead to a lead. Detective Matson, whose Saturday tour was officially over at 4:36, had relayed the request to Detective Kerner, and Kerner arranged it, so that was done. With that much accomplished, Brymmer had made what had now come to seem like a thousand phone calls, prodded the crime lab, and written reports. Ross had come up to him, wildly excited *("Manic depressive and off of her meds!")* and Brymmer'd suggested that Ross himself should return to Walgreen's and purchase a pill.

"She isn't moving," he said.

"So?"

51

"So leave it alone till we've looked at the hair. If it doesn't match, you'll have wasted time."

"Like time better spent watching spaniels squat?"

"The squatting spaniels could lead to a witness. So could the busses. You're checking the busses?"

Ross threw his hands up and stalked to his desk.

Brymmer felt stiff from the hours of sitting. He paced to the window and looked at the street. The Russian Embassy, facing the precinct on 67th, was silent and dark— a stolid *Nyet* in the midst of Manhattan. He finished his smoke and went back to his desk, gave the finger to Bloomberg and woke his computer.

He typed in *Clawson.*

Computer crashed.

He poured some coffee and tried it again.

He got a message. *Files updating. Try again later.*

He tried something else.

He wanted to know how the crime was reported. He'd read the story, like everyone else, but he'd been off duty and hadn't been called. It was just a murder— something the squad from the local precinct could handle itself. But the missing crotch had been inside buzz; he was almost certain it hadn't been tipped to the general public, and that was the thing. The thing that could point to a serial killer, opposed to a one-off, opposed to a fluke, opposed to a copycat. Nothing was sure, but it tilted the focus— broadened the picture— changing the lay (as it were) of the land.

RICHARD CLAWSON, MERRILL EXEC, FOUND SLAUGHTERED (*The New York Times.*) The story was level and unexcited. A Wall Street wizard was found in his home with some multiple stab wounds and "mutilations." (There was the word again.) Nothing more.

MILLIONAIRE MANSION, A HORROR CHAMBER. "BLOOD WAS

EVERYWHERE." (*New York Post*). And once again, there were "mutilations." Also a photo of Clawson's house—a gated townhouse on West 11th. A shot of his widow — "the former model, Andrea Clawson" (age 36)— who'd been "seeking divorce" when the murder occurred.

BLOODY NEW YEAR (*The Daily News*). The murder had happened, as best it was known, in the early hours of New Year's Day (a Thursday morning, as Brymmer recalled) but the body lay rotting till Monday morning, much to the horror of Clawson's maid. Nothing was said of the crotchless wonder the woman had witnessed at 7 A.M.— another "impossible thing before breakfast" that surely would haunt her for the rest of her days.

"You spending the night here?" Brymmer looked up: Reginald Kerner, precinct detective. A man he respected and wished he could nab, if presented the option, to fill out the team. Kerner was balding, with rimless glasses, a bony frame and an arrogant nose, more apt to get "made" as an English professor than anyone vaguely connected with "cop," and smart as ratshit.

Brymmer said, "No," and shut the computer. The research could wait. He belonged on the street. In a couple of minutes, the tour, as officially defined, would be over, the room would be empty, the floor would be dark, but persistent detectives would be out on the street.

"Then I'll see you tomorrow," Kerner said, yawning. "Man oh man but we're in for a bitch."

"Let's hope we catch her."

"All I can say is I'm glad I'm married. It lowers the odds."

"But just to be safe, better hide your razor."

"I use electric."

"Then sleep well."

## 13

*Sunday, January 25th:*

Ross had arranged to get a message texted to the night-shift drivers who'd been driving the bus routes— uptown and down—in the four-block radius from Lexington to First.

The message was hazy but the best he could do:

Did anyone remember having picked up a woman (likely a looker, probably a blonde) between 4 AM to 7, 59th to 63rd, who'd attracted their attention [full stop] or attracted their attention on account of acting odd?

He got one (count em) taker. An overnight driver on the M15 line. Ross arranged to meet him in a bus drivers' coffee shop at just around breakfast time, the end of the man's shift. As soon as Ross entered, the driver, who was settled in a booth, rose and smiled.

"You the guy?" he said.

"The *which* guy?"

"Policeman."

"Is it written all over me or what?"

"Like my uniform." The man grinned and pointed at himself.

Ross was wearing cords and a navy blue pea coat. He nodded resignedly, ordered a black coffee, and slithered into the booth. The driver, who was built along the lines of Ralph Cramden, by inordinate coincidence was also named Ralph. Ralph was indulging in a mug of black coffee and some lemon meringue pie that looked as though it might have been extruded from Crayolas.

"So tell me about the woman."

"Not a whole lot to tell. Not really. Picked her up around five, five-thirty. Sixtieth, I'm sure."

"And Second."

54

"That's right. She was standing there alone and the bus here was empty. Not unusual, really, for the middle of the night. She was drunk, is what I think."

Ross took a swallow of the foul-tasting coffee as he prompted, "Why'd you think?"

"She was wobbly, to start with." The driver shoveled pie. "Kinda shaky on her feet. So she navigates the aisle, goes directly to the back which I think is kinda funny. I mean usually, the bus being empty, they're in front, except she bee-lines— well actually, she wobbles— to the rear. After that, she starts giggling."

"Giggling."

"Well... kinda laughing to herself. I can't see her, just hear her but there's no one else around. That's about what I can tell you."

"And where'd she get off?"

"Couldn't tell you. Forty-Second, Thirty-Fourth, you get a crowd. Twenty-Eighth, you get the nurses. There's a Bellevue there, you know."

"Do I know," Ross inserted.

"And, aside from that, she must've gotten out the back door."

"Describe her."

"Just a girl."

"Just a girl," Ross repeated. "Not a woman. How young?"

"Hey look. I'm forty-seven. Forty-*two* to me is young."

"Take a stab."

"I dunno. Twenty-eight? Thirty-one?"

"How tall?"

"Aw look. I mean I really couldn't say."

"Hair color."

Just another head shake and shrug. "Like it's win-

55

tertime, you know? Like the ladies bundle up. They got head scarves and ski caps and seventy kindsa hats. They got coats that make em look like an igloo that's walking."

"Was she wearing an igloo?"

Ralph thought it over. "Well no. I don't think. Just an ordinary coat and don't ask me what's the color since I'm colorblind anyway."

Ross threw a couple of dollars on the table. "For the coffee. Or whatever that shit was," he said.

"Was I helpful?"

"Very possibly." Ross liked to lie and he liked to keep in practice.

"Nice meeting you, Detective."

"Nice meeting you too."

## 14

On Sunday, God rested. To the men of the Manhattan Homicide Task Force, He cackled, "Fat chance," and then added, in a slightly majesterial undertone, that "Vengeance is *mine*, but you guys can do the legwork and then we can talk."

And so it ever was, and so would ever be.

Brymmer, who'd been out on the streets before the sun, had— after dropping off his shirts at the laundry and loading up on bad frozen dinners at Gristede's— spent the better part of the morning in the grips of his computer, perusing all the DD5's about Clawson. Every detective who had dealt, or was currently dealing, with a case, filed a mandatory end-of-day summary of his work on a form (Number 5) that was issued by the lords of the Detective Division. When Brymmer had begun his career on the force, the forms had been a triplicated bundle of paper that was filed at the precinct. Now that the Department had glommed to computers, the forms were available at anybody's desk, so Brymmer didn't have to go traveling downtown and rifling through papers.

Except that he did.

A form was essentially a "just the facts ma'am." But the fullness of any story lay in flickering impressions — the never-stated glimmerings of savvy detectives who were far too savvy to write them all down.

So Brymmer sat talking to Detective John Ritter— a 30 year veteran who was scarfing down his lunch at a battle-scarred desk at the 13th Precinct. Ritter had hold of a club sandwich. He looked up at Brymmer, grunted, and bit. Tomato and mayonnaise blasted his face; the turkey slid out and plopped on his desk. Ritter sighed. "There are days…" he said.

Brymmer just nodded and watched as the man reconstructed his sandwich. Ritter had the tough, line-scoured face that seemed to be given to thirty-year cops instead of the gold watch and the Dinner. Ritter wiped mayonnaise off of his nose. "So—" he said, "tell me what else you want to know."

Brymmer spread his hands. "Just tell the whole thing."

"Whole thing." Ritter sipped at some coffee. "Whole thing. Okay, so he attends a big New Year's Eve party—Clawson, that is— gets totally plotzed. Guests confirmed it. Totally plotzed. In fact, passes out. Two of his buddies—"

"Merino and Jacobs?"

"Yeah that's the ones. They decide to take him

home. They're buzzed but not plotzed. *Also* confirmed. They get a car-service car. They tell the driver to wait. Shlep Clawson up the stairs, toss him gently on the bed, strip him down to his undies, go back, take the car. Driver confirms this. Says they were gone about only ten minutes and they didn't look ruffled and they didn't look bloody and they didn't look like guys who'd just de-genitaled their chum."

"Hold on. Was he told about—"

"The whack-off? No. I was speaking metaphorically." Ritter took another quick bite of his sandwich, losing turkey as he went. This time he left it. "Okay. So the driver drives both the guys home—"

"Separately?"

"Yeah. They had two separate homes. And they're easy all the way. Buzzed but not plotzed. They talked, the guy said, about Bolivian futures."

"And what the hell's that?"

"Beats *me*," Ritter said, "but you can't pronounce 'Bolivian futures' if you're plotzed. What I mean is, they were not beyond the realm of making sense. However, they're buzzed enough, they just can't remember what they did about the gate. Here— Let me show you."

Ritter pulled a photograph up on his computer. Brymmer saw a townhouse— a three-story limestone with a decorative six-foot wrought iron gate that made a cage between the sidewalk and a small stone courtyard that fronted the house itself. The gate was electrified. A sign in the window said *Protected by Holmes*.

"They entered using Clawson's keys from his pocket. One of those keys was for the gate on the street and the second for the house. They remember leaving Clawson's keys on the dresser—and we found them on the dresser— so they didn't lock the house but they just can't remember what they did about the gate which has an automatic lock. You slam it, it locks. Did they leave it half open for anyone to see? Did they close, but not slam it? Or did they, after all. Slam it, I mean. So you see where that gets us."

"I don't know," Brymmer said. "A random burglar who's a maniac perv? In any case, it sounds as though the place wasn't burgled and a burglar steals your Rolex, he doesn't steal your cock. So what else is there? A Charlie Manson and his merry band of freaks? A stalker? A stalker who's waiting on the street? Was it random or personal? Was it someone with a key who just figured he'd be ripped by the end of New Year's Eve? Or discovered he was ripped and decided to have fun."

"Some fun," Ritter said. He shook his head slowly. "Those are all the right Q's to which we ain't got the A's."

"But you do have the hairs."

"The blonde ones. Yeah. On the other hand, they didn't have a time stamp on em, so who the hell knows."

"We found some at Starrett's."

Ritter raised his brows.

"I thought we might at least get the lab to compare them."

"You got it," Ritter said.

"Something else I'd like to have— his contacts. To see if we can match them to Starrett's. Any girls they knew in common. Hell, even any *guys* they knew in common. We're fishing," Brymmer said. "Now tell me about the wife."

"You want to take a walk? I need air on my head."

———

They stopped at a deli. Ritter bought coffee. Brymmer bought coffee and a toasted bialy. There were benches by the door of the School of Visual Arts. They sat. It was cold but there was no ripping wind. People passed by with the Sunday *New York Times*— all twenty-three pounds of it. Ritter said, "I didn't think they did that any more."

"What?"

"Read papers. That generation?" He pointed at a girl. "Only thing they read is the lint in their own navels.— Where were we?"

"The wife."

"Andrea. You want my opinion, she'd be It."

"Except."

"Except for that alibi. Right. Car picked her up for a party in Connecticut. Three other people and the driver say it's so. Not only that, but she stays there the weekend. Witnesses confirm. Still, she had everything to gain from his demise and she was sure as hell angry. Didn't even disguise it. She's informed, she says, 'Oh.' Like that. Just 'Oh.' Then she says, 'Well, the sonofabitch had it coming.'"

"Marriage," Brymmer said.

"Hey, don't knock marriage. I been married twenty years. I got a sweetheart."

"Yeah, well you're lucky," Brymmer said.

"On the other hand, I don't have the forty-million bucks that would make me worth killing."

"That what Andrea got?"

"Yeah. They'd been divorced, she'd've only gotten two, poor baby. As the widow, gets it all."

"So why was she angry?"

"He's a lush who fucked around. But the point was, he found a younger version of Andrea and wanted to

60

trade her in."

"So it was he—"

"Not exactly. According to their agreement—and I'm talking pre-nup—if it's *him* that left *her*, she'd've bagged a lot more, so what he wanted was both ways. Stay married, bring the other lady into the apartment."

Brymmer laughed and said, "That was no lady."

"Yeah. *That's* the truth." Ritter shook his head. "What's *wrong* with these people?"

"Boredom," Brymmer said. "They've tried everything there is and they say, 'Is that all?' and they invent something else."

"We thought for a while about a contract..."

"Say what? You mean a contract killer? Well there's an idea. Here's ten thousand bucks to go to bed with my husband, right after which I'd like you to whack off his dick. And since nobody sane would take up that proposal..."

"I know," Ritter said. "So we're left with it's a nut. As you know, we checked the downstate mental asylums. There was nothing. Only dick-whackers known to them were guys. And those guys are in the lockup for the criminally insane."

They were silent. Brymmer balled up the paper from his bialy and tossed it into the now empty well of the paper cup.

Ritter looked at his watch. "Nice chatting with you, Burt," he said, grinning mordantly. "I wish you good luck."

## 15

*New York Post, Sunday, bottom of page 42:*

ACTOR FOUND DEAD IN EAST SIDE APARTMENT

Monty Starrett, 31, an actor who appeared on several episodes of television's CSI in recent years, was found dead in his apartment at 293 East 62nd St. on Saturday afternoon. The death has been ruled a homicide. Mr. Starrett died of multiple unspecified knife wounds, according to police. An autopsy has been scheduled for Monday afternoon. The investigation will be headed by Sgt. Burt Brymmer (rhymes with skimmer) of Manhattan's Major Homicide Task Force. Brymmer had no comment at this time.

It was 4 PM. Brymmer was sitting with Captain Parisi and Lieutenant Meyer in the Captain's office. Parisi and Meyer were calm and well-rested— the Captain, as always, particularly dapper. Parisi affected those three-piece suits and the black tasseled loafers and the ruby signet ring that made him enjoy making gestures with his hands. Brymmer suspected that he also got manicures. Sometimes his nails were unnaturally bright. Brymmer sat sprawled in the second of the leatherette visitor's chairs. Discounting the something like four hours off in which he'd slept, eaten, showered, shaved, shopped and come back, Brymmer'd worked, straight now, for 24 hours. So had his men.

"So?" Parisi asked.

"So nothing," Brymmer said. "No witness, no weapon. We're looking into websites. We're checking out the local loony asylums for anyone they might've let go of too soon but the Ritter guys have pretty much done that to death so I doubt it pays off. We got a bunch of blonde hairs and we're waiting on the lab. Aside from that, we'll just keep doing what we're doing, then do it all again. I'm widening the canvass. We'll go back, talk to everyone we've talked to before. Keep checking Starrett's contacts. See if there's any kind of nexus with Clawson. The only thing I know about the girl is she's careful. And pretty damn lucky."

"And blonde," Meyer said.

Brymmer shrugged. "Time will tell."

"Time," Parisi said. "We have to talk about time. Time which is money. I don't have to tell you how the city's cutting back. Of course they're not cutting back on the limos for the council, or the Health Department ads about how you drink a Pepsi and your toes'll fall off, or that contractor ripoff cost forty million bucks, so the cutbacks are us. So first, I have to tell you how I can't give you any more men to help you out and then I have to tell you how days off are cancelled. Double tours when you can."

"I've done that," Brymmer said. "I could still use some men."

"Hey," Parisi said. "I just told you. Can't do." He shrugged. "The old can't-do spirit of New York."

"So," Meyer added, "just do the best you can."

"Or can't," Brymmer said.

## 16

*Wednesday: January 28th:*

Report from the Medical Examiners office: Starrett had eaten six hours before dying (a healthful combination of salmon and greens) and had ejaculated shortly before the main event. No vaginal secretions had been found on his body which was not too surprising considering the general nature of the wound. He'd also had some alcohol riding in his system and he'd mixed it with Valium. That was not what had killed him.

Report from Forensics: The blood was all Starrett's. If other blood was there, it was too commingled, or otherwise corrupted by the bleach in the Comet, to be able to be read. Zero fingerprints other than Starrett's were found in the bathroom. The soap cake was gone. A towel (which potentially was lousy with skin cells to test for DNA) appeared to be conspicuously missing from the rack.

Report from Forensics: Word had come back on the exfoliated hair. It was natural hair. Not from a wig. It was natural blonde. Not bleached. It was healthy hair. No split ends. It was twenty-point-oh-oh-six inches long with resins of polyvinyl acetate on it or, in other words, plastic or, in other words, hair spray. In other words, the boys in the lab all agreed: the long blonde hair was a long blonde hair. And identical to hairs that were found at Clawson's.

There were other reports. Starrett's laptop had revealed he had very little interest in blogs, or in hookup websites, or online games. His tweets were insipid. His Facebook page was a paeon to himself. His address book had given over twenty-six names and, with seven detectives now sifting through the list, nobody'd turned up anyone they "liked." Most of the women had provable alibis, wrong-color hair, bleach jobs, niceness, double pneumonia, or other excuses that let them off the hook. None of the men (4, count em, 4) had admitted to having had relations with Starrett, though one added "Darn it."

Brymmer looked up. It was 8 AM and for the whole of his squad, as opposed to just half, it was a turnaround day. Detectives who'd been working the second tour Tuesday, worked the first tour Wednesday, at least for this week. Brymmer'd come early to check the reports. He glanced around the alcove (it did not have a door) that served as the offical task force office— a crowded little nook that afforded only room for six desks, six chairs and a filing cabinet, with not a lot of space left for anything else except a coat tree, microwave and bulletin board. Ross was approaching through the frame of the archway, looking morose and entirely downed. Ross took his coat off, announced that it was colder than his mother's heart, was so cold that *wages* had actually frozen which proved that you couldn't trust Democrats either and further, after six hours off from Starrett, he'd decided that the butler had definitely done it.

Clark walked in in the middle of this and, shaking his dark bald-shaved head, had succinctly remarked, "*What* energy crisis?" and Brymmer broke up.

Dubisky and Kerner had now straggled in along with McAllister and finally Corelli. Corelli was the newest member of the team, having transferred directly out of Narcotics, and still looked as though he were an undercover geek.

Everyone sat now and stared at Brymmer.

"We wondered why you called us here," Dubisky prodded.

"Yeah. We were having such fun," Ross said.

Brymmer was about to say something incredibly funny and tremendously obscene when the Captain passed by and Brymmer said, "Yeah. Okay, as I was saying, I think we're gonna have to pursue both lines," which saved him from having to think of something funny and tremendously obscene.

"*What* both lines?" Ross said crossly.

"The ones I was saying," Brymmer replied. "Has your mind gone drifting again, Detective Ross?"

The Captain disappeared through a door at the side.

"All right," Brymmer said. "The hairs at both Starrett's and Clawson's were a match. Are we looking at a psychopath who knew both men and who thought she had a wacked-out reason to kill them? Or she picked them at random. I believe we're down to that. If it's the first, we've got a prayer. If it's the second…" He shrugged. "And in any case, we keep on looking for a witness."

"So what about the Symington hair?" Ross pursued.

"No report. And from the rest, we'll get no DNA. These were hairs without roots. So they weren't yanked out, they were broken or shed."

"She's a shedder, all right," Dubisky agreed. "Like it's molting season for vampire bats."

"Something else," Brymmer said. "Starrett had Valium and booze in his blood. So I figure must've had a few shots at the bar, come home and at some point popped in a pill. There was a glass at his bedside. Which possibly indicates he'd taken it to sleep. Which throws in a clinker."

"I don't exactly follow," McAllister said. He was large, thirty-one and the youngest on the squad. A man who didn't look as though he'd ever lost sleep.

"Because why," Kerner said, "if you're making it— or let alone planning to make it— would you want to go to sleep?"

"Un*less*," Dubisky said, "he took the Valium after.

Maybe they had a fight. She leaves. He's upset. Takes a pill. She comes back. Anyway explains why he might've been groggy. Especially if he mixed it."

"Un*less*," Clark suggested, "he took the pill *first* and then surprise, there she is. Knock-knock. Hi, honey."

Brymmer said, "Which still doesn't tell us who she is."

McAllister reported that the street cameras hadn't recorded any action— "at all," he said— between exactly 3:21 and 5:47 when a dog walker—guy with maybe six, seven dogs—had been captured on a pooper-watch at Sixty-Third and Third. McAllister had suffered through a six hour session with the street-camera files, covering the time between 2 AM and 8. He'd even seen Starrett as he headed back home— heading east off of Lexington at 3:07.

Ross reported on behalf of himself, Dubisky, and Clark that she didn't take a cab and then added as an afterthought that cab drivers lied about as badly as they drove and they did it in a range of unfathomable accents so you couldn't really tell if they were making shit up or just being Pakistani. Brymmer said, "You want to repeat that in English?" Ross said, "She probably didn't take a cab."

The telephone rang: A woman reporting that her cat was up a tree. "Is he dead?" Corelli said. "Or you've got the wrong number."

The telephone rang. Kaplan, who'd been working on the dog walker gleam, had a witness with a possible description of the girl.

## 17

They called it The Green Room because it was green—
a converted file room with the words *Interrogation
Room* written on its door which made innocent people
nervous and the guilty ones shrug. There was, as in the
Hollywood version of the room, a long wooden table
and a few never-comfortable straight-back chairs, but
the who-are-you-guys-kidding two-way mirror had been
long ago replaced by the video cameras that connected
to monitors in the room behind The Room. Looking at
them now were Kerner, Dubisky, McAllister and Kaplan
who'd brought the man in. Matson, who was busy on
a case of his own, would of course be immediately and
thoroughly informed about the fruits of his magnificent
idea about the stakeout.

On the inside of the room were Brymmer and Ross
and a Harold Ziegler, a guy of twenty-seven with curly
brown hair and a heavy blue sweatshirt and the sniffles
of a cold.

Brymmer let Ross do the basic prelims. The put-
ting-the-guy-at-ease and the Thanks-for-stopping-by.
This was not, after all, a criminal interrogation. While
Brymmer sat lazily in a tipped back chair and Ziegler
eyed him furtively and then looked away, Ross began
asking him to "start from the beginning. —Where were
you coming from?"

"Home," Ziegler said. "Oh! I guess you mean
geo*graph*ically, right? I'm on East Sixty-Second Street.
Just west of Third. I was walking Hillary."

"The dog," Ross said. "And what time was it,
about?"

"I don't know. After five. Between five, five-thirty."

"And where'd you see what?"

"At the corner of Second."

"And where?"

"Sixty-second."

Ross didn't blink. But with that, Ziegler'd placed her in the shadow of Starrett's door. Ross said, "Go on."

"So anyway, that's where I happened to see this girl. She'd just fallen on the ice. Crack! You could practically hear it when she hit."

Ross looked at Brymmer who was looking at the camera and imagining Dubisky who'd be punching his own palm, going *Yessss! Yessss!*

"And what did you do next?"

"I went over and helped her up. I said, 'You okay?' she said, 'Yes, I think so,' and I guess we said some more stupid stuff like that and that was basically it."

"And where did she go from there?"

"I believe down Second."

"Was she limping?"

"A little. I mean, she was just a little wobbly on her feet."

"And you. Where'd you go?"

"Turned around and went home."

"Describe her," Ross said.

"She was really quite pretty. Maybe medium height. Thin, I suppose. Or at least not heavy. Her eyes, I dunno. I believe they were kind of light but don't ask me for more specifics."

"How about her clothes."

"Um...wool coat...Dark. Boots. I remember boots. And this crazy little hat."

Brymmer leaned forward. "Describe it," Brymmer said.

"It was...I dunno...it had these braids coming down."

Brymmer and Ross locked eyes for a second.

"So," Ross said, "you didn't get to see her hair?"

"Uh-uh. I didn't."

"Okay. Will you talk to an artist?" Ross said. "Let him try to get a picture?"

"Sure." Ziegler glanced up at Brymmer. "What she do?"

"I really don't think you want to know," Brymmer said. "But just because you saw her doesn't mean that she did it.—Can I ask some more questions?"

"Sure. Why not? But I told you what I know."

"Like...why were you walking your dog at that hour?"

Ziegler shrugged. "I work nights. I get home, I walk the dog. Otherwise the dog'll have to wait until noon and a dog, well you know it. A dog's gotta go."

"Just out of curiosity...you mind just telling me where it is you work?"

"Maybe, Maybe Not."

"Like you'd mind it or you wouldn't?"

"No. That's the name of the place that I work. It's a hot club in Chelsea. Thought everybody knew."

"Some of us are less cool than others," Brymmer said. "What time does it close?"

"Officially? Three."

"And *un*officially?"

Ziegler got an Uh-oh look on his face.

"What time did you leave there?"

"Um. Am I allowed to take the Fifth Amendment?"

"Sure. You can also refuse to answer. You can also call your lawyer.—Come on." Brymmer laughed. "What time did you leave?"

"About a quarter of five. I tend bar. There's a whole lot of cleanup to do."

"Oh, man," Brymmer said. "Look. I don't care if you lock up the doors, snort stash, or if the place turns into a brothel. That's not what we're about, and I wouldn't follow up. I'm just trying to determine the condition of your head. How reliable you are."

"Okay. I admit I did a line," Ziegler said. "But it didn't screw my head. And my girlfriend would probably kill me if she knew. She's a stickler on that."

"You live with her?"

"Yeah. She's a nurse. She works nights. It works out for us fine."

"Was she there when you got home?"

"Yeah. Why?"

"Just curious, that's all."

"*Okay*," Dubisky said. He was sitting on his desk and exuding smugness.

"And if you add 'I told you so' you're dead," Brymmer said.

"But at least we got something."

"Or to quote Mr. Ziegler, Maybe, maybe not. Look— we know from Alfie that the girl lost her keys. So she might have stayed over with a friend in the neighborhood. It's not necessarily as exciting as you think." Brymmer took a pause. "Though I hope to hell it is."

"What now?"

"Now I think we want to track her to the bus. If the girl is our girl, it could help at least to know if she was heading downtown." Brymmer turned to Ross. "You said Kathy has the hat. Go get it, bring it in and you can show the thing to Ralph. See if it anyhow rings a faint bell. That, plus whatever we can get out of Ziegler." Brymmer paused again. "And, while you're about it, you can call in your girlfriend."

71

"My girlfriend."

"Carmen. She seemed to get a pretty good gander at the girl. So next time you see her, whenever it might be, you can have her come in and see the art department guys. And Alfie. Why not? Let's see what we can get."

"Ya know?" Ross said. "Sometimes I think you're not as stupid as you look."

"What? About Carmen?"

"Never mind," Ross said.

"Okay—" Kerner seemed to be impatient with the drift— "so even if the driver ID's her, what then? And besides, it seems her most important feature is a hat."

McAllister laughed. "So I got it. We could put out an APB. 'Calling all cars. Be on the lookout for a woman in a hat.'"

"I don't know," Brymmer said. "I don't know what's next. But we know she was hanging at McGinty's at... what? maybe seven to eight? So I guess you go back and check the street files again. See if you can find her heading into the bar. Or out of it. That'd give us something to go with. A picture we could show."

"And aside from that?"

"We go over Clawson's stuff again. We look for something Starrett and Clawson had in common. Though at this point, I doubt it's something obvious," Brymmer said. "And keep interviewing girls."

"Under the circumstances," Ross said dryly, "that's not such a wonderful assignment, after all."

# 18

*Thursday, January 29th:*

It was snowing. Again. The Global Warmists were getting alarmed.

Nothing much happened.

The interviews with Carmen, Alfie and Ziegler had resulted in the likenesses of three different women, none of whom were vaguely familiar to Ralph though he did, however, think he might have seen the hat.

Ross said that Kathy couldn't find the thing at all and decided that she'd probably left it at her sister's. Brymmer said, So go buy another one, stupid. You said they were selling them somewhere near the park, and Ross had said he wasn't so stupid after all because he'd looked for the vendor but the vendor wasn't there. "Well, perhaps he'll be back by the summer," Brymmer said.

The surveillance camera files had indeed shown a girl walking out of McGinty's, alone, around eight, but the overhead cameras didn't really catch a face and in any case she'd instantly opened an umbrella.

Brymmer inquired about the Symington hair and the lab replied "*What* Symington hair?" and Brymmer'd said, "Find it." Three hours later, the lab called him back and admitted they'd lost it.

Ross was upset. Brymmer said, "There's always some more where it came from. You can always go wee-wee in her bathroom again."

"If you really think the hat-lady might not be It—"

"Hey look—I never *said* that she might not be it. I just said there could also be another explanation for why she hung around. And at the moment, it's moot."

"Then I'd really like to think about the Symington some more."

"Why?"

"Because for now, she's the only game in town,"

---
**19**
---

*Sunday, February 1st:*

# JACKIE THE RIPPER??

Someone had leaked the full story to the press. The *Post* and the *News* had a field day with it, and a radio shock jock, not quite amused enough with "Jackie the Ripper," had called her Cock Robin'.

---
**20**
---

*Saturday, February 14th:*

"All right. All right. I'm coming. Who is it?"

"Um…well actually you wouldn't know my name but Ramona sent me."

"Ramona *Pike?*"

"My goodness. Do you know any other Ramonas? I'm sure she'd be hurt."

"No. I don't."

"Okay. So I was sent by the one and only Ramona Pike."

"And you want?"

"I want what Ramona wants. She recommended you highly."

"You should have called first."

"I know. But I was feeling spontaneous tonight. I was passing by the neighborhood and thought I'd drop by, take a chance.— Want to open up the door? Take a chance yourself?"

"I can't. I'm not dressed.—So, wait a second. How come the doorman didn't buzz me?"

"He did. You didn't answer but he said that you were home."

"Okay. I guess he could've. I think I fell asleep. But listen, this wouldn't be a very good time. Really. I've got this incredible cold."

"Everybody does. It's been going around."

"It might be the flu."

"I've already had it. I believe I'm immune. David? How about it? My back aches awful and I really really-*really* need a massage. Really. Would you *please* open the door?"

"Well…okay. Just wait till I get a robe."

"Do you really need one?"

"Well, I guess not."

## 21

*Monday February 16th:*

"Sergeant?"

"Oh Jamie. Don't you ever give up?"

"Nope."

"And how the hell do you know where I'll be? I mean, even before *I* do?"

"Easy. We listen to police calls, Sergeant."

"Ah."

75

"Don't *you?*"

"No. I was listening to the Knicks game, in fact.—Watch it. There's a big patch of ice on the street. And stop following me, will you?"

"It's a public sidewalk."

"I'll have you arrested for reckless walking."

"So is this one connected to the others, Sergeant?"

"To *what* other sergeant?"

"To Clawson and Starrett. Otherwise you wouldn't be the first on the scene. It seems to me the case was directly sent to you. No one else has showed up except the squad car guys.—Sergeant?"

"I'm fresh out of answers, Lady. "

"Mmm. Are you also fresh out of leads?"

"And I'm running out of patience. I haven't even *been* to the crime scene yet, and —"

"Can you just tell me something? Anything? Please? I'm trying to make the eleven o'clock news."

"You can't use the tape if I swear on it, right?"

"No. Wrong. I can edit it out."

"Oh. Shit."

"So what can you tell me? I have to make air-time in twenty-five minutes."

"You see that good-looking blond over there? That's Detective Ross. Why don't, the next time, you go bother him?"

"I'm rather enjoying bothering you. Do I bother you, Sergeant?"

# 22

They rode to the seventeeth floor in silence. Clark, Dubisky, Brymmer and Ross and Alonzo Ramirez, the building superintendant. The story, as he'd told it to the first two officers, was basically simple. David Tanner wasn't answering his phone. He hadn't been well and his employer, an expensive little East Side gym known as Let's Get Physical, had called the superintendant who'd discovered why Tanner wasn't answering his phone.

The superintendant showed them in. He was quiet, cooperative, and hadn't seen Tanner in "practically a week. Of course, I'm not always here," he said, "I'm in the apartments. Leaky faucet. Stopped toilet. There's always something bad."

"Stick around," Brymmer said. "We'll want to ask you some questions. If someone has a stopped-up toilet, tell em, wait."

Ramirez seemed happy for the temporary leave from latrine duty after what had been a rough day. "You want me, I'll be in my apartment. You knock."

On the way to the bedroom of the Tanner apartment, they passed by a room that had a long mirrored wall and a massage table in it. Apparently, its owner "got physical" at home.

The bedroom was... The Bedroom. Deja vu. Tanner had been sandy-haired and very well built.

Dubisky said, "Christ. You gotta see it to believe it."

Brymmer said nothing. He turned, flicked his eyes at the bedside table: Kleenex. Aspirin. Afrin. Vicks.

Clark said sardonically, "I guess he had a cold."

Ross said, as flatly, "And a very sore throat."

Brymmer ignored them and scoped out the bed: The spread-eagled body. The wide open neck. The wide open crotch. The hand, reaching out across the pillow, tightly curled— its now-swollen fingertips encrusted in his blood. Bending now, Brymmer put a flashlight to the bed. He scanned it all thoroughly. No yellow hairs. He now turned his flashlight on the tightly curled fingers and something very nasty started curling in his gut. Caught in the fist, as well as under the fingernails, were long stiffened hairs. He looked up at Ross and then pointed with his thumb. Ross bent over now and looked at the hair.

Ross just stared at it, focussing the light.

"Red," he admitted after a while.

"Red." Brymmer nodded.

"Red," Ross agreed.

They were silent for a time. Clark and Dubisky came over to inspect.

"Or maybe," Clark said, "it only *looks* like it's red on account of all the blood."

"Maybe so," Ross decided.

Brymmer didn't say a thing. He leaned in close and took a picture with his phone. Then he turned to Dubisky. "It'll be what it is."

Sanders from the Crime Scene Unit arrived, mumbling to Brymmer, "Mass producing em, eh?"

Brymmer said, "You'll want to put a bag on the hand," and then exited the room, pulling Ross along with him. Silently, they moved to the bathroom, looked around. Ross checked the cabinet, prying it open with the tip of a pencil; Brymmer, touching nothing, took a look at the tub.

"Doxycyclene," Ross announced.

"Okay. What's it for?"

"Hell, it's for anything from acne to clap.—Pepcid …Lunesta…"

"Never mind. Just c'mere."

Brymmer, bending down on his knees above the tub, pointed down at his finding: the long blonde hairs that were poking through the drain.

More men were arriving; voices in the hall.

Brymmer grabbed a cigarette out of his pack, stuck it in his mouth and then ambled to the hall. He leaned on a closet, not-lighting up his smoke, as he talked to the arrivals. He suggested Dubisky go and interview Ramirez.

While Sanders took pictures, Rieger started fishing for the tokens in the tub.

A cop siren wailed. It was Brymmer's ring-tone. The call was from the Borough Commander's office, from Kluger, Padillo's second in command. "We got a live one," Kluger said. "He can ID the perp. Commander wants you over there in person like now."

"Where's 'there'?" Brymmer said.

"Beth Israel. Downtown."

"Who'm I looking for?"

"Who do you think?" Kluger said. "A poor sad sonofabitch without a dong."

## 23

The man was in the Emergency Room, in Bed Twenty-Six. There wasn't much they could do except shoot him with antibiotics and tetanus vaccine and infuse him with blood. "And then we called *you* guys," the intern said. "He was hollering all the time, you know? 'She did it! She did it! Get the police!'"

Brymmer nodded. "He still conscious?"

"Yeah. Flat with shock, but he wouldn't let us give him any drugs till you got here. Says he wants to talk."

They were standing in the corridor outside Emergency. Brymmer had brought Clark, leaving Ross to contend with Tanner.

Clark said, "So how did he get here and when?"

The intern shrugged. "Called for an ambulance."

"Himself?"

"Oh yeah. You can check the dispatcher. He got here, eleven. Eleven, give or take. I can tell you, man, we looked at him, the shape he was in, and the first thing we thought about—"

"Save it," Brymmer said. "Just tell us what's his name."

"Carson. Jack."

"Age?"

"Twenty-two."

"He live in the Village?"

"Yeah. West Eleventh."

Brymmer looked at Clark and then back at the intern, a tired blond kid with some blood on his blouse. "Let's go," he said.

The intern led them down the hall.

Jack Carson was lying in a curtained-off cubicle. Skinny— a long, pale, clean-looking boy with curly brown hair and large fevered brown eyes. A *young* twenty-two, Brymmer considered, and wondered how old he'd let himself get; what window, pill, or river he'd choose, or whether he'd manage to adapt, survive.

He pulled up a chair to the edge of the cot. "Hello, Jack," he said. "I'm Sergeant Brymmer." He flicked with his thumb. "And that's Detective Clark. So take it very slow now and tell us about it."

Shaking his head, the kid looked at Clark and then suddenly shivered. He looked back at Brymmer. "I—

80

I can't—I—" Slight southern accent.

"Just take your time."

"It hurts. Oh Christ, it really, there was just so much... much blood."

"Yeah. Look. Why don't you let them give you a shot? It won't— it won't put you out all at once. You'll still be able to talk to us."

"Yeah?"

"Yeah."

"Okay. Yeah. I gotta—I just gotta—look, oh look, does *he* have to be here?"

"Who?"

"*Him.*"

Brymmer looked at Clark. "See if you can find a nurse with a needle."

Clark just nodded and backed through the curtain.

Kid shivered again.

Brymmer said, "I'm the one that usually scares people. Were you scared of him?"

"No. I just don't like em."

"Cops?"

"Black guys."

"Oh." Brymmer nodded. "I thought you looked scared. Do black guys scare you?"

"Can I have a cigarette? They said I can't smoke here."

"Sure." Brymmer lit one and handed it over. The kid's hand was shaking.

"Black guys scare you?"

The kid made a quick and robotic little shrug. "Those guys beat me up. Two of em."

"When?"

"Long time ago."

"Why?"

"*Why?* Oh Christ, how do *I* know why? They just did. They were crazy."

"And what about the girl? Tonight. Was she black?"

"Oh no. Jesus, no. No. She was blonde." The hand that was holding the cigarette shook; dropped it.

Brymmer quickly picked it up from the floor. "Listen, I'll hold this for you, okay? Just tell me when you want it."

"Thanks." The kid nodded. He licked at his lips.

Brymmer said softly, "Just start at the beginning. How did you meet her?"

"Just met her on the street."

"What street?"

"I don't— I don't know. Around— around Sheridan Square."

"What time was it?"

"Nine?"

"And where were you coming from?"

"I don't—I don't remember."

"All right, son. Just take it slow. Just...try to give it a second and think."

"Some...some bar. I don't remember its name. And it's not important anyway."

"You're right. Go on."

"Can I have some cigarette?"

"Sure." Brymmer held it and let the kid puff.

He was starting to cry. "I...I don't know why I'm crying," he said. "I really don't cry. I'm not a crier."

"Everybody cries."

"I don't want to cry. I...hate criers."

"Then tell me what happened."

"I...met her on the street. She said, well, you know, she said 'You want to?'"

"Just like that? First thing? 'You want to?'"

82

"No. No, first she just asked me for the time."

"Yeah."

"And then we sort of talked for a while. And then she said, then she said, 'What do you like to do?'"

"What do you like to do?"

"You asking me?"

"Yeah. I mean, what did you tell her?"

"Just— just regular stuff, that's all."

"She talk about price?"

"No, nothing like that."

Brymmer just nodded. "And then what happened?"

"We went back to my place." The kid grew quiet. His eyes started shifting. He shivered again.

"And then you sucked her," Brymmer said softly.

"No! Jesus, no!— Why would you think I'd do something like that?"

"That's regular stuff, isn't it?"

"Oh. Yeah. I guess."

"But you didn't."

"No. No. We didn't do anything."

"Nothing?"

"No. Just the regular stuff."

Brymmer nodded. "And then what happened?"

"I—I fell asleep. And—and then… and then when I woke up, it— she—it was the cut that woke me up. And then— and then—and then she went away."

"With your penis?"

"She…threw it out the window. There's a window by the bed."

"And *then* what did you do?"

"Bled. Oh Christ, I bled. It hurt. Oh, Christ, it hurts now. Can I…can I just…can I just hold your hand?"

"Sure."

"I'm sorry."

"It's okay. Dig into it."

"It's just that it hurts."

"I know."

"I'm scared."

"I know. I know." Brymmer let a long moment go by. He drew in a breath and got ready to dive—his instincts telling him he'd land, quite safely, in a deep muddy pit. "Listen," he said. "You want to tell me the truth?"

"What—what do you mean?"

"I mean what really happened."

"I told you."

"It's all right," Brymmer said gently. "You don't have to. I know."

"What do you mean? Oh Jesus. What do you mean by *that?*"

"I mean...I know."

"You're wrong. I didn't do that. I wouldn't. I told you. They're crazy. My God. I *hate* them."

"I know. You hate wanting them."

"I don't. I don't. I swear to Jesus, I don't. I swear on my mother's—"

"Hey, it's okay," Brymmer breathed. "So maybe the guy forced you. That happens sometimes. Big strong black guy? Happens all the time. Is that what happened?"

"I—" The kid shook his head back and forth, and then cried for quite a while, pounding on the cot. "I didn't—I didn't — no, I didn't want to. You gotta believe that. Oh Christ. You believe me?"

"Sure. Sure I do. It just...wouldn't be so bad if you did."

"I didn't."

"I know." Brymmer took another high-diver's breath and expelled it in a sigh. "Jack...it wasn't bad enough to do that to yourself. To take a razor and do that. That's what you did though, isn't it? You picked up a razor and you—"

"No! Ohno. Ohno. I didn't do that. No." He was shaking his head so rapidly it looked as though he actually might shake it off. Or was trying to. "No. Ohno. I didn't do that. *He* did. After he forced me. He was big."

Brymmer whispered, "He was gone."

"No-no. He—"

"No. You."

"No Ohno, ohno, ohno, ohno, ohyes, ohGod, ohChrist, ohJesus get outta here, get outta here, get outta here, get outta here, get ou—"

A nurse hurried in with two large orderlies. "Get *out* of here," she yelled at Brymmer. "Get *out*. My God, what are you? Some kind of monster?" The orderlies were holding the boy down forceably, giving him the shot. "Get *out!*" the nurse hollered.

Brymmer just nodded.

Clark had been waiting outside the curtain. Silently, the two of them walked down the hall. There was a bench in the hall. Brymmer stopped in front of it, rubbing at his jaw. Suddenly sighing, he allowed himself to sit.

"I had to do that," he said in a while.

Clark nodded. "I know you did."

"Better call it in. See if we can get a few guys to go look for it. Maybe some genius here can glue it back on."

"Sergeant?" The intern was passing by the bench. "If they find it, use ice."

"They'll know that," Brymmer said. He unfolded from the bench and, while Clark punched a cell phone, he started down the hall.

"Sergeant?" The intern was calling him again. "I don't think you really want to go the front way. There's reporters in the lobby."

"What's your name, Doctor?"

"Finkel."

"So thank you, Dr. Finkel. Where's another way to go?"

"Down that way. Hang a left." A pause. The young doctor frowned thoughtfully at Brymmer. "Take care of yourself, Sergeant."

Brymmer made a short, fast, humorless *hah.*

The air outside had turned sharp and bitter. It had snowed again, coming down softly in the night, and the snow in the lot hadn't yet turned to soup; it was piled, white. He was watching his feet, so he really only saw her from ten feet away, sitting on the hood of his blue Camaro. She was wearing that same fur-collared coat that she'd had on at Tanner's with a fuzzy wool cap pulled down around her ears. For a snowy midnight, she looked pretty happy. For a sunny noon, she looked pretty happy. She looked pretty happy. She was swinging a long, tan-booted leg. She cocked her head. "I figured you'd take some sneaky way out. I remembered your car. Small wonder."

He froze. "Get off of it, Jamie."

She stopped with the foot; stared at him.

"Look.—Whatever you might've heard that brought you here," he said, "you heard it wrong, so move your ass."

"You mean it—"

"I *mean* that I am deeply in the mood now to punch out windows so *get…off…my car.*"

She didn't. Get off. Her grey eyes widened; she nodded, then said very softly, "You look tired."

"I *always* look tired," he growled deliberately. "This is how I look. Now for Chrissake—God*damm*it!" His anger was suddenly totally real. He was striding towards her, grinding his teeth. "You want to play kid-games, we'll play kid-games. Foot-in-the-door, ass-on-the-hood." He lifted her, scooping her up off the car, intending to drop her right in the snow. But she smelled of gardenias and the fur of her collar was tickling his neck and he just kept moving, out through the lot, not looking at her.

"Where are you taking me?" she said evenly.

"I thought I might take you to a landfill and dump you."

She said, "You're too tired."

He put her down quickly. "Exactly. Goodnight."

He turned abruptly and walked to his car.

## 24

*Early Tuesday morning: February 17th*

At exactly 1:30, with Brymmer on his way from reporting to the Chief, Ross was still pacing through the empty apartment. The apartment was telling him nothing at all. If walls had ears, they did not have mouths. Ross felt like pounding his fist on a wall, reading it first its Miranda Warning, but then just pounding it straight to the moon. (To the *mooooon*, Alice.) He stopped in the living room and leaned on a wall, glancing around at the dregs of the "scene." The place had been dusted, the body was gone, the sheets had been stripped and sent to the lab. Ross didn't pin much hope on the lab. The blood and the semen would there be examined by all the most modern forensic techniques, and the news would come back: The red stuff was blood and the sticky was come. Except for an occasional hit with DNA, forensic procedures mostly led you to zip, though that, in all fairness, he had to admit, was as much of the criminal's fault as the lab's.

Criminals rarely left you their prints. Instead of just placing their hands fair-and-squarly on a slick metal object, they tended, inconsiderately, to move them around, leaving a smudge. Or not to touch slick metal objects at all, but beach towels, table cloths, and warm fuzzy dogs. If a criminal happened to bleed on your scene, the chances were he bled too little or, unconscionably, did it on the floor where the blood got commingled with the Johnson's floor wax, or the victim's breadcrumbs, or something like that and was therefore "too impure to be typed." And then for the rest—the other details— the hairs, threads, buttons, paint chips, powder, lipstick, hangnails, dandruff, snot and blended Egyptian cigarette ash— Ross hardly ever found them at a scene unless it was maybe a scene from a 3 A.M. rerun of *Columbo*. The hairs they'd been happily finding so far had therefore been a truly remarkable find, almost, in fact, like a present from the killer. Or as Brymmer had observed before he'd departed, "It's almost like she's telling us 'Kilroy was here.'"

Ross had thought Brymmer had something on his mind, but there hadn't been the time to think about it then. Ross had been otherwise busy at the scene. The M.E. had told him that the death time was very likely

Valentine's Day— two days ago; Saturday— but really couldn't say if it was daytime or night because the heat was left on (later bulletins expected). Ross had then welcomed reinforcements from the squad who'd been canvassing the building and been learning not much. No one'd noticed anything fishy on Saturday. No one'd seen Tanner since at least Tuesday night when he'd sneezed on a baby in the elevator cab and which the Mother still resented. ("You'd think," she'd told Kerner, "he'd've done it on his sleeve.") Also, Ross learned, from Dubisky through Ramirez, that the cameras in the stairwells had been out since the spring so the cameras in the elevators wouldn't, necessarily, tell the whole tale.

Oh yes, there was one other thing to tell Brymmer but... here he was now.

"I heard," Ross greeted him. "Your boyfriend told me." Clark had come back and was looking at the elevator scenes even now in some warren at the precinct. Ross said, "You look like dogfood, by the way."

"Everybody's suddenly concerned with how I look. I'm touched," Brymmer said. He sat on Tanner's couch. "Fill me in on what's doing."

Ross filled him in. "I think you want to talk to the doorman, however."

"You didn't?"

"I did. But there's a changing of the guard. The night guy I talked to's a newbie to the building. He says to see the day guy. The day guy is yours."

"When's he on?"

"Eight to four."

"So tomorrow," Brymmer said. "What you learn from the night guy?"

"I learned there was a Valentine's party down the hall. Seventeen-J. Guy named Levy. Lotsa people in and out. I learned he told the night guy he didn't need to bother about buzzing people up on account of there'd be lots, so if they said they're for the party he should just let them go."

"And did you talk to Mr. Levy?"

"Mr. Levy wasn't home. Still isn't. I've been watching."

"So tomorrow," Brymmer said. "What Levy knows Monday, he'll also know Tuesday."

"It's al*ready* Tuesday."

"See?" Brymmer said. "And what about the weapon? Any theories about that?"

"Poultry shears."

"*What?*"

"Something strong and serrated. Dr. Thompson thought poultry shears. I said to him, 'What's more appropriate for a cock?'"

"Of course you did."

"So what are we doing?"

"Going home."

## 25

It was quiet in the house. Not a creature was stirring. Ross walked in through the quiet foyer, tossed his coat on the sofa and headed for the kitchen, thinking vaguely of coffee, sandwiches, whiskey, sex, and how goddam exhausted he was, and how nice it would be to just crawl into bed and find her there, sleep-warm, purring a little, and to run his hand down the smooth of her rump and to have her roll over and other such wild impossible dreams—

There was blood on the floor.

Fat, red, puddles of blood.

His eyes went up to the side of the sink and a twelve-inch bloody serrated knife and the streaks of blood, and he raced to the bedroom.

Kathy wasn't there.

The kid wasn't there.

He went back to the kitchen and looked at the floor. As blood puddles went, it wasn't that bad. He opened the cabinet under the sink and looked in the garbage and pulled up the red, still-frozen bagel she'd been trying to slice, and cursed, and went rapidly back to the hall, and leaned on the bell of Apartment Six.

"Hell, you might at least have left me a note," he barked at the woman who opened the door.

"I'm sorry," she said, and her tone was wry. "I didn't think."

Ross rubbed his eyes. "Yeah. Well I'm sorry I yelled at you, Sally. Where did she go?"

"Hospital. Wouldn't let me go with her."

"Bad?"

"Wasn't good. She cut through her palm."

"So. You got the kid?"

"Yeah. He's with mine."

"He scared?"

Sally Davis lifted her shoulders.

"Well, let me see him before I go."

"If you mean to the hospital, never mind. She called. She's already on her way back."

"Oh."

"Yeah.— Come in or go home before you fall down."

Ross went in. And found himself staring at Sally Davis's beautiful boobs. They were hidden under cover of a brown flannel robe, a dark coffee brown about the color of her skin, but the soft, round, deep, warm, incredible swell of them practically seemed like a pillow for his mind. Sally was Mrs. Davis and she lived quite alone with her nine year old kid, and if there happened to be anybody else in this world who Ross could fall in love with, really in love with, it was Sally Davis, with her easy mind and her beautiful boobs and her nine year old kid.

She stood there now with her hand on her hip, and said, "If you're lookin for your son, try the bedroom."

Nodding slowly, Ross turned around and felt her eyes still on him, still warm on his back. He followed the sound of a Road Runner rampage into a darkened green-and-white room where Jimmy Lee Davis lay on the covers of his neatly-made bed, and Billy Ross sat in his chair in front of an ancient twelve-inch set, with tears and drool coming down his face, and Jimmy Lee saying, "It's all right, Bill." And suddenly Ross had the urge to cry. To cover his face with his hands and weep. It had something to do with the sound of "Bill," and Jimmy Lee's handsome, bright little face and everything else in the goddam world.

Instead he said, "Got a towel or something?"

Frowning, Jimmy Lee nodded his head. "I dunno, Steve. He was really okay. We was watchin the show and laughin okay and all of a sudden—"

"I know," Ross said. "Just get a towel."

The kid went off and Ross took the radish's hair in his hand and smoothed it back from the crazy face and said, "It was just a cut on the hand. Listen, it isn't the end of the world," and added, "Listen, *you've* got your health," and turned off the set and the doorbell rang and Sally was saying, "Well look at that," and Jimmy came back with a Mickey Mouse towel, and Ross took the towel and walked to the door and there was Kathy, with a giant bandage around her hand and a nightgown sticking out from her coat and he looked at her and said, "Since we're out of bagels, I hope you've got some Thomas's English Muffins."

Kathy said, "oh," and started to cry.

Sally gave him a head-shaking glance. "Why don't I just keep Billy tonight. Maybe you two want to fight in peace."

Kathy said, "No," and Ross said, "Fine," and took Kathy by the cold, unbandaged hand and led her through the door.

In their bedroom he said, very gently, "What are you trying to do to yourself? Sprained ankles...cut hands...?" but all she wanted to do was cry. Didn't want to be held. Didn't want to be touched, so Ross went out to the living room couch and, after an hour, he fell asleep.

## 26

He took a Valium. He hated the goddam pills but they let him sleep, made the machine in his head click off. He stretched on the bed, set the alarm, turned on the radio. Soft voices sang, about arms...charms, and Brymmer looked up at the black window and found himself trying not to think, at all, about Jamie Rogers, how she'd felt in his arms. Nothing in that, he told himself. Nothing but another kick in the gut. Twice in his life he'd let himself want something warm and bright, something that cocked its head at him and grinned, and

93

93

looked at him with wide, steady eyes, and twice he'd
learned it was the fastest way to hell, and the second
time had hurt much more than the first because when
Nancy came along he'd been almost thirty-five and
should have known better, did know better, and ignored
what he knew, fooled himself, or tried to, and just for
a moment, as the drug slowed him down, he flashed
on Nancy, climbing under his covers, "Hey *cop*," she
said, and ran hands down his chest and he slowly closed
his eyes. She'd called him Cop. In her Wellesley accent,
she'd called him Cop. And it ended when he'd called her
a badge-crazy bitch, because that's what it was; she was
slumming that year. Daddy had bought her a gallery
in Soho, which featured, she'd told him, "experimental
art," and that's what she was doing—experimenting—
broadening her artist's palette, as it were, getting in a
little blue collar action before she reverted and eloped
with the Count. Or the stock broker. Or whatever he
was. "Hey *cop*," she said, and he was glad he'd taken
the goddam pill, that it was pulling him away from the
sound of her voice, from the scent of Jamie Rogers, the
sight of Tanner, the plight of that poor scrambled kid in
the bed, away from the radio blatting out the news that
Jackie the Ripper had struck again, that police had no
leads, that McDonald's was fixing his Egg McMuffin....

## 27

"You're really gonna hate this," Ross said, grinning.
"Yeah? It'll have to work hard," Brymmer said. "It's
got stiff competition."
They were heading for Tanner's. Brymmer had his

coat on. Ross had one of his arms in a jacket and the other one extended with a printout in its hand. Brymmer raised his eyebrows and reached for the printout. Ross held his hand up and pulled it back away. "Uh, uh, *uh*," he said. "I get to tell it first." He put the printout in his pocket and his arm in the sleeve.

"Remember how yesterday you burbled how we oughtta keep looking for a link between Starrett and Clawson?"

"As though it were yesterday."

"Guess who found it?"

Brymmer said nothing, just opened the car door and then waited till the engine had brought itself to life. "Spill," he said, pulling from the curb into traffic.

"In Clawson's contacts."

"DiAngelis checked them."

"*Cross*-checked them, did he? Side by side?"

"Right," Brymmer nodded. "And didn't find a thing."

"Because he didn't know everything."

"Spill," Brymmer said.

"Jennifer Symington."

Brymmer swerved quickly to avoid a damn bike. "Go on," he said. "Don't make me grovel for the news."

"She's in Clawson's Iphone."

Brymmer looked sideways.

"And she wasn't in Starrett's, not his Droid or his Mac, because Starrett didn't care and then he knew how to reach her, he could knock on the ceiling. And DiAngelis—"

"Right. Didn't know of her at all." As they crossed Park Avenue, Brymmer kept thinking as he circled around north and started heading for the Eighties. "So what do you want to do?"

"Well I thought we'd bring her in."

"Ask her what? Confront her with the bloody switchblade? Tell her we discovered her footprints on the wall?"

"Make her nervous. See what happens."

"I will take it under advisement."

"Does that mean you'll take it seriously?"

"I think so," Brymmer said. "I'd want to think about it, though."

He pulled up at Tanner's— a parking space right smack in front of the front door.

The doorman, Tim O'Fallon, was heavyset, fiftyish, and talkative as hell. He was, in fact, the male Irish version of a yenta.

"Listen, if you want to talk suspicious kind of characters, then mostly it's the tenants. Second, it's the nannies, and tied with that, the aides. You got people in and out of here I wouldn't want to trust to even babysit a guppy, but they have em wash their mothers. And they always rob em blind. You got girls, they're walkin outta here with two, three shopping bags they didn't come in with. Do the old ladies know it? I wouldn't want to bet. I mean some of the old ladies aren't compos in the mentis if you know what I'm tryin'a say. So, sure, I could tell you who was in and out Saturday or generally speaking. The only ones we really keep a list of is the prikes."

"Is the what?" Brymmer said.

"Puerto Ricans on bikes. Messengers. Delivery guys. Some of em are chikes."

Brymmer squinted. "Chinese?"

"Yeah. You catch on. Now you ask about the cameras. The ones in the stairwells. The ones that're on the blink. Now you know why that happens? The management is cheap. You got condos here, people paying five grand a month except the ones that's still stabilized but management is cheap. What they figure is that people see a camera, think it works. So why *pay* for it to work, if you follow what I'm saying. So anyway, a person could get off of the elevator anywhere at all and walk up and down the stairs without a person being wiser. You follow what I'm saying?"

"I follow," Brymmer said.

Ross cleared his throat and said, "I'll meet you up at Tanner's," and beat it to the back.

Brymmer said, "I heard there was a party on the floor."

"Levy. I heard."

"Is Mr. Levy here now?"

"No. On vacation."

"Oh? When'd he leave?"

"Sunday."

"Uh-huh. And you wouldn't, I suppose, know how long he'll be away?"

"Nope, but I figure he'd be down in Key West, San Francisco, like that, if you follow what I mean."

"You might've lost me," Brymmer said.

"I mean he's light on his feet. Couldn't say what his business is, I think he does well. Like a ballet dancer, maybe, or a hat designer, say."

Brymmer nodded. "Now tell me what you know about Tanner."

"Now, *there's* one." O'Fallon started grinning ear to ear. "Got a nifty little business. He works at some gym but he also works at home, if you follow what I'm saying. Does 'massages' upstairs. A lotta ladies in their fifties got some pretty bad backs, if—"

97

"I do." Brymmer nodded. "I follow what you're saying.—Any regular customers?"

"Oh yeah. Though I couldn't start to tell you who they are. Mrs. Smith and Mrs Jones, if you follow what I'm saying. I think he gives em one or two hours. Afternoons."

"Any *Mister* Smiths and Joneses?"

"Not that I could say. But then it wouldn't surprise me. You work at this job, you see everything. Twice."

"Any ladies on Saturday?"

"Nope. He was sick."

"And would you recognize the usual ladies if you saw them? Or if someone came over here and showed you a drawing?"

"Oh yeah. I got an eye."

"And did you ever eye a hat that had braids coming down?"

"Braids? What do you mean?"

"You don't follow what I'm saying?— Braids." Brymmer illustrated. "Braids down to here."

"Not that I know of, but I couldn't say for sure."

"Okay," Brymmer said, "if you think of something else, there'll be cops in and out of here, say, another week."

"That's fine," O'Fallon said. "And if they need me," he added, "I'll be more than glad to talk."

"I'll bet," Brymmer said, and went up to join Ross.


Ross said, "I know you're gonna think I made this up." He was lying on the massage table, hands behind his head. "I was poking into whatnot's."

"And what?" Brymmer said.

"Appointment book."

"And?"

98

"Symington. Three or four times every month. Six PM to seven." Ross pulled the book out from underneath his head. "I believe," he said, grinning, "this is called a trifecta."

"Let me see it," Brymmer said.

Ross handed it over. Brymmer flipped the pages: Jennifer Symington: three times a month and going back to September. Brymmer closed the book. "Okay, we call her in."

"Like tomorrow?"

"Could be. I want to look her over first."

"Look her *over?* How so?"

"Never mind," Brymmer said.

## 28

Six-thirty, he was home. Lay down. Fell asleep and started dreaming about hair. Blonde hair and red. In the dream, he was waiting for the lab to call in and was wondering if the red hair was actually red, and if it was, would it be leading him to two separate killers, or a redhead planting hairs? Or neither. If the killer could have planted the blondies, she could also plant the reds. If the reds were really red. He woke, and was wondering exactly the same thing. Only one thing was certain: He would not find a whole lot of answers in his bed.

He got up, took a shower, and shaved while the bathroom was still full of steam. Returning, he carefully made up the bed and picked up the pile of yesterday's clothes. Disorder bothered him. Loose ends; leftover pieces. They made him restless. He liked to come home to things-in-their-place, to a surface of calm, an illusion of order. He'd once heard a radio playing Bach and it seemed to encapsulate the things that he craved:

Mathematical melody. Answered calls. Contradiction encompassed, fused, and explained. And yet, he reflected as he shucked off the towel, as much as he longed for the neatness of order, as much as he tracked it like some kind of grail, that much did he test it, probe it, suspect it, and finally expose it for what it really was: an *illusion* of order, a *surface* of calm.

At the closet, he selected his clothes with some care—pulled out a good pair of cavalry twills and a soft tweed jacket, and picked out a tan, turtleneck sweater. Cashmere. He'd once considered strangling Ross for whistling loudly at the same sweater, and Brymmer'd gone on to make everything worse by attempting to pass the thing off as a present when we all know that nobody gives Brymmer cashmere. Stupid, he certainly had to admit, but what made the whole incident tougher than that was that Brymmer— no fool about human nature, and sometimes even no fool about his own— had managed to notice the Terrible Truth behind his reaction:

He was *vain!* A folly beyond belief. He'd believed, right up to September the Twelfth and the Infamous Transaction at Barney's Warehouse, that dressing well was, at best, revenge, or at worst, a crutch, an apology even. But Ross's whistle had cut through that, and just in case Brymmer had missed Ross's point, Ross had gone syrupy as southern breakfast and sang about "My how the thing do cling," showing off Brymmer's "beautiful biceps, terrific torso, and wonderful waist," in fact, enhancing the whole remarkable six-foot, hundred-and-sixty-pound body and, not only that, Ross had observed, it really sets off the color of your cock.

Fuckit. He reached for and strapped on his holster, pushed in the gun and, armed with Pringle and Smith & Wesson, went off to do….whatever he'd do.

## 29

He parked, as before, at the station house curb, tossed the card on his dashboard *(New York City Police Department/ Restricted Parking Plate)* and walked the two blocks to the Fox 5 studios. He'd phoned in advance. Told her he wanted a private screening, not a big deal. She'd told him she'd arrange it for a quarter-after-eight when she'd be finished on air and with the newsroom conference.

It was twenty after eight. The facade of the building was a bright shiny metal and reflected like a mirror. Walking east, as he was, it observed him from the left and he glanced at it, thinking that he looked almost normal, or at least from the left.

In the lobby, he told them "Miss Rogers expects me," signed his name in a book, and averted a pass through the metal detector by flashing his shield at the monitoring guard and then quickly, discretely, pointing at his rib cage to indicate the gun.

An elevator took him to the fourteenth floor. She was waiting in the reception room— a knockout redhead in an emerald green dress.

"Merry Christmas," Brymmer said.

"What?"

He said, "Nothing." And continued to say nothing as she led him into a corridor and into a maze of halls and then finally to a dim, overheated little room about the size of a closet—just spacious enough to hold a single console, two midget-sized chairs and a free-standing monitor. He stood there, silent. She sat at the console and slightly cocked her head. "You want to take your coat off? It's hot here."

"I know." He shucked off the trench coat, leaving

on his jacket, for which it was also too warm in the room, and then took a seat— the only other seat he could possibly take, the one to the left of her, the one that put his ugliness right in her face.

"Okay," she said, "what's here is, I gave you the whole thing. I mean, it's unedited. Everything we shot. So if you want me to fast forward, just tell me and I will."

He nodded and she reached for a switch and dimmed the lights.

And then there she was on the dark snowy evening, the red hair spilling on the bright yellow coat, holding up a Fox 5 mike to McCain, the uncomfortable rookie who'd been first on the scene.

"What's the story?" she was saying.

"It's a homicide. Man, it was brutal," McCain offered.

"How?"

"You mean how was it was brutal? He was slashed."

"Who was 'he'?"

"Look I really shouldn't talk to you at all. Just wait for a while and there'll be some detectives."

"You look pretty shaken."

"Well I gotta say I am. But listen, you can talk to the detectives later on."

"Was it multiple stab wounds?"

"You'll have to ask *them*. And actually, Miss, I should move you to the curb."

"Okay."

Brymmer said, "You're a persistent little thing," as the camera kept recording the confusion on the street and then focused back on Jamie.

"Will he get into trouble?" she said now to Brymmer. "I'm aware that he broke the rule. I mean he fraternized with the enemy."

"You're not the enemy," Brymmer said, his eyes staying on the screen. "Simply put, there's just the factors we reveal to the public and the stuff we keep to ourselves."

"I understand that," she answered him. "My cop was a father."

He turned now and looked at her, observing she was flustered, very slightly turning pink. "I meant," she said carefully, "my father was a cop. What the hell. I'm Irish."

"Rogers?"

"Rogers was a husband," she said.

"Oh."

"*Ex* husband."

"Ah."

"Here's the segment where the neighbor comes in."

At the left of the monitor, a cab door opened and a woman came out. She had light blonde over-the-shoulder-length hair and a short purple coat and was blocked from moving further towards the stoop of her building by Tomasi and Kell.

Now enter Jamie: "Do you live here?"

"Yes. What the hell is going on?" The woman seemed angry at the rank inconvenience.

"It's…apparently a murder."

The woman seemed no more appeased by the excuse. She looked up at the building. "Oh," she said, and paused, looking thoughtful for a moment. "Not surprising. He must've played one too many games."

"Of what?"

"Chance."

"Did you know him?"

"In a way. What happened? He get stabbed with an

103

ice pick in the heart?"

"I wouldn't know," Jamie said. "What kind of a guy was he?"

"A guy, that's all."

"Good looking?"

"Oh yes."

"How old?"

"I'm not sure. Early thirties, I believe."

"Could you tell me his name?"

"I don't think I'm supposed to. Don't they usually wait until his mother gets the news?"

"Well usually, yes. —But you really think someone might have stabbed him in the heart?"

"Actually, I don't believe anyone could find it."

"Even so," Jamie said, "you start to wonder what it was. I was thinking about that New Year's murder in the Village, that… whatsisname… Clawson. Did you read about that?"

For a moment the woman seemed to… blink? or was it wince? Then she shrugged and said, "Actually I wouldn't be surprised. I mean it *could've* been the same. I mean anything's possible, isn't it?"

Tomasi now walked up to Symington and said, "If you can show me your keys, I'll let you in."

And the monitor went to black.

Brymmer grunted. "Can you send me a copy of that scene?"

"Sure," she said. "I'll do it right now if you like. Why? Do you suspect her?"

Brymmer said nothing, just immediately gave her his email address. "Are there any other interviews?"

"Nope. Only you and that Detective Matson. Do you want to see yourself?"

"Hardly ever," Brymmer said. "But you can fast-cut

104

to Matson."

He watched her fast-forward. Then Matson— looking red and important in the lights. Flashbulbs popped at him. Microphones flattered him from outreaching hands.

"It's a homicide," he said. "The victim's a male and there's knife wounds inflicted."

"Can you tell us who he is?"

"We're looking into it."

"God have mercy," Brymmer groaned.

"Can you tell us something else?"

"I can say he got a...what you'd call, assorted mutilations."

Brymmer shook his head.

"Can you be more specific?" That one, from Sydney Talbot at the *News*.

"Just that we're engaging in a full investigation and we're sure to get our man."

"So the killer's then a man?"

"Man or woman," Matson said. "And I need to get moving now and get myself to work." He leaned away from the microphones and then angled back. "Let me clarify," he said. "Starting now we'll have a full team of experts on the team and I'm sure we'll get our woman, that's unless we get a man."

Brymmer's laughter came rollingly. "And therefore, the popular image that we're dumb. Jesus. He's straight from Central Casting, isn't he?"

"Sort of." She was laughing now, a merry little sound. "Movie's over," she added. "Want to buy me a drink?"

He studied her steadily and then mumbled, "Why?"

"Well why do you think?"

"I guess because you want information on the case."

"Then I'd have to be pretty stupid since I've noticed you're a clam."

"Then you'd want to know something about homicide procedures."

"If I wanted to know *that*, I could read it in a book. I—" She suddenly stopped, a hand flying to her mouth. "Oh Lord. Are you married? I didn't see a ring so I—"

"No. I'm not married."

"Do you live with someone?"

"Yes." He was watching her, taking in the 'Oh-well' shrug that was slightly contradicted by the reddening of her cheeks. He nodded and then added, "Yes. With a cat. But the arrangement's not romantic."

She laughed. "You have a *cat?*"

"And is that so surprising?"

"You're just... not the type. Perhaps a pit bull..."

"Right. I found the cat at a scene. He was locked in with several corpses for a week. He was starving. What could I do?"

"So how about dinner, then? *I'm* starving too."

He appraised her again quickly, then shrugged. "Why not?" and then suddenly held his hand up. "Wait! Do you jog?"

"Do I *jog?*" she said. "No. Did you want to go jogging?"

"There are two other questions: Are you terrified of steak? Do you run in hysteria from secondhand smoke?"

"I am mad about steak and I occasionally smoke, though I'm trying hard not to."

"All right," he said finally. "So go get your coat and I'll bring around the car and I'll be waiting at the door. I'm pretty sure you know the car."

She looked at him somberly and nodded. "It's blue."

## 30

The building was at 73rd Street and Park, and Ross, whose Beetle was again on the blink, had had to walk from the station house, trudging over curbs that were slush piles of black, degenerating snow that had seeped through his shoes and was watering his socks which were sticking to his toes which would soon have blisters.

The doorman, who did not open the door, and who was dressed in the flashy epaulletted getup of a Prussian officer in a Marx Brothers movie, announced Ross's presence on a gold-plated phone and then pointed at a couple of gold-plated elevators waiting at the side. His carriage thus awaiting, Ross stepped inside and then punched Number Ten. The elevator carriage had a lot of dark wood and a small velvet bench, in case you discovered you were really too tired to stand all the way to your tenth floor triplex. But that then, of course, would be the tenants' problem. Ross's problem, at the moment, was his shoes, so he scraped the soles quickly on the elevator rug. There. Nice and tidy for his upcoming date.

The elevator opened its gold-plated jaws on the tenth floor landing where there seemed to be one— only one— apartment. Its entrance was across from the elevator door in a small, wall-papered, carpeted hall. The door had a buzzer that was onxy rimmed with gold.

He buzzed.

High heels clicked on polished parquet. It would, he imagined, be polished parquet.

The door popped open. The floor was parquet. The woman was a blonde, or had been once and was now once again. The hair was coiled in a knot on her head.

Joanna Whitlaw. One of the appointments in Tanner's little book, though not exactly among the most recent. Whitlaw's name had stopped appearing in November. Ross gave his name. She looked at his shield and then up at his face as he also looked at her: tall, anorexic, and over the hill, but a hill it might have paid Tanner to climb, considering the diamonds that flashed at her ears. On the other hand, considering the face-lifted face, the hair-lacquered hair and the flesh-eating eyes, there might have been a few things that just wouldn't climb. On the other hand, Ross could be guessing it wrong. For instance, she might have been Tanner's aunt.

"Mrs. Whitlaw?"

"Mmm. About David, of course." The voice had a smooth whiskey bite. "Come in." She was wearing a long blue dress. "I was on my way out," she said over her shoulder, beckoning Ross through a mirrored foyer. "To a party," she added, "but I guess it can wait." She looked at a small diamonded watch. It was 8:30 on Ross's watch but he wondered if time flew faster on diamonds. She led him to a small dimly-lit study, turned up the lamp a notch, and studied his face.

"The police are certainly improving," she said. She licked at her smile.

Ross said neutrally, "Tell it to the press. We've been under their guns."

She didn't pursue it, but sat where she'd apparently been sitting before, near a table with a more-than-half-empty glass of Scotch. When she sat, a long slit in her skirt fell aside, revealing a firm, silky thigh. She left it that way and picked up the glass, giving him an openly appraising look. He wondered idly if she thought he would do, and *what*, precisely, she thought he would do. "Freshen my drink— would you?" she said and

108

extended the glass. "Scotch on the rocks."

"Uh-uh." Smiling, Ross shook his head. He sat on a chair directly across from her. "Sorry. Not allowed to fix drinks on duty."

Her laugh was deep. "You just made that up."

"Uh-huh."

"Well at least we know where we stand."

"Uh-huh." He pulled out a notebook and pen. "When was the last time you saw David Tanner?"

She nodded slowly and nipped at her drink. "Late last night," she said. "He didn't look well."

"I beg your pardon?"

"He was wrapped in a bag. The television cameras hardly ever show more."

"Uh-huh. And when was the last time you saw him?"

"December seventh. The night of his birthday."

"And what did you give him?"

"His walking papers." The fact, or the wit of it, pleased her a lot. He waited till the laughter went to a smile and the smile got licked before he said:

"Why?— Why was that?"

"He was really a bore."

Ross just nodded. "How often did he bore you?"

She frowned, cocked her head. "Are you clever enough to have just made a pun?"

"No ma'am," he said, looking Genuinely Puzzled. "I just want to know how often you saw him, how long you knew him, that kind of thing."

"Oh. Well I saw him a few times a month for a couple of months."

"Could you be more specific?"

"Occasionally I brought him to parties." She shrugged. "All in all," she said, "I guess I must have

109

known him since May."

Ross nodded. "So he didn't bore you all the time. I mean, you brought him to parties."

"That's true," she said, responding on the literal level. "At first he seemed refreshing."

"Refreshing."

"He was into Vedanta," she said.

Ross squinted.

"That's an Indian religion," she explained. "Very spiritual."

"Ah. So your relationship was spiritual then, not sexual?"

"Yes."

"Uh-huh. Where'd you meet him. At the gym?"

"Oh no. At a party at Dana and Ralph's."

"Beg pardon?"

"Dana Brent. He's a fashion designer."

"Uh-huh. And was David their... particular friend?"

"Of theirs? I don't think he'd even met them before. He came with a friend of mine. Ramona Pike."

"And why was he boring?"

"His manners were boring. He thought he could say exactly what he thought—*about* anyone, *to* anyone."

"And that's why you dropped him."

"Yes."

"And the fact that he gave you gonorrhea had nothing to do with it."

The frozen face froze. Her mouth came open and the bright red lips seemed suspended in an Oh. She watched him for a moment with glittering eyes. Finally, she lowered them and briskly shook her head. "And how in the hell did you learn about *that?*"

Ross said nothing, meeting her gaze before he shrugged and, for the hell of it, decided to cough. The

110

thing was that Ross hadn't actually *learned* it, he'd only half-learned it. From checking out the bottle of Doxycyclene that was dated 12/1. Tanner's doctor had helpfully informed him of its actual purpose. From there on, Ross had made a calculated leap.

Mrs. Whitlaw was annoyed. Her movements became abrupt. Abruptly, she reached for a cloisonné box and came up with a long, brown cigarette. Ross leaned forward with a friendly light. "Don't worry," he said. "It goes no further."

She looked at him coldly. "It's gone far enough."

"And so had your...sort of lying," Ross said, leaning back in his seat. "I can well understand how you must have been angry. You might even—"

Laughing, she barked out some smoke. "You mean was I angry enough to kill him? Oh Lord, deliver me. The middle-class mind. Let me guess. Your next scenario would likely include my enraged husband rushing furiously to David's to wreak his revenge." Shaking her head now, she crossed to the bar where she built a quadruple Scotch on the rocks. "I suppose you're allowed to *watch* people drink?"

Ross just nodded, watching her face as she took a long pull from her crystal glass and looked at him levelly over the rim. "Let me tell you something, Detective, the only possible thing that would bother my husband would be if this story got out to the press. My husband doesn't give a damn what I do as long as I do it with appropriate discretion." Sipping her drink, she went back to her chair. "And there's a detail, Detective, that you seem to have gotten wrong. David didn't give the little present to *me*. No, Detective, I gave it him. Because my husband gave it to me because his lover gave it to *him*. And note I said his lover and not his mistress.—Got the picture now?"

"Yep."

She studied him again with a sour smile. "How very Boy Scoutish you look just now. I bet you're married to a sweet little thing who washes your sweaters and irons your shirts and does absolute wonders with tuna-and-noodles."

"And two great children. Timmy and Sue. So just for the record, on Saturday evening, where—"

"At a party. I hosted a party. With seven people. Would you like the guest list?" She checked her watch. "And if not, we're finished."

He said, "We're not."

She heaved a sigh full of bored impatience.

"Sorry to keep you from the party," Ross said. "I truly understand that the evening is young and the story is old, even possibly boring, but here's the thing. There's a corpse in the morgue that was David Tanner. You had your fun with him, gave him the clap, and you booted him out for whyever you did and you aren't too deeply concerned that he's dead. But, see? the strange part of this is that I am. I'm trying to figure out how he got there. You might know something that might be of help. Do you know any places that David hung out in. Or any women who might have—" he paused— "might've killed him like that?"

"No. Honestly." She looked a bit chastened, but only a bit.

"Did anyone love him? I mean, was there a woman he seriously hurt?"

"There was a girl once. I haven't the foggiest what's her name and I never laid eyes on her. I think they were both quite smitten for a while, till she learned who he was."

112

"Was he bi?"

"You could buy him, if that's what you mean. Who he sold his services to, I wouldn't know."

"How about kinks? Did he have any kinks?"

"No. Not with me. And none that I ever heard. He comes from Wyoming," she added rather vaguely, as though that could override the very idea. She seemed to grow thoughtful, or else just drunk. "I think... I think he was in over his head. I don't think he planned to become what he was. I think it just happened."

Ross said nothing.

"Sometimes," she said, "you get knocked off your course. You start off thinking the usual thoughts, and you plan on living the usual life and then you get sidetracked. Or kicked in the teeth. And then you start figuring, Well, why not? And then all of a sudden your whole damn life is a whole damn series of Well, why not?"

Ross said nothing.

She finished her drink.

## 31

He took her to the Water Club. Partly for the food and the relative quiet but mostly for the view. From the banks of the river on a cold starry night, and from a reasonable distance, even Queens could look attractive. They sat by a window. Brymmer ordered Scotch and she ordered a glass of wine. He asked her if she'd like something first, she said no, so he asked for the menus since she'd said she was starving. As they studied them silently, he noticed she was looking at his scarred right hand that was lying on the table; he left it there, allowing her to take it all in and pretending he didn't notice.

He said You don't have to have a steak if you don't want it, and she said she really did and was tired of being made to feel guilty about it and tired of the people turning food into sin, and Brymmer'd said no, they were making it a crime—A health crime, he'd said, and she picked it up and played with it, adding, Any day now I imagine we'll get busted for ordering an egg, and he told her they'd been drafting the official rules of engagement: Don't shoot until you see the whites of their eggs. She laughed. He was aware that they were Making Conversation. He was also aware that he was Doing His Part, and further aware that he was both There and Not-there and somewhere in between— the tireless observer observing the participant observing the observer. He willed the observer to get the hell away.

"Have you ever," she said, "shot anyone, Sergeant?"

"Sure. I shoot people six times a day."

"But seriously."

"No."

"I feel kind of silly here, calling you Sergeant."

"You could try Lieutenant."

"And as long as I'm trying, I could also try Commander."

"No," he said, "I wouldn't want to be a Commander. You could also try Burt."

"Burt."

"What?"

"Nothing.—I was just trying it," she said.

The dinner arrived and she didn't have to prove that she wasn't scared of steak. She really dug into it.

114

"So how did you decide to be a television star?"

"Reporter. I started at a newspaper."

"Where?"

"Binghamton," she said. "I was born there. I started at the hometown paper. My father used to say I was born curious. The news questions kind of hard-wired in my head. The Who, What, Where, When and definitely Why."

"'Why,'" Brymmer said, "is the luxury question. Interesting, but mostly it's entirely irrelevant."

"Why?" she said, and laughed and grew serious again. "I mean, why's it irrelevant? It's the point of things, isn't it?"

"Why did the chicken cross the road?" Brymmer said.

She angled her head at him from over her wine glass. "Meaning?"

"Who cares? Because now you've got a chicken on the other side of the road, and the problem is, what're you gonna do about it, see?"

"Well..." she said, taking his proposal in earnest, "suppose you learned the chicken went to the other side of the road to get a juicier kind of worm. If you didn't want the other chickens plowing over the road, you could bring them the better worms."

"Crime prevention."

"Sure. Why not?"

"It doesn't work. You get huge social programs, lotta bureacratic graft, and at the end of it, you're still getting trumped by human nature."

"So the answer is?"

"You keep all your chickens in a coop."

The waiter interrupted to ask if things were fine. They both agreed things were fine.

"Okay," she said. "So why did you decide to be a cop?"

"Oh, for the usual reasons, I suppose. Truth… Justice… The American Way."

"You know?" she said, "you're so awfully good at doing deadpan, I really can't decide if you're being sarcastic."

"I'm being sarcastic. The American Way has very little to do with truth and almost nothing to do with justice. It's not the Americans' fault, it's just the nature of things at large."

"So then what keeps you going?"

"I like to see the badguys hollering in hell."

"So that's justice then, isn't it?"

"That," he said, "or pure unadulterated rage.— Have you ever stopped to think about what's the use of parsley?"

"Of parsley?"

"They stick it on your plate all the time. It's stupid to look at and it's terrible to eat. So why," he said, holding up a sprig, "do they bother?"

She grunted. "That's the worst segue I ever heard."

"Right. And you news people do it so well. 'Three bodies were found chopped up in a freezer. And speaking of freezing, Carol, what's with the weather?'"

She laughed. She had a very nice full-throated laugh. Genuine. Musical. He tried not to smile out his pleasure at her laugh.

As the waiter cleared the plates she said, "I really don't believe that."

"What?"

"That you're only in the business out of rage. I think, like me, you're obsessed with solving puzzles. Engaging in the game."

116

"Colonel Mustard in the kitchen."

"Oh well."

"The thing is, there's not a plot to puzzle out. At least not in most cases. And your Why's are the least of it. Look. You find a gun-shot body on the street and it doesn't have a wallet and there's marks on the neck from where a chain was ripped off, then your Why, at least ninety in a hundred, is a robbery, which doesn't get you zilch. What gets you there is who saw the robber run away, or who snitches on him, maybe what you know about the nabe. Mostly it's pretty straight-forward and pragmatic. Or else it's off the wall. You want to hear some examples?"

She nodded, interested.

"Guy buys a puppy. Puppy takes a crap in the neighbor's back yard. Next morning the neighbor comes over and shoots him. Not the puppy, the man. *Why?* Okay? Here's another example and it's one of my favorites. Middle class couple, not married, just living together for a while. Couple starts preparing dinner together. Decide to have a fight about whether it's good or bad for your health to eat the seeds of a tomato. You know how it ends. Guy pulls a kitchen knife and stabs her in the head. You want to conjure with that one?"

He watched her grow thoughtful. He liked the way she looked when she was thinking something through. Open, but not taking anybody's word. He smiled because he knew she was thinking of a comeback. He liked that too.

"Okay," she said, not in the way of a concession, "okay, so what you're saying is that people go ape but it still leaves the question as to *why* they go ape."

Brymmer shook his head. "I'm saying you could drive yourself crazy with the Why and it doesn't really matter. The only thing that matters is that somebody's dead and somebody did it. Beyond that, you're either into Jesus or Freud and by then you've got another body in the alley or the kitchen or the yard.— You want coffee?"

"Do you?"

"What I want's a cigarette. When I gaze upon a coffee cup, I want one even more."

She nodded. "Okay. I've got some coffee in the house.— And some ashtrays," she added.

To the hovering waiter, Brymmer turned and said, "Check."

In the car, as it idled at the curb by her door, she said, "I think you can park around the corner. It's free and—"

"You know?" he said, "I think I'll take a raincheck on that."

"Why?" she said

"I have to go home and feed the cat."

"You're kidding."

"I am. Because I don't have a cat."

"You lied about a cat?"

"I'd *like* to have a cat. Or a dog. Or a Venus Fly Trap or something."

"What's *wrong* with you?"

"Everything."

"*Aside* from that."

"Everything else," he said, laughing.

He was idling the motor.

"Seriously," she said. "How hard do I have to throw myself at you before you catch me?"

"And why would you want me to?"

"Oh, I dunno. Because you're whip-smart and

118

funny and you're totally fucked up and I'm a sucker for all three. And besides, I like your looks."

"You're a scar-fucker, eh?"

She sucked in her breath and blew it out in exasperation. "Just forget it, all right? I'm just making such an absolute idiot of myself and...I'm sorry." She turned from him and reached for the door.

Reflexively, he reached out and grabbed her by the wrist. "Don't," he said.

"What?"

"Play with matches," Brymmer said.

She looked at him searchingly. He still held her wrist and was hoping that she hadn't noticed his erection. Apparently, she had. He let go and moved back and she flushed and said, "At least you seem to find me attractive."

"But you've known that," he said, "from the moment I extracted your foot from that door."

"Then why—"

"Because you nailed it. I'm totally fucked up."

"But you want me."

"Goodnight."

She shook her head ruefully. "Goodnight, Sergeant Brymmer."

# 32

*Thursday, February 19th, New York Times:*

## 50 DETECTIVES NOW HUNT "JACKIE" UNDER CENTRALIZED COMMAND

With evidence linking the murders of Richard Clawson, Monty Starrett and David Tanner, police have taken steps to coordinate and strengthen the investigation. The three local detective squads that once provided manpower under separate commands, have now been combined into a 50-man unit under the supervision of Sgt. Burt Brymmer.

Brymmer's Manhattan Homicide Task Force had been assigned a key role in the police investigation since the Starrett murder in late January, but departmental kinks in the chain of command had left him scrabbling for help amid a sea of red tape.

Chief of Detectives Roger Hammett, announcing the move at a press conference today, said that it was

Flashbulbs had popped in his face. The room had been floodlit with television lights. He had not wanted to be there. He'd have liked to have sent in a body double. So when he saw himself later on the six o'clock news, he expected to see himself looking as he'd felt: scowling, slumped. Instead, he was surprised to see a Brymmer on the screen who merely looked stolid. He'd sat there listening as Hammett reeled smoothly from cliche to cliche, followed by "a few words from the Mayor," and he'd looked the way soldiers look when presidents speak and they know they're being used as political backdrop: perfectly erect and attentively blank. The cameras had been kind; they'd shot him from the left or from a three-quarter view, though whether this was done to protect his own image or the delicate appetites of six o'clock viewers, he wasn't quite sure. When reporters had asked him, "What do you want to do with your newly expanded team?"— a question he considered to be totally fatuous— he'd resisted the impulse to respond, "I thought maybe we could take in a movie and go for some beers," and gave them the kind of crap the occasion seemed to call for. He'd said, looking serious, "I plan to work their tails off," and then, in case they thought it was an inadvertent pun, he'd squinted, laughed, and said, "figuratively speaking." The room had responded with a tension-breaking laugh and his reviews had been good.

Now he sat looking at Assignment Sheet forms and wondering what to do with them. He now had a total of 51 detectives, including himself, to fit into a grid that encompassed seven days at two tours a day, allowing for the usual two days off after four days on. He didn't know the names, let alone the abilities, of the new detectives yet and he didn't want to step on too many toes— especially not Ritter's— and he hoped that he could pair the detective with the task (Who was better at doing What) but for now he just wanted to get a feel for the Numbers.

However, he had always had trouble with Numbers. He had a decent feel for chemistry, had even acquired a certain mastery of physics, but Numbers defeated him, evoking brain freeze. He could neither divide or multiply fractions unless he reduced them to the nearest percentage, but the way this was happening, it seemed he could either have 13.375 detectives on duty at all times or concentrate the force within the most productive hours to be working on the case. If he knew what those were.

One thing he knew was, he'd have to have a couple of teams working Tips. Calls were coming in by the hundreds every day. From psychics, astrologers, psychiatrists, numerologists; from women who were happily implicating rivals, and men who claimed they'd dated, been engaged to, or married to the Harridan from Hell, all of whom were Jackie.

Another thing he now had to deal with was the press. He decided that as much as possible, in the future, he'd steer them to the smartest of the working detectives, the guys, unlike Matson, who could string together sentences and, unlike himself, would not need the courtesy of camera angles.

Ross, for example.

## 33

*Friday, February 20th:*

Ross had been an actor before he joined the force. Kathy'd been an actress. They weren't successful but they always paid the rent. Then Kathy got pregnant and Ross got serious. He entered the Academy. Kathy miscarried, but Ross carried on. He found he liked the work plus the fact that it was steady and, for evenings and matinees, enjoyed the role of Cop. He brought to it not just the talents of the stage but a quick-flash intelligence and a gift for improvisation. And then, of course, Kathy'd given birth to the Onion and, for better or impossible, Ross was locked in.

Brymmer watched him now as they planned to

interrogate Jennifer Symington. Ross, like the rest of the squad, had seen the file to which Ross had said, "You see why I thought to get the hair? That the fuckin lab lost?"

"Relax," Clark suggested. "I mean maybe you can reach out and pluck a few more. Like, 'Wait! Is that a spider crawling on your head? Oof. Yeah. Got it.'"

"I don't know," Brymmer said. "You want the hairdresser role? You could run your hands over it and say, 'You know I think you'd look fab with a perm.'"

"Very funny," Ross said. "In the meanwhile, I think we do the usual routine. You Butch, me Sundance."

"And maybe you could *shoot* the hair off her head."

Actually, you couldn't. This time the hair was pulled back in a pony tail, revealing an architectural face, very carefully made up. She had what Brymmer thought of as a "Gym Body"— one of those bodies that were resolutely built through immoderate exercise and grueling self-denial. He'd bedded those bodies on one or two occasions and found them pragmatic: sex as Phys Ed. This one was packaged in a brown woolen suit and stilettos that could pass for a lethal weapon. She entered briskly and settled at the table as though she were about to have a business meeting, perhaps the kind of meeting at which she might preside. Brymmer then planned to disabuse her of that notion, only quietly at first. Sundance, on the other hand, was all Thanks-for-coming and, as Brymmer sat silently, he launched the first round.

He started out gently. Asking her to repeat what she knew about the night that Starrett had been killed. She said once again that she'd slept through the night and had seen and heard nothing. He asked her what she knew about Starrett as a person. She said he was an actor who also tended bar. She knew nothing of his "love life," as she rather quaintly put it. Had she ever herself slept with him? She paused for some breathing time before she decided "No."

Brymmer, in the meantime, was trying to gauge the power of her slightly masculine hands with their forty-dollar manicure—the perfectly-trimmed cuticle, the long polished nails. For the rest, he just eyed her with particular skepticism, as though he clearly doubted every word that left her mouth including "a," "the," and "of." He noted that she noted it and how she looked away from him and how it made her squirm.

It was Ross's turn now to begin to make her squirm and he asked, matter-of-factly, with a sudden turn of the screw:

"Have you ever used any kind of psychotropic drugs?"

"Psycho *what?*"

"Medication for altering your mood."

"I take Ambien to sleep. Not often but I do. Is that what you're asking? if I slept through the murder because I—"

"Valproate," he said. "You ever take any Valproate?"

"Valproate? No. Oh wait. Yes I did. I was given it for migraines last summer. Last...July. It was awful. And, aside from that, it didn't really work."

"You've got migraines," Brymmer said.

"Yes."

"Did you have one the night you killed Starrett?" Brymmer's tone was conversational.

"No. Hey, what are you getting at here?"

They let it linger for a while.

"And how long were you dating Richard Clawson?" Brymmer said.

124

"Oh God," she said. "You think I'm a suspect or something?"

"How long?" Brymmer said.

"About…two or three months."

"And from when until when?"

"Well I didn't exactly carve all the dates on my heart, but I'd say it was last winter. Last winter into spring."

"Last year," Brymmer said. "And was he married at the time?"

"Richard never got divorced. It would've been too expensive. So yes, he was married."

Ross added, "So you didn't expect him to marry you."

"No. No I didn't."

"So why'd you break up?" Ross seemed to be sympathetic. "Did he treat you very badly?"

"Not worse than most do."

"Do most men treat you badly?"

"Most men—" she said dryly, "treat *all* women badly."

"So most men are bad?"

"No," she said. "They just… it's a buyer's market.—They get away with what they can."

"And what do they get away with?"

"With treating us badly."

"Did you care about Clawson?"

"You mean did I love him? No, not really. But he took me nice places. I thought, very briefly, it could be a nice life."

"As his mistress."

"If you will."

"Did he have another mistress? I mean at the same time?"

125

"Unbeknownst to me, yes."

"And Starrett," Ross said. "Did Starrett treat you badly?"

"Uch, *Mon*ty!" She rolled her eyes. "What a trip and a half *he* was. I can't believe *any*one would fall for his line of crap, you should pardon the expression."

"Then why did you sleep with him?"

She shrugged now, conceding it. "Okay. He was there. I was horny. He was handsome and um..." She let it trail.

"*And?* Please go on."

"He was... ummm..." She spread her hands about ten inches apart.

"Well endowed," Ross concluded. "So why did you break it off?"

"We were finished, that was all. Look, I always knew what he was after was a job. I'm in advertising."

"So?"

"So he wanted to be the sharp handsome guy in the Lexus. Or the guy going mmm-mmm-mmm at a can of soup. I knew he was using me which was, after all, how I got to use him."

"Were you also using Tanner?"

"*David?* You're kidding. David was half-queer and the other half gigolo. He works at my gym and gives magnificent massages, which is how I got absolutely rid of my headaches. Okay, not entirely but really they're much better."

Brymmer leaned forward now and gave her the raw Full Monty of his face. "And how did you know Starrett died exactly like Clawson?"

"I didn't," she said

"Sure you did. Or that's what you said to that reporter."

126

"What reporter?"

"Stop screwing around with me, Jenny. You said it to that reporter."

"It's the *reporter* who was saying it. I simply went along. I said I wouldn't have been surprised."

"And were you?"

"Surprised?" She thought a while, fiddling with the tail of her blonde hair. "Well, I really couldn't say."

"You couldn't say if you were surprised?"

"Well... he really did ask for it."

"Did he?"

"He was playing roulette on his mattress. He picked up anything. And actually, he managed to break a few hearts. He might even have driven a girl or two crazy. Either that, or he simply must've picked up a psycho. I don't know. Things happen."

"And you think it's coincidence that things 'just happened' to three men you know?"

"Well it has to be, doesn't it?"

"Not necessarily." Brymmer let it sit. Then he looked at her with a dead level animus in his eyes. "New Years Eve," he said. "You still had the key to Clawson's house."

"New Year's Eve I was in Hawaii. And I never had his key."

"Where in Hawaii, from when to when?"

"December twenty-second to January third. The Luana Hotel."

"And how about Valentine's?"

Symington shrugged. "You got me there," she said. "I'm afraid I don't have one. Valentine, I mean."

"I wonder why," Brymmer said.

She apparently missed his point. "Men," she said. "They're just so... slippery, that's why."

"Well," Ross said, "I suppose she could be a psycho. I mean she was pretty cool.— We could check on the migraines."

"And Hawaii," Brymmer said. "But I don't think she dunnit. I don't think she cared. And that cock of his had given her far too much enjoyment."

"So maybe she wanted to enjoy it on her own."

"It gets shrunken after a while. And it stinks after a week."

"Unless she stuck it in her freezer."

"Cold comfort?" Brymmer said.

They were entering the squad room where the others had been watching through the closed circuit loop.

"So?" Brymmer opened.

Nobody seemed impressed.

"But if that's Miss America, we're in trouble," Dubisky said.

Kerner said thoughtfully, "I thought she was sad."

"Sad?" Dubisky argued.

"Disappointed. Resigned. Embittered," Kerner said.

"Disappointed, my ass. The trouble with those babes is they want to be macho and they want to be adored. It just doesn't *occur* to them," Dubisky said hotly, "that one cancels the other."

"Dear Abby," Brymmer said. "Any other advice for the lovelorn?"

Dubisky said nothing.

"Good," Brymmer said. "So where does that leave us?"

"Are we crossing her off the list?"

"What list?" Brymmer said. "We got an unknown

hat on the corner of Sixty-Second. We got nothing from any canvass. Two-hundred-seventy apartments in Tanner's building and nobody saw a thing. Most of them didn't know him. Files from the elevators show us a lot of people going up to Tanner's floor for a party at Mr. Levy's. Mr. Levy, reached in Maui, said he didn't recall the guests, he could only recall a few because people were bringing people, it was kind of an open house. And the couple of names he gave us didn't notice a bloody thing including other murderous guests."

There was dead stony silence.

"Getting back to Jennifer Symington," Clark said carefully, "she was right about something. I looked at that interview. It *was* the reporter. She dragged in Clawson from the edges of left field. So what made her do that?"

Brymmer said, "The officer had told her it was brutal. He also said 'slashed.'"

"Is that sufficient?" Clark wondered.

McAllister interrupted, appearing through the arch. "I got a lab report," he said. He gave the printout to Brymmer.

The red hair was red. The five recovered strands of it were all varying lengths and were structurally and chemically different from the blonde ones. A few had roots so that ultimately the DNA could be sequenced which would not mean bupkas if they didn't have the hair, or the skin or the juices of the actual killer. It could only be useful in ruling someone out.

Brymmer initialed it and passed it to the squad.

## 34

"It would have been so simple if I hadn't found the hair," Ross said. "The red one."

"*You* found."

"Well....*Yeah*. After you found it, I found that it was red."

Brymmer said nothing, just stared ahead at the road.

"Kinda changes the whole complexion."

"So to speak," Brymmer said. "Crap!" He cursed loudly at the green Jersey Jag that was cutting him off at a curve. Traffic was bearable on the East Side Drive; the city, still battered by intense freezing winds, was staying home under the covers with its heaters on High. Grumbling now, Brymmer pulled out past the Jag.

"Tanner," Ross said. "Hadn't left his apartment. No visitors, either."

"Or maybe there were. And O'Fallon or the other guy at night didn't catch em. Or maybe this killer just knocks on the door. 'Hi, I'm collecting for Girl Scout Cookies.' And David Tanner, who swings both ways, swings—"

"And misses."

"And loses his bat."

"Or," Ross said.

"Right. Or."

Brymmer was silent, driving the car. Ross stuck a cigarette in his mouth and lit it by scratching a match with his thumb. He sat, blowing smoke at the frosty window and thinking of several hundred Or's.

"And besides," Ross added. "The three things were much more the same than different."

"Knife, razor blade and poultry shears. Right."

"Also slit throats and sordid mutilations."

"Stockbroker, bartender....I don't know, how do you classify Tanner?"

"Dead," Ross explained.

"Right," Brymmer nodded. "Right.—*Or?*" He squinted at Ross with a side-eyed challenge.

Ross took it in, then let out a yawn. "Is this a particularly wonderful Or?"

"Right. It's the Or with the heart of gold. It's also the painfully *obvious* Or. An Or so easy a child could do it."

Grimacing now, Ross looked up. "Some of us," he said, "are slower than others."

"Right. Some of us are beautiful but dumb."

"Some of us, being physically perfect, have not had to bother developing brains.— C'mon. What's your goddam fucking Or?"

"It's a team," Brymmer said.

"A team."

"You never heard about threesomes?" Brymmer said. "The redhead distracts him and the blonde does the job."

"Or?" Ross said.

Brymmer was silent, driving the car. "Or," he said, "we either have one smart killer or two separate killers or else..." He let it hang.

"Or," Ross prodded.

"Or how about a group? What if it's a whole big organized gang? Maybe there's some kind of feminist underground. A group that has regular meetings and dues. Sisters in Crime. Murderess Inc."

"You're punchy," Ross said.

Brymmer said nothing. He made the turnoff at East Fourteenth Street and kept going west, heading for

131

Ross's incredible rent-controlled four room apartment. "Or," he admitted. "We're a whole lot further up the creek than I thought."

## 35

*Tuesday, February 24th:*

*New York Post, "Cardin's Corner":*

### SERIAL KILLERS, HARDEST TO CATCH

#### by Pete Cardin

So I ask a cop friend of mine, what are the odds that Jackie gets caught? And he says what every cop who's worked homicide knows: If you don't catch a killer in the first days or weeks, the odds take a nosedive, and serial killers often operate for years.

The Boston Strangler racked 14 victims in 18 months, New York's Son of Sam was actively at large for over 2 years. Then you've got the guys like John Wayne Gacy—30 victims over 3 years; The Green River Killer in Washington State, 50 victims, took 20 years to catch, and the Zodiak Killer in California was never caught at all...

Brymmer and Ross had their regularly scheduled two days off and with all leads cold and a hundred more legs now doing the legwork, that leave wasn't cancelled. Brymmer'd spent the full two days holed up, sitting in his living room and reading Dostoyevsky and falling asleep. Not that *Crime and Punishment* was boring him; in fact, he was finding it intense, but the overwhelming need to just sleep overcame him. His mood, like the weather outside, remained foul.

Ross spent the two days babysitting Billy so Kathy could get out. She needed to get out. And by the end of Day Two, Ross had found a sudden new sympathy for prisoners and a new understanding of "stir-crazy," too.

At nine, he phoned Brymmer. "So— what do you say?"

"Nothing. And I'd like to keep it that way."

"My, you sound cranky."

"I am. I am cranky, crappy and cross."

"Then you need to get drunk and laid," Ross observed. "I want to take you to a party."

"No thanks."

"It'll perk you right up," Ross pursued.

"I don't need any perking and I want to stay cross. I enjoy being cross.— Where are you?"

"Right now? I am visiting a friend."

"Well, good for you."

"Officially, I'm working. You called me at suppertime and said to come in.—Now about that party."

"Forget it," Brymmer said.

"Right. So I'll pick you up in...say, half an hour."

"In your non-working Beetle?"

"It's a Honda," Ross said. "And it happens to be Carmen's."

The party was downtown. A large party in a loud loft. The host, a friend of Carmen's—a man who taught online courses in poetry and didn't, by the look of things, do it for the money—was longhaired and forty and surrounded by a chorus of adulating girls. Ross introduced a glowering Brymmer, who'd been ready to execute a u-turn at the door, as "my friend Jackie Hunter. Be kind to him," he said, "he's a decorated hero. Winner of the Distinguished Medal of the Cross."

133

One of the women, who'd apparently misheard it or was too dumb to get it but whose dumbness didn't stand in the way of her convictions, said, "You ought to be ashamed. Don't you know that the army is a tool of imperialism?" at which point another, rather sweet-looking thing said, "My brother's in the army. He was wounded in Iraq and I think—" she said, looking up at Brymmer and his Wound— "that we owe every soldier our unquestioning support and our expressions of gratitude."

A gratitude she later expressed to its fullest in her Chelsea apartment. Afterwards, reclining on a pink-striped comforter, she'd even shared a joint—a treasure she'd extracted from a box in her dresser. When she said, very softly, "Will I see you again?" Brymmer had explained that he was visiting on business, that he lived in Cincinnati, but the next time he visited, he'd surely give a call. The next morning, in a move of uncharacteristic kindness, he sent her some roses, "From the Cincinnati Kid."

## 36

*Tuesday, March 3rd,*

*Headline: New York Daily News:*

### COPS CATCH KILLER OF 10 DOGG KNIGHT

A rap star was shot in front of a recording studio in Soho. The Task Force wrapped it up in three days flat. Thanks to the brilliant work of Sergeant Burt Brymmer and his all-star team. But the press was only interested in Jackie the Ripper who remained still at large.

*New York Observer, Business Section:*

## JACKIE RIPS INTO NIGHTLIFE PROFITS

Business, especially in singles bars, is off by up to 40% in all five boroughs according to both owners and staff. "Unless there's some kind of game going on, the guys aren't coming," said Jimmy Casal, owner of The Turnaround Bar in Brighton. "The guys are just scared. Like, 'yeah, she looks cute but is she Jackie,' you know? The girls—well, the girls seem to think it's kind of funny. It's almost like they're glad to see the guys running scared."

## 37

*Wednesday, March 4th:*

"I ordered you a refill."

"You mean just now? While I was powdering my nose? Well that was very nice of you, Mister uh—"

"Bill."

"Mr. Bill."

"Just Bill."

"Mmm-hmm."

"And then you would be...?"

"Angel."

"Angel. That's nice. Short for Angela?"

"Short for Avenging Angel."

"Ah. Very funny. And what do you avenge?"

"I concentrate mostly on subway-car defacing. Hopscotch cheating. Horseshoe theft."

"And there's a lot of that going around, I suppose."

"The statistics are absolutely shocking, Mr. Bill. And I'm ready to stop this when you are."

"Huh?...Oh. I get it. I think. Dealer's choice."

"Well in that case, the dealer chooses— mmmm... let's see... then the dealer chooses hearts. Have you ever played hearts?"

"Is that something like bridge?"

"*Real* hearts, I mean. It's a game that's not a game. People talk to each other. People actually sit around and talk to each other, care for each other. Don't screw around. Oh Lord, I'm so sorry. Don't look so alarmed. The fact is, I just broke up with my husband."

"He cheated."

"He's probably cheating as we chat. So I was simply wondering, in a casual way, if there were actually any men with any feelings still around or if that sort of thing went out with the mambo. But really, Mr. Bill, you do look as though you're a very decent man. If you *are* a decent man, then I'd like to have a nice quiet dinner with you tonight. I'd even like to see what happens after that. You're probably only in town for the evening..."

"Till tomorrow."

"Then I'd really like to be with you tonight. Do I shock you?"

"Are you trying?"

"No, I don't think so."

"Okay then. So.... Are we talking about money?"

"I'm insulted that you'd ask. That was merely an open, straightforward proposition."

"Shall we start with some dinner then?"

"How about room service?"

"Hey. Dealer's choice."

## 38

*Early Thursday morning, March 5th:*

"Gore City," said the sleep-deprived chief of security. "And it looks like it's Jackie." He was leading Brymmer and Ross down an ever-winding corridor, carpeted in green institutional geometrics and dotted with dead Room Service trays. The man was a scowler named Terence O'Toole, an ex-Lieutenant, Robbery Squad; fifty, steely, burly, tired. He was obviously angry at having been awakened and angrier still, perhaps, at not having rank. In any case, he was angry.

"Got the call at a quarter after midnight," he said. "Ring-ring. 'There's a body in Room Nine-oh-one.' It was Room Service called. They're open till midnight. Quarter of midnight, guy in Nine-oh-seven calls down for a sandwich. Kitchen messes up, writes the seven like a one. Order's then going up to room Nine-oh-one. Room Service knocks. No answer. Knocks again. Kid wants to get home. Figures the occupant is maybe in the shower. Maid passes by. They use the key to get in. Like I say," O'Toole said, "it looks like a Jackie."

Ross said, "I guess he got room service, then."

"*What're* you? A wise guy?"

"Probably. Yeah."

"'Probably. Yeah.'" O'Toole repeated it in sing-song mimic. "You guys think you're smart? Pulling down lousy municipal pay?"

Brymmer said nothing. The hallway turned. He could now see the uniformed cop at the door; hear voices leaking out.

O'Toole said, "There's two other dicks in the room."

"Including the victim's?" Ross said flatly.

O'Toole built a quick, hard, unpleasant grin. "You

137

think you're so smart."

A precinct detective came out of the room. Poll, his name was. Poll said, "Christ. I was clocking out at one. Now this." He jerked his head at the innards of the room and, turning to a tall beanpole of a man, said, "Outta here, Kurtz. The marines have landed." Kurtz made a small disclamatory shrug. "He just had a baby. He wants to get home. Meanwhile, I guess we're on overtime tonight."

"I'd guess," Brymmer said.

"What we know is, he registered as William Mc-Connell. Came in for some manufacturer's convention which started on Sunday but he got here Friday. Credit cards, money and watch are still there."

Poll hollered, "Kurtz! Start knocking on doors. Before the big boss here assigns you to do it."

Ross looked at Brymmer. "Everybody's shoulders got chips on tonight. You notice that?"

Brymmer walked into the room.

The naked body was sprawled on the bed, eyes staring dryly up at the ceiling; a nasty congealing stab wound to the head; entering through the vulnerable wall of the left temple; just behind the eye. He was lying in a puddle of his own blood and shit with a tag on his toe and a gutted crotch. Brymmer looked up from the crotch to the throat which was not slit open, not even scratched.

"Pattern-buster," he announced flatly.

The pattern was busted in a few different ways. First, the victim as an out-of-towner, and now, the specifics of the murder itself. Then, too, the man looked to be somewhere in his fifties, though trim, very tanned, and with graying blond hair. He looked to be dead for just a very few hours.

138

O'Toole reappeared now, opening the door. "The management wants you to keep this quiet."

"Shit," Ross said, "and I just put a call in to Rupert Murdock."

"Press hasn't gotten any wind of this yet, but they follow you around like dog follows tail."

Brymmer was still peering over at the bed. On a sheet that was pulled way over to the side, he saw the faint, drying gleam of something viscous and sticky. "Come," he said, showing it to Ross with a sigh. "I hope he died happy."

"Or maybe he was just jerking off," Ross proposed. "And he killed himself later. Likely out of guilt." Ross bent closer and peered at the stain. "Yep. Looks to me like it's jerkoff come. The milk of human blindness."

O'Toole said, "You creeps are disgusting, you know? You always clown around like this at a scene?"

Brymmer said, "Only when we've got an audience," and looked at O'Toole with such hard narrowed eyes that the ex-lieutenant reddened, and then said, "To hell with you," and quickly slammed the door.

Brymmer looked at Ross as he scratched at his jaw. "Sometimes," he said, "we could do without the jokes."

Ross looked sober. "Yeah. I'm sorry."

"Yeah. You're sorry." Brymmer was making some notes in his book. "You know maybe that fine irrepressible charm of yours had damn well better learn to get itself repressed."

Ross turned slowly. "What's eating *you*? I *said* I was sorry."

"Right." Brymmer didn't look up from his notes. "Now go out in the hall and be nice to Poll and Kurtz. Make them feel wanted, needed, and loved."

"Why?"

"Because it's going to be a long night."

A guy from the M.E.'s office came in. The Crime Scene Unit was clanking down the hall. The photographer stood in the doorway, looking in. Brymmer conferred with them and then left the room.

## 39

At 1:47, with Ross at his side, Brymmer knocked at the door of Room 623. There was no answer. He rubbed at his jaw, feeling the stubble bloom through the pits, and then knocked again louder, palming the wallet that showcased his shield. At the moment he felt about as tired and seedy as a house detective in an old B Movie. A lot of times he felt like a house detective in an old B Movie. A lot of times *life* was like an old B Movie. He knocked once again.

This time a muffled male voice said, "Shit!" and then louder, "Who is it?"

"Police," Brymmer said. "We'd like to ask a few questions."

"*Now?*" The voice was a raw nasal bark.

"I'm sorry. I realize it's the middle of the night but time is important."

"Well...just a second." Brymmer heard the creak of an inside door that was probably a closet and the low husky whisper of a female voice as the man whispered louder, "For Chissakes, ssshhh!" and the woman muttered, "Oh my *God*, you're a coward," and the door to the hallway opened very slightly, blocked by a tall, silk-enrobed man with thick sandy hair and a faceful of sleep.

Brymmer said nicely, "You're Harry Mannis?"

Mannis dropped his eyes from Brymmer's face to his shield and then warily raised them, checking out Ross who presumably didn't look like a bandit. Ross just hovered and didn't say a word.

Neither didn't Mannis.

"I'm Sergeant Brymmer and he's Detective Ross. Did you happen to be in the bar off the lobby at about seven-thirty?"

Mannis squinted. "And what makes you think so?"

Sighing, Brymmer flashed the tab from the bar; it was signed *Harry Mannis, Room 623.* Timed 7:32. "This makes me think so."

Mannis nodded.

Brymmer almost yawned, knowing the next few minutes by heart. Entering hotel rooms was always tricky, requiring both persuasiveness and absolute vigilance. Almost as tricky as checking out cars, which was how about an eighth of all badguys were caught. A traffic cop notices a car making speed, tells the guy, Pull over, and next thing, *wham*, he's got a gun in his face, or otherwise he turns up a kilo of smack, a corpse in the trunk, or the loot from a neighborhood liquor store heist. Hotel rooms could also be that kind of scene but in this case Mannis was either with a pross or protecting a girlfriend, or protecting himself and a *Mrs.* Mannis who was probably still back at home in Sioux Falls.

Brymmer said wearily, "May we come in?"

Mannis remained, blocking the door. "What's this about?" he asked, cagey.

"Routine investigation."

"Of what?"

"Homicide."

"Oh. Could you come back later this morning?"

"No," Brymmer said. "She can hide in the john or *you* can get dressed and come down to—"

"Oh Harry. Don't be abs*urd*," the woman's voice said, and then she appeared, muscling Mannis's arm to the side, a sheet wrapped around her like some kind of toga. She was clutching it closed with a handful of short wine-colored nails. The girl was brunette, about twenty-seven, fairly well-built and fairly attractive and she looked at Brymmer with fairly intelligent light brown eyes. She wasn't a pross and he guessed by her tone that she wasn't a pickup. She said to Brymmer, "Well, come on in. I really don't think we should stand in the hall."

Brymmer said to Ross, "Go back to the ninth floor," and Ross just nodded as Brymmer walked in.

The room was the usual chain-hotel bedroom with the usual king-sized and bounced-upon bed. Sourly, Mannis walked over to a chair, the room's only chair, and sat in it, staring at the dregs of some drink set beside it on a table meant to double as a desk. The girl was enjoying the man's discomfort and, doubtless to annoy him, curled herself cozily up on the bed. Brymmer took it in, partly amused, and pulled out the photograph of William McConnell as appearing on his drivers license from Spokane. At Brymmer's suggestion, Dubisky and Clark had been checking out the tabs at the four lobby bars and Dubisky had found one signed by McConnell. They were now in the process of checking other guests whose tabs showed they'd also been around at the same time.

Brymmer showed McConnell's picture to Mannis. "Did you see this man in the bar when you were there?"

Mannis studied it, shaking his head.

"You sure?" Brymmer said.

"Yeah. I'm sure. I never saw him before in my life."

Brymmer rolled his eyes. It was one of those beautiful canned phrases. It was also, his instinct told him, a lie. Mannis sulkily drew on his drink which was mostly melted ice. He was lying, Brymmer reckoned, so as to not "get involved." So to hell with him. Brymmer showed McConnell to the girl.

Mannis said, "She wasn't even with me in the bar."

The girl looked faintly surprised at this news.

Brymmer said, "Oh? I kind of figured that she was. The tab was for two martinis and a Scotch."

Mannis threw his head back and looked at the ceiling, inquiring of the whimsical gods, Why me? and also why the hell this was not his day.

The girl said, "Yes. I talked to that man. I was waiting for Harry—" she looked at Mannis who was still communing with invisible gods— "You were late, you know, Harry." He continued to commune.

Brymmer said, "About what time did you talk?"

She said, "Between sixish and six-twenty-five.— You were nearly a half-hour late on me, Harry."

"So I've heard," Mannis said.

"Well I didn't exactly stay mad," the girl answered. She turned back to Brymmer, her bright young eyes full of tired old plaints. Brymmer said, "First, I think I'd better get your name."

"Sure," the girl said. "Carolyn Klein. Of one-twenty-seven West Fifty-Eighth." Brymmer looked over at Harry Mannis who was pointedly ignoring the whole damn thing. Brymmer wondered idly if Mannis got through life by pointedly ignoring the things he didn't like, and then how far it got him. Judging by the silk of his heavy silk robe and the five-grand Rolex on the dresser, far.

Brymmer turned back to the girl and said simply, "Carolyn? Go on."

"With what?"

"With what you were saying. About the man."

"Oh, yeah. As I was saying, when you leave a girl in a bar, all alone for half an hour, a guy will start talking to the girl, wouldn't you say? So this guy in the picture comes up to me and talks. He was very attractive. He was tall, very tan—"

"Did he tell you what his name was?"

She thought a minute. "Bill."

"Uh-huh. What did he say?"

"Why don't you sit down?"

"That's what he said?"

"No.— That's what *I'm* saying to *you*." She patted the bed. "Why don't you sit down?"

Brymmer shook his head. "What else did he say?"

"Well he was kinda nice. Asked me what I did. Things like that. Like most guys, you know, when they try to pick you up they only talk about themselves. They tell you about their business and their great golf game and the great car they drive, and then they sort of sneak in a mention of their wives so that later, just in case, they can say that they were 'fair,' and then maybe an hour later, if it happens you're still there, they say, 'Oh. By the way. What's your name?'"

Mannis growled nastily, "And how the hell would *you* know?"

Shaking her head now, the girl looked at Brymmer. "Guy wants a nineteenth century mistress." Turning, she laughed. "I got news for you, Harry. They used to be kept. You know—rent paid? Little diamonds for the ears? So what do you expect? You come here once a month from your goddam Topeka—To*peka*,

144

f'r chisssakes— and the wife and the kiddies and the cute little dog and you buy me some dinner. What's *that* supposed to buy?"

Harry was flushing. "Jesus! I never heard you *talk* like this."

"You never asked me."

Brymmer cleared his throat. "About this guy Bill. You happen to notice if he met someone there? picked someone up?"

"Yeah. I think." Carolyn Klein ran a hand through her hair. "When Harry came in, we moved to a table and I think this other woman moved over, took my seat. She was standing at the far other end of the bar and she moved to the seat."

"Can you tell me what she looked like?"

Carolyn shrugged. "Long brown hair. Attractive. Thin. She was wearing a dark green Donna Karan suit. Wool. And she had this giant handbag."

"Brown," Brymmer said.

"The handbag? No, I think—"

"I meant the hair."

"Oh yeah. It was brown, except I think it was a wig."

"And why would you think that?"

"I'm a makeup person. I do makeup for models. You know those fashion shows they do in Bryant Park? I do makeup for that. And sometimes for television. And sometimes even for female politicians. Like before they make a speech. So I know about wigs. This wasn't, you know, a real wiggy kind of wig. I mean it wasn't a cheap one. Most people wouldn't guess. But it wasn't exactly a great one, either."

Brymmer zagged away. "Did you happen to notice if the two left together? I mean Bill and this girl?"

145

Carolyn looked up, her eyes getting wide. "You said *homicide?*"

"Yeah. That's right."

"Was she *killed?*"

"No."

"Oh. Then okay." Carolyn Klein built a fine indifferent shrug. "No. I don't know if they left together or not."

"They didn't," Mannis said. He was up now and pacing. "The guy left first and the girl went to the bathroom, came back to the bar again and finished up her drink. She was some— well, she had this little ass-swinging walk. And I know she was sitting at the bar when we left."

"Talking to anyone?"

Mannis shook his head.

Carolyn said, "Seems you were pretty busy looking."

Mannis said spitefully, "And what do you expect?"

Brymmer scratched his jaw. "Look—" he said.

Carolyn raised a finger. "Something else. I don't know if it's important."

"Take a stab," Brymmer said.

"Well after we left the bar, we went out to a movie and then we came back to the dining room to eat. And while we were eating I... um...got gas. So I came up to the room to get some of Harry's Gas-X— God love him, he wouldn't get it for me himself— and as I'm coming down in the elevator, I notice this woman—she was already in the car—and I'm thinking, that's funny. She looks like the woman who I saw down at the bar, except now she's a redhead. I couldn't say for sure because now she had a coat on so I couldn't see the suit but it was definitely red hair and kind of curlyish and wild so I suspected it was real though I couldn't really tell."

Brymmer leaned forward. "What time was this?" he said.

"What time was it, Harry, when I said I had gas?"

Harry said flatly, "I don't time your stomach."

"I would guess," she said, "somewhere in the neighborhood of ten."

Brymmer said, "Tomorrow you'll come down to the station—both of you—as early in the morning as you can. Here. Here's my card. See if you can help us get a picture of that girl."

"Oh Christ," Mannis said.

"It won't take that long."

"That's not what bothers me."

"Yeah. I know. Listen, you can come dressed as Ronald McDonald if that'll make you happy. We don't release names."

At the door, Mannis whispered, "So what do you want the girl for?"

"Nothing," Brymmer said. "Just questioning, that's all."

Mannis made a grunt and then closed the door swiftly. Brymmer stood in front of it, listening from the hall. After a beat, he heard Carolyn's voice saying, "So! First you're late and then you're *girl*-watching, right?"

## 40

"Sergeant?"

"We have to stop meeting like this."

"Tell that to Jackie."

"Next time I see her."

"And you can't tell me anything?"

"Yes. I can't."

"Are you frustrated?"

"That was a stupid question."

"You're right. It was. On the other hand, *Jackie* doesn't seem to be stupid. She keeps on going and she's gone without a trace."

"So you think Jackie's smart."

"Well she's outsmarted *you*. Well I didn't mean *you*, what I meant was the police."

"Pretty snarky tonight, huh?"

"I'm working. It's my job."

"So what do you want me to say?"

"Something quotable, if you would."

"Four score and seven years ago, our fathers—"

"Oh you're cute."

"Goodnight, Jamie."

"Goodnight, Burt."

## 41

*Thursday, March 5th:*

# JACKIE STRIKES AGAIN!
*-New York Daily News*

## WHACKY JACKIE TAKES ANOTHER WHACK
*-New York Post*

## SERIAL KILLINGS STUMP POLICE
*-New York Times*

## BATTLE OF THE SEXES: ROUND 4 TO JACKIE
*-New York Newsday*

## SEX IN THE CITY?
## BETTER COOL IT, SAY DOCS
*-Men's Health Magazine*

## 42

*Friday, March 6th:*

The meeting was held in a large conference room at One Police Plaza on the 14th floor. At the head of the room was an oblong table and, provided with microphones, were three psychiatrists, each of whom specialized in criminal behavior. They were, left to right, Dr. Herman Roetgen of NYU; Dr. Milton Merkowski, the head of a department at Columbia P&S, and Dr. Johnathan Paine of Bellevue Psychiatric. At a dais to the side, and also with a totally unnecessary microphone, was Borough Commander Anton Padillo.

The attendees, who were seated at a large oval table— all, including Brymmer, dressed in dark suits and ties—had been conveniently provided with lined yellow pads, the ubiquitous blue-and-white ballpoint pens, and glasses filled with tepid municipal water. They included Roger Hammett, the Chief of Detectives; Lieutenant Archie Walsh, representing Manhattan South, plus a dozen or so detectives, including (by invitation) Matson, Ritter and Poll and a highly recalcitant Sergeant Brymmer who'd dragged along with him Kerner and Clark.

Brymmer was doodling O's on his pad as Padillo cleared his throat— far too loudly and straight into the mike— and announced the agenda. The following presentation would come in two parts. "First," he said, "we'll background the history of the crime and then, with the help of our expert panel, we'll try to establish a practical picture of... well, of Jackie.— Have I got that right?" He turned to the panel which nodded yes. "Then I'll turn this over to Dr. Roetgen."

Brymmer looked up. Roetgen was a clean-looking pink-and-white man with a yellow bow tie but a humorous mouth.

"It's rare," Roetgen said. "I suppose I ought to add that it's thankfully rare. Most of the cases of criminal penectomy are fairly anomalous." He looked around the room. "Unusual," he said. "Or in other words, cutting someone's dick off is rare."

Brymmer and Kerner exchanged glances.

Roetgen continued. "Undoubtedly you're versed in the case of Lorena Bobbitt. Nineteen-ninety-three. Husband falls asleep and Lorena, in the kitchen where she wants a glass of water, has the sudden epiphany that kitchens have knives, and the rest is history.

Afterwards, distraught and, she claims, still in shock, she gets into her car, starts driving around, and discovers to her horror that she's still got the penis, right there in her hand, so she throws it out the window. Lorena goes to trial where she pleads self-defense combined with our old friend Temporary Insanity on the grounds that he abused her, which apparently he did. And Lorena gets off. Not guilty, says the court.

"Then we've got another case. Two-Thousand-Five. This one's in Alaska where the mistress of a man who'd been promising divorce but who'd kept on postponing it, finally decided enough of this crap, so she tied him to the bed in post-coital languor, and so on and so on. She got twenty years.

"The other case I know of is in Liverpool, England at about the same time though it wasn't quite the same. In this case, the lover'd stopped seeing the woman and rebuffed her advances. They fought, in the course of which she yanked off his ball and, when confronted, tried to swallow it. This one got two-and-a-half years for assault.

"The rest of the cases are all male on male or else self-mutilation which can often result in death from infection or blood loss or heart attack, of course."

Two of Brymmer's O's were now injected with a pendulous U in between them which could either be interpreted as an icon for Groucho Marx or a fully assembled package.

"That's it," Roetgen said.

"Not quite." Dr. Paine held a finger in the air. "There's the famous epidemic of penectomies in Thailand. This was back in the 'seventies. It was almost quite the fashion. Women who were cheated on were doing it in droves. They'd wait till their husbands fell asleep and

151

then whack. And since many of these people were in rural Thailand and were also raising ducks, these women, they'd throw it out the window for the ducks. In fact, there was a common saying in Bangkok, 'I'd better get home before the ducks get a treat.' If you don't quite believe me, then google it," he said. "It's in quite a few journals."

There was silence in the room. Except for the sound of men squirming in their seats.

"All right. So with that much stated," Padillo said, "there doesn't seem to be any pattern here at all that would seem to fit Jackie. Each of those women had a personal motive. Which, if I get it, was jealousy or revenge."

"Ah yes, but it isn't that simple," Paine said. He paused to sip water and to finger a mustache which was tenderly growing. "What I mean is, these were all pathological, too. There's a difference between... I dunno... Frenching somebody's bed, making phone calls and hanging up or reporting your errant lover to the folks at the IRS, and engaging in dismemberment. So what you're talking about here entails a strain of internal violence. And additionally a failure— or, in some cases, an absence of the filter that reins it in." He again checked his mustache to be sure it wasn't lost. "In other words, we're getting past the limits of normal jealousy or even what you might call the normal gamut of rage."

"What's the normal gamut of rage?" Hammett called out.

"Throwing a lamp. Throwing a punch. Throwing a tantrum. Shooting a gun. That's—Bang! That's practically a reflex," Paine said. "You're not grabbing a razor blade and actually cutting flesh."

"So then who grabs a razor blade?" Hammett

persisted.

Padillo held a hand up. "I think that's the subject of the next part of our— what shall we call this?—discussion? So why don't I toss it to Professor Merkowski."

Brymmer's ○'s now developed a downward-curving bridge and then sprouted a pair of stems. Merkowski, wearing big, round, dark-tinted glasses that successfully hid his eyes, had the look of a sneaky owl. Brymmer started to draw an owl.

Merkowski moved the mike in closer to his mouth. "There are many and varied profiles that connect with this crime, and abuse— I mean a history of having been abused— is most definitely one. Abused people snap. They lack resilience. It's not temporary insanity, it's recurrent insanity. And some people manage to control it very well until it suddenly slips out. Something triggers it."

"Well like what?" Padillo asked.

"That depends, of course, on the person. Could be anything. Even if she hadn't been abused, either mentally or physically, but had merely been cheated on, even once or twice—"

"Or was forcefully rejected," Roetgen cut in. "Love," he said, "is truly a many-splendored thing, unless or until it becomes destructive. A person falls in love and then the love becomes obsessive. A normal— well...a *seemingly* normal person can suddenly go berserk at the moment of rejection. It's as though she's been suddenly rocketed into hell and she reacts like a hell-cat. It's what I call the curse of the 'Stay Moment Thou Art Fair'" He glanced around quickly at the phalanx of blank faces. "That's Faust," he said. "Does anyone remember the tale of Faust?"

Faust, Brymmer recalled, had sold his soul to the

devil, but he didn't recall the rest.

"Faust," Roetgen said, "sold his mortal soul to the devil but the devil could only claim it if Faust discovered a moment— a moment in mortal life— that he wanted to last forever. 'Stay moment, thou art fair.' And the moment that Faust thought it, the devil would claim his soul and he'd be bound as a slave in hell. So that's what I'm talking about. Rejection is hell. And hell hath no fury like a woman who wants Forever when Forever is saying No."

Brymmer now added an N to his ○.

"So in other words," Paine appended, "there are people who suddenly snap and seek revenge on specific men and then apply it to men at large. And then too, it isn't even as simple as plain revenge. It's a desire to completely humiliate the victim. It's not enough to kill him, he has to be deeply humiliated too. Even posthumously so. And there's nothing more humiliating—"

"—to any man living or dead—" Roetgen said.

"Exactly," Paine agreed.

Again there was silence. Even the members of the panel seemed unnerved. A lot of water got sipped.

"And of course, we've got the actual psychotics," Merkowski said. "The ones hearing voices. God, instructing them to do His bidding and 'this is the bidding I want you to do.' The serial killers like Son of Sam. David Berkowitz. Look it up. Thought God—or a dog, which is God spelled backwards— was seriously telling him to 'Kill the harlots.' On top of that, there's always the paranoids, the schizos. The people who believe that humanity as a whole is out to destroy them and they narrow it down to Who. The man at the newsstand who told them 'Good morning' when it was patently after noon. That was the secret warning that he's definitely out to get them. So the newspaper guy is shot. Can a detective 'figure it out'?"

Again there was silence.

"Anything else?" Padillo inquired.

Paine said, "Of course we have to mention the Ted Bundy's. They're very clever and very charming and they totally lack a soul. They're sociopaths, we call them, but in other times and places we'd have simply called them evil. And they're smart as all hell. They lack emotion but they know how to act it. They mimic feelings and they lure people in. They're likely articulate, seemingly normal, and even attractive. Bundy was that. He was also successful. A brilliant student. Came from a family that offered him love. There was just no 'reason' why he was what he was. No abuse, no rejections. People *liked* him, in fact. And given all that, he was able to murder about thirty-six women. Some say a hundred, and some say it's more."

"If I might," Roetgen said, "I don't mean to interrupt, but it's frequently quite simple. For some, it's just a potent impulse they can't control. A kick. An empowerment. An addiction, if you will. These are the kinds of people who torture animals when they're young."

"And one other pointer," Merkowski threw in. "Most of these people are eager for ink. They like the spotlight. They follow the press. Son of Sam, as I recall, was writing letters to Jimmy Breslin. Breslin at the time was with the *Post* or the *News* or with one of those papers, I now forget which. And a lot of them try to get close to the police. They'll try to get friendly. They'll offer you 'help.' If you ever get a call from a woman being helpful, it might be your killer. So stay on your guard."

Again there was silence.

Padillo said, "Well... are there any questions?"

155

The assemblage was mute.

Padillo grew anxious. He glanced around the room. "Was that of help to you, Sergeant Brymmer?"

Brymmer looked up at him. "Yes sir," he said. "Jackie either does or does not hear voices; she also either was or has never been abused, and is seemingly normal or congenitally nuts."

Padillo was scowling.

Roetgen laughed aloud. "But he's got it exactly. That's exactly what we said."

Brymmer decided he liked Roetgen.

He also decided that he'd like to read *Faust*.


## 43

"There's a fair chance we're dealing with something else here," Brymmer said. "Some *thing*. Some *one*. Else," he repeated. He'd carefully ditched the tie just as soon as he'd hit the station. The jacket lay folded, almost neatly, across his desk. He was pacing around the room which, in light of the extra staffing, was now standing room only. "Out-of-towner. Hotel. In the head. Not the throat." He decided to sit down. "So as I pointed out to begin with, we pursue both tracks. Meaning Jackie and not-Jackie. — Does anyone disagree?"

Nobody disagreed.

Brymmer swiveled in his chair.

"McConnell," Brymmer said. "What do we know about McConnell? We know that there were no blonde hairs in the guy's room but we found some in the closet. On the navy blue jacket of a navy blue suit. Also on the pants. Or to be more specific on the inner part of

156

the thigh." He looked quickly around the room and then addressed the smirking faces. "Want to speculate, gentlemen?"

"Is it possible," one of the new guys suggested, "that a *Mrs.* McConnell, back home, could be a blonde?"

"On the pants?" Kerner said.

"Or how about a Labrador Retriever," Ross tried. "There are blond ones, aren't there?"

"His wife," Dubisky said, "is a salt-and-pepper gray. We found her picture in his wallet."

McAllister protested, "Are you certain it's his wife?"

"Would you carry around a picture of a salt-and-pepper lady if it *weren't* your wife? Come on," Dubisky said. "We all know the answer.—Sergeant Brymmer? Spell it out."

"Well having a dirty mind like the rest of you," Brymmer said, "it's a blow job, fully clothed.—Which gets us to?"

"Seeing if there's saliva on the zipper?" Dubisky asked hopefully.

"Sure. Why not? Since we're desperate," Brymmer said. "But we also found a ripped piece of paper in his pocket. 'Vanessa,' it said. And a telephone number."

Ross raised his hand. "Can I have that assignment?"

"If you eat all your spinach.—Continuing," Brymmer said. "Once again, we have no direct witnesses on the floor. And I also note we didn't find a cell phone in his room, which I'm inclined to think is odd. I mean nobody doesn't have a cell phone any more and especially not a businessman. So who swiped the phone? The killer? or the chambermaid. Or maybe he just lost it. Anyway, I mention it and think we ought to pursue it.—Reggie? What do you know?"

"A fair lot," Kerner said. He was seated on his desk,

his feet in their sensible Brogans, hanging down. "I corralled the concierge. A pretty sharp lady named Maribelle Lee. So Maribelle tells me that he visits fairly often, maybe six times a year, staying mostly for a week. Told me that he often ordered theater tickets, limos, reservations to hot restaurants. Also ordered flowers."

"Well a lot of that could also've been business," Clark said.

"With the cards signed 'Always' and 'Thinking of you'?"

"Well," Clark temporized, "maybe he loves his job."

"Which was what?" Dubisky said. "I mean what'd the guy do?"

"Ran a factory," Brymmer said. "Auto parts. Business called McConnell and Claib."

"Let me finish," Kerner said. "So I talked to the maids. Corelli and I did. They remembered him well on account of his flashy tips. They also remembered how frequently they didn't change his linens in the morning since the bed wasn't slept in."

"Hold it," Brymmer said. "You mean this time around?"

"Uh-uh. In the past."

"From which we conclude what?"

"He had a mistress in New York."

"But he didn't see her *this* time."

"Uh-uh," Kerner said. "This time he went to the convention, that was it. No theater, no flowers. No sparing of the maids."

"So we conclude they broke up?"

"I don't know," Kerner said. "Do we leap to conclusions?"

"I don't know," Brymmer said, "but why the hell not? We're just spitballing, anyway.—Did you check with the flower shop?"

"Do dogs check the tree? Unfortunately, they only keep records for six months and the last time he visited was back in September."

"Terrific. Anything else?"

"Yeah. We got your two prize witnesses," Ross said. "The lovely Carolyn and Harry? Came up with different faces. They were close but not identical. Harry's had a woman with some longish dark hair and Carolyn had both— the long dark and the curly red. Not to mention that they didn't match at all with the ones from Starrett though the batch that we got from Starrett didn't even match with themselves."

"It's an inexact science," Kerner added irrelevantly.

"Like astrology," Ross said.

Brymmer waited. "Anything else?"

Nothing.

"Okay. Then it's my turn to spritz. I've been thinking about Jackie. What she does with her souvenirs. We got whatshername Bobbitt, she threw it out of the window. Kim Tran—the Alaskan one — flushed it down the john."

"And the Thai ladies," Kerner said, "who fed it to the ducks." He shook his head slowly. "I will never eat pâté de foie gras again."

"And do you eat it a lot *now?*" Dubisky asked airily.

"The question," Brymmer said, "could be where do you get formaldehyde?"

"Oh," Dubisky said.

"Who works with it? Where do you buy it? Look into it." Brymmer paused now and lit a cigarette which meant Ross and Dubisky now lit cigarettes as did six other guys. "Not to say," Brymmer said, "that she doesn't toss it out with the coffee grounds in the morning, but still— worth a shot. Second point," he said, "I've also been thinking a lot about the hair. Here's a working hypothesis. I'm ready to hypothesize that Jackie is a redhead. What Tanner caught in his fingernails was pulled, not broken. He could have pulled it during sex, he could have pulled it as he was dying. But the blonde hairs were planted. Blonde herrings, if you will."

There was general thoughtful silence.

"I said it's a hypothesis."

Brymmer rose again and then aimlessly paced the room. "The hairs at all the opening scenes were identical. Broken. No roots. Not shed, not pulled. So I've been thinking about hair. About where you'd get hair. There's a neighborhood in the Twenties where they sell it. Lots of stores. It's like the Diamond District, sort of, except this one, it's for hair. West Twenties. Around Sixth. And then it might have come from salons or whatever the hell they call them. Beauty parlors. Floor scrapings. Think about it."

"What do we do with it?" Wright, from Ritter's group, said.

"I haven't," Brymmer said, "the vaguest fucking idea. I'm just spritzing is all. You want to do something, do it."

He paced to the back wall where a bulletin board with pin points was marking the fatal scenes. "All of em in Manhattan," he noted in passing. "And all classy nabes."

Again there was silence. Eyes followed him.

Corelli, who'd been sitting around like a log and letting Kerner do the talking, said, "She'd have to be pretty smart. Like for instance she's been planting her little blondies in the drain. How'd she know that we look at drains?"

"Like anybody else," Dubisky said. "From TV."
Then he squinted. "On the other hand, the hat-girl in
the bar, if I remember from that report, said her father
was a cop."

"And her brother," McAllister said. "And I'd also
stop to consider if she just 'happened to' know where all
the surveillance cameras are. So she could dodge them
the night of Starrett."

Dubisky looked doubtful. "So how'd she know
*that?*"

"You can google it," Brymmer said.

"No kidding."

"You can google almost anything," Brymmer said.

"So why don't we just google us a 'Who the hell's
Jackie?' and be done with it?" Clark said.

"Because we'd all be out of a job."

## 44

Late Friday night, Brymmer visited Areola who'd
been highly recommended by Tony Corelli and was
known to give a special discount to police. Why not?
Brymmer'd thought. It was good clean hundred-dollar
no-fuss sex. No feelings involved. No roses required.
Lying there now, he was all-in-all content.

On the other hand—and Brymmer had a headful of
Other Hands (always reaching into the cookie jar and
stealing all the Mallomars)— on that other hand, he
was perfectly aware that contentment always existed in
direct proportion to his lack of expectation. Expecting
nothing, Brymmer was content. It was only on the rare,

blighted occasions when hope sprung, infernal, that Brymmer knew despair.

He felt himself slip-sliding out of his nest.

"Hey Brymmer—is almost three o'clock," the girl said.

"Mmm-hmm."

"You tell me to tell you when it's three."

"Mmm-hmm."

"You have to be working now at eight."

"Uh-huh." He moved languidly and opened his eyes. He scrabbled a cigarette off of the table, struck up a match, rolled to his back, and blew out his smoke at the mirrored ceiling. He wasn't nuts about mirrored ceilings. He didn't like looking at himself, at all, in any mirror, at any time, let alone at the less than heraldic image of Brymmer Rampant on Corelli's Whore. Watching her now, by way of the mirror, her Asian hair fanned out from her head like a black sunburst against the pillow, Brymmer was filled with nothing at all. The sex, after all, had been a humorless fuck and its ephemeral pleasure had a half-life of seconds.

Getting up quickly, he crossed to the window and looked at the weather through a slat in the blind.

"A deluge," Brymmer said, and laughed. "*Après moi.*"

"Huh?"

"It's raining. Very hard," Brymmer said. The girl had pulled the comforter up around her chest. He stepped into shorts and the business suit pants. "You got any coffee or something in the kitchen?"

She nodded. "Yeah. You want me to fix?"

"No. I'll get it." He reached for his shirt and then ambled to the kitchen, a small spare room, not dirty, not clean. While water boiled in a tin pot, he went through his wallet and pulled out the bills.

Sipping at some watery Nescafé, he went back to the bedroom, folding the bills, a crisp pair of fifties. The girl was propped up against a Ralph Lauren pillow, still chastely wrapped up in her Ralph Lauren sheets and was fiddling with the dial of a slick- looking radio. Standing near the dresser, he hesitated. What should he do about the bills?

She tilted her head at him. "You like me, yes?"

"I like you fine." A jewelry box was up on the dresser, a rather handsome Indian box. He slipped his donation under the lid, aware that she saw it. "I'll call you," he said. "Another time maybe. If that's okay."

She nodded, grave. "You... very good body."

He laughed at that. "Mutual, I'm sure."

"No. I mean this. Very good built. Others—" she hovered her hand atop her stomach and gestured with a wide arc in the air. "How you saying this?"

He strapped on his gun. "Paunch."

"Paunch," she repeated.

He reached for his jacket.

"Also," she smiled, "very nice cock."

He flushed, which embarrassed him so much that he flushed. He picked up his trench coat. "Well... so long."

She smiled again and reached out a hand from the covers and said to him earnestly, "You shake me goodbye?"

Brymmer thought a handshake was a novel con-clusion but who was he to argue?

He shook her goodbye.


His phone was ringing as Brymmer was opening the door to his apartment. He pulled it from his pocket, saw who it was, and waited till he'd tossed down the soaking wet coat and gone over to the sofa before he clicked it on.

"I didn't *think* you'd be sleeping," Dubisky said hoarsely.

"No. What's the matter?"

"Nothing's the matter."

"At four in the morning, something's the matter. What's the matter?"

"Nothing's the matter. I just couldn't sleep. I wanted to know if you'd seen the paper."

"No. What paper?"

"Actually the *Post*. Tomorrow's."

"No."

"Look it up online."

"Something bad?"

"Something funny."

"For funny," Brymmer said, "I can wait till tomorrow. What's the matter?"

"*Nothing's* the matter. So she takes the two kids and goes off to L.A.. Right? Her new husband gets a *business* trip there so she pulls em out of school for a whole damn week and she doesn't even *tell* me about it till tonight when she sends a fucking e-mail."

"So?"

"So tomorrow's my weekend with the kids."

"Except days off are cancelled. You're working tomorrow."

"To hell with it. You're missing the *point* of this, Burt. The point is she sends me a fucking e-mail. Subject line: Kids are in California. Opening: Harold got an all-paid trip. Goddam sonofabitch Harold gets a trip so she pulls em out of school."

"They'll go to Disneyland or something. They'll

have a good time."

"Yeah I know," Dubisky grumbled. "I know about that. And I'm also aware that I'll be working tomorrow. So why'm I so mad?"

"Because it's four in the morning."

"Yeah."

"Go to sleep. Harold eats it."

"So true."

"And they'll be home again in a week."

"So you really think McConnell might not've been a Jackie?"

"Go to sleep," Brymmer said. "Have a drink. Go to sleep."

## 45

*Saturday, March 7th, New York Post:*

# McCONNELL WIDOW BLASTS POLICE
## Tells Good Morning America
## "They lied about Bill."

"It's a vast, wing-tip conspiracy," Brymmer said.

## 46

*Monday, March 9th:*

According to the Medical Examiner's report, McConnell had been stabbed with a 7-inch blade that had severed the Sylvian fissure of the brain which separates the frontal and temporal lobes. The knife had not only been thrust, but levered, doing maximum damage. It had not only severed the carotid artery, causing mas-

165

sive internal bleeding, but had mangled the centers for speech and motion, proving that there were, indeed, Fates Worse Than Death. How quickly the man had died was a matter of speculation but he'd probably been unconscious when the mutilation occurred.

The last meal he'd eaten was apparently his lunch. His blood level of alcohol was moderately low and he hadn't taken drugs.

The killer once again had left no clear fingerprints or vaginal secretions— nothing from which DNA could be determined— and a check of the plumbing system indicated that nothing of biological interest had been flushed down the john.

Kerner tossed a written memorandum on Brymmer's desk, right on top of the morning *Post*.

*Formalin – dilute formaldehyde (40% by volume, 37% by mass) – used to preserve animal parts by permeating and subsequently hardening tissue and preventing decomposition – is available to veterinarians, research biologists, museum curators and licensed embalmers through wholesale medical and funeral suppliers while everybody else can get it everywhere online, including at Amazon.*

Brymmer looked up. Kerner looked baleful.

"I suppose I could pester those online sources and see who's been ordering Formalin in New York...?" Kerner left it dangling.

"I suppose," Brymmer said. "But my request for your services has just about elapsed." He paused and then shrugged. "Everything we do around here is ad hoc and what it means is, I have to keep hocking some Lieutenant when I need to add staff. I meant 'hocking' in the—"

"Yeah. I know what you mean. It's Yiddish. Means pestering. Banging on about something. Just surprised you'd know the word."

"Yeah? I washed dishes in a deli one time. So what do you think, Reggie. If I asked for you permanently…"

"I'd grab it," Kerner said.

"Then I'll see what I can do."


At 11:45 when Brymmer got back from a command performance at the mayor's office, Ross walked over and sat on his desk. "You gotta hear this," he said. "Don't worry, don't worry, I'll write the damn report but you really got hear it. You ready?"

"If I weren't, would it stop you?" Brymmer said.

Ross took a good long chug of Brymmer's coffee. "Vanessa Peters. Not only is Vanessa in McConnell's pocket, she's in Clawson's address book."

Brymmer bit his lip. Everything told him this would be a shaggy dog.

"Vanessa," Ross said, "turns out to be a blonde which, being a rat-smart detective, you'd've guessed. In fact, it turns out that we already talked to her. Ritter's guys, anyway. Vanessa is a stew. A flight attendant, for-mally. Vannessa is a gorgeous blonde flight attendant stew. I go down there with Clark. Quarter after nine. So she opens up the door in this little pink shortie with the—"

"Skip it," Brymmer said.

"So she says to us, Is this about Richard again? and we tell her No, no. It's about Bill McConnell, and she says What about him? and Clark tells her what. And she screams—not yells, but screams. Eeeeeee-aaaaaah. She gets totally hysterical. Her roommate appears. The

167

roommate, who's bundled in a terry cloth robe, is an Asian-looking stew named Olivia Park. The roommate goes off and reappears with some Valium. Vanessa takes it down with some instant coffee while the roomie says Vanessa's had some dreams about Bill. About Bill's being dead. And Vanessa says she's started to believe she's a witch. Vanessa gets carried away with this theme, reeling off instances of possible witchhood. The convenience store she buys her potato chips at had been robbed around Christmas and the owner, she informs us, was 'practically shot.' That, for example. Then Clawson. Now this."

Ross paused briefly for some more of Brymmer's coffee.

Brymmer said nothing. Ross, like an engine, was merely warming up.

"Okay, so she tells us how she told the other cops how the one and only time she ever saw Richard Clawson was in possibly November when she met him, where else, in a first class cabin from whence they adjourned to spend a night and the entire following afternoon in some suite in some Sheraton in San Francisco. So we ask about McConnell. Well him, she says, she met on a flight from Spokane and it was, put poetically, love at first flight. Specifically in the bathroom."

"I hope it was early in the flight," Brymmer said. "Those bathrooms get disgusting."

"Agreed," Ross said. "All the wadded paper towels. And the piss smell. I'd figure that was *their* problem, though, but I'd hazard we could now explain the hairs upon the pants."

"Go on," Brymmer said.

"So later that night—which is a week ago Friday— she goes to his hotel."

"He invited her?"

"Nope. She just went there on her own. But I gather he didn't look the gift horse in the mouth. So they're rolling in his room or as Vanessa now puts it— this is all in italics— it was *only last week!!* and she lay, God help her, on *that very bed!!* Did she, we ask, ever see him after that? Oh no. Not again. 'And it just drove her crazy,' Olivia now adds.

"'*What* drove her crazy?' Clark asks nicely.

"'I was *never crazy*,' Vanessa hollers.

"'You were crazy,' Olivia corrects her sweetly. 'You were totally out of your fucking bird.'

"'*What* didn't drive you crazy?' Clark asks.

"'That he just never called her,' Olivia offers. 'She wanted to love him,' Olivia adds. 'Either that, or to kill him. She wasn't quite sure.' Olivia is very calm when she says this. Vanessa's going totally out of her fucking bird. 'Are you trying to get me *arrested?*' she hollers. 'What are you trying to *do* to me, Olivia? I didn't want to kill him and *I wasn't crazy*. My God! It's just bad enough being a witch.'

"'She needs therapy,' Olivia explains to us calmly. 'She really gets too upset about men. She expects something of them. They drive her up the wall. If you ask me,' she says to us, 'whoever did a job on those four rotten bastards did an act of public service. Revenge for all the girls they leave waiting by the phone.' She looks up at Clark and says, 'I hope you don't catch her.'"

Ross paused to breathe.

Brymmer raised his brows. "Is this, by any long shot, building to a point?" Brymmer kept a good firm grip on his coffee.

"We ask her where she was on the night McConnell died."

"Olivia or Vanessa?"

"Both of em."

"And?"

"Olivia was in Vegas and Vanessa, L.A."

"That's it?" Brymmer said.

"Mostly. I checked with their supervisor."

"And?"

"Olivia was in Vegas and Vanessa, L.A."

Brymmer gave Ross a long up-from-under look. "That's all?" he said.

"Yep."

"Thanks for sharing," Brymmer said.

<br>

## 47

*"Suppose,"* Dubisky said over Subway sandwiches, "suppose that mysterious brunette with McConnell was in fact his ex-mistress."

"That's doing quite a lot of supposing," Brymmer said. He was squinting at a large piece of lettuce on his cheese and removed it just in case it might involve nutritional value. "But go on. Where does it go?"

"Well...nobody else heard what they were saying in the bar. So what if what she said was, 'Hey there, Billy. Long time no see. So how about for old time's sake we have a boff?' And then, for discretion's sake, they don't leave together, but she trundles up later. We can pretty much say she left ten minutes later. Or later than McConnell. Or the bartender says it."

"And then what?"

"She whacks him for dumping her, of course."

"So our imagined ex-mistress, we imagine, is brunette."

"Or maybe she's a redhead."

"Or maybe our Carolyn got it wrong," Brymmer said. "After all, it was pretty damn dark in that bar. And even *she* wasn't sure that the redhead was the same."

"Still and all," Dubisky said, "it would be a pretty trick. Go up as a brunette, come down as a redhead. Avoid identification."

"That's the obvious part, isn't it? *If* Carolyn's right. I don't buy that it's the mistress."

"Well think about it though."

"I think about everything."

"If you don't want your lettuce, can I have it?" Dubisky said.

"You actually want lettuce?"

"Gotta fill myself up. This diet is killing me. I walk around starving."

Brymmer looked him over. "Well you've lost a few pounds."

"I will lose the prescribed twenty just to prove that I can."

"And then," Brymmer said.

"I will gain it all back."


The call came at 4:25 from the front desk. A Mrs. McConnell had arrived at the station and she wanted—well actually, demanded— to see Brymmer. Did Brymmer happen to know if Brymmer was still there?

Brymmer decided that he had to be there.

He met her at the door to the general squad room and, for privacy, took her to the Green Room down the hall, offering, on the way, his condolences for her loss.

She said nothing, merely looked at him with glowering disapproval. Since the days of that much-discussed wallet-size photo, she'd gotten a little grayer and she'd

171

put on a little weight but then, generally speaking, it was not an unpleasant face. In fact, she had the settled look of Everyone's Mother, or as Corelli later suggested, of Everyone's First Wife.

She sat across from Brymmer, occasionally tugging at the too-tight jacket of her sober gray suit and opening and closing the clasp of her handbag, which made a distracting *Click*.

"I thought I ought to visit here and tell you to your face," was how she began it, "that you're being unfair to a very decent man. You've been spreading awful stories that somehow this... *thing*... had something to do with his being with some... woman."

Brymmer said gently, "We don't write the headlines. I can understand your feelings but your quarrel, if you have one, is likely with the press."

"But the police are their sources."

"Not necessarily."

"So what is it you tell them?"

"Just the facts," Brymmer said.

"But what facts are those? That my husband was some kind of... sexual opportunist?"

"That particular phrase would have never crossed my mind. In fact, Mrs. McConnell, we tried to keep it quiet. For a number of reasons. The hotel wants it quiet. The mayor wants it quiet. It's apparently bad for business."

"But you told them—"

"It leaked. It was leaked in ten minutes. There are chamber maids, porters. What happened is what happened. Listen. I'm sorry. I'm genuinely and deeply sorry for your loss. I'm sorry for the circumstances."

"You don't *know* the circumstances. You simply presume. You've got a whole series of murders that you haven't been able to solve so you simply blame the victims. And you lump them all together. And you make it all dirty. And it just…isn't…*right*."

Brymmer said nothing.

She looked at him sternly. "You're an *ugly* man with an *ugly* mind."

Brymmer said calmly, "Well murder's ugly too. Maybe you need someone like me to deal with it."

"I'm sorry," she said suddenly. "I didn't mean to be rude."

"Be whatever you like."

"I'm not like that. I'm not rude. I always told my children that most people really can't help how they look, they can only help what they do."

"Never judge a book by its cover," Brymmer said.

"Exactly," she agreed.

"Did your husband have a cell phone?"

"Yes. Of course he did."

"Do you know what kind it was?"

"One of those fancy ones that does about everything."

"Iphone? Droid? Blackberry?"

"Oh good Lord. I wouldn't know about that. But why are you asking me?"

"It wasn't in his room."

"You see?" she said. "Doesn't that prove it was a robbery? Someone broke in and then it all went awry."

Brymmer didn't remind her that the wallet holding credit cards and two K in cash, not to mention the gold wedding ring (left in a dresser drawer) had been somehow or other overlooked by the thief.

"We're looking into that," he said. "We're exploring every angle. Would you allow us to have access to his home computer?"

"It's at home," she said rather densely, "in Spokane."

"We can partner with local law."

"But why would you want it anyway? He was *killed* in New York. Why would you need to go poking into his business? You're implying something again. What? That he was cheating? I assure you he never did."

"Would you have left him if he had?"

"I—-I don't know. I— no. I'd forgive him. To err is human. But I don't have to worry about anything like that since it didn't ever happen. And if that's what you were thinking—"

"I was actually thinking about cyber stalking."

"What do you mean by *that*?"

"Someone your husband got to know on line. Could have been for any reason. Politics. Business. I mean, there're very strange people out there."

"Well my husband didn't 'get to know' people on line. You don't know what he was like. He was a hard-working man. You have no idea how hard that man works. To give us our beautiful home. The tuition for the children. He built that business from— I almost started to say 'from the ground up' but it began under the ground. From our basement in Tacoma. We struggled. It was hard. I can't say that I minded. Those were even happy days. And he always put us first." Her eyes challenged Brymmer. "I know my husband. I've known him for thirty years, and here you come barging in and trying to destroy him. I won't let you do it. So, no, Mr. Sergeant, you can't have his computer. I'll at least protect that."

Brymmer just nodded in tentative acceptance. Obviously the woman had a lot more vested in preserving the image of her (decent, dedicated, hard-working) husband than in tracking down his killer. Nor did that seem so unreasonable, Brymmer thought. The satisfaction of catching whoever the hell it was would at best be ephemeral; the image, however, was something she could clutch until death did them part.

And therefore, if McConnell'd had a mistress in New York, and if the mistress had anything to do with it at all, they would just have to look for her in some other way.

"Up to you," he said pleasantly, and rose from his chair. "My apologies," he said, "I have to go to a meeting." She would understand Meetings. "However, if you feel you'd like to talk to someone else..."

She sighed. "I guess not," and then gradually rose, ironing the wrinkles from her skirt with her hands.

"You've got the case number," he said as he walked her to the stairs. "You can call us for updates. And of course we'll call you if we should get something good."

She started down the steps and then turned, looking fretful. "You *are* looking into the robbery thing, yes?"

"Absolutely," Brymmer said. "We leave no stone unturned."

### 48

*Tuesday, March 10th:*

*Syndicated column by Dr. Dill Bradley:*

## ARE MARRIED MEN SAFE?

Even faithful husbands have begun to watch their wives at the breakfast table lately and wonder: Has she ever gotten so really angry or maybe disappointed or otherwise bored....

Kathy said, "I had a really terrible dream."

She was brooding into coffee at the kitchen table as Ross, in his undershirt, was entering the room. Billy was plunked between them like a wall. Ross walked over and tousled his hair. "Hey there, kiddo. Yep. Lookin more like your dad every day." For an answer, Billy drooled and went into some tremors. Ross wiped the drool off and stroked the kid's arm. He walked to the table and poured out some juice from a lopsided carton, looking at Kathy who stared at her cup while she chewed at her lip. It was going to be a neurotic day.

"Yeah?" Ross picked up his glass. "What about?"

"That you're going to be a victim."

"Yeah? That's a switch. I thought I was the villain." He swallowed his juice and put down the glass.

"You're going to pick up the wrong girl and you're going to be a victim." She looked at him now. "Like the cases you're on."

Ross just stood there and tilted his head. "Would that make you happy?"

"We're not talking," she said, "about making me happy, we're *talking*," she said, "about what I dreampt."

"Yeah? Well, Freud says they're both the same thing. Even nightmares are wishes. Ask me anything. I've been studying up on psychotics." Ross put his foot up on one of the chairs and picked up a cup that was filled with coffee. He sipped it, watching her over the rim. She said nothing, looked perfectly calm.

Finally she said, "So you think I'm psychotic."

"Oh Christ. I didn't say I thought you were psychotic. I said I was reading Freud because I'm *reading* about psychotics because whoever's been *doing* this sure as hell is. Now that's what I said." Shaking his head, he put down the cup. "Jesus, Mary and Joseph! Kathy! –

176

Is there just any way – I mean any way at all – to get off of this rat-fucking ride to disaster and just have a reasonable conversation? Good God, I don't expect to be greeted in the morning with warm and tenderly loving hands, let alone with a warm plate of Aunt Jemima pancakes – God only knows I've given up on *that* – but *some*time, I'd just like to get out of bed and not find you sulking, or otherwise bitching or sniping or zapping. Listen – I'm having it right up to here. I am going berserk. Hey– you want to talk about who's going nuts? *I'm* going nuts. My time consists of going from the laugh-filled world of murder to the laugh-filled world of murder. You want to know who's killing me? *You* are killing me. You see that onion in the chair over there? That's half your genes, baby. Twenty-four fine little Hanson chromosomes and, man, I am goddam fucking *sick* of taking a hundred percent of the fall *ev*ery morning and *ev*ery evening and every other fucking second of my life! I'm sorry, Kathy. I'm truly sorry. I wish you could be Miss Movie of the Week. I wish I could take my kid to the ball game. I wish a *lot* of things, Kathy. I wish I had money, I wish I had luck, but most of all I *just wish I had a wife!*"

She looked at him calmly, nodding her head then tracing a finger over her lips. He stood there watching her watching him glare.

"Do you think," she said slowly, lighting a smoke, "you could read that again with a little more fire?"

Ross threw his head back and laughed out loud.

# 49

Brymmer was sitting with Captain Parisi and Lieutenant Meyer in Parisi's office.

Brymmer said, "So what do you *want* me to do?"

Parisi said, "Something."

Brymmer said nothing. As far as he could reckon he'd been doing a lot of something. He'd canvassed and recanvassed. He'd followed every even half credible-sounding tip and dived into local and FBI files. And was doing all the other somethings he was doing.

"Like," Brymmer said.

"Like," Parisi said, "how about you have a bunch of guys in the bars."

"They'd like that," Brymmer said, "only where would that get us?"

"Well," Meyer said, "we have reason to believe that both Starrett and McConnell met the killer in a bar."

"True," Brymmer said, and then found himself wrestling with the old Shall I Argue With The Boss Now problem, which perfectly defined a lose-lose situation. If you argued and were wrong, you would never have a future. If you argued and were right, you would never be forgiven.

"However," Brymmer ventured, attempting to look thoughtful, "the thing is that Tanner and Clawson didn't."

"Of course not." Parisi looked Brymmer in the eye. "But we have to do *something*. The something we have to do doesn't have to be something smart, it just has to be…something."

"Ah." Brymmer nodded. "Public relations."

Meyer smiled approvingly. "Yes," he said. "A little something for the press."

"And the mayor," Parisi added. "And the nightlife community who are feeling a lot of pain."

"Which means," Meyer said, "that they're paying less taxes."

"So in other words, we babysit," Brymmer said flatly.

"We prefer to call it something a little catchier," Meyer said. "Something like a Public Safety Patrol."

"How many of my guys would you require?" Brymmer asked.

"Oh, five ought to do it," Meyer said with a smile.

"Five," Brymmer said, thinking there were two thousand bars in the city. "Well then, that's fine."

"We're announcing it tomorrow," Parisi said, rising. "Of course, we won't mention the *size* of our patrol…"

"Gotcha," Brymmer said.

Brymmer rose too.

Parisi extended a manicured hand. "Nice working with you, Burt."

"Same here," Brymmer said.

## 50

The bulletin board at the back of the room now held, among other push-pinned data, a map with the pinpointed "Jackie Attacks," the five composite faces as described by everyone from Carmen to Harry, and a blue woolen hat with braids coming down that Dubisky had bought from a sidewalk vendor at 12th Street and Broadway near the Strand Bookstore. There was also a list that might have been, but wasn't, headlined cleverly as "Secondhand Smoke." These were the hazy and ques-

179

tionable factoids that had so far been gathered from the possible (or possibly mistaken) witnesses who might or might not have seen the actual Jackie and/or Jackies, plus the few other items that were actually corroborated by physical evidence:

| DESCRIPTION | SOURCE |
| --- | --- |
| Pretty | All |
| Hat with braids | Carmen/Alfie/Ziegler/Ralph? |
| From out of town? | Alfie |
| Cop link? Father/Bro? | Alfie |
| Wobbly (on 1/23) | |
|     From injured ankle | Ziegler |
|     Drunk? | Ralph? |
| Lives south of 60th? | M15 downtown bus? |
| Blonde | Evidence: first 3 scenes |
| |     Planted? |
| Redhead | Evidence: Tanner's hand |
| | Carolyn (maybe)? |
| Brunette | Carolyn, Harry, Bartender |
| Smart, articulate, abused, cheated on, vengeful, psychotic, sociopathic, normal | The Experts |

Brymmer held a dart, just about poised to get leveled at the chart, as good a way as any, he decided, to decide.

Kerner approached him with some papers in his hand.

"People who bought Formalin." Kerner sat down, backwards, on the straight-back chair beside the desk.

"Go," Brymmer said.

"One of those people was a Mr. George Levy. The gentleman who lives down the hall from Tanner. The guy who was giving the party that night."

"Go on," Brymmer said.

"He ordered it online from a place called Applix on January second."

"Six weeks before Tanner who was killed by a woman."

"I thought you'd find it interesting." Kerner looked hurt.

"I do find it interesting."

"So what do you want to do?"

"I think you grab Corelli and pay Mr. Levy a friendly little visit and just for the hell of it, see what he's up to."

"That's what I thought you'd think." Kerner was grinning.

"Welcome aboard, by the way. You're all ours."

At 7 PM, when it was 4 on the West Coast, Brymmer punched a telephone number in Spokane, and got shuttled into Hold where he was treated to a repertoire of vintage Beatles while he waited to connect to the object of his call: Randy Claib of McConnell & Claib. And since, whenever possible, Brymmer liked to "see" whoever he was talking to— the better to gauge how the talking-to should go— his computer screen was flashing him a photograph of Claib as featured on the company website ("About Us"). If the picture had been taken within the last decade, Claib, like McConnell, was half into his fifties and looked like a high school athlete going soft. He also had a Hard-Working Family Man face and was pictured wearing jeans and an ordinary workshirt with his arm around a machine.

When he finally came on, he came on with "Sergeant Brymmer, this is Randy. How can I help?"

"Well I hope you can help, Randy. I'd like to ask a couple of fairly basic questions. Starting with simply, How long did you know McConnell?"

"Oh we go back. In fact we all met in college. Bill and Marianne and then Lucinda and me."

"Lucinda's your wife?"

"Yep. Of thirty-one years."

"And did you and McConnell start the business together or—"

"Oh yeah. Together. Yeah, together."

"Would you say you were close friends— I mean, right up till now?"

"Yep. Like brothers."

Brymmer said, laughing, "Well, except brothers don't always get along..."

"And don't I know *that*. My own, I tell you. But yeah, Bill and I were the closest of the close."

"And would you say, as close friends, that he was happy in his marriage?"

Slight hesitation. "Yeah. I'd say yeah."

"Randy— this'll get a little delicate here— but as Bill's close friend, did he ever tell you about a woman in New York?"

Heavily-breathed sigh. Silence. Then, "Yeah. I suppose you found out about it, huh?"

"Yeah," Brymmer said. "I was hoping you could just corroborate what we know. So we can start with her name."

"Nora."

"Nora what?"

"Just Nora, that was all. Never said a last name."

"And what else did he tell you?"

"That she worked 'in fashion.' No idea what that means. Clothes, I suppose. I think she was a fairly sophisticated girl. Sophisticated taste. He told me one time she made him go to ballet and then he said he kinda liked it and I said to him, 'Man, you gotta really be in love, she gets you likin ballet.'"

"Was he? In love?"

"Smitten, I'd say. Well, more than that maybe. I don't know if it was her or the idea of her, you know?"

"Yeah. I think I do. I mean I think I understand.— How long was he seeing her?"

"Oh. Three years on and off. He'd make these excuses, like to go to New York. Business deals that weren't. That kind of thing. I was uncomfortable covering, but that's what friends do. But it kind of made me feel as though I was cheating too."

"Did he talk about divorce?"

"Oh yeah. That was part of it. Got himself in a real bind over that. Telling her he would, and then he'd get home here and think that he couldn't. Too much with Marianne. Too many people involved to get hurt. But he'd go back and forth."

"So did *he* do the breakup? Or the other way around?"

"Oh. Him with her. Told her he thought it was the decent thing to do. Said she took it real hard. Threw a real screamy tantrum."

"And when was the breakup?"

"September, I think."

"Did she bother him after that? I mean write him. Phone him. Make calls and hang up?"

"That last one, I think."

"Called and hung up."

"Right.—Wait a second. Are you leading to it's something to do about his—"

"Listen, just a few other questions here, Randy.

183

Did the hangup calls stop?"

"Yeah. Thanksgiving, I think it was the last."

"Do you know how old she was?"

"Mmm. I believe he once told me thirty-two? Something around there."

"Did he describe what she looked like?"

"He showed me her picture. Blonde. Looked expensive."

"Pretty?"

"More, um...more glamorous than pretty. Like all dolled up."

"Would you know if that picture would be somewhere in the office? I assume it's not at home."

"Pictures were on his phone. Couple of em, in fact. I don't think he printed em out."

"Uh huh. One more question. Do you think you could let us have access to his computer? I mean his office computer."

"Nope. Marianne came and took it this morning. Understand, we don't have any big fancy set up. We've just got some laptops. It was business property really— a new Mac Pro— but you know, what the hell."

"Did you clean it up first?"

"What? Oh. Christ. Didn't think to. On the other hand, he might've dumped Nora on his own. I hope so."

"Yeah. For Marianne's sake."

"Right. —Now you think this has anything to do with his—"

"No. I don't know. But if you think of someone else he might have possibly confided in—"

"There wouldn't be. Hard enough time telling me."

"How about some business friends in New York?"

"Didn't have any really. Or none that I'd know. Most of our business is in Michigan, some's in Carolina, like that."

"Well, if you think of something else about Nora, let me give you my number."

"I've got it already on the caller ID."

"Well, there you go."

"Technology," Claib offered. "It's something else, isn't it?"

"Yep," Brymmer said. "Yep, it sure is."

"Okay," Brymmer said. "So let's just suppose— as Dubisky has supposed— that in this particular case, as opposed to the others, that it's Nora, the fashionista and recently-spurned lover. Doesn't meet him in the bar. Phones him on his cell. Goes up to his room for that one last fuck and is ready to make sure that it's *his* last fuck. Does the job, steals the phone. No record of her call, no record of her number or any remaining pictures."

"Sounds good," Corelli said. "Except that you were urging us to check out his phone. Long story short: Iphone. Verizon."

"Break it gently," Brymmer said.

"GPS found the phone. It was stolen by the maid. Her son, little technie, had erased McConnell's stuff and erased it from the server."

"Well...there you go. Technology," Brymmer muttered. "It's something else, isn't it?"

## 51

*Wednesday, March 11th, New York Daily News:*

### POLICE ANNOUNCE PUBLIC SAFETY PLAN
### BARS TO BE COVERED, UNDERCOVER

Could be that the next time you order a beer at your local tavern or a $12 whiskey at a fancy club, the man (or woman) at the next stool or table will be a detective casing the scene for the killer now known as Jackie the Ripper. "This ought to make bar-goers feel more secure," said Captain Alfonso A. Parisi...

*Sunday March 15th: New York Post, "Cardin's Corner"*

### BAR BIZ DROPS FOR FEAR OF COPS
by Pete Cardin

Bars owners say the threat of an army of police detectives invading their turf has cost them business at a time they can least afford to lose it.

"You go to a bar to let loose," said William "Rocky" Caputo, owner of The Rocking Pony in Soho. "You don't want to feel that you're being spied on." Other owners report the same...

It was midnight again. Tomorrow was turnaround: night tour to day. Nothing had been accomplished. Much had been done except nothing more was known.

Kerner and Corelli were reporting about Levy, the guy who'd bought the Formalin.

"Giant apartment," Corelli said. "Huge. Rent stabilized, too. Levy's been living there for seventeen years. Got the lease from his father, also a Mr. Levy."

"Is this relevant?" Brymmer said.

"Do we know any more what's relevant?"

"True. Okay. So go on. How old a guy is he?"

"Forty," Kerner said. "Took a crowbar to get that out of him, too. I'd say in good shape."

"What else?"

"Lots of Avedon photos on the wall."

"Avedon."

"Fashion photographer. Dead. He's got photographs of Audrey Hepburn on the wall. Of Judy Garland in a black mink coat."

"Am I supposed to get the picture?"

"You got it," Kerner said.

"So?"

"He got cagey when we asked him what he did. I mean did for a living. Said 'What's this got to do with what you've come here about?' We had 'come here,' of course, about his Valentine's party, what he knew about Tanner. He gave us the same song and dance as on the phone. Blah-blah and blah-blah. So we give him a little room and then Corelli throws the corkscrew."

"Right," Corelli said. "I asked him if his business, whatever the hell it was, required the use of Formalin. Threw him for a loop but he recovered pretty well. 'Oh that,' he goes. Yes. He was planning a trip to Maui where he planned to go fishing and do some diving off a reef and if he caught something exotic, he wanted to preserve it."

"He added," Kerner said, "that he'd always been interested in exotic marine life."

Brymmer started to laugh. "And you got the impression he was much more interested in exotic marines."

Now Kerner was laughing. "Nail on the head.—So what do you want to do about him?"

"Shit. I don't know. Let me think about it."

"Good."

A couple of minutes later when Brymmer got back from a quick trip to the bathroom, Dubisky said, "You just missed a telephone call."

"From?"

"Carolyn Klein."

"So what did she have to say?"

"Her telephone number. She said you could call her any time up to one."

When Brymmer got through, she said, "Yeah, this is probably not that important but I know when I was down there and helping to do the drawing that I never really got it. You know, you gotta choose from those face shapes and whatnot and they weren't the right shapes and I never got it right."

"That happens," Brymmer said. "And I'm sure you did your best."

"Yeah, well the thing is, I saw her again tonight. At least someone she looked like. The elevator woman?"

"Yeah. Okay. So where did you see her?"

"On television."

"So. Are you saying she's an actress?"

"A news person. One that does the *On The Spot News*."

"*Jamie?*"

"Yeah *that* one. I think that's her name. Rogers?"

"Uh-huh. And you think she's the woman on the elevator."

"No. I don't know. I'm just saying that she *looks*

like the woman on the elevator. Same kind of hairdo. You know, kind of wild. So if you want a more accurate description of the woman you should tune in tomorrow. *On The Spot News.*"

"Well thanks." Brymmer rolled up his eyes to the ceiling. "I'll certainly do that."

"And one other thing. She was wearing the same coat. What I mean is, the same as the elevator woman."

"Describe it."

"Anne Klein."

"Beg your pardon?"

"The designer."

"Doesn't help me," Brymmer said.

"Brown wool. Fur collar."

His eyes rather suddenly dropped back to earth and started picturing the coat. The coat Jamie'd worn when he'd pulled her off his car in the hospital parking lot. The coat whose fur collar had brushed against his cheek. And still, it meant nothing.

"I'll look for her," he said. "And thanks a lot for the tip."

Dubisky said, "So?"

"Nothing," Brymmer said. "The redhead in the elevator looks like Jamie Rogers."

"The news girl?" Dubisky took a long thoughtful pause. "You know?" he said carefully, "Clark had a point. Like the way at the Starrett scene she buffaloed Symington. She pulled the 'like Clawson' stuff right out of air."

"She was leaping to conclusions from the givens," Brymmer said. "Unlike, of course, you."

"Never mind about me. And from the second you arrived—and remember I saw the tape— she's going,

189

'Hey, is this related to the Clawson case, Sergeant?'—
She was angling for something."

"A story," Brymmer said.

"And when you asked her where she got that, she
tells you it's from Symington which wasn't how it went."

"Which, of course, makes her Jackie."

"It doesn't make her Jackie but it makes her worth
a thought. Hey look," Dubisky said, "it was you, I
believe, who said Jackie is a redhead. And *Rogers* is a
redhead."

"And so's Lucille Ball."

"There's a difference. Ball's dead."

"Ah but she comes back from the grave," Brymmer said. "Takes vengeance on Desi on account of he
screwed around. Follow up on that, will you?"

"You know?" Dubisky said. "What I've always really liked about working with you, Burt, is that you never
dismiss cockamamie theories out of hand. You always
say tactfully, 'I'll think about that.'"

"Well I won't," Brymmer said, "think about *that*."

Except, briefly, he did. As he drove through the
Central Park Transverse, heading home to his West Side
walkup, two things teased his mind. First, that both
Clark and Dubisky had a point. On the sidewalk at
Starrett's, she'd been angling for something and it wasn't
just a story. Her connection of Clawson to Starrett was
a leap and it was not based on givens. It had bothered
him, in fact, from the moment that he'd looked at
that interview with Symington; he just hadn't let it.
The second thing that came unbidden to his mind were
the words of Merkowsi: *"Some of them try to get close to
the police. They'll try to get friendly."*

190

## 52

*Early Monday morning: March 16th:*

At two o'clock in the morning, for reasons entirely unrelated to anything either personal or business and simply from the merest and idlest curiosity (or so he convinced himself) Brymmer got online and googled Jamie Rogers. Sitting on his bed with the laptop on his lap, wearing an old sweatsuit against the persistent cold, he found himself squinting at the opening menu. There were twelve of her, apparently. A Target store manager in Tuscaloosa, a nurse in Moline, a guitarist in La Jolla, an assemblywoman in Maine; she was an anarchist advocating "bombs for peace;" she was fumingly indignant about the lack of sufficient drainage in the Halleluia Valley, and even more indignant about the unleashed dogs running loose in Clyde Park.

He added the single word "reporter" to his search, and yes, there she was. *Jamie Rogers, On the Spot News.* Observing that her facebook and twitter account pages were obviously written and managed by the station, he moved to the various news clips about her from which he learned the following:

Her age was thirty-four. She'd been hired as a reporter for *On The Spot News* two years ago, July. Before that she'd worked for a Fox affiliate in Southern California, as a print reporter for *The New York Sun* and, earlier than that for a local television station in Binghamton and, earlier than that, at the *Binghamton Gazette.* The daughter of a policeman, she was "interested in crime." Her favorite indulgences were Haagen-Dazs ice cream and "roast beef, rare;" her favorite music was retro jazz, and her favorite sports were ice skating (click for photo) and tennis.

He clicked for photo. Smiling broadly, she was whirling, arms out, on the Central Park rink accompanied by a tall wavy-haired guy identified only as "with a good friend." She was warmed by the layers of a long knit muffler and a short down coat and a knit woolen cap that had braids coming down.

He double-clicked back and then clicked on the link to *The Binghamton Gazette* (established in 1874). He checked through its archives, counting back the years to when she'd probably been hired ("I started at my home town paper," she'd said) and observed the only byline with a "Jamie" at the head was a "Jamie O'Brien" ("I'm Irish," she'd said). He skimmed thru her stories, watching her advance from covering city hall to crime beat reporting. She'd done a whole series on a serial killer—a rapist who'd carved his initials on the breasts before slicing up the bellies. She'd done a good job. She'd also done a series on "Women Behind Bars," and on the use and abuse of the insanity plea. She was certainly, as she'd stated it, "interested in crime."

He checked out Binghamton, a small hopeless city of 48,000, lost in the wilderness of economic slowdown, its factories shuttered, its mayor trying valiantly to rebuild its image. He clicked on a tab that led to Binghamton High. He didn't know why except presumably she'd gone there. Maybe there'd be pictures of a Jamie O'Brien as as teenage cheerleader; editor, perhaps, of the *Bing Hi News*. The site told him nothing. The school would be closed because a blizzard was expected. A tab at the left offered Famous Graduates. Brymmer took a chance. The most Famous Graduate was Rod Serling, the prodigious creator of *The Twilight Zone*. He scrolled down further under Famous Graduates and found Jamie's class. And, yep, there she was.

Listed as "Jamie (O'Brien) Rogers, Nightly reporter for *On the Spot News*." And right there next to her was Kate Marrott, "assistant producer for network television's *Living on the Edge*."

Kate Marrott. Two R's, two T's. The woman who'd been seemingly wounded by Starrett and admired by Jerry Siegel.

Brymmer lit a cigarette and blew out the smoke. For a time he just sat there and squinted at the screen. And then suddenly his fingers seemed to move without his will: The name of the high school yearbook was *The Chronicle*. He rummaged through its archives:

"*Jamie Rogers—. Most likely to succeed (at pestering people with a million questions.)*" Despite himself, he laughed.

Kate Marrott turned out to be a plain-jane brunette. "*Our favorite Aunt Eller in Oklahoma. Is she destined for the stage?*"

He scrolled around further. Picture: The two of them, standing on a bench. "*Best Friends Forever: Jamie and Katie at the Homecoming Game.*"

He stubbed the cigarette.

Clearly, he would have to get in touch with Kate Marrott. But first, there was something more difficult to do. If only to neutralize Dubisky and Clark. He would not even think about appeasing himself.

## 53

*Monday, March 16th:*

The television series, *Living On The Edge*, had been permanently cancelled; its production office had been permanently closed and the message was simply that "the number you have dialed is not in service."

It wasn't a tough trick to get Marrott's home address and a landline number that rang twenty times (ten each on two tries) and had no machine. The cell phone number said its owner was not available. A visit to the residence— the 1200-unit Murray Hill Towers— yielded total indifference from a daytime doorman and a "whaddaya expect from me with all these people I should know where they are? I should even know I seen her or I haven't in a month?"

Brymmer went to visit a man named Barrett at the management office. Barrett had an Aussie accent and a lisp which made for interesting conversation. Barrett told Brymmer that Marrott's apartment was among the last few that had remained rent-stabilized since the buildings went condo about seven years back. He also told Brymmer that, being out of a job, she'd applied to have a roommate to help pay the rent. Permission had been granted "becauth," Barrett said, "her leathe ith up thoon— I believe in July— and, in any cathe, it taketh uth that long to evict her." And, in any cathe, Barrett had "athumed that Myth Marrott wath thtill in rethidenth" since Marrott paid the rent with her own personal checks, and that was all that he had to know.

"When," Brymmer asked, "had she applied for the roommate?"

"January," Barrett said, "the end of the month."

By 4 in the afternoon, it had seriously started raining, a rainfall predicted to be "heavy at times, lasting into the evening." This suited him fine.

At 6:27, in a driving rain, he drove around the corner and re-parked his car in front of a bar called the Arizona Zoo that was right across the street from the Fox 5 entrance. He'd brought with him a sandwich, a thermos jug of coffee, a bag of potato chips, and copies of both *The Weekly Standard* and *The Nation* (political slugfests amused him on occasion); that, and some Carmen McRae CD's.

The rain let up at about 6:40, then started again, even harder than before.

At 7, he stopped reading and gazed out the window.

At 7:37 he started— and then idled— his engine.

At 7:43, she emerged from the building, immediately blasted by the wind and the rain, her umbrella blowing out. He moved into traffic and caught her at the corner, honking his horn and pulling over to the curb. "Hey, Miss," he called out. "Want a free ride home?"

She looked at him quizzically, standing on the sidewalk as the rain beat down, then quickly rushed over as he opened the door. She came in smelling of spice and wet wool: "Well *you're* a surprise."

"Well...so are you."

Carmen was singing *Still We Dream*. Retro as all hell. The windshield wipers played a contrapuntal bass.

She shivered against the cold. "Are you on duty or off?"

"Actually," he said, "I was heading for Jamaica."

"The island?"

He looked at her sideways. "Queens. The forensic lab's there.—Should I turn up the heat?"

"No, this is fine."

He drove up Third and then doubled back to Second and started downtown. "Okay, so what's happening in the news tomorrow, huh?"

"Tomorrow," she said, "you are going to win the lottery if you pick the numbers one-two-three-four-five."

"How about instead I find Jackie tomorrow?"

"Well how about."

"I thought you might tell me about the wonderful breakthrough I'm going to get tomorrow. The tantalizing link. Something I might have missed."

She looked at him slowly. "I'm afraid to respond."

"Hmm?"

"My response would be to ask you a lot of questions and you'd only get pissed at me and not say a word."

"That's true. I mean the part about I won't say a word but I've never been pissed at you. Well, except once. But if you did know something, you'd tell me about it, huh?"

"As soon as I get my crystal ball out of hock."

"Well," he said, shrugging, "that's good enough for me."

At her door he said, "I think you still owe me a cup of coffee. I mean if that's okay."

"You are weird," she said.

"True."

"You can park around—"

"Anywhere." He gestured at the tow-away zone across the street. "So just tell me what apartment."

The apartment was nice. The living room was mostly done in blues, greens, yellows with a lot of warm wood. She hung his wet coat on the shower rod with hers and then moved to the kitchen.

"How do you take your coffee? Black, no sugar?"

"Black," he said. "Sugar."

"Oops. Pegged you wrong."

He spotted a collection of silver-framed photos on a cabinet at the side. She came back as he was holding one of them in his hand.

"Mmm, that's my brother's wedding," she said.

"That's the whole O'Brien clan. Two sisters and one brother."

"Is your brother on the force?"

"No. Why do you ask?"

"Just making conversation."

"Funny, though. He actually went to the Academy but then he dropped out and decided to be a lawyer."

"Criminal?"

"Yeah. Well...public defender."

"Truth, justice, The American Way."

She groaned at him and then went back to the kitchen. He could hear the clank of china. He was still scanning the photo. Aside from the brother, there was one other man, almost startlingly handsome.

"Who's the other guy in the picture?"

"That's the ex. He's the hunk in the lower left corner."

"What happened?"

"He got even lower and left."

Brymmer laughed aloud.

She came back with the coffee cups and set them on a low glass table between the couch and a wing chair that made a right angle from the side. "Are you sitting down or what?"

He sat; in the wing chair. "What did he do wrong?"

"Who?"

"Mr. Rogers. I mean if you don't mind..."

"Oh well," she said thoughtfully, "I guess I don't mind. It's actually pretty basic. Charlie started out as a literary agent. Then he became a Hollywood agent. Then he became a...how can I put this...a Hollywood agent. In other words, an arrogant, full-of-himself coke-head. It was all very glamorous and quite not for me."

"So it was you did the leaving."

197

"Actually, yeah. But— well, never mind. But by then, it was obviously rather mutual, too."

She sipped at her coffee. Brymmer sipped his.

"It seems to me," she said, "that in the interests of pure fairness, I could ask questions, too. No, not about the case."

He shrugged. "You can try. Doesn't mean I have to answer."

"Okay. That's fair. I mean I had the same choice.— So how about you? Have you ever been married?"

"Uh-uh."

"Ever want to be? Wait. I take it back. Let's try... Have you ever been deeply in love?"

"*Deeply?*" he said mockingly. "Geez, I don't know. How deep is 'deeply'? In over my head? Yeah. Maybe once. Sort of. I don't know. I know I thought so at the time."

"And what happened?"

"She got even lower and left."

"Ah, back at me, huh?"

"It's a pretty good line. On the other hand, the question was intrinsically sappy."

"Let me ask you something else—"

"Like if I were a tree, what tree would I be?"

"Stop it." She flushed. "No really something else. There's a dinner," she said slowly. "It's a kind of a television journalist dinner where they're giving out awards..."

"You expecting one?"

"No. I'm just invited, that's all. So I wondered, well, maybe I could bring you as my guest. I'm allowed to bring a guest."

He shook his head No.

"Gee! And you didn't even ask me when it was so

198

you could tell me you had to work."

He shrugged. "You like lies? I just wouldn't want to go. I can't talk to those people."

She gave him a fish-eye with her head to the side. "You can *talk* to anyone."

"Sure. It's my job. I can psych people out. But that isn't exactly a social conversation. I'm lousy at conversation. I'm remote from it. I don't participate, I manipulate."

She paused for a moment with her cup in mid-air. "Are you manipulating me?"

"If I am, how'm'I doing?"

"Very well, I'm afraid."

"Come on," he said patiently, "you're not that naive. I mean, everyone manipulates everyone, Jamie. Guy buys you dinner. Tells you you're beautiful. No matter how sincere he is, he wants something of you and he thinks he can get it by…buying you dinner and telling you you're lovely."

"Ah well. At least you haven't told me I'm lovely."

"You're beautiful, Jamie. Most beautiful thing I've ever seen in my life."

"And now you're just schmaltzing."

"Right. I saw the Sistine Chapel once in Rome, beats you six ways to Sunday. And besides, you're not nearly beautiful at all, you're just passably cute."

She shook her head slowly. "You're inscrutable."

"Then don't try to scrute me, okay?— Do you mind if I use your john?"

"Well of course not." She pointed rather vaguely off at the hall where he again passed the table with a scarf and the pairs of gloves and the recent *New Yorker*, and the hat with the woolen braids.

In the bathroom, he ran knowing hands through

her comb and plucked a gleaning of red hair. He bagged it, opened the hinge of the small mirrored cabinet, checked out the contents, flushed, ran water and collected his coat.

"Gotta go," he said, returning. "And thanks for the coffee."

She stood, looking thrown and trying gallantly not to show it.

"I told you," he said. "I have to get to Jamaica."

At the lab, he gave the freshly bagged hair to Shari Cruz. "Check it out," he said. "See if it matches the hair at Tanner's."

## 54

*Wednesday, March 18th*

### WILL JACKIE STRIKE AGAIN?
### CITY ON EDGE

Having nothing to report, the papers were reduced now to speculative nightmare. Anything to keep up the pitch of hysteria that was boosting circulation.

However, indeed, there was nothing to report. Even within the task force: nothing to report. There were no working theories since no theory worked. There was just the vague notion that the first three killings had been somehow connected— a redheaded Jackie who was planting blonde hairs— but that McConnell was (at least potentially) a sport— a copycat who hadn't quite known what to copy except for the obvious and salient wound.

Dubisky's concoction, then, was still on the table, cell phone or no. Which would mean there was a "Nora" "in fashion" to be found on the nonetheless odds-against chance that she was It.

Ross had been in touch with a place called The Fashion Club— an organization that functioned as a combination trade group and self-appointed Insiders Circle for the people in the biz. This included every area from actual designers to fashion mag editors to advertising writers to glitzy hangers-on. He'd asked if he could look at their membership enrollment which happily turned out to be a published registry, available for only $55 (for which he'd be reimbursed) and which he rummaged for Noras while Clark and Dubisky were obtaining education at the public library, leafing through volumes such as *Who's Who in Fashion*, *Who's Who in Publishing* and *Women in Rags*. Bleary, they'd quit to return later on, but had still found the time to create a fine limerick and leave it for Brymmer:

> There once was a lady named Nora
> Who had a magnificent aura
> But she'd take you to bed
> And she'd puncture your head
> And leave other terrain even sora.

That Brymmer was less than appreciative had little to do with the quality of the art but with the state of his mouth. Brymmer had been stricken in the middle of the night, when such things always strike, with a ferocious toothache and had therefore spent the morning in his dentist's office being told that he'd irreparably fractured a molar from grinding his teeth. He could either try a two-week prescription of antibiotics, which invariably made him sick, at the end of which he'd undergo a root canal procedure which would probably not succeed because the fracture was that deep or he could simply have it out. He decided to have it out, being also reassured that, as a back upper molar, it would not be a great loss. However, an hour later when the numbness had worn off, he was rocketed with a pain even worse than it was before, and with a mixture of codeine and something even more fantastic in his system on top of a sleepless night, he decided that he'd just go to bed and sleep it off.

In the meanwhile, no possible Noras had been found.

## 55

*Wednesday evening, March 18th:*

It was not too surprising that the Arizona Zoo, being right across the street from the Fox 5 studios and right down the block from the precinct station house, would get a mixed crowd: sound engineers, on-camera talent and off-duty cops. So Ross was not surprised when, at 7:30, Jamie Rogers walked in with a couple of her female friends from the station.

Ross and Dubisky had been hanging there from just about a quarter after five. Dubisky, because he didn't have a home to go home to, and Ross, because he did. They were, at 7:30 then, pretty well plowed and, since tomorrow was Day Off, they had plans to continue on.

At the particular moment when Rogers hit the bar, Dubisky had left the booth to relieve himself of six or eleven previous beers and Ross was on his fourth (but who's counting) double Scotch. He was watching her idly as she hung up her coat, started settling into a booth, then noticed him, excused herself and headed across the room.

"You're Burt's partner, aren't you?"

Ross cracked a grin. "'Burt,' is it, eh?"

"Sergeant Brymmer."

"Uh-huh."

"I just wondered. Is he around?"

"Someplace," Ross said, searching idly under the table. "Why?"

"Well, I called him. In fact, I called him twice and both times I left a message…"

"Uh-huh."

"Well, he didn't return either call so I wondered—"

"—if he's around?"

"If you'd ask him, when you see him, if he'd call Jamie Rogers."

"Uh-huh." Ross nodded. "And who was the lady calling? Sergeant Brymmer? or 'Burt.'"

"Both," she said, flushing.

"And would this have been business?" he inquired, "or pleasure."

"This is business," she said.

"Uh-huh. Okay. You want to interview him or what?"

"It's not that kind of business."

"Siddown," he said, aware that his voice was becoming slurred — a fact that he found pleasant; the slur meter being such an excellent barometer, providing a good gauge of his own, internal, barometric pressure.

Jamie Rogers sat slowly at the farther end of the booth and then looked at him quizzically, saying nothing at all. Ross studied her; he'd only seen her rarely on the air and on the m-peg with Symington, so now he tried to quantify the rate of her relative charm. Close up, she had a look that reminded him of Kathy or of what he'd come to think of as Kathy The First. The original Kathy, that Kathy that he'd met on another planet. That incredibly, remarkably vivid Kathy. That flaming red hair and the tinge of a true fire. And he thought of how he'd loved her and the way she'd loved him and how that was another country and alas the wench was dead.

"You know...." he said. "If Burt doesn't call you, he doesn't want to and that'll be just that."

"No, really," she said, "it's business."

"Really really? Or just 'really'?"

For an answer, she stayed silent.

"Oh man," he said, "you'd really be skunked at poker. Really really," he said.

She shrugged.

"You like him?"

He watched her. The way she took her lip between her teeth as though afraid of what she'd say but then nodded gravely.

"Hang in there," he said. "Be tough. And just learn to ignore him when he growls. He won't mean it. He's confused. And besides that, the man is better-guarded than Gitmo."

She nodded. "Thank you."

"De nada," Ross said. She was starting to get up as Dubisky returned. "Ah hah!" Dubisky burbled. "The non-Jackie. Congratulations, non-Jackie. It seems you didn't do it."

She laughed. "Was I suspected?"

"*I* suspected you. Yes. I confess that I did. Well, I didn't exactly. I just sort of did, but your hair didn't do it."

She said: "My hair?"

Ross had aimed a lethal boot at Dubisky's ankle but he couldn't quite reach it. Dubisky sat heavily. "Ya know," he said, "The *hair*. The hair that you gave the Sergeant. The hair. It didn't match."

"The hair that I....Ohhhh," she said as it dawned. "Yes. Of course. I can't tell you how relieved I am at the news."

She stood there for a moment looking absolutely punked and then quickly walked away.

"Nice going there, Abe."

"What?" Dubisky said. "What? What did I say?"

Ross said nothing, just watched as Jamie Rogers grabbed her coat from the brass rack, spoke briefly to her friends, and then stalked to the front door.

## 56

*Thursday, March 19th:*

Even though Thursday was the first of his days off, he'd come in to the station to make up for yesterday. He didn't have to but he did. There were things to catch up on. Reports to be read.

He read his messages: Jamie Rogers. Called. Twice. His hand was on the telephone even as it rang. He answered: "Brymmer."

"You dirty...rotten...sneaky...sonofabitch."

"That's redundant," he said. "I already said 'Brymmer.' So what's on your mind?"

"You *stole* my *hair*!!?"

He was stunned into silence. He couldn't figure out how she'd possibly know it but she obviously did so he wouldn't deny it.

205

He said, "I can explain that."

"Oh I *bet* you can! But I don't want to hear it. I don't want to hear another word from your lying mouth."

"I don't lie to you."

"Hah! You even *lied* about a cat."

"That was different. I was playing."

"What? Cat and mouse?"

"You're no mouse," Brymmer said.

There was stone silence. Within it, he could hear her take a long angry breath. "I should have listened," she said. "I should have listened to what you said. You manipulate, that's all, and I really don't think I want to talk to you again."

Click!

He held the phone in his hand for a long while, eyeing it as though it were a desktop grenade, and then placed it on its cradle and reached for his jacket. He walked down the stairs and to the porch of the station house and did what he always did: Lit a cigarette and exhaled it as a sigh. The day had turned warm. It was practically spring-like, though a spring that would never last. Even now, the forecast was for late-in-the-week snow. A man and a woman passed by with a dog; they were laughing about something—some antic of the dog's. He wondered if he'd rather be the man or the dog. He decided on the dog. Eat, crap, rut, and then occasionally chase a ball. He dragged on his cigarette and realized he was tired. He was tired of smoking; he was tired of drinking; he was tired of winter, murder, New York, humanity, inhumanity, insomnia, hysteria and frozen macaroni; he was tired of himself, of his own insistent sarcasm, his shortening temper, his congenital...loneliness. Well, there it was.

He stubbed out the cigarette and went back to work.

206

## 57

*Sunday, March 22nd:*

### COPYCAT KILLER CAUGHT IN QUEENS

#### JILTED GIRLFRIEND ARRESTED, CHARGED

Within 7 hours of what appeared to be the fifth of the so-called "Jackie The Ripper" killings, police arrested Karla-Maria Balodis, 27, of Elmhurst, Queens for the brutal murder of Anton Lutz, 34.

Police say the woman, who still had the keys to his Chelsea apartment, had left a string of threatening messages on his phone and had also left her bloody palm prints on the wall.

A spokesman for the Major Homicide Task Force, Detective First Grade Steven R. Ross, said, "This one was easy. She was caught red-handed," referring, of course, to the palm prints on the wall....

Brymmer was sleeping on Ross's converted convertible sofa. Ross had been much too drunk to drive home and Brymmer had seen him safely to his bedroom where he dumped him on the bed on which Ross was now lying in leaden slumber. Kathy had offered him a cup of coffee and confided her concerns about Billy's virus. Billy had been to the doctor that day for a respiratory virus and the doctor had told her to watch how he was doing and if things were getting worse, to take him to the hospital. Kathy had then suggested that if Brymmer would stay the night it would greatly relieve her mind because if lousy should turn to rotten then she'd need somebody's help to get Billy into a car and with Ross's car in Soho and with Ross himself inert...

Brymmer had indulged her with a quick look at Billy, decided he was breathing as easily as anybody else with a bad cold, but decided that for Kathy's sake, he'd really better stay.

He'd been sleeping for just about the span of an hour when his shoulder got tapped on. Kathy, in her flannel pajamas, sitting down. "Move over," she said, "please. He's snoring like a lawn mower. Putt-putt-putt. Whenever he snores like that, I take to the sofa but it seems you're on the sofa."

Brymmer moved over. "As long as you keep your hands on the top of the covers like they taught you in Catholic school."

"Why?" she said, pulling up the comforter to her chin. "You wouldn't like them underneath?"

"I wouldn't like your husband to *think* they were underneath."

"Shit. You think he'd care?"

"Yeah. I think he would. I think he does care, Kathy. You ought to give him a chance."

"You mean I ought to give him a break."

"Same thing," Brymmer said. He was drifting back to sleep.

"If I weren't married to Steve," she said slowly, "would you want me?"

"Honey? What I want right now is to go to sleep."

She sighed. "I'm such a hag."

"Hardly. But you might try to gain a little weight."

"I can't eat. I look at food and I feel... what I think they call existential nausea."

"Take an existential Tums."

He rolled over on his side and felt a hand on his cheek. "Don't," he said.

"Why?"

"I don't like to be touched there."

"You ought to. You ought to get petted there a lot.

What's the line from *Othello*?"

"I really wouldn't know."

"'She loved me for the'...something...'for the dangers I had passed and I loved her that she did pity them.'"

"Christ. I get Shakespeare and Sartre in one night."

"You're a very lovely person."

"Oh yeah. That's me."

"You are. You're sympathetic. It was nice of you to stay."

"Uh-huh."

"Put your arm around me for a while?"

"Sure."

"That's better."

"Now try to go to sleep."

"Yeah. You too."

## 58

*Monday, March 23rd:*

Not succeeding at first, Brymmer tried again. He dialed Kate Marrott, tapping his ballpoint pen on his desk. It was 8 o'clock at night. This time, the phone call was answered. Fourth ring.

"Miss Marrott?" he said.

"No, she's not here."

"This is Sergeant Brymmer at the Nineteenth Precinct. You know when she'll be back?"

"Um...she's not here."

"Yeah I know. You said that. And then I said when will she be back and then things kind of stalled. You know when she'll be back?"

209

"Well...she's out of town."

"Uh-huh. You know where?"

"What's this about?"

Brymmer sighed. "Routine investigation. She's not in any trouble."

"Oh. Well...how do I know that you're a cop?"

"If you don't believe me, you can call me right back. The number's—"

"I'll look it up in the book." Click-buzzzz.

Brymmer stared at the buzzing phone and clunked it back down. Shaking his head, he swiveled in his chair and looked up at Clark who was hanging up a phone. Also shaking his head.

"His wife is Jackie."

"Amuse me," Brymmer said.

"He knows it on account of she's a vengeful little bitch. Always *was* a little bitch. The whole time they've been married."

"How long?"

"Fifty years."

Brymmer built a shrug as his telephone rang. "Brymmer," he said.

"Yeah," she conceded. "I guess you really are. See, how it goes, I'm here on a sublet but the way we've been doing this, it's not exactly l-e-g-a-l."

"Uh-huh. Well don't worry about it, Miss, uh—"

"Lubin. Lottie Lubin."

"And where's Kate Marrott?"

"I don't know. All I know is, she got out of Dodge and she did it pretty fast."

"When?"

"I couldn't say. I started paying rent here on February first, but she told me when I met her I could move in sooner. So I did."

210

"Did when?"

"Um, January...um...twenty-ninth? It was a Thursday morning."

"And when did you meet her?"

"Well...I kinda knew her slightly all along so I don't mean met her like Hello, the first time. I meant met her about the sublet."

"Right. When was that?"

"The Monday right before. See, I was living in this studio apartment with these two other roommates. The place was like a zoo and even then we were paying twelve-hundred, that's apiece. So I'd bitched about it plenty. The way I knew Kate was from working on the show—"

"You mean *Living on the Edge*?"

"Yeah, I used to joke that I was living on the window ledge and just about to jump. I mean, the place was like a zoo."

"So she called you on Monday which would be the twenty-sixth."

"If you say so."

"I thought *you* did."

"I wouldn't know from the twenty-sixth. I just know it was the Monday —"

"Okay, I got it. So what did she tell you? About why she was leaving."

"New York, she said, was why. She hated it. She said it was a great place to work but it was no way to live."

"She say anything further?"

Lottie Lubin gave it thought. "And she said if you stayed here you'd never get married and you'd start to hate men. She also said everyone's crazy in New York and she had to get out before she went over the edge." Lubin paused. Brymmer heard the sound of ice clinking

211

glass. "I don't know," she said slowly. "Ask me, I think she'd already gone over."

"The edge," Brymmer said.

"Yeah, I thought she sounded...frantic. Or maybe like she's, I dunno, scared?"

"And what would she be scared of? Any idea?"

"Nope. She just seemed in a real hurry to go."

"She take everything with her?"

"What do you mean by that?"

"Furniture. Clothes. Papers," Brymmer said.

"Furniture's here. So she'll maybe come back. Or she'll worry about it later. She took all her clothes, both summer and winter. Her computer, of course. A couple of CD's. She did leave some other stuff. Papers. In a box. At the top of the hall closet."

"And what did she say to do with it?"

"Nothing. Leave it alone. She said she might send for it. If not, I should dump it."

"And what do you do with her mail?"

"Mail? Who gets mail? I mean nobody gets letters. So there's junk mail and mainly the utility bills which I pay with my own account. Like Con Ed really cares. You want to come, look around?"

"Not yet," Brymmer said. Checking Marrott's papers would require a warrant and he didn't have a reason he could get one, not yet. "And not me. Someone else."

"Too bad. You sound cute."

"Uh-huh," Brymmer said. He tilted back in his chair. "So what makes it illegal? Your being there, I mean. I thought you were legally registered as a roommate."

"Yeah, well...yeah. But in order to be a roommate, um, Kate would have to stay. Otherwise, it's a sublet and nobody'd let her do it. They want these apartments. See, once you move out, they go up to the market rate which would be about triple."

"So explain to me how you cheat."

"You're sure you won't rat on me?"

"Our motto," Brymmer said, "is 'To protect and to serve.'"

"And you don't protect landlords?"

"Hey, I've got my own."

"Okay. Then the way we go about it's like this. At the end of every month, I arrange this direct deposit to Kate's account. I send the proof to this friend of hers who mails me a check of Kate's that's made out to the landlord. Like they're all predated, like there's one for every month. Then I leave it with the doorman."

"Who's the friend?" Brymmer said.

"Well her name's Jamie Rogers. I think she does the news."

"So...what?" Clark said. "So what do you want us to do?"

"Call her in. Ask her questions."

"You and Sundance?"

"No. You. Pick Dubisky if you like. Hey Dubisky! You want to be the badguy for a change?"

Brymmer's phone rang again.

"Brymmer."

"It's me."

"So it is." He waved the others away with a quick hand. "So what's on your mind?"

"I was thinking.—You know I tried to reach you last week."

"Twice," Brymmer said. "I wasn't here on Wednesday and Thursday you weren't ever talking to me again."

213

"Well I'm *still* not talking to you *personally*," she said. "And I still think you're sneaky and manipulative…"

"True."

"But I think you figured out that I knew something. Something that I really should have told you. In the car, you were asking me to tell you and I didn't."

"Also true," Brymmer said. "But you want to tell me now."

"I would have told you last Wednesday. That's the really silly thing."

"All right. Tell me now."

"It's a very long story and it's not for the phone."

"Where are you?"

"At the station."

"Okay. I'll buy you dinner. Pick you up in half an hour."


## 59

He handed her a bag marked P.J. Bernstein. "Dinner," he said. "It's a pastrami sandwich."

She said, "I'm not hungry."

He said, "There's coffee."

They were waiting for a light at Sixty-Seventh and Third.

"I think I'd like a cigarette."

He handed her the pack. "But just don't accuse me of corrupting your morals."

"My morals," she said, "are now questionable at best."

She looked pale, he thought. Strained. He handed

her a lighter as he drove across Third.

"Not that it's entirely important," she said, "but where are we going?"

"Who, what, where, when, why," Brymmer said. "Ever heard of rendition? I'm rendering you to the Saudis for some wicked interrogation. We're meeting my good friend Abdul in the park."

"Oh," she said. "Him."

"Uh-huh. You can start talking any time you like."

She took a deep breath. "Hard to know where to start."

"The beginning," he said, "is usually the spot."

"It involves a good friend. Who I'm probably betraying."

"Kate," he said.

"Yes. I began to figure out that's the thing you'd likely know. It's the only thing *to* know."

"Is it." He didn't frame it as a question.

"Yes," she said. "It is. And even that— I don't know..."

"Just begin at the beginning then." He headed into the park and then swung to the East Drive.

"She phoned me on...whenever it was the Clawson story broke. She was frantically upset."

"About Clawson?"

"In a way. But you have to let me tell it, and I promise you it's long. So be quiet, please."

Brymmer said dryly, "As a mouse."

He pulled into the dark empty parking lot of the Boathouse with the lake in the near distance, the lights of the city a notionally incongruous three blocks away. He quickly cut the engine and listened to a bullfrog complaining into the night. It was just that quiet. He waited. She stubbed her cigarette in the ashtray.

215

"So I met her," Jamie said. "I met her for a drink and she tells me this story. It seems that on the early afternoon of New Years Eve she had a hairdresser's appointment but the place, or its computer, or somebody messed up and they'd double booked the appointments. The place says they're sorry but if everybody waits, which could even be hours, they'll be sure to get done. They even provided some sandwiches and wine.

"So this one group of women, the group that Kate's in, starts talking to each other and they talk, as most women invariably do, they talk about men. And someone starts the topic of Who's the worst bastard you've ever been involved with, and they start swapping stories, getting higher as they go. At least Kate's getting higher. She could never hold liquor. We used to tease her about it too."

Brymmer cracked the window and lit a cigarette.

"So later, when it's just down to six of these women— they're alone in this anteroom—it somehow evolves. Wouldn't it be satisfying to murder these bastards." She stopped, looked at Brymmer. "I'm sorry," she said, "to keep using the word 'bastards' but that was the whole point."

"Why 'sorry'?" he said. "You afraid I'd take it personally?"

"No, I just—"

"Hey. Skip it. Go on."

"And then somebody said, 'And after, we could cut off their'—well, the... thing they cut off."

"Aw say it," Brymmer said. "Why suddenly shy? You're not afraid to say words."

"Dicks."

"There you go."

She looked at him. "Why did you want me to say it?"

"Why were you restrained?"

"I don't know."

"Just go on."

"So *after* that, somebody said, 'We could do it. We could actually do it. Like what if we each did another person's guy? Like no one could ever trace us. There wouldn't be any kind of link to the guy.' And they started to plan it. How they'd be careful. How they'd work it out. And it ended when they all wrote the names and addresses of their personal bastards and dropped them in a hat. Not all of them did. One of the six women said she wouldn't be a part of it, even as a joke. So the five of them were left and they each drew a name, except one of the women got stuck with her own bastard but she said never mind, that she could find another partner who'd be willing to do the swap."

Brymmer took a long deep drag of his cigarette and leaned back to think it over—the ultimate implications of the missing Somebody Else. He'd have to puzzle it out later. He turned and said evenly, "But Kate drew a name."

"Kate thought it was a joke."

"But still," he said, "she wrote Starrett's name and address."

"So you know that too."

"I know the connection. I sure as hell didn't know the rest of this tale. Only an idiot could think that one up. But keep going," he said. "I reserve my questions."

"So when Clawson was killed— and there was nothing in the news about what was cut off— the papers just described it as a 'bloodbath' and 'stabbing'— Kate was still convinced that it was somehow connected. I told her she was nuts. That it had to've been a joke and I think it calmed her down. But when Monty was murdered, she went into panic. I *still* said, 'it has to be coincidence, Kate,' but she wouldn't believe me. She said, 'I'm responsible for Monty's getting killed and someone's expecting me to kill someone else.' And with that, she left town. So the thing—"

Brymmer held up a finger. "Be quiet. Put a bookmark in it." He opened the deli bag and grabbed one of the two cooling coffees and sprung the lid.

"How, when and where did you meet Monty Starrett?"

"Oh," she said. "How did you know that I did?"

He wiggled his eyebrows. "I'm a detective."

"At Bloomingdale's," she said. "It was purely by accident. I was shopping and I ran into Monty with Kate. Only time I ever saw him, though of course Kate had spoken about him. Quite a lot."

"And what had she said?"

"She thought he was Mr. Right. I mean Monty really gave her a dazzling rush. So she said he was handsome, tremendously charming, very romantic and— that's what she said."

"And what did you think of him the day that you met?"

She met Brymmer's eyes now. "Not very much. I thought he was using her."

"You tell that to Kate?"

Jamie shook her head. "Never. That's the kind of thing your bad mother tells you. 'For your own good.' Uh-uh. It wouldn't have done any good, and after I'd told her she'd have just hated *me*. And besides, I kept hoping that I might've been wrong."

"But you weren't."

"Guess not."

"So how did it all end?"

218

"How cold is that coffee?"

"It's tepid," Brymmer said. "But you might as well drink it and you might as well eat. We're gonna be here for a while."

She opened the bag and then opened the coffee. "She got pregnant is how. She didn't even get to tell him she was pregnant. He dropped her in a very...ungentle-manly way, and she had an abortion. She was very... distraught."

"Because he dropped her."

"That too. But the abortion even more. She just wept for a week and after that she withdrew. I didn't see her very much. But she told me," Jamie said, "that when she wrote down his name and just dumped it in the hat, that she felt...I don't want to use the corny word 'closure' but she felt as though a stone had been lifted from somewhere. She said she felt good."

"But she thought it was a joke."

"Yes. I believe that. Who knows? Perhaps it is. And perhaps it has nothing to do with this at all."

Brymmer slid down and leaned his head against the headrest and stared at the visor. "When you met him— at Bloomingdale's— what happened then?"

"Then? What do you mean?"

"I mean what happened then. You shopped for tableclothes together. You went and had a drink. I mean what happened then."

"Oh. Well, we had a cup of coffee at the corner and I walked with them to Second where I got on the bus."

"So you passed by his house."

"Yes. To be exact, we all parted on his stoop."

"Ah," Brymmer said. "I figured it'd have to be some-thing like that." He pulled out a sandwich and began to unwrap it. He was suddenly hungry. He was pleased with himself. "So that's why you were asking is it tied in to Clawson. You knew Kate's story and you knew, without knowing what apartment he was in, that it was Starrett's building."

She nodded now. "Yes.— That sandwich looks terrific."

"It ought to. It set me back fourteen bucks. You believe it? When I was a kid back in Latvia, we fed the entire army for fourteen bucks."

"Latvia," she said.

"Latvia... New Jersey, it's all the same thing. What's the name of that... 'salon'?"

"I don't know. She didn't say."

"And you didn't think to ask? Jesus. And I thought you're Miss Questions R Us."

"Look. I'm with a friend and she's hysterically upset. I was trying to calm her down. I wasn't trying to solve a crime and I wasn't trying to get a story."

"And didn't ask for the women's names?"

"Even Kate didn't know them. She said she only knew a couple of first names and that's all she said she knew. Or that's all she remembered. And again, it wasn't really any part of the conversation."

"Where is she?"

"I don't know."

"Now you're stretching my credulity and it's already pretty stretched."

"Honestly. I don't. She told me that she didn't want anyone to know. And very likely for this reason. So I couldn't tell the police. I only talked to her on the phone. She told me she was leaving and then she asked if I could do her this ongoing favor."

"Any other favor except for the checks?"

She looked at him in astonishment. "Boy. You are

really good at your job."

"I'm just thorough and occasionally lucky," he said. "And what's your answer to the question?"

"No; that was it."

"Now eat," he said, holding out the other half of his sandwich. "Pastrami loosens tongues."

She glanced at him obliquely and then took the food. "You're right," she said, after taking a first bite. "I will now spill the plans for the Normandy Invasion."

"It's Kate's plans I'm after. Where do you think she'd go? Would she go back to Binghamton?"

Jamie shook her head. "You know everything, don't you."

"Right. So don't give me any jazz and we're cool."

"She wouldn't go to Binghamton. She wouldn't involve her parents and besides, there's nothing there for her."

"Okay, so what's something? And where would she go to get it?"

She shrugged. "I don't know. Except maybe she'd want a job."

"And where do you think she find it?"

"California?" she offered, and suddenly looked away, out the window.

He waited. "Okay so what's the other place that's fluttering through your mind?"

"Are you a mind reader?"

"No. I read faces. I read yours."

"Canada," Jamie said. "A lot of production goes on in Canada. Toronto. Montreal."

"Thanks."

"Is she in trouble now? I mean with...the law?"

"It depends," Brymmer said. "It depends on what she said, it depends on what she did, and it depends on

what she tells me when I eventually track her down.—
And don't be too certain that she told you the whole
truth. For all you know she committed murder. After
all, she drew a name. Whose name?"

"She threw it away."

"Unread?"

"I wouldn't know. And don't look at me that way,
please."

"How'm I looking at you?"

"With doubt."

"Because the premise remains doubtful."

She gathered a deep breath and put the sandwich
back in the bag. "Listen, I can tell you this with absolute certainty. She'd never commit a murder. I've known
her my whole life."

"Right. And Mrs. McConnell's known her husband for thirty years. You'd be surprised what you don't
know."

"I know Kate."

"If you think so."

They were silent for a time.

"Am *I* in trouble now?"

"For what?"

"Well, for not telling this sooner?"

"Ask your conscience," Brymmer said. "To the law
you're just hearsay. The story was bizarre and you didn't
believe it. You want trouble, though, then hide what
you know about Kate. Hide her whereabouts if you
know them. Or warn her I'm coming and advise her to
run away. Ask your brother, why don't you. The public
defender."

"Sweet Jesus."

"I imagine you could try him too.—You want a
drink?"

"I could use one."

He opened the glove box. "I'm extremely well-prepared. Pour your coffee out the window." He reached for the unopened bottle of J&B, cracked the seal with a snap and poured a shot into her cup. While he was at it, he poured a shot into his own. "Cheers," he said dryly, and lit another smoke. Again there was silence. Except for the frog.

"I understand," he said finally, "exactly how you'd feel. You've got a friend, and your friendship's important. It hangs heavy."

She said, "Yes it does."

"So altogether, I think we have to cut it after tonight. If I happen to ask you questions, you answer. That's it. You ask nothing. We don't talk. If you still want to talk to me when it's over— *if* it's over— I'll take you to dinner and explain what went down."

"And tell me I'm lovely?"

"I'll give it some thought." He started the engine.

"You think too much."

He backed up the car and said, *"Cogito ergo sum."*

"Now you're just showing off."

"Yeah? Showing what?"

"That you graduated college."

"Brat!" he said. "What makes you think I went to college?"

"I googled you," she said.

"Sneaky."

"Well at least I didn't burgle your hair."

"So maybe I just wanted a lock for my locket."

"Tell me honestly," she said. "Did you really and sincerely think I might have been Jackie?"

He looked at her levelly. "Who says I don't still?"

223

## 60

*Tuesday, March 24th:*

"Okay," Kerner said, "so we could buy the whole story but why can't we buy that it's something in left field? No link. Coincidental. Including Starrett's death."

"We could," Brymmer said, "I'm not saying we don't. But it sure as hell accounts for an incredible lot of things. The hairs for example. From a beauty parlor, no? The different choice of weapons. And, potentially at least, if we're talking about the motive as 'Kill The Worst Bastard You've Ever Been Involved With' there are motives at least for three. Andrea Clausen's. Kate Marrott's. And, of course, Nora Nora's."

"If we knew," Corelli mumbled, "who Nora Nora was."

"Or where," Dubisky added. "Like maybe Nora Nora's in Tora Tora Bora."

"Write a limerick, why don't you." Brymmer looked at Clark. "What?" he said.

"Nothing. However...." Clark paused. He liked to do that—pause—get everybody's attention. "I checked the Manhattan phone book. You know how many beauty parlors are listed in Manhattan? About thirteen hundred, about seventy-five percent of which are below Ninety-Sixth Street where the skinny white people play."

"So you're assuming, I assume, that the Jackies are all white."

"I am, but I acknowledge it's a racist assumption. But the *point*," Clark insisted, "is what do we do with *that*? Walk into a thousand beauty parlors and what? Ask em what? Ask em anything you can think about, the answer's 'Where's your warrant?'"

"Question," Brymmer said. "Why would you think we'd do that?"

"I wouldn't. That was the point."

"Well…" Brymmer said, "you sure took the long way around to get to the obvious." He glanced around the room. "Any other ideas? Aside from pursuing Marrott — for which I'm almost practically sure I can get a warrant if I sacrifice the right goats to the right gods…"

Nothing. Silence.

"Okay," Dubisky said. "We got a thousand salons? We get a thousand detectives. We put em all in drag, send em in to get a haircut."

"That's presuming," Kerner said, "that detectives have hair."

"Well the *girl* detectives do. We put *them* in drag too. And then we call it a dragnet."

Brymmer crossed the room, poured coffee and, against his better judgment, took a sip. "Or how about, instead, we put a tail on Andrea Clawson. If the gimmick works at all then she'd've had to've taken part and she'll eventually get a haircut or whatever a woman gets."

"Not bad," Kerner said.

"But not now," Corelli added. He looked around the room. "Like nobody else here reads the gossip page in the *Post*? Andrea Clawson's in Milan."

"In Milan," Brymmer repeated. "Why the fuck is she in Milan?"

"Well I'll read you." Corelli moved his coffee cup from the *Post* and started quickly thumbing its pages. "Okay, here you go. 'Guess who showed up at Antonio Fabuloni's jam-packed Fashion Week show in Milan? None other than the recently bereaved Andrea Clawson, and she wasn't wearing black.' Unquote," Corelli said. He looked up at Brymmer who was glowering in accusation.

"Why the *fuck* do you read the dumb fucking gossip page in the *Post*?"

"Because I wanted to make your day."

"Mission accomplished," Brymmer said. He paced across the room. "And speaking of dead ends, there is, in all likelihood, another body to go. Or at least if the story's true and if nobody's chickened out."

"I don't get it," McAllister said. "It's six women. Minus one. The one who balks at the very start. Minus Marrott— if Marrott's gone and the little angel she's claimed to be— so that's four and we've got four. Clawson. Starrett. Tanner. McConnell."

"It's five," Kerner said. He looked patiently at McAllister. "Maybe go back to school and do remedial subtraction? Look. Starts with six. Sixth woman drops out. But so, for some reason or other, does the *fifth* who says she'll get somebody else. The somebody else would demand a swap. So the somebody else, who's out of the circle, which means she's anywhere out in the world, would have a bastard choice of her own. So altogether, we're back to six. Minus Marrott which gives us five."

"Thanks, Professor," McAllister said.

"And that's assuming Marrott is out. And that the woman she's crapping out on doesn't find a somebody else."

"Which could mean that we're back to six. Or even seven," Dubisky added.

"Hey, Steven—are we keeping you awake?" Brymmer said. "I haven't heard you so quiet since the Mets hit the wall."

"I am present," Ross said. "I've had forty minutes sleep and my mouth isn't working. My ears are okay so

I'm listening, that's all. I believe what you're saying is we need to get lucky before another ding is donged." He sat squinting. "Dong is dinged. See what I mean about my mouth?"

"On the other hand," Corelli said, "if we knew where the place was, we could look at their appointment book for New Year's Eve day, maybe bag ourselves the others."

"And how," McAllister said, "could we know where the place was?"

"Well Burt could pressure his source."

"Except my source says she doesn't know."

"And that's bullshit," Dubisky said, "*All* women know. At least they know what's the place to go. It's like the birds that know where to migrate. It's like the bats that travel on sound. It's in the air and they pick it up. Just standing around in the supermarket, a message passes between them. Which Kardashian got her butt-lift at which doctor and off they go."

"And you're aware of this how?" Corelli inquired.

"I used to be married," Dubisky said grimly. "And I paid for a butt-lift, believe it or not."

"Okay, so you can go ask your ex," Corelli said.

"I wouldn't give her the satisfaction."

"Either way," Brymmer decided, "I suppose we should ask around. And if we manage to narrow it down to, say, a reasonable number of places, we can go with a Plan B. We'll get one of the lady officers here to call and make an appointment. 'I forget,' she'll say, 'my buddy Kate Marrott named me a place where she got this terrific haircut and I'm practically sure it's yours but can you tell me please, is one of your customers Kate Marrott?'"

"This is desperate," Kerner said.

227

"Absolutely," Brymmer agreed. "Any other, better ideas?"

## 61

"Hello?"

"Yeah, it's Burt."

"Oh. And I thought we weren't talking to each other."

"Except for the part about me asking questions and you giving answers."

"Oh. Okay.

"I'm not waking you am I?"

"It's only eleven-thirty."

"Okay, so you don't know exactly where it was that Kate got her hair done, but how about a ballpark?"

"I don't think a ballpark would do a good perm."

"Funny. But you know damn well what I'm asking. Like what *kind* of place? Or just name me the top ten."

"The top ten what? Places in New York? Except most people really don't go to the top ten. Sometimes the smaller shops are hot for a while and otherwise people just go in the nabe."

"Okay, that's a thought. But now tell me what's 'hot.'"

"Gee I really wouldn't know."

"So you mean you don't go to some hot, in place?"

"I don't go at all. Remember, I've got make-up people at the studio. One of them does hair. So once every month or so she gives me a little trim. Otherwise, I just let it do what it wants to do. Like it's basically kind of wild."

"Kind of wild," he said slowly.

"Are you drinking?"

228

"I'm thinking. Why? Do I sound drunk?"

"A little."

"Then I'll stop."

"Drinking?"

"Thinking."

She laughed.

"So the night when I tossed you off my car—"

"You didn't toss me. You carried me rather gently, I recall."

"When you were sitting on my car, you were looking pretty cheerful. Why were you looking cheerful?"

"Oh. Because the rumor was the victim was a kid, like he's twentyish or something. So I figured that it couldn't be connected in any way to the...well, you know what, and I figured it would have to mean that Jackie was a Jackie and that Kate was off the hook."

"Ah," he said.

"Pardon me but wasn't that a Why? I mean, 'why was I cheerful?' I thought you once told me that the why's didn't count."

"My statement wasn't meant as categorical," he said. "And I vaguely recall that I also said the why's could be interesting but rarely...dispositive. Or germane. Or whatever the hell I said."

"Was it interesting, then?"

"Moderately," he said. "But surprisingly germane."

"To what?"

"To my seeing how you get to your conclusions and whether or not to trust them."

"Am I trustworthy?"

"No, not entirely," he said. "But you're logical enough."

"Hmmm." She was silent for a very long beat. Then she said thoughtfully, "How come you're always so honest when you shouldn't be and not when you should?"

"I guess because I lack proper manners," Brymmer said. "Which undoubtedly comes from being raised by wolves."

"In Latvia."

"The Latvian wolves are the worst.—Goodnight, Jamie."

"Yeah. I guess so."

## 62

*Thursday, March 26th:*

*Online edition, New York Daily News (posted at 6:45 PM)*

# JACKIE AGAIN!!
# FIFTH BODY FOUND

The mutilated body of Harrison Kramer, 42, a corporate attorney with Beasley & Johnson, was found in the bedroom of his Greenwich Street loft. Sergeant Burt Brymmer, head of the Manhattan Homicide Task Force, the team that's been following the blood trail of "Jackie," said police were "closing in," and when asked by reporters to explain what that meant, said "whatever you want it to" and got into his car.

Mr. Kramer, once selected as *New York Magazine's* "most eligible bachelor," was about to tie the knot with Octavia Villanova, a dancer with the Met. Ms Villanova is in seclusion. Kramer's colleagues have described him as....

*Online edition, New York Times (posted at 8:47 PM)*

## CITY COUNCILMAN CALLS FOR
## KNIFE REGISTRATION

"Why not knives?" said City Councilman Ramon Riviera (D, Bronx). "It's not just guns that kill people, is it?" The proposal, which already has attracted co-sponsorship by Manhattan Councilwoman Cindi Park-Lane would also ban the internet sale of...

### 63

*Friday, March 27th*

"It's me."

"Mmmp."

"Am I waking you?"

"Yeah. It's okay."

"It's only eleven-thirty."

"Jamie, it's okay. Only how'd you get my number?"

"You called me once, remember? You had to press star-eight-two to get through and it unblocked your block."

"Oh yeah. I forgot." He'd fallen asleep with the radio on and a female disc jockey burbled on his bed.

"Oh. Are you busy?"

"Am I *busy*?"

"I thought I heard voices."

"Oh them. Yeah I've got thirty-seven girls in my bed but no, I'm not busy, it's entirely platonic."

"Oh. Poor girls."

"Stop it."

"Well *you're* the one that brought up the girls."

"Right. You were asking was I busy doing yard

231

work." He turned off the radio. "What's on your mind?"

"Hairdressers."

"Good."

"I did some research for you. The hot place in town is called Michel DePierre."

"I thought you said hotness wasn't really a factor."

"Well, I got a whole lot of other places too. I figured if you figured out the hairdresser place, then you wouldn't bother Kate."

He almost came back and said "Bad thinking, kiddo" but instead he just yawned.

"I could email them to you."

"Yeah. That's good.— How are you?"

"I'm fine. And you?"

"I'm fine."

"I'm sorry I disturbed you."

"You always disturb me."

"Good."

"Sez you."

"But listen, have you noticed, with the fifth murder and all, that I haven't asked a question?"

"You just asked a question."

"Oh. Guess so."

"Goodnite, Miss Rogers."

"Sleep well then, Burt."


## 64

*Saturday morning, March 28th:*

Before he met them, Ross liked to imagine what people would look like based on their names. Harrison Kramer, the FIFTH BODY!, had in fact looked exactly like a Harrison Kramer (until, of course, he'd looked like a FIFTH BODY!) —a tall, lanky WASP with that lank blond hair and that thin-lipped smile that wasn't merry as much as snide. What undoubtedly had added to his all-around charm was the fact that he was also one of *The* Kramers—of Kramer's Root Beer, Gingerale and Tonic ("When you care enough to mix with the very best") and whose family's invention of the lo-cal mixer in the 1950's had led to a fortune now reckoned in the Bils.

His friends called him "Harri" (which sounded like "Harry" though they noted, when he wrote it, that it ended with an "i") and described him as "the smartest guy I ever met," a product of everything Exeter, Yale and Harvard could manufacture. That his life, like his death, had turned out to be chaotic could have never been predicted from his name or from his face.

Such things were on his mind now as Ross parked his Beetle at a curb in Murray Hill in preparation for Lottie Lubin. A girl named Lottie Lubin, in Ross's imagination, would be overweight, brunette, have a probably-fixed nose and what her friends would all describe as "a terrific sense of humor."

Ross rang the bell of Apartment 6C.

The woman who answered it was overweight, brunette, but had not yet undergone any surgical intervention. She was more or less Barbra Streisand at twenty-seven in an Indian kaftan of irridescent blue.

"Hi," Ross said, "I'm—"

"Yeah-I-know," she said. "You called."

She opened the door wide to a narrow foyer that led to a living room that seemed to have been done with a taste for the Oriental.

"Want some coffee or something?"

"Sure," Ross said. And while Lottie was in the

kitchen, he used the opportunity to quickly look around, looking mostly at the dark, red-lacquered bookshelves for a measure of Marrott's mind, which apparently included an interest in *Police Forensic Procedures* and *Murder and the Law.*

Lottie returned and handed him a mug with a faint spot of lipstick remaining on its rim, taking obvious notice of the wedding ring on the hand that accepted the warm offering, and registering a short weak sigh of resignation. He offered her a "Thanks," and then settled on a chair with a nice coat of cat hair and pretended to relax. "Nice place here," he said.

"Yeah. Well it's just like I told the other guy, I'm pretty lucky to've got it." Lottie sat tentatively on the end of a red couch and looked nervously over her cup. "So," she said, "I sure hope whatever's going on here is not gonna—"

"No." Ross said. "Don't worry." He took a short sip of coffee from the colorless side of the cup. "So I heard that your television show got cancelled. When did that happen?"

"October thirty-first."

"Did you get another job?"

"Still looking," Lottie said. "It's pretty tough right now."

"I imagine," Ross said. "It was a cop show, wasn't it?"

"Yeah. You never saw it?"

Ross shook his head. "So what did you do for it?"

"Me? I was kind of an assistant assistant. Basically, I typed. Lists. Like who'd be wearing what in what scene and what scene would shoot when."

"And Kate?"

"Oh Kate was an assistant producer. Like she'd sit

234

in on everything. Meetings with the writers, the technical advisors, the well, with the everything."

"The technical advisors." Ross leaned back in the cat-covered chair. He hadn't taken off his coat but he tried to look At Home and Engaged in Conversation. "So what did they advise?"

"Well mostly they'd tell us how procedures really worked and what would and wouldn't happen and then, of course, the writers would entirely ignore them and have the characters do stuff that real cops would never do."

"Like solve crimes," Ross said.

Lottie Lubin laughed.

"But Kate would be in on all the meetings with these guys."

"Yeah. She'd show em scripts and take notes on what they said."

"Uh-huh.— She have anything to do with the casting?"

"No. Not really. I mean she could have put in a word for someone maybe but the casting was someone else. Maria. Maria looked for guys that had grit."

"Grit," Ross said.

"Yeah. Not slick. Not handsome." Lottie Lubin looked him over with a smile. "Like you'd never get a part."

Now Ross had to laugh. "So anyway, Kate would know actual procedures. What a crime scene unit would look for at a scene."

"Yeah. And what stuff could really trip a killer up. Like street cameras, stuff they'd erased from their computers..."

"Uh-huh," Ross said. "Did she ever confide about her personal life at all?"

235

"No. Not to me. We're not on the same level. Like Kate, she was more of an executive type."

"Did she ever happen to tell you what beauty shop she went to?"

"Was that a serious question?"

"Yes."

"No."

"Okay," Ross said. He took another sip of coffee.

Lottie cocked her head. "Is she in some kind of trouble?"

Ross said, "We're trying to help her out of it, Lottie. But before we can help her, we first have to find her." He looked at her levelly. "So that's why I'm here."

"Yeah *but*—" she said, "I already said to the other cop. She didn't tell me. I wouldn't know."

Ross nodded. "On the other hand, she left you a box of papers."

"Yeah. Up in the closet. You want to see them?"

Ross shook his head. "I'd need a warrant," he said, and left it, pausing a moment, seeming to think. "On the other hand," he said almost tonelessly, "you wouldn't."

"Wouldn't what?"

"Need a warrant."

Comprehension dawned in her eyes.

"Look. She left a box. In a closet. In your apartment. You want to open it, that's okay. I mean it isn't against the law. And if you also happened to tell me, voluntarily, that is, what you found when you opened the box..."

Lottie Lubin bit her lip.

"You don't have to," Ross said.

"But if I did," she said carefully, "what would I be looking for?"

236

"Appointment books…bank statements…credit card bills. I don't know," Ross said. "You'd just tell me what you found." He looked her in the eye. "It's not required of you, Lottie. You can tell me to go to hell."

Lottie Lubin looked away. "It's sealed," Lottie said. "She's got packing tape around it."

"You got scissors?" Ross said.

## 65

Kramer's large loft was on the top (sixth) floor of a building that had once, in the dead ancient past, contributed to the economic life of the city by manufacturing something— something that by now had undoubtedly been banned or whose production had been transferred to a previously desolate Pakistani province.

Brymmer used a code to get into the old but now renovated building— noting, once again, the keypad and the lineup of buzzers at the door— and then sprung a half-key to enter Harri's apartment. The squad had put a new special lock on the door, a lock that had the other half-key loaded in, so that only Brymmer's jig-sawed half could connect with it and *click!* move the door.

Once again, he marveled at the acreage of the place, its windows looking out on a landscaped terrace whose plantings were obviously changed to fit the season. Now it bore fir trees in huge orange pots. He walked to the bedroom and again circled the bed on which Kramer had been found by his hysterical fiancée at two o'clock in the morning of the previous Thursday though she'd first called her agent and second her instructor and

237

finally her publicist before she'd seen fit to dial 911 at approximately seven-thirty. Her claim to having been "in a numbed state of shock" was particularly understandable considering the vividness of what she'd come home to after spending the evening at the top of her tippy toes.

Kramer had been found with his wrists bound tightly to the stout bars of his headboard— an Art Deco triumph of malachite and brass. They'd been tied there with heavy silk hundred-dollar ties and, with his open-throated head turned slightly to the side and his crotch-gutted body spread-eagled on the bed, he'd presented, in a rough and obscene parody, the pose of a horizontally-crucified Christ.

This, in itself, had raised a few questions. Was Harri a regular dabbler in S&M or was this a chance sport? Was his death, in fact, even connected to "Jackie" or merely the upshot of a pleasure-pain session that had somehow, in Marianne McConnell's locution, "simply gone awry"? Had he buzzed up his killer or how did she get in? But once she'd gotten in to the building's ground floor, she'd efficiently disabled the elevator's camera with a pinpoint laser. All it had recorded was a gash of red flame with a starburst of yellow. The fact that she'd left a few clear sweaty fingerprints to taunt them from a few brass columns of the bed was of too little consequence, at least at this point. The prints had matched nothing in anybody's files. Nor were they the prints of the grieving Octavia who'd also provided them with specs on the maid whose prints they weren't either. However, the maid had rather pridefully informed them that she'd "polished all the brasses" on Tuesday afternoon ("with Brasso!" she'd said) so the chances were the prints could be eventually useful. If they ever found anyone to match the prints *with*. And, oh, incidentally, there weren't any hairs.

So. There it was.

Brymmer retired to the living room area and stood for a moment looking over at the trees before turning to the room and its eclectic contents.

The furniture was cold-cut leather-and-steel Modern, but the kind where every chair was worth ten thousand dollars and the couch about twenty. They sat on a rug that was probably woven by tenth century monks in some corner of Shangi-La and, surrounding them, backed against the muted green walls, were the ebony bookcases crammed with such items as weird African artifacts, old French porcelain, and a nicely-framed cover of the first and original Superman comic book (Superman hoisting up a Dodge coupé). As further examples of Harri's far-ranging approach to culture were the leather-bound (and actually thumbed through) novels of Conrad, Dickens, Dostoyevsky, DeFoe, going all the way around, in alphabetical order to the X, Y and Z's, which included the memoirs of Zhou-en-lai.

Brymmer took particular interest in the records— original vinyls with labels like Deutche Gramaphon and Angel but selected a recording of Billie Holiday. He placed it on the bed of a custom-made turntable, fig-ured out the tuner and, pouring himself a short shot of vintage cognac, considering (but not taking) a Cohiba, he sprawled on one of Harri's twenty-grand cushions and listened to Billie commanding willows to weep.

Well, *someone* had to weep for poor old Harri, cut down (as it were) in the prime of his rich life.

The swanlike Octavia, who'd seemed to resemble a piece of modern sculpture, had, when interviewed, sworn she knew nothing whatsoever about kinks or that Harri had entertained them. And Brymmer, who believed almost nothing and no one, had been willing to concede that she probably hadn't known, that the patently aloof and refined Octavia had fulfilled the Deutsche Gramaphon part of Harri's life and was, or was intended to be, kept on another shelf. Nor did his straight and unremarkable male friends seem to offer any insights into darker preoccupations. The next woman to interview, as soon as they tracked her down, would be Harri's previous girlfriend, a paramour who'd lasted, according to male friends, for the duration of two years and in fact up to the advent of the virginal Villanova.

The turntable only played one side at a time, so Brymmer crossed the room again to flip to Side Two with its offer of *Easy Living, Gloomy Sunday* and *Strange Fruit*, an activity which caused him to lean into the shelf which in turn caused him to notice that the fluted edge of the bookcase had a subtly carved notch and another similar notch about five inches down. Pondering this oddity, he learned that if he grabbed and then tugged at the notched portion that it pulled away from the shelving and revealed a couple of buttons. And if he pressed on one of the buttons that... nothing at all happened, but if he pressed on the other button that the bookcase swung from the wall, almost hitting him as it went, and swung out to a right angle, exposing another bookcase that was cleverly set in the wall.

Its contents were such that left Brymmer cocking his head. He recognized the obvious paraphernalia of S&M—the whips, masks and chains— but there were items for which he honestly couldn't figure out a purpose and then, once he did, was profoundly sorry he had.

So that answered that.

The next thing to wonder was: where do we go from here? If Harri had an obsession that Octavia couldn't salve, then the question, more precisely, became...where did *Harri* go? He hadn't gone to a bar. The elevator cameras had shown him arriving home at approximately 7:30; his internet cruisings had shown nothing out of the way and the leather bar waiters said they'd never seen him at all. So it seemed, Brymmer thought, that if Harri hadn't gone to extremes to get his erections, those extremes could have come to him. New York being a town where you could order in any-thing— 24/7— from a Mooshu Pork with Noodles to a dominatrix, Brymmer now considered the possibilities of a Service. That could explain a lot, though it wouldn't quite accommodate the use of the silk ties when such a trove, including handcuffs, existed at close hand. Still, it was worth a shot and he knew the man to shoot it.

He reached for his telephone and punched out some numbers. "Hey Tony," he said to Corelli. "I want you to do a job."

## 66

Brymmer was printing out the list of hot salons that was clipped as an attachment to the message from Jamie Rogers. The message reading, "Hope this is helpful. J.R."

Printout in hand, he went directly to Alice Cotton, the best-looking female officer on the force. Alice had a long dark swinging mane of hair. "If you want to," Brymmer said, "I could borrow you for a job."

241

Alice said, "Probably, but tell me what first." Handing her the copy now, Brymmer said, "Phone calls. You want to find out if Kate Marrott's their customer so you say you're not sure if it's the place she recommended, could they look it up and see."

"So why don't I ask Kate?"

"Because Kate's out of town."

"And what if they say yes?"

"Then you make an appointment. You go, fish around, maybe see if they do a Nora. I'll explain later on. That's it. Can you do it?"

"Of course I can *do* it."

"So why do I sense a 'but'?"

"*But—*" Alice said, "no one fucks around with my hair." She was actually scowling.

Brymmer raised his brows. "If you're scared," he said dryly, "I can send a pinch hitter. Just strikes me that any girl who can collar two muggers in the park on her own—"

"But they didn't have scissors."

"True. They had a P.38, I recall. Don't sweat it. This'll wind up as nothing," Brymmer said. "But thanks for doing the calls."

Upstairs, he found Kerner who was eating a hot dog and saying into the phone, "I'll put the squad on it, madam, and we'll crack it by tonight.... Yeah, me too."

"What's that?" Brymmer said as soon as Kerner hung up.

"My daughter. Found her guppy lying dead in the tank. She believes he was murdered by an alien invader."

"I wouldn't dismiss it out of hand," Brymmer said.

"By tonight, if I remember to stop off at PetCo, he'll have come back to life."

242

"Like magic," Brymmer said.

"She's five. What the hell."

"Mr. Levy," Brymmer said. "I've been thinking of Mr. Levy. So how about this? We pin a tail on him Monday. Starting around seven. We see where he works."

"And what'll that tell us?"

"Just where he works. You said he was cute about telling you where.— Why?"

"I don't know."

"So you get out your gumshoes and fill up your tank. You can go with Corelli. You're good as a team."

Ross was back from lunch. "Should I have brought you a taco?"

"No. I'll catch a something or other later on.— What else you got?"

"A Lottie. Or a little," Ross said and then filled Brymmer in. The best he'd come up with was some credit card bills. "But of course they only covered up to January twelfth. And on January twelfth—"

"Monty Starrett was still alive and God was still in his blue heaven. I got it," Brymmer said. "What credit card was it?"

"A Citibank Visa."

"Any other kind of cards?"

Ross shook his head.

"Any hairdresser charges?"

"I'd've mentioned it, wouldn't I?"

"So maybe you were saving it for last," Brymmer said. "Like the diary," Brymmer said. "The one where she admits to every murder since Abel."

"That one. How could I forget it," Ross said. "You want to swear out a warrant?"

"Forget it for a while."

"Why? What's up?"

"A Felicia," Brymmer said.

"A Felicia as in Spiderman's cat girl?"

"I suppose we could ask her," Brymmer said.

Felicia was a model. Felicia was entirely composed of cheekbones and large violet eyes which reflected an indeterminate level of intelligence; sometimes she looked stupid, sometimes she looked smart. They were sitting in her apartment, a nice little aerie across from the UN. From her thirtieth floor windows, you could look at the flying flags of the many united nations or, preferring to look elsewhere, you could look at Felicia Martin— on the covers of *Vogue*, *Elle*, *Glamour*, *Cosmo*, and *Harper's Bazaar*, all delightfully framed in silver and suspended along the walls.

Felicia, in the middle of a Saturday afternoon, was wearing jeans and a sweatshirt with apparently nothing under it but small bony breasts. Her hair was in foam curlers. It was blonde although, at this point, it didn't exactly matter.

"I wouldn't know," Felicia was saying of her ex-boyfriend Harri, "I have absolutely no idea who'd want him dead."

She was drinking a Diet Pepsi from a can in her left hand. Brymmer focussed on the hand, noticing a thin red line of discoloration that ran from the knuckle of her thumb to her wrist.

"You have a cat?" he asked idly.

"No.— Why would you ask?"

"You just look like you'd have a cat."

"You mean I look like an old maid?"

"Oh hardly," he said "No. Just for the record," he added flatly, "where were you on Wednesday night?"

"I was in bed," she said defiantly. "And I've got a couple of witnesses." She waited for a reaction. Not getting one, she giggled. "My parents. They stayed over."

"Uh-huh. What are their names?"

"Sam and Cherri. They live in Flatbush. We ate at Blotto. We saw a show. And I didn't kill him, you know."

"I know. You might have wanted to, but you didn't."

"Why would you say that?" she argued. "Why would you think Id've wanted to?"

Brymmer shrugged. "Ex-girlfriends frequently do. And then especially when they've been dumped."

"Well, there's that," she admitted. "Yes. And after two really creepy years..."

"Why creepy?" Brymmer inquired.

"Just creepy," she said, "that's all."

"Define creepy."

Felicia shrugged.

"Maybe chains, leashes and muzzles," Ross injected. "It creep you out?"

"It wasn't that," she said nonchalantly. "That's... whatever it is turns you on."

"Then what was creepy?"

"He'd make me read a lot of those books he adored so much. And I'd have to report on them. Jesus Christ. He made me suffer through *Moby Dick*. And then he'd ask me 'So what's the whale?' Do I give a flying fuck what's the whale? Another time it was *Winnie The Pooh*. He'd get these enthusiasms, you know?"

"And you found it creepy."

"Well wouldn't *you*? An entire *eve*ning where Harri blats about Eyeore and Piglet? I'm ready to woops."

"So why'd you put up with it?" Ross pursued. "You could've got yourself thousands of guys."

"I sort of loved him," she said, "in a way. And he said we'd get married which solved a lot. I'm only good till I get to thirty and then I'm over. I like to plan. And I guess I'd invested a lot of my time."

"And then you got bumped by the ballerina."

"And just as lousy," Felicia complained, "he asked me to hang around on the sidelines, kind of visit and do his thing. Like he said he'd pay me? I told him, listen, Buster, I'm good for a grand an hour and all they want me to do for *that* is sit and sulk in a Vera Wang."

"It made you angry."

"That's not the word. I could have killed him," she said, then caught herself and added, "Of course I didn't."

In the elevator Brymmer said, "You notice the stuff on the walls?"

"Mirror, mirror. You mean that?"

A Saturday couple got on the car. Brymmer was silent, watching the floor numbers blink their way down to L.

"There's a cover shot on a *Vogue*," Brymmer said when they hit the curb, "on which she's wearing a dark coat. So I think we should get a copy, photoshop it to add the hat, and then we show it to some of our friends. Like to Carmen, Alfie and Ziegler."

"So you think she's the girl in the hat?"

"I don't know. You look at her thumb? She had the line of a fading scar."

"And thus the question about the cat?"

"They're unpredictable," Brymmer said. "They're even pissy to those they love. Whatever it was, it was some kind of cut. It was very narrow but almost clean. Could've come from anything. Maybe a can, or maybe

246

a razor or maybe she slipped while she's dealing with onions. I wouldn't know. We do the picture and see what we see.— Are you still seeing Carmen?"

"We parted friends."

"That was very noble."

"I try to be nice."

It was almost twenty of three, getting cloudy, planning rain, by the time he got to the station, got some coffee, got to his desk and made a call to the Crime Scene Unit.

Jack Sanders picked it up with a "Yeah. What's on your mind?"

"Grout," Brymmer said. "Specifically the grout around Starrett's bathtub. Did you ever check it for blood?"

"Probably," Sanders said. "We couldn't check it the night we came. Too much bleach. It foxes the test but it disappears if you give it a day. I think it was Henderson followed through."

"Could you do me a favor and look it up?"

"You mean *now*?"

"If you wouldn't mind."

"Well I would but I'm doing it now.— You want to share with me your sudden intense interest in Starrett's grout?"

"Same as usual," Brymmer said. "I want to know if she cut her hand."

"Well I can tell you, top of the head, that the only blood in the drain was Starrett's."

"I'm aware of that," Brymmer said. "But I'm simply imagining what if she did. Not very deeply, but just enough. I'd say the cut's on her left hand since she did the immediate work with her right. So the left's for leverage. Holding him down. Suppose he moves and she cuts her thumb."

"It's not unlikely."

"It never was."

"If she bled on the sheets, it was too commingled. We couldn't read it."

"I know that too."

"And she didn't drip it on any floor. Damn this computer, it's freezing again. So how does she get from the bed to the tub?"

"You want the rest of my fantasy, Jack? She covers the thumb with her right palm. It's the right palm that retains the blood. She turns on the faucet, using her right and the blood drips down and it gets in the grout."

"And the grout would hold it for twenty years.— Wait. Here's the file...Hummm hummm-hummm. Well it was Henderson. Him and Lodge. And they only looked at the drains and bowls. Jesus Christ. Not even the walls. You want it done? I could send McLane. The apartment empty?"

"Yeah. I checked. The lease is good till the end of the month and the family held it. You'll still need a warrant. There any chance you could do it today?"

"So all of a sudden you want it today? What kinda ants've you got in your pants?"

"Must be the red ones, I think. They sting. In another few days we could lose the apartment to painters and carpenters."

"Yeah, I suppose. I suppose you want me to swear out the warrant?"

"I guess it figures. I mean you're the man."

"And what should I say for my probable cause?"

"That somebody notably messed it up. And it's

now your humble but expert opinion that somebody notably messed it up. And what the fuck. It's an empty apartment."

"An empty apartment that won't be for long."

"'Exigent.' Use the word. The judges love it. It's now or never. Suppose the landlord tears down the walls and wants to do marble instead of tile. Let me know if they give you trouble. Call on Steve when you want the key. I appreciate this, Jack," he added quickly and hung up.

After that, he swiveled his chair and looked at the screen of his own computer which showed him the form for a warrant request. He gathered his thoughts and then started to type, pleading the case for a different warrant—another path to another ring of the five-ring circus he happened to own.

## 67

STATE OF NEW YORK      IN THE GENERAL COURT OF JUSTICE
NEW YORK COUNTY      SUPERIOR COURT DIVISION

IN THE MATTER OF      ATTACHMENT TO APPLICATION
Kate Marrott, w/f, 5.11.82      FOR SEARCH WARRANT BY
New York City, New York      Sergeant B. Brymmer

### Description of Items to be Seized:

I am requesting any and all credit card information retained by Citi Corp Credit Services Inc., 7799 Third Avenue, New York City, NY, 19946, as it relates to the account of Kate Marrott for the period extending 6 months prior to the date of this warrant to the date of its execution, which shall be no later than 10 days following its issuance. This request is for all relevant bank records including, but not limited to, debits and credits, and the names and addresses of all businesses involved in any and all such transactions.

249

Description of crime:
Homicide (UF61-2143)

Probable Cause Affadavit

Qualifications of Affaint:

I, Sergeant Burt Brymmer, have been a law enforcement officer
with the New York City Police Department (NYPD) for 15 years,
8 months. I am currently assigned as a Supervisory Sergeant to the
Manhattan Major Homicide Task Force. I have investigated homi-
cides for10 years. I received my training in law enforcement at John
Jay College from which I was graduated with honors and at the New
York City Police Academy. I am conversant with the laws involving
arrest, search and seizure as well as all aspects of criminal investigation. I have conducted investigations that have led to the arrest and
prosecution of many individuals who have committed crimes under
New York State law. I have obtained and executed countless court-
approved search warrants in the past that have helped lead to these
successful prosecutions.

Circumstances of Request:

The NYPD is currently investigating the murder of Montgomery
Starrett. Marrott's troubled involvement with Starrett has been
determined by statements from various independent witnesses. So
has the fact that she abruptly fled the city, cutting all ties, within days
after his death. Obtaining these records will enable the Department
to determine her current and still unknown whereabouts and potentially lead to ascertaining the level of her involvement in Starrett's
murder and may lead to her providing further information that will
help our investigation into other currently open homicide cases.

Conclusion

It is believed throughout the Homicide Task Force that the information we seek will be found among the aforementioned documents (in
any form they take, electronic or otherwise). Therefore, I respect-
fully request that a search warrant be issued for the above listed
account to recover any information pertinent to this, and perhaps
other, homicide investigations.

SWORN TO BEFORE AND SUBSCRIBED
BEFORE ME ON THIS DATE         APPLICANT
SANUEL J. ROBERTSON, MAGISTRATE   Sgt Burt Brymmer

250

## 68

Ross met Sanders at the Starrett apartment at a quarter after six. The apartment was empty. All traces of the dead Monty Starrett had disappeared. The floors, covered with dust in which the tracks of the moved furniture were written into the wood, held the shell of an empty carton and an ashtray with three butts. Sanders said, "It looks like we got here just in time." He had a camera bag on his shoulder and was hauling a metal tripod and the usual black bag.

"Well...I don't know about that," Ross said. "They'd have some trouble finding a tenant."

"You gotta be kidding me," Sanders said. "They could fill up the Bates Motel if they made it cheap enough."

"Yeah. I guess." Ross had trailed him up to the bathroom.

"In or out," Sanders said.

Ross decided to step in; Sanders, closing the door to block the light from the other rooms. "You wouldn't mind if I watch you work."

"If you'll be invisible," Sanders said, "and if you promise to ooo and aah."

Ross sat quietly on the toilet seat and watched through the ambient gloom as Sanders set a $6500 Nikon on the mount of the metal tripod and aimed it with precision at the faucets over the tub. After that, he linked the camera to a cable line with a trigger; then clicked the remote trigger, took some shots and checked the results.

"Okay," he said. "Magic time."

"Ooo," Ross said.

Sanders shot him a look from under bushy red

brows. "My kids," he said, "love this." He removed a bottle of Bluestar Luminol from his bag and sprayed it evenly over the tiles around the faucets and rim of the tub. The tiles remained white but there were places along the grout that turned a bright irridescent blue— little dots, like blue sequins, that glittered eerily on the wall.

"There we go," Sanders said, as he clicked off a carefully-timed series of gaudy pictures before the sequins had disappeared.

"Blood," Ross decided.

"Ninety-seven percent sure. Any bleach would be long gone. And that's only if it penetrated the grout to begin with. More than likely it never did."

Ross didn't say a word. He wanted to say "So how come you putzes blew it before?" But he didn't. He just watched as Jack Sanders took a scalpel-like instrument out of his case and then, checking out the photographic map of the tiled wall, started scraping out the tiny dried flecks of the killer's blood. Or hopefully, the killer's. Or hopefully, blood at all.

"This is good. We can get DNA from this," Sanders said.

"How soon?"

"Sooner or later." Sanders grinned. "That's a rough guess."

"Sergeant Brymmer will not be happy."

"Is he ever?" Sanders said.

With nothing more to accomplish on any other front, Ross made it home at an early quarter of eight to find Kathy, still in her nightgown, watching *Dora The Explorer* and drinking coffee while Billy slept.

"Honey-I'm-home!" he tossed at her archly. "What's

252

for dinner? A rack of lamb? Perhaps a steak tartare à la mode?"

"There's stuff in the kitchen," she said. "Frozen. Defrost whatever. I already ate."

He went to the kitchen where only a plate with the sticky remnants of mac and cheese and a glass with tomato juice soaked in the sink. He returned to the sofa. "Like hell you did! You might've fed *him* but *you* didn't eat."

"Ah, the detective."

"C'mon," he said. He yanked her up by the crook of her arm. "I'm fixing you dinner."

"I don't want dinner."

"I don't give a fuck," he said. "You will eat."

He sat her down at the kitchen table, gave her a watchful and warning glare as he pulled out the butter, the eggs and the bread and, prowling the cabinet, got out a pan. "Okay, I've been thinking," he said, "that as soon as we've gotten Jackie or given it up, we should take a vacation. I've got the time and I think we should use it. We get away."

"A family outing," she said. "What fun."

"You know what I'm saying." He watched her again as she fumbled a cigarette out of a pack. "Billy can stay at that place he can stay at. You and me. Mexico, maybe. Maybe Aruba. Remember Aruba? Piña coladas. Lie in the sun."

"I couldn't do that," she said. "You know that I couldn't do that."

He cracked the eggs into sizzling butter. "Of course you could."

"He wouldn't know why his mother left him. He wouldn't know I'd be coming back."

"He doesn't *know*," Ross said, "that you wouldn't.

253

He doesn't *know* any fucking thing. Or else allow me to put it this way: Of the things that he needs to *know*, he needs to *know* that life isn't Jello. And as for *you*, what *you* need to know is that all of this mothering bleeds you dry and that what you need is a good transfusion."

He buttered the toast and dished out the eggs. There were two for himself and he dug in hungrily.

"Hey! Listen!" he said brightly. "You want to ask me about my day? We saw a model. A famous model. She's perfectly fine doing whips and chains but she's truly disgusted by Winnie the Pooh."

"Perhaps it's the Pooh," Kathy suggested.

"Well I think you could have a point.—Now would you pick up the fork and eat?"

"My Jewish mother," she said.

"So maybe your Catholic mother could come to New York. She could take care of Billy a couple of weeks. And you and me, we escape to the islands, there to recover paradise lost."

"Lost is lost," she said with detachment, and stabbed her cigarette into a yolk.

## 69

Brymmer could score at bars when he selected the right bars— not the hot hookup places clearly meant for the young and the fair, but the sawdusty local taverns, the dingy neighborhood pubs wherein collected the tired waitress, the lonely teacher, the death-weary nurse— the huddled misses, yearning to breathe a purely-imagined air of adventure, or to find themselves a tempest-tossed and equally horny soul who, if given enough huzzah, would lift his lamp at their golden door. The twitching hour, he'd learned, was the hour before closing, when only the desperados would be left at the quiet bar— the not-pretty-enough girls who had earlier been rejected, the half-pretty girls who'd rejected the earlier guys, always thinking that something better would come around through a later door until later became too late.

He'd fallen asleep at 11:30 but suddenly wakened at quarter-of-two, feeling disconnected and slightly horny. After trying a couple of drinks that hadn't managed to put him to sleep, at 3:30 he was up, out and into McCavity's Bar, an Irish tavern on West 82nd. He got his pick of preferred seating— end of the bar with his side to the wall— ordered a whiskey to add to his buzz, and looked at the woman who sat at his left across the span of some empty stools, just enough of a distance away to either ignore her or start to play. It was she who started to play.

"You look interesting," she began.

"Why not?" he said, shrugging. "So what are you interested *in?*"

"I'm interested," she said, "in finding out if you're interesting."

He nodded. "Fair enough.—How could I indicate that I was?"

She was plain, but not unattractive, had eyes that didn't look dumb, and seemed to be in her late thirties, maybe older in better light. "I suppose," she said, "I could start with the old reliable 'what do you do?'"

"I'm a homicide detective."

"Well *that* sounds interesting. But I think you're putting me on."

"Okay, you can take your pick. I'm a creative direc-

255

tor of an advertising agency. I'm a child psychologist. A theoretical physicist. Does any of that interest you? Ask and it shall be so."

She just looked at him, head to the side.

"Oncologist? Concert pianist? Come on. Give me some help."

"Oh well," she said, laughing, "I was right about one thing. You are, in fact, interesting."

Brymmer pulled at his drink. "*That* was easy. How about you?"

"I'm a pediatrician," she said.

"Are you now." He nodded. "Well good for you. That's a wonderful thing to be."

"I'm also Sandra."

"And I'm... Steve.— How old are you, Sandra?"

"That's a truly horrible question, Steve. As you know."

"But I ask it because I'm *actually* a social anthropologist and I'm doing a major study."

"And you're also a little drunk."

He nodded. "Right. I am a little...drunk...social anthropologist and I'm still conducting a study. About women in their thirties. And why women in their thirties are so pissed off at men."

"Because the men let them get to be women in their thirties who don't have a man."

"Wow. Simple as that."

"Ya know? I didn't know I was going to say that at all but, yeah, simple as that."

"Have you ever been pissed enough at a guy that you'd want to kill him?"

"You mean *actually* kill him?" She shook her head no. "I once, however, wished that he'd flunk his final exams."

"And did he?"

She shook her head.

"Lost your mojo there, did you." Brymmer drank from his drink. "So what's the *other* part about? I mean 'the men let them get to *be*'? No female responsibility? Nothing they did wrong? No suitors they might've rejected?"

"The rejected ones never count."

"They don't reckon in the reckoning."

"Right. They don't count."

"Interesting. It's sort of like the Marx Brothers' line: 'I wouldn't belong to a club that would have me as a member.'"

"You lost me."

"Never mind.— So you offer your life to children."

"They're wonderful."

"And you want to have some children to call your own."

"Oh definitely. Two or three."

"Then reconsider the guys you rejected."

"No," she said. "No. I still believe there's gotta be love."

"Where's it written there's gotta be love? Who promised? Who says? Show me where it says in the contract."

She was silent.

"You want a refill?"

"They're closing," she said. "You want— if you want to talk, or another drink, I happen to live around the corner..."

He shook his head at her very slowly. "No, I'm sorry. I'm sorry, Sandra. Very sorry. Sorry indeed. I haven't got a thing that I could offer a pediatrician with an eager and tender heart. I could give you a roll in the hay but that's not what you're after. So....I'm sorry. For many, many things. I'm sorry the world is loveless. I'm sorry that men are louts, or shmucks, or whatever we are, and I'm sorry that women are sad or become bitches through disappointment, and I'm sorry about the whole fucking mess that we've made of the world. But you and I, my ubiquitous Sandra, we ain't gonna fix it so let it be. It was nice talking to you, Sandra. I appreciate the offer much more than I think you know."

## 70

*Tuesday, March 31st:*

On Tuesday afternoon, after two days off, Brymmer had presented his court-approved, signed-and-sealed warrant to the bank. Specifically, he'd been guided to a snarky young woman who apparently disapproved of policemen in general based upon a set of ideological principles she'd internalized at Yale. Icily, she informed him of what he obviously knew: that Ms Marrott would be "informed of this invasion of her privacy." Brymmer wondered idly if Ms Snark had ever witnessed an "invasion of privacy" that was centered on the warrantless seizure of private parts but decided, in the interests of Community Relations, that it was better not to ask.

He returned to the station, arriving at 4:30, to find a pile of paperwork and few people around. He felt, simultaneously, determined and discouraged. It was nearly three months since the butchery had begun, and there was nothing to show for it. Puzzle pieces floated on the bulletin board, unjoined, forming no coherent picture.

The working theory now was the on-the-wall Strangers At The Hairdresser's Plot which, in turn, had set the premise of The Fearless Girl With A Grudge which was nice, intellectually, but even were it true, offered nothing to take to court.

The push-pinned descriptions of the once singular "Jackie" had been buried under a new and more fascinating chart:

| Girls with Grudges | Grudgees |
|---|---|
| Andrea Clawson | Richard Clawson |
| Kate Marrott | Monty Starrett |
| ? | David Tanner |
| Nora Nora | Bill McConnell |
| Felicia Martin | Harri Kramer |
| X | Y |

Brymmer thought a final victim could still be out there regardless of whether Marrott had excused herself or not and, if she had, perhaps either one of Question Mark or X had found another intrepid trader and the killings would still go on. And on. And perhaps on. Like some chain letter from hell, or some pyramid swindle where the last sucker in is the only one to get burned.

Then, too, a single item floated airily on the board:

### George Levy, Tanner's neighbor, bought Formalin

Reading that, one could wonder, as everyone did, what Mr. Levy could have to do with the bisexual (?) David Tanner, but then Levy had had an alibi and hadn't done it himself and there was nothing except proximity and poorly-explained preservative to implicate him at all.

Nonetheless, after dropping off the envelope on his desk, Brymmer headed for Reggie Kerner who'd tailed Levy the day before.

"Nothing," Kerner said. "You thought we'd tail him to where he works? It doesn't look like he works at all. Where he went was, he went shopping. Ralph Lauren on Seventy-Second. Down to Bergdorf's. Back to the Carlyle where he met some friends for a drink and then home again, hippety-hop. I start to imagine he clips coupons, makes his living from some kind of trust."

Brymmer shrugged. "Try him tomorrow. Possibly Monday's his day off.—What did he buy, just by the way?"

"A silk bathrobe."

"I have never grasped the need for a silk bathrobe."

"Me neither," Kerner said, "but I imagine we lack class."

Corelli had been looking into phone-order S&M. There was nothing on Kramer's phone but still Corelli'd known where to look. "Martha Maple," Corelli said. "A nice all-American name. Kinda sounds like Betty Crocker or Aunt Jemima or Sara Lee."

"Except..." Brymmer prompted.

"Except she runs the dirtiest shop of horrors west of hell."

"And he called her the day he died."

Corelli laughed. "We should be so lucky."

"Why did I know that?"

"Because we're cursed. Nevertheless, he's one of her clients. And pretty steady for several months. But she hadn't heard from him. Not in a week."

"And was that unusual?"

"So she said."

"He did that *weekly*?"

"And often twice."

"Well, sure." Brymmer nodded. "Or what's money

260

for?— Go on. Or was that it?"

"So I ask her a couple of questions. What're the names of the ladies he likes and would he be likely to call someone else—like another service. Martha says no. Martha says Harri was scared of exposure. He paid her a fortune to button her mouth. And my other sources were telling me no."

"Did you talk to the ladies?"

Corelli nodded. "These are heavily scary chicks. Lisa and Luna. Just for the record, they had a play-date for Wednesday night. Doing *what* is another planet but they probably provably did, and they turned in the money as though they had."

"Which leaves us nowhere."

"Except for knowing the shit at Harri's was Amateur Night."

"Which leaves us nowhere."

"That's what I said."

The only rainbow had come from Alice who'd told Dubisky she'd found a salon that had boasted the custom of Kate Marrott. The girl on the phone had said "Yeah, I know her. She works for the cop show. Is that still on?" so Alice had gone there to check it out.

He'd left the envelope on his desk— the history of Kate Marrott's Visa transactions— a 7-page printout going back to the past July that either would or would not (no; did or did not) tell him all he needed to know. Like the hole card in Black Jack, it would be what it already was whether he looked at the thing or not. The alternatives to that would be time-consuming and iffy, but if fate was about to fuck him (*again*, Brymmer thought) then he'd play with the cards it dealt because wherever the woman was she was central to everything else. Only she could tell him the story; name the names; place the place. So paradoxically, Brymmer thought, Kate was the only game in town and the question was which town. *Have some fun*, he said to the universe. *The envelope, please.*

| 1/26 | United Airlines | $400.76 |
| 1/28 | Fedex, New York, NY | $208.47 |

Okay, he thought. Right. For shipping out her clothes.

Ace, ten.

1/29    The Alameda Hotel, Los Angeles, CA

He phoned the front desk there and asked for Kate Marrott. He was told she'd checked out about two weeks before but left a forwarding address. He was given that address. He did nothing else with it except carefully write it down. He then called the office of the Chief of Detectives to arrange for permission to travel out of town, got it with an almost unprecedented speed, and got a flight that would land him at eleven the next night. Eleven by his head, only eight by California's.

He then got to work.

A map of Los Angeles showed him the address of Kate Marrott's new hangout was somewhere in a quadrant with La Brea on the east and West 3rd Street on the south. A google search showed him that the place was a bungalow: a small stucco building with a red-tiled roof and a red-tiled porch and a bed of poinsettias basking in the sun. A check of county records showed the bungalow was owned by a Lola Montenegro, who'd inherited the property in 1993 from her paternal grandmother who'd owned it since the fifties. Meaning if the house was worth a million bucks now, its original purchase price was 22 K.

He telephoned the number.

A woman answered cheerfully and Brymmer said, "Lola?" The woman who answered said, "No. She's out of town. Are you a friend of hers?"

He laughed. "I'm not an enemy," he said. "How's she doing?"

"I suppose you ought to ask her for yourself. You want to wait? I'll get the number."

The number turned out to be somewhere in Nevada. "That's her mother's place, you know. Lola's mother broke her hip so Lola went to help her out."

"Ah," Brymmer said. "And then you would be… who?"

"I'm the house-sitter, actually. Well the cat-sitter, really. You know— the three cats?"

"Uh-huh," Brymmer said. "Well thanks for the helpful information, Miss—"

"Kate."

"Yeah. Thanks again."


There were no Visa charges on December 31st. There were no charges anywhere that sounded like a salon though he could, if he wanted to, probe through the underbrush of corporate identity and maybe, in a week or so, pull out the plum. Or otherwise, tomorrow, he could find the girl and ask.


Ross slapped the photoshopped cover on the desk: Felicia, all pout beneath the braided wool hat. "Should I take it to McGinty's?"

Brymmer looked up and then glanced at Ross's watch. "Except Alfie's off at seven."

"Except Carmen's on at night."

"Oy," Brymmer said. "And I thought that was over."

Shrugging, Ross grinned. "I'm a plaything of the gods. And should they will things otherwise, I'm helpless in their hands."

"What's the name of that goat-god?"

"Pan, I believe."

"Well then, I hope it pans out for you."

"Shit. Jesus. You couldn't resist that, could you."

"Nope. And if it happens to work into your schedule, maybe you could venture in to Maybe, Maybe Not and see what Ziegler has to say. And catch Alfie tomorrow."

"Yes, sir."

"I just hit some paydirt," Brymmer said. "Kate's in California."

"And?"

Brymmer pointed at the still-warm printout of his online ticket.

"Well," Ross looked at him with envy, "have fun."

"Some fun," Brymmer said, and went back to his paperwork.

Report from Dubisky: Felicia Martin's father, Samuel Martin, was not a policeman though he might, in some fantasy, have told himself he was. His occupation was listed as "retired bank guard." Her brother was not a policeman either but a student at Rutgers in New Brunswick, New Jersey and had graduated, mid-term, on February 8th.

Therefore, if Felicia was the face in the barroom, she'd built herself a story out of fragments in her head, or to further bait Starrett who for seven whole episodes had once played a cop. All of which presumed that Alfie hadn't made up the dialogue himself.

264

Brymmer looked up to where Alice Cotton stood glaring in the archway. Alice Cotton, with short fluffy hair and very dark angry eyes.

"It's kinda cute," Brymmer tried.

"Don't cute me," Alice said. "I never in my whole entire life went for cute. I only want to be sexy."

"Okay so you're both."

Alice shook her head. "It's either one or the other. And—" she said sullenly, "my boyfriend's gonna kill me."

"So you've come to the right place, then. We'll catch him and make him fry.— You want to tell me what you discovered?"

"Nothing! The worst part. Kate Marrott used to go there but not since the fall. Guy says to me, 'What's the matter? She doesn't like us? She recommends us, she doesn't like us?' So I said she'd been out of town. And also, by the way, her friend Nora was never there, and that's the freaking end of the news."

"How it goes," Brymmer punted. "So why did you let him cut you? I mean, if you want it long?"

"You don't know," Alice said. "You don't know how these guys operate. First thing, he just kind of picks up a clump of hair and goes 'Hmmmmmm.' He gets this visionary look on his pasty face and then, bam! I'm catching my breath and half my hairdo is on the floor. So what do I do *then*? The thing with these people is, they see themselves as artists. They don't care what the customer wants. You tell them, it's like the canvas telling the painter what he should do. It's like Why should I listen to *you*?"

"Okay," Brymmer said. "But really. I think it's cute. But sexy," he added.

"Just stop with that 'cute' stuff already," Alice

snapped. "Have I finished with this assignment or you want me to carry on till they shear me a Mohawk?"

"Uh-uh. We're done. In fact...I think we're just about ready to get a break. Hey Alice? Thanks. Sincerely. For the help."

"Yeah," she said, "sure," and then turned, ready to go. Then she suddenly turned back. "Hey—" she said. "You really *really* think it's cute?"

## 71

"Hi."

"It's Jamie."

"I know. I see your number."

"Did I wake you?"

"Just got home. I was working the second tour."

"Oh I'm sorry."

"About what? That I was working the second tour? Or are you sorry you didn't wake me?"

She laughed. "In a way. You're very nice when you're half asleep."

"As opposed to how crappy I am when I'm awake."

"I'll admit. You can be fairly crappy when you're awake."

"You know? For two people who aren't talking to each other, we've been talking an awful lot."

"I know. Except, in this case, I've really something to say."

"By all means, then. Go on."

"I've been thinking— this is serious— I've been thinking that if you do— that if you manage to find Kate, she'll figure out it's because of me."

266

"Not necessarily. I knew about Kate before you opened your pretty mouth."

"Okay. But as soon as you ask her about the swap, she'll have to know that it came from me."

"Again," Brymmer said, "not necessarily. There were other women involved."

"Oh." She grew silent. The silence grew a beard. "What?"

"I was occupied with not-asking questions. Questions like... well... Have you managed to find Kate? Did you track the other women?"

"I admire your self-restraint."

"In any case, she will, I mean she'll definitely think it's me and I'm having a... tremendous problem with that. I mean the fact that it *was* me. But then I get to thinking that, No, I wasn't wrong. I mean, for *Kate* I wasn't wrong. I can't imagine how she'd ever live comfortably holding back. But I still feel... immoral. Or treacherous. Or something. So listen, if you see her, would you just please tell her... just tell her... just tell her that I love her and I wasn't trying to hurt her and I—"

"Oh. Hey Jamie."

"What?"

"You're crying."

"Well *yeah!* This is *tough!*"

He took in a breath and said, "How can I help you?"

"No. You can't. It's just difficult, that's all."

"Oh hell," he said. "Everything's difficult."

"No. No it's not. Just the difficult things are difficult."

"May I quote you on that, Miss Rogers?"

"No. And just please don't try to make me laugh. I just really need to cry."

"Oh Christ! I never know what to do with a crying woman."

"Take her gently in your arms and then whisper, 'There, there.'"

"There, there."

"I'm hanging up. I'm not angry. I need to cry."

"Okay."

Click-*Buzzzzzzzzz*.

## 72

*Wednesday, April 1st:*

On his way to the airport, he was thinking of the old Western television series: *Have Gun, Will Travel.* He remembered watching reruns in Mackabee's basement, after he'd fled from the fourteenth foster home and Mack took him in, and thinking at the time that he wanted to have a gun; and travel. Knowing, too, right then, that he wanted to be a cop. A police officer. An Officer of the Law. On the right side of the law. Only now he was thinking that he wanted to be Paladin, the hero of the series; pack heat, get a horse. Because now it was something else.

He had to arrive early at the dull, crowded terminal on account of all the crap he had to go through with the gun. First, he had to prove that both he, and then the weapon itself, were "legitimate" (that Smith, having married the expectant Miss Wesson, the resulting offspring had been blessed by the state). Then he had to show them that the gun was in a box, that a lock was *on* the box, and that the magazine was nowhere to be found in the vicinity. After which, he had to get the

usual other crap of being picked as a Usual Suspect—
the exacted retribution for having a villain face—and
get the full-bore attention of a cretinous little thug,
get the table turned on its head. Shut your mouth.
Stay where you are. Hands up. Pat down. And with the
irony still remaining that if Terror threatened the air,
his prescriptively useless weapon would be locked in the
space below.

Upon arrival, he lit a smoke amid the fumes of
the smoggy air and claimed a Mazda from National.
From New York, he'd booked a two-night stay at The
Alameda, stressing on the phone that he wanted a
"smoking room," a preference he'd pronounced with
the emphasis on "room" instead of on "smoking" to indicate his preference for a smoldering accommodation
in which a once-raging fire had been recently banked.

The Alameda, where Kate had spent her first
frantic days, turned out to be a vintage pink stucco
building with palm trees predictably swaying around
a court which, in turn, was enclosed within the walls
of the building. Two stories high, it had rooms that
either opened directly on the court or on the second-
floor balcony that spanned its facade. Smoking rooms,
plotted on the "smoke rises" theory, were arranged on
the top floor.

He settled in to the room which had a dwarf refrig-
erator, an electric coffee pot, a mini microwave, a wi-fi
connection and a television set that got pornographic
channels. He sprawled on a bed that had "Magik®
Fingers" and leafed through the pages of the bedside
phone book to find the location of the nearest precinct.
Two cigarettes and one small jigger of airline Scotch
later, he paid them a visit— a bit of professional courtesy
but also a play to prevent any hassles and to possibly

provide him with strategic or moral or informational backing. At the station house, he talked to a Lieutenant Baker and a Sergeant Dunham and told them the general outline of his business. In return, as a courtesy, they gave him a green "park anywhere" card with "Los Angeles Police Department" printed on the top. He promised to return it before he left town.

Somewhere between the hotel and the station, he found a little Mexican joint on a corner where he had some buritos and one single beer. Leaving the restaurant and heading for his car, he stopped on the dark and half-deserted street and then squinted at the car. A kid in a sweatsuit was busily working on the driver's side door with a wedge and a hanger. Brymmer moved quietly and took a position about six feet behind him, stood with his arms held loosely at his sides and announced, half in wonder, "You can't be that stupid. *Nobody's* that stupid."

The kid didn't move, kept working at his job. Not thinking he could possibly be the object of that remark.

"Police," Brymmer said. Evenly. Flat. "Drop the hanger, don't move, put your hands up on the roof."

This at least got some attention. The kid looked at Brymmer passingly, over his shoulder, then looked for an escape route, hanger still in hand.

"Not smart," Brymmer said. "You run, I catch you, and we add to it something like 'fleeing from the scene.' Drop the hanger, face the car, put your hands on the roof."

This time the kid at least sullenly complied. He was slim— five-nine, one-forty, Brymmer gauged. Fifteen or sixteen. Black-haired. White. Brymmer did a pat-down. Nothing. Not so much as a joint or a knife.

"You a cop," the kid said, "you better show me your

270

badge."

"I'll show you my knuckles in your face," Brymmer said. "Now c'mere." He grabbed the kid by the back waist of his pants and then forcefully yanked him to the front of the car. "Now you see that card on the dashboard?" Brymmer said. "I want you to read me what it says on that card. Just read me the first line."

Nothing.

"Aloud."

"Los Angeles Police."

"*There* you go. You see the value of education? How reading can take you far? So next time you go to boost a car here, bozo, read the warning signs first. Now sit on the hood and then sit on your own hands."

The kid eyed him angrily but sat on the hood.

"And the hands," Brymmer said.

He waited. The hands went slowly under the ass.

"What's your name?" Brymmer said.

"Juan."

"Juan what?"

"Juan Two Three."

"Oh funny. Let me give you a few tips for survival. Mouthing off to cops is not in your self-interest. Memorize that."

The kid just tilted his chin up defiantly.

"Why did you want the car? You saw there was nothing in it, so why did you want the car? Chop shop?"

"I wanted to go somewhere."

"Where?"

"Somewhere. Anywhere."

"Somewhere-anywhere usually ends in jail. You don't want to go to jail. I think what you're saying is, you want to get away."

Now the kid nodded. "Yeah. Away."

"Second rule of survival: Learn to accept that you can't get away. You can't get *out* of it, you have to get *through* it. You have to endure. Understand what I'm saying? You know what endure means?"

"Yeah. I think so."

"What?"

"Survive."

"Third rule of survival is that: Survive. Then you have to ask yourself, Survive as what? Who do you want to be? Where do you want to go? It's not somewhere-anywhere, it's someplace specific. You don't get there in stolen cars. Fourth rule of survival is, you need to have a friend. A friend who hangs apart from your crappy neighborhood, your idiotic school and your miserable home. Someone who'll remind you of what's your self-interest. Your long-*term* self-interest."

"And who the hell's that?"

"Yourself," Brymmer said. "Now pick up your tools before I bust you for littering."

"You mean I can go?"

"What would *I* want with you?"

He drove the few blocks to inspect Marrott's house. There were lights on inside and a silver-gray Acura parked in the driveway. It would wait till tomorrow. It would wait till he had a plan. Sometimes, instead of asking "What would Jesus do?" (a question that had never occurred to him in his life) Brymmer would ask himself "What would Ross do?" which wasn't always legitimate but usually worked out.

He went back to the Alameda.

When he got to the balcony that rimmed the top floor, he saw the light of a cigarette, a beacon against the dark, and a woman's voice, nicely burnished with booze, said laughingly, "Welcome to the leper colony."

He turned, looked down across the faintly lit space. She was sitting on the red tile floor in front of a room, her back against the wall, an ashtray and a bottle of whiskey beside her and a glass in her hand. From where he was standing, he couldn't really tell if she was thirty or fifty, but even in the thin light of a pale moon he could make out the curves of an agile body and the lines of a dark-haired, sensual face.

"Are you a leper?" Brymmer asked.

"We all are. Smokers. We've got five whole rooms here. All in the same corner. You'll notice there's a scarlet S on your door."

He looked, and there was. It wasn't on the door but beside it on the wall. An S, and it was red.

"Well I'll be damned," Brymmer said.

"You want a drink?"

"I'll get a glass."

He returned with an Alameda bathroom glass and then joined her on the floor. She poured him a fine, generous shot, clinked glasses, said, "Cheers," and then studied him and added, "Are you permanent or transient?"

"In what sense of those words?"

"The Alameda," she said. "It either rents by the moment or it rents by the month."

"In that case, transient. — You?"

"Permanent, I guess. Till the money runs out." They drank in silence. Something chirred in the court. "You don't happen to be in the movie business, do you?"

"Don't happen to be, no."

"So that's good in a way. In fact... *very* good."

"Should I follow this conversation? Or you want to just riff?"

"It's good since you don't seem to know who I am, or was, and it's bad because I guess you can't cast me as the interesting but overage trollop or the mother of the mother of the mother of the bride."

Brymmer laughed. "I would cast you as an interesting trollop in a heartbeat," he said. "Why are you permanent?"

"My house was foreclosed and I can't get arrested."

Brymmer knew from Ross what she meant by arrested. In actors' circles, meant "can't get a job."

"I went back to New York and auditioned for some plays. At least in the theater there are actual stories that have actual words. Here it's just visual. Special effects. Once in a while, a character says 'fuck' and they call it a movie." She said, "You want to fuck?"

"If you're not too drunk to know what you're doing."

"I *only* know what I'm doing when I'm drunk. And I'm not very drunk but I *am* just drunk enough to know what I'm doing."

"Then you're on," Brymmer said.

### 73

*Thursday, April 2nd:*

Dressed in a beat-up windbreaker and jeans so as to look "California," he drove to Kate Marrott's place at 6 in the morning and parked across the street. He did not want to wake her. He noticed a newspaper sitting on the pathway that butted on the porch. Under normal conditions, she'd come out and collect it; he'd wait till she did.

274

However, she didn't. At 6:45, she emerged in a sweatsuit with a matching backpack and started to jog, thus killing her chances as Dubisky's second wife. Brymmer decided to follow her on foot. He didn't have to get close; the streets were as empty as the California mind.

After several blocks, she turned, heading right, and went up a grass hill. The grass was still damp and the bright morning sunshine sparkled on the dew. At the top was the long plateau of a park. He hoped to hell she wouldn't want to jog around the park and, obligingly, she didn't. Instead, she went directly to a food concession, bought coffee and a muffin, and settled at a white metal table in the sun. There were few other people in the park at this hour and none were around her. He could talk to her here.

Brymmer bought coffee and stood for a moment in the shade of the concession, watching Kate Marrott. She did and did not look like her picture in the high school yearbook. She'd acquired what he imagined women called "style." An angular haircut. A slight loss of weight that put cheekbones in her face. On the other hand, her whole presentation was pragmatic. A straightforward face atop a straightforward body.

He watched her as she fumbled around in her backpack and pulled out a manuscript in a red vinyl cover. She opened the manuscript and opened the coffee. He waited till she seemed relaxed and engrossed. Then he moved to the table and simply said, "Kate."

She looked up at him, frowned and then said, "Do I know you?"

He showed her his shield and then watched as her eyes grew immediately wide and she essentially froze. "I'd just like to ask you a couple of questions."

She made an indeterminate sound in her throat but continued with the deer-in-the-headlights impression. Her dark hazel eyes, though, were gathering thoughts, so Brymmer sat down at her little white table, not directly across from her, but more at an angle, angling left so as not to distract her, not to alarm her, to possibly coax her, at a crucial juncture, to look him in the eye.

She continued to stay silent, her hands tightly folded, thumb rubbing thumb.

"I don't bite," Brymmer said. "I just want to ask questions." He appeared to be relaxed as he sipped at his coffee and seemed to look away.

Kate Marrott found her tongue and said, "According to Miranda, I don't have to answer."

"True," Brymmer said. "Except she isn't in the room. We're just having a conversation."

She slowly shook her head.

"Okay," Brymmer said. "But let's now consider the alternatives, should we? You know what they are? What they are is, I call a Lieutenant Baker. I tell him you're a suspect in the murder of Monty Starrett. Lieutenant brings you in. He tells you all the jazz about your right to remain silent or to get an attorney and if you can't afford an attorney, the court will appoint one. So now you're on the radar as a murder suspect by the precinct around the corner at which point you either answer the same questions I'm going to ask you now or you hire an attorney at six bills an hour or take a court-appointed dolt. Otherwise, you sit in this nice sunny garden and we have a conversation. So. What'll it be?"

She sighed and then shivered. "*Am* I a suspect?"

He shrugged at her. "Are you?"

They looked at each other through the sparkling air.

"Actually," Brymmer said, "I just wanted to ask

some questions."

"Wait!" she said, suddenly alert. "How'd you find me? I didn't tell anybody—"

"Uh-uh," Brymmer said. "I'm sorry, Kate. It isn't that kind of conversation. But I bet with some thinking, you can answer that yourself.— Okay?"

"I guess it has to be."

"Yeah. How it goes. Okay, so let's begin with a basic proposition. I heard a story from...well, let's call it 'another woman.' But I need to hear it again. I need to hear it from you. So let's build to it step by step. Exactly where were you on December the thirty-first— New Year's Eve in the afternoon?"

Her lip trembled slightly. "You know the answer to that, I guess."

"You're not guessing, you're answering."

"The Salon de— Guy Laval's beauty salon."

"Right. And what's the full name of that salon?"

"Le Salon de Laval."

"And where is it?"

"On Madison at the corner of Sixty-Ninth."

"And how long were you there? On December the thirty-first."

"My appointment was at one. I was there till about six."

"Because the place had been double-booked."

She nodded. "They said somebody else could take you sooner but if you wanted to wait for Guy, they simply told you, wait around. So a lot of the women did."

"Why?"

"He's supposed to give a very good cut."

"'Supposed to'. Had you never been there before?"

Kate Marrott shook her head. "I got his name quite a while ago from an actress I worked with. I decided, oh

277

well, new year, new me. So I made that appointment."

Brymmer just nodded. "And how many women were waiting around for Guy?"

"About a dozen, I suppose."

"And they're all sitting around telling badguy stories?"

"No. By then I'd say a couple of women left."

"And by the time you got around to talking about murder?"

"Six. But that was only just at the beginning. When someone said, 'You know? we should just kill them all and then whack off ...' you know, and everybody laughed. And the sixth women said That's really not funny, and then she got called. Went in to get done."

"Uh-huh. And how long did it take to get done?"

"Mmm...Guy himself took at least half an hour. And then you went to somebody else to get washed."

"Okay, so for the next half an hour, there were five."

"Yes."

"Who were they?"

"You mean...their names?"

"Yeah. That's the usual meaning of 'who.'"

"Listen—I'd never seen any of them before. And I didn't get the feeling that they knew each other either. It was just like strangers sitting around a waiting room or maybe, you know, when the train gets stuck, or the plane's on the runway but it doesn't leave for hours. People start to talk. Sometimes they say very intimate things but they don't give their names. Or sometimes, if they do, they'll give their first names only.—Wait a second!" Suddenly suspicion changed her face; tightened it. "Something doesn't track here," she said. "You couldn't've traced me through any of those women. If anything, they'd only have known my name's Kate.

So how could you have possibly—"

"How about I checked the receipts at the front desk?"

"Oh," she said, nodding.

"Go on," he said. "So what were the first names, then?"

"I'm not sure I caught them all."

"Do your best," he said, and took another pull at his coffee.

"I remember a Nora. She happened to give her name before the talk got serious. The only name I'm sure of, or believe that I'm— no, that I'm definitely sure of, is Andrea Clawson."

"And why would you be sure if she didn't give her name?"

"Because her picture was in the papers. When the story broke of the murder, her picture was in the *Post*."

"You didn't recognize her before?"

"I'm not up on society news."

"Describe her."

"She looked like her picture in the paper."

"What color was her hair?"

"Auburn. Dark red."

"And after it hit the papers, were you sure of it right away?"

"I suspected it right away. I wasn't certain till later."

"Till Monty," Brymmer said.

"Yes," she said tightly. "And that's when I started to believe that it was real." Her eyes had gone misty. "And then—" she shrugged helplessly—"I didn't know what to do."

"Understandable," Brymmer said. "You were frightened. You didn't know what you'd gotten yourself into. And you still weren't totally convinced that it was real."

She nodded, looked relieved. Swallowed hard and looked away.

Brymmer glanced around the park. Nobody nearby. He had all the time in the world. He said, "Your muffin's getting stale."

"For some reason," she said dryly, "I'm not exactly hungry."

"Is that a script?" He pointed down at the shiny red binder. It looked like a screenplay. "How's the job search going?"

"Horribly, thank you."

"I'm sorry to hear that. Times are pretty tough."

"It's a freelance project. I'm advising, that's all."

"A police story?"

"No."

"Can you describe the other women? The ones you couldn't name?"

"One was very pretty—almost like a model— but all of them were attractive. Slim. Well-dressed. Looked fairly well-off. One was a little older. Like fortyish, I'd guess. She had a gypsy kind of look. Dark hair. With bangs. Very thin and intense. She had a quirky sense of humor. The rest of them—I mean aside from Andrea, were blondes. Nothing special about them. They were just a group of rather successful-looking women."

"Let me show you something." Brymmer took the phone out of his pocket and scrolled to the unshopped photo of Felicia. "Ever seen this woman?"

Kate Marrott looked briefly and nodded. "She was there."

"You're certain."

"Yes."

"Okay, so they were telling their stories," Brymmer said. "Their Worst Bastard stories. So tell me a few plots."

She shrugged. "Just the usual kind of plots, I suppose. Most of the stories involved cheating, crapping out, leading on, acting piggy..."

"Those are usual stories?"

She nodded. "Oh yeah."

"Was anybody beaten? Physically harmed?"

"One of the women—the gypsy with the bangs— and actually I didn't get to hear the whole thing, I had some phone calls to make — but she called him a... mmm, I forget what it was but I know she said something like he ruined her body or—wait... what she said was he 'scarred her for life.' Really, at the time, I didn't think she meant physically but maybe she did."

Brymmer gave it thought, tried to place it in the universe of what he now knew. It didn't quite fit, but he'd think about it later.

He drank some more coffee. "What was Andrea's tale of woe?"

"Her husband— well, we know who her husband was now— her husband wanted to have another woman live in the house and wanted to screw her out of some money."

"And the cover girl?"

"Was dumped. Said her boyfriend was all of a sudden getting married but he'd offered to pay her for... well, having sex."

Brymmer nodded. "She happen to mention what kind?"

"What *kind?*"

"Of sex."

"I'm sorry," Kate said, "I don't follow what you mean."

"And how about Nora? You remembered the name

Nora."

"I think she's the one that had the married boyfriend."

"And what did she look like?"

"Nora? I don't know. Not pretty but not not."

"Did she happen to mention what she did for a living?"

"Not directly, though I gathered that she worked at the Met."

"The opera?"

"The museum."

"Was it something to do with fashion?"

"I really couldn't say since *she* didn't say. But they do have a huge collection of costumes."

"See? This wasn't as hard as you thought."

"Oh but it will be."

He nodded. "That's right. You know the tricks of interrogation. —How'm I doing so far?"

"I'm too subjective. I couldn't tell."

"Too bad. I thought you'd give me a few notes on my performance." He drank some more coffee, leaning back again in his seat. He wanted to scratch his face which was itching in the sun. He wanted a cigarette which usually prevented him from scratching his damn face. He drank some more coffee.

"Would you recognize the women if you saw them all again?"

"Yes. But I sure as hell hope I won't have to."

"Right. But you sure as hell know that you will. Come on, Kate. You're not a stranger to this stuff. What would happen in a script?"

"In a script," Kate said, "I'd be called in to testify and the day before the trial I'd be found in the river."

"Which one? East or Hudson?"

She glared at him. "You think this is funny?"

"No. It's not. But if we ever got to trial, and that's a very big if, we'd have it six ways to Sunday and your death would be pointless."

"Well *that's* reassuring."

"What I'm saying is, you'd live. You could even come back to your rent-controlled apartment."

"Stabilized."

"Whatever." He let her have a break, a little time to catch up with him, before he continued.

"Whose idea was the killing? I mean *seriously* killing. Which of the woman said, 'Listen, we could do it' or 'why don't we do it?'"

"Andrea."

"Uh-huh. You're sure of that?"

"Yes."

"Whose idea was the swap?"

"That was Andrea's too."

"So then aside from the stories and, I'd also imagine, the names of the perps—"

"We weren't saying their names. It was just 'my boyfriend,' 'my ex,' 'this guy'."

Brymmer squinted. "But you must've eventually given names—"

"We never said them as I recall. We only wrote them. At the end."

"Along with the addresses."

"Yes, with addresses."

"Something's missing."

"What do you mean?"

"John Smith, One-eleven West Whatever doesn't work. How'd you know how to get him?"

"We gave each other clues."

"Clues," Brymmer said. "How'd you clue them

about Monty?"

"God forgive me," Kate sighed.

"Ask him later," Brymmer said. "What did you say about Monty?"

"Where he worked. Where he *wanted* to work. As an actor. His ego. How he'd likely make a pass at Hello."

"And you wrote it all down?"

She again nodded grimly.

"On what?"

She cocked her head at him and squinted. "On paper?"

"Describe it."

"Oh. It was memo-pad paper. About....I'd guess about seven by nine. Green. It was lying around on a table."

"In the waiting room."

"Yes."

"And how did it feel? Writing those names. Playing that game."

Kate Marrott grew thoughtful. A shoulder reflexively lifted and dropped. "I don't know if you can understand this," she said, "but it was sort of like at college. Girls sitting around in the dorm late at night and, you know, smoking weed, and then pretending we're doing witchcraft. It was silly but still sort of thrilling in a way. And embarrassing, really, if you think about it later."

"Did you ever do witchcraft?"

"Me? No. Nor did anybody else. And besides, *doing* anything was never the point. It was thinking you could do it. Imagining power."

"Magic."

"Yes."

"Okay, so what then? After you wrote it down."

"We folded up the paper till it made a tiny square, and wrote a number on the top."

"Why?"

"So you wouldn't draw your own guy."

"Were the numbers then random?"

"Yes. Exactly. So no one would know whose number was which. You'd only know which of the numbers was yours, and then you'd avoid it or throw it back in."

"And the purpose of that was...?"

"To kill any links. So no one could say, if it came down to saying, that so-and-so asked me to...well... you know."

"And you all drew a name. All five of you?"

"Yes."

"And which of you quit and said she'd get someone else?"

"That was Andrea."

"Why?"

"Because Andrea drew last. And it turned out the only paper left was her own. Andrea said, Fuck! And then somebody else suggested we could throw them back in and do the whole thing again, except two of the women had looked at their chits, so Andrea said No, she said she'd get someone else and she even said 'I think this'll work out better.'"

"I don't know about better, but it must've worked pretty damn fast," Brymmer said. "Considering that Clawson was murdered that night."

"I thought of that too. At least a friend of mine did."

"You told this to a friend?"

Kate Marrott bit her lip.

"Don't worry," Brymmer said. "I won't ask the friend's name. But just what did the friend say?"

"That it didn't seem likely to get a killer that fast. The friend said you'd hardly get a *plumber* that fast."

Brymmer laughed. "She did, did she."

"I didn't say it was a she."

"Just guessing," Brymmer said. "But the next time you see her, tell her the improbable happens all the time." He surrendered now and rubbed very briskly at his jaw. He was seeing it— the five slick women drawing lots. Like a parlor game. A beauty parlor game. What the fuck. "So," he said, "after you'd all drawn the names, one of you must've got called to see Guy. Which one of you was first?"

"Andrea," Kate said.

"And half an hour later, who after that?"

"I was."

"And after you were done, what then? You go back to the waiting room?"

"No. I went home."

"And what about Andrea? Did Andrea go home?"

"No. She came back to the waiting room, in fact. She came back as I was called."

"So you don't know what happened or was said after that."

"No. I don't."

"What else?"

"About what?"

"Sorry," Brymmer said. "I was talking to myself. What about the timing? Was there some kind of deadline?"

"No. It was just like...as soon as you can but as clever as you can. And we all made a promise that we wouldn't crap out."

"Whose name did you draw, Kate?"

"I threw the thing away."

"Whose name did you draw?"

She appealed to him with her eyes. "You do believe me that I threw the thing away."

"I don't believe you 'threw the thing away' unread. So what's the guy's name?"

"It was Eric Raven."

"C-r-a—"

"No. Raven. Eric...Raven."

"Address?"

Kate Marrott again shook her head. "It was Central Park West. I really didn't pay much attention to the number."

"And what were his Gets?"

Again, she met his eyes. Hers were level but clouded. "I didn't— I swear to you— I didn't read far enough to get to his Gets. I just read his name and then I tore the thing up and then I threw it in the garbage and I tossed it down the chute. I didn't want it in my house."

"Why not? If you really believed it was a joke?"

"Because it struck me that, even as a joke, it was sick."

"Uh-huh. Well, better late than never," Brymmer said. He paused, looked around, clearing his mental palate. A kid rode a skateboard. A man walked a dog. There were flower beds, pushing up the first spring tulips. The sunlight danced off the table where he sat. Kate Marrott, Jamie's friend, picked tensely at a nail.

"So let me just try to get it straight," Brymmer said. "One of the women says that her boyfriend's getting married and wants to pay her for having sex, and another woman says she's got a married boyfriend who's been jerking her around, but when everyone draws a name, you don't know if it's the name of Felicia's boyfriend or the name of Nora's jerk. And on top of that, you don't even know who Nora is or Felicia or Andrea or anybody else."

Kate nodded. "And that's why I thought it was a joke."

"I wouldn't blame you," Brymmer said. "It's worse than a joke. It's the goddam stupidest movie I've ever seen. Or it was until you gave them your technical advice." He looked at her directly. "So what did you tell them?"

"I thought we were joking."

She was toying with the muffin.

"But what did you tell them?"

The innocent muffin was now getting shredded—a really compulsive two-handed shred that left the raisins popping out in a shower of tortured bran.

"Kate?" he said. "What did you tell them, Kate? Exactly. I need exactly."

She gave him the list.

## 74

Like the kick-me character, Major Major, in the classic novel *Catch-22*, Clark's first name just happened to be Clark. And actually it did just happen to be. His mother was not a cruel woman; she did not intend to make a joke of her son. She named him Clark because that was the name of the man who got her pregnant, a merchant seaman who had shipped off to sea after one amazing unforgettable summer and left her, unknown to him, six weeks with child. Her fatherless child had had her own last name (Jackson, in fact) but she'd wanted to give him the feeling, no matter how remote and abstract, of having a tangible paternal line. And who could have known then that, four years later, the wandering seaman would return to port, remember that girl and that memorable summer, and phone her ("Hey, girl. You remember Bill Clark?") and that the rest would be the happily-ever-after kind of ending that usually doesn't happen.

The result was that Clark, who had to contend with tiresome grillings and idiotic jokes every time he so much as made a restaurant reservation, was devoted to his family, which consisted, at this time, of two children under four. Clark believed that children under four needed fathers and a fatherly presence, so when Brymmer was working up assignment schedules, Clark had requested a first-tour-only, at least for the duration. Getting home at five meant dinner with the family, a chance to read story books and tuck children in.

Therefore Clark, who'd been previously scheduled for the four-to-one tour, was delighted to be partnering with the morning-hating Ross at 7:30 A.M. as they parked across the street from the Tanner building on 82nd between Lexington and Park in the hopes of pursuing the mysterious Mr. Levy to see what, if anything, he did for a living.

Ross was dispirited by Clark's good cheer. He was further dispirited by the freezing weather, his own lack of sleep, and the general difficulty of tailing in Manhattan.

If Levy took a cab, you could lose it at a light and get stuck behind a bus. If Levy took the bus, you could likely climb aboard, but the rush hour busses, like the rush hour subways, were jam packed with people and you couldn't always move to get off at the right stop; you were often left helplessly staring out the window, crammed between several large-butted ladies, while your subject walked quickly and merrily down the street or the platform or whatever. So Ross was not pleased.

As they sat drinking coffee— just a little, not a lot in case the stakeout dragged on— Ross had asked Clark would he please stop whistling. Clark had asked Ross would he please stop grousing. Ross had decided that if that were the tradeoff, Clark could keep whistling.

They stared at the dark green canopied entrance. By 8, there was a changing of the guard at the door and Ross could see their favorite doorman, Tim O'Fallon, pacing back and forth, opening the double glass doors for the tenants, whistling for taxis, accepting the deliveries of laundry and food. There was no sign of Levy.

At 9, Ross rolled down the passenger window and lit a cigarette. "What do you want to bet that the bastard sleeps till noon?"

"We're in a car," Clark reminded him. "We're not freezing either of our asses on the street."

"Miss Sunshine," Ross groused.

For an answer, Clark whistled.

At 9:23, Clark hit the radio in time to get the news which included the weather. It was twenty-three degrees with a wind chill factor that made it fourteen.

At 9:35, Ross left the car to feed money to the meter. At 9:35 and 17 seconds, Levy emerged in a camel's hair coat with a mink collar and matching ear muffs.

"What do you want to bet he's a cab man?" Ross said, his eyes glued to Levy, his hand on the handle of the open car door.

"No. Not with ear muffs." Clark had his hand on the key in the ignition, ready to pull it fast and get out of the car.

Levy started heading on foot towards Park, allowing an empty cab to go by.

"Go," Clark said.

Ross started tailing as Clark reached over and closed Ross's door and then tossed down the "Fuck you, Meter Maid" card on the vinyl dashboard. Clark then exited, following Ross.

While Levy walked the side street, Ross hung behind him by a reasonable distance. By the time they made Park— a double-wide avenue with an island in the middle— he could peripherally see Clark moving briskly on the opposite side of 82nd and also heading west.

Levy crossed Park. Ross timed his movements to remain on the curb when Levy hit the island, then get to the island in time to move forward while the light was still green. Meanwhile Clark had already crossed the street.

Levy continued heading west on the side street. Ross pulled a muffler up over his ears which were stinging in the wind. His gloves were in the car.

At Madison, Levy made a turn to the left and started heading downtown. Stopping to browse in every fucking window! Every fucking boutique! Missoni. La Maison du Chocolat. Carolina Herrera. Ross had read somewhere that rents on this strip ran to fifteen-hundred dollars and up a square foot, and Levy seemed to want to get his sidewalk money's worth, dawdling and dallying on the streets lined with gold, and every time he stopped, Ross too would have to brake and pretend to be browsing at the shop next door, or lighting a cigarette, or looking for a cab. He decided that the looking-for-the-cab bit was good since there weren't any cabs and if Levy, who wouldn't be expecting a tail, should particularly notice him, well, he was just

291

another man-wanting-cab, giving up from time to time before searching again.

At the corner where the Whitney Museum used to be, he and Clark traded places, Clark crossing over to the west side of the street, while Ross pursued the downtown route on the east.

In passing, Ross mumbled something to Clark about "lovely day for a stroll" as Levy, in his mink-lined cocoon, kept strolling and Ross's eyes watered from the biting cold.

From Prada right down to Dolce & Gabbana, as though these were actually stations of the cross, with each requiring special prayer and meditation, Levy made his leisurely way down the street, until finally he entered a two-story building at the corner of Sixty-Ninth.

Clark, on the Levy side of the street, could only observe, through the plate glass door, that Levy climbed a flight of white marble stairs. He could not yet follow. Nor could he see the sign that was printed in gold on the second floor window.

Ross, across the street, could read it with ease. It read, in gold, Le Salon de Laval.

Ross watched as Clark very slowly opened the door and appeared to be reading from a plaque on the wall. Clark came out and crossed over to Ross.

"It's a hair salon," he said.

"I know." Ross was staring through the wide, clean window. They stood there together, watching it a while. Through it, they could see what looked like a line-up of pale green barber chairs whose sides faced the window and whose fronts faced what might have been a long bank of mirrors.

"Maybe he's getting a haircut," Ross said.

"You ever seen a barbershop with pale green chairs?"

"I believe I was joking, but I'm too cold to tell."

A few minutes later, Mr. Levy appeared in a pale green sweater with some scissors in his hand as an auburn-haired woman moved swiftly to a chair.

Levy ran gesticulating hands around her head, and then started to cut.

## 75

He had no illusions of great accomplishment. If everything he'd heard this morning were true, even truly explanatory, as tidy as it was or might turn out to be, in the realm of reality he was nowhere at all. Without any evidence, aside from a couple of hair strands at Tanner's and a thumb print at Kramer's, he didn't have anything to bring a D.A. If anything, the hard part was waiting to begin.

With nothing else to do, then, he drove around town if only because there was nothing else to do. Incuriously, he cruised around Hollywood Boulevard, passing the spot where the footprints and handprints of long-dead movie stars nestled in cement; had lunch at a delicatessen on La Brea; then drove down the coastal highway to Venice and inspected the boardwalk where fortune tellers clamored to tell him his fortune and girls, so alike that they seemed to be hot off the same production line, skateboarded by, and stands offered endless varieties of yogurt; drove up the highway and checked the Palisades, settled on a bench whose green wooden slats bore a beautifully hand-painted "No Smoking" sign, and lit a cigarette against an enemy wind. Looking

293

at the ocean, he briefly contemplated ruiners of bodies, and wondered which body now moldering in its grave had ruined the body of which vengeful witch. The closest he could get to that was Harri Kramer, but Harri seemed to settle on the self-wounding "M" side of hard S & M, and the image didn't quite seem to fit David Tanner.

He pulled out his iPhone and checked it for the time. It was only 1:30 (4:30 in New York) so he ferreted out the number of a Raven, Eric (MD, it turned out) on Central Park West, and discovered that it led him to an answering service, an actual person, who informed him that the doctor was "currently out of town and attending a medical convention in Paris." Brymmer thought of phoning Raven in Paris and warning him to shun any sudden *voulez-vous coucher avec moi*, but decided he was probably out of danger in Paris, if not entirely in New York. "So what kind of a doctor is he?" Brymmer asked. "Sir?" the woman said, "I'm just the answering service. I don't know that kind of thing." Swell, Brymmer said, and did the answering service know when the doctor was coming back? "In two weeks," she said, "I think." Brymmer left a message for the doctor to call him—to call him "day or night"— and as soon as he hit town.

It was now a quarter of two and he remained without purpose. He thought about calling Ross (an illusion of purpose) but decided that he wasn't in the mood for conversation and the Marrott story could wait. When he got to his car, he discovered a young couple was leaning against his fender, locked in embrace. The boy's cheap guitar was strapped to his shoulder, and the girl, whose arms were wrapped tightly around his neck, held a lighted joint in her hand. Brymmer could smell its pungent sweetness in the air and he wondered idly if they'd also found a pungent sweetness in each other.

"Sorry," he said softly as he opened the car door and the couple quite indifferently shrugged themselves apart and then instantly walked off in their opposite directions, neither one of them looking back

He drove through the long winding roads of Bel Air past a surfeit of mansions, had a drink at the Loggia at the Beverly Hills and, struck with his aimlessness, drove back to Hollywood, stopped at a liquor store for two fifths of Scotch— one Johnny Walker and one J&B— then parked at the precinct where he found Lieutenant Baker, asked him to keep a loose eye on Kate Marrott to be sure she stayed put, handed in his green "park anywhere" card, and vulnerably piloted back to the Alameda where he hung the little gift-wrapped bag of Johnny Walker on Ann Gray's doorknob. Just left it; no knock.

Back in his bedroom, he showered, stepped into a clean pair of briefs, lit a cigarette, poured himself a good stiff shot of J&B, and sprawled on the bed thinking about the long pointless evening ahead of him and how he could kill it. Looking down at the bottle, he decided that drowning was the most humane way.

There was knocking at his door.

He hollered, "Who is it?" and got, for an answer, "The girl next door. Open up," she said gaily, "in the name of the lawless."

He didn't have a robe but he figured, what the hell, they'd been naked last night, so he padded to the door and opened it a foot.

She stood looking up at him with mischievous eyes. She was dressed in white ducks and a loose v-neck sweater with the sleeves pushed up and she smelled of

295

something nice. Her hair was pulled over to the side in a braid and she was holding a shopping bag with lurid pictures of vegetables and fruits.

"Aside from thanks a hell of a lot for the booze, I wondered," she said, "if you were busy tonight or if you'd like to have dinner."

"I'd like to have dinner."

"Good. Then open up because we're going to have a picnic. I've got lovely pâté, with truffles and everything, and a pleasant white wine and some other good things."

"What'd you do— win the lottery?"

"The alimony check, pitiful as it is. Are you going to open up?"

She went straight to the kitchen area of the room and began to unpack.

He looked at her quizzically. "I'll put on some clothes."

"Uh-uh-uh! It's a come-as-you-are party, dear. In fact, I'll come as *you* are." And with one swift motion, she yanked off the sweater, under which was nothing but smooth round breasts, and wriggled out of the ducks to a white lace bikini. Then blithely continued unwrapping the groceries.

"Here," he said lightly, "let me help you with those." He moved up behind her and cupped both her breasts.

*"Those,"* she said, "don't require any help. And just for the record, they're a hundred percent mine."

"On loan," he said, "for the evening." His hand slid down across the well-muscled belly and started to descend. She playfully slapped it. "First we eat, naughty boy."

"Boy," he said. "I don't think I've ever been called a boy. Not even when I was a boy."

"Mmm. You were undoubtedly born mature."

"Oh bullshit," Brymmer said. "There was a time when if anything was absolutely knock-down dangerous and stupid, I'd be the first to do it."

"Is that how you got your... distinguishing marks?"

He laughed and said, "No, but I suppose that I could've. I used to do things like ride on the top of an elevated train and jump cars while it was moving. I once stole a Harley from a Hell's Angel."

"Death wish?"

"No. I was saying Fuck all. I'd already been 'distinguished' by the time I was eight which tends to limit your options. You can either try to join the closed club of the normal and you wind up, at best, being pitied or bullied or you say Fuck all and be dangerous and feared."

"Were you feared?"

"I don't know. But the Frankenface and Creature Feature bullshit ended. At least I was left alone."

She looked at him appraisingly. "So what made you change?"

"Who says that I changed? Except for the part about dangerously stupid."

"Tough-guy," she said. "I believe you're still tough but you're surprisingly gentle."

He laughed. "That opinion is not widely held."

"You hope."

He laughed again and then lit a cigarette. "All right," he said. "I'll tell you a story, if you like."

"Oh good," she said and grabbed the cigarette from his hand, took a drag and gave it back and then leaned against the counter.

He leaned against the wall. "Okay, so I'm just about turning seventeen and I decide to hit the road. So I steal twenty bucks, which I notice pretty fast doesn't get

297

you very far, so I decide I'm gonna burglarize a liquor store at night. I case it. Ideal. It's got a window on an alley and a rinky-dink alarm. I come back around midnight, crowbar in hand, make a fool of the alarm, make shards of the window and I'm halfway into it— head in the storeroom, legs dangling down, ass in the air and a voice says, 'Police. Hold it where you are.' I am smart enough to hold it. Turns out that the brother of the owner is a cop. Off duty at the time, came to check on the premises. So there I am, literally ass out the window and he says 'Hold it there.'"

She winced.

He shook his head. "What's the matter? This is funny."

"I was picturing the shards poking into your stomach."

"Get past it," Brymmer said. "I don't remember my descent but I remember there was sort of this courtyard in the rear. It was a hot August night and Mack, the officer, was coming off tour— his wife had just died— and maybe, I don't know, he might've just felt in the mood for conversation, but he sat me down on a garbage can and hollered, 'What the *fuck* did you think you were doing?' and I said, 'I was doing a half-assed burglary,' and I remember his saying, 'Well you've got a sense of humor,' to which I responded, 'No, but God does' and he looked at me and said 'Any kid who can say that may be due some salvation.' So he saved me," Brymmer said.

She was silent for a time. "That's a wonderful story," she said. "Is it true?"

"As it happens," Brymmer said. "And I'm getting pretty hungry." He reached for an olive.

"Well, darling, if you want to be demanding," she

298

said as she pulled out a long, thin loaf of French bread, "you can gather up a few of those chintzy little over-bleached Alameda bath towels and spread them on the bed for a picnic blanket and then when you're finished you can open up the wine."

"Yes ma'am," he said.

It was quite a fine feast, and not a vegetable in sight. He leaned against the headboard; she sat in a yoga position across from him and asked about his day and then asked him if he'd "seen my paw prints" on the Strip. He regretted that he hadn't. They'd been left there, she said, "a few truly unmentionable decades ago," in the summer of her prime. She'd been discovered, she explained, by a then-hot but now, alas, long-dead director; had even been featured on the cover of *Time* which had labeled her a reincarnation of Ava Gardner.

"I was such a little hick, I wasn't even quite sure who Ava Gardner was and I doubt I knew the meaning of reincarnation. *Now*, of course, I find I look forward to it."

"Oh? And what do you intend to come back as?" he said.

"I happen to have given it a great deal of thought and decided that I want to come back as a teapot."

He laughed. "Not a stable future in that. They're breakable."

"I know. But they're pemanently hot."

"I think you've got that part covered right now.— You know," he said, "it's hard to concentrate on food when I'm staring at your boobs."

"Then I'll distract you with conversation."

"Wanna bet?" he said.

She stuffed some pâté in her mouth, licked the rest

299

off her fingers. "Did you always work homicide?"

"Nobody always works homicide," he said. "I started in uniform like everybody else. But then pretty soon into it, the brass called me in. They wanted to train me for hostage negotiation." He shrugged. "I understood why they wanted me for that."

"Why?"

"Because most of the creeps who take hostages—even in a botched-up robbery, for example—they're mostly the kind of people think society's screwed them. They see themselves as victims. They'd look at me, they'd think they weren't talking to The Man but to another fellow victim. That I'd see their position. That I'd be sympathetic."

"And how about you? You ever *feel* like a victim?"

"Uh-uh. Only feel like an alien, maybe."

"Like someone coming down here from Krypton to save us?"

"Save you? No. Just to see if your planet's worth colonizing, though."

"Hmm." She cocked her head. "Are you allowed to cross-breed with us?"

"Any time you're ready."

She was much more than ready. She folded up the towel with the food still on it and tossed it to the floor and then bam! they were at it. She was hungry for everything. Like a cat, she growled, clawed, purred. She was playful. She made him laugh. Her abandon sparked his, and when they'd finished and lay groaning, she said to him happily, "Fun, wasn't it?"

"Fun," he said. "Yes." He'd never before had sex that was fun. Occasionally passionate, but mostly just a practical release of tension. But Ann Gray was very definitely fun.

300

"You know why?" she said.

"No. Why?"

"Because I want nothing more of you than this. And I also know you want nothing more of me either. Just a good ole rollicking roll in the hay. I made myself a vow that I will not go gently into sexual oblivion but I'm not at all inclined to fall in love again either. I've had four husbands, darling. Passion burns bright but it eventually burns out and then you're left with those squabbles about money and fidelity and finally with who forgot to pick up the laundry."

Eyes closed, body sated, Brymmer said, "Remind me, then, not to fall in love."

"Do you need some reminding?"

"I think so," he said. "God only knows I'm trying very hard not to."

"Well, I suppose it depends," Ann said. "Is she worth it, though?"

"Nobody's worth it," he said.

She was silent for a time. "Want to go another round?"

He looked at her. "God, you're an insatiable bawd. You want to give me a few minutes?"

"All right," she said tauntingly. "But life is short and gets shorter by the minute."

"Patience is a virtue."

She was silent again, lying on her side, curling into his chest. "I want you to know though," she said very softly, "that while I am, as you've noted, an insatiable bawd, I'm also a surprisingly selective one too. No reason for you to know that. But the fact is, I find you tremendously attractive. You have substance and depth. You have green eyes that know things, green things and black things, and competent hands, and a very fine body that's been riding rough weather. I like the way your voice sounds. I like the way you look. You're like a wild animal with exotic markings. Rather dangerously beautiful."

He squinted, sideways. "Jesus. You think that's a tad overdone?"

"Should I tell you it's a speech from a movie I was in?"

"I'd believe that," he said.

"I know. More's the pity."

When he finally got around to looking at his phone at six the next morning before he hit the airport, he found two messages.

The photoshopped picture of Felicia Martin had merited three thumbs-up ID's, from Alfie, Carmen and the dog-walking Ziegler.

And George Levy was Guy Laval.

## 76

*Friday, April 3rd:*

When Ross arrived at the station at four, he saw Brymmer on the porch, a cigarette gripped between his thumb and third finger as he squinted against the wind. He looked tired and dead-eyed and Ross could see the duffel bag resting at his feet. Ross climbed the stairs and said, "Batman returns."

Brymmer just nodded. "Flew all the way over on my own tangled webs."

"Just landed?"

"Uh-huh."

Ross lit a cigarette to be companionable. "All in all, was the Marrott thing productive?" he said.

"I guess that depends on what you mean by productive. You know how it is when you go to the doctor with a really bad cough and he asks 'is it productive?' and he means have you been coughing up a lot of bad junk?"

"Yeah."

"Well, she coughed up a lot of bad junk. Known as getting it off her chest."

"Was it useful?"

"We can dream."

"How was California otherwise?"

"Well, I had a very fine night last night and a totally disgusting plane ride this morning."

"The hand that giveth also taketh away."

"You've noticed that, have you.— Come on. Let's go in. I want to hear about Levy and I don't want to tell all the Marrott stuff twice."

With the expanded Task Force, Brymmer had eleven detectives on the tour, half of whom now sat waiting in the squad room which Brymmer'd commandeered. Waiting for the others, he repaired to his own digs where he poured a cup of overcooked coffee from the pot. Ross tried to read the expression on his face but found it unreadable. Knowing Brymmer, he knew that something not very wonderful was up and it was better not to ask. Yes, Ross thought, it was a "Don't ask," expression.

Dubisky seemed to lack the same God-given instinct for self-preservation. Dubisky looked at Brymmer and whistled. "Holy shit. You look like you died and forgot to get buried."

"Get fucked," Brymmer snapped. "My fuse at this moment is about this long." He indicated Nothing with clenched fingers.

Ross watched as Brymmer went over to his desk, tilted back in his chair and then briefly closed his eyes. He stayed in that position for several minutes as the squad room was filling. Then he stood up, looking totally composed, and strode into the room, took his place at the head of it, and essentially called the meeting to order.

"Okay," he said, "I clearly haven't read the reports so I may ask a few of you to fill me in now. But I'll start with Kate Marrott. Basically, the Rogers story is confirmed. Only let's not forget that it's that: a story. I'll try to break it down into usable components of which there are few. Let's start with the fact that our coven of Jackies first met at the Levy-Laval salon."

There were murmurings in the room.

"That's the major bombshell, though the guys tailing Levy may have figured that out. And I hope the rest of you are up on Levy. Yes?"

There was nodding.

"Andrea Clawson. According to Marrott, she was not only there on the—what shall we call it? That Fateful Afternoon? but she initiated the plot. Or the game. Or conspiracy, or whatever you want to call it. That she was there, we can prove from the records at the shop. According to Marrott, it was Andrea who said she'd get an outside partner. So Andrea's the link to the missing outsider and the missing outsider most likely killed Clawson. If," Brymmer said, "we go along with the story. And finally, Andrea Clawson is a red-head. Auburn."

"And what the hell's auburn?" Rickler asked.

"Dark red. Like a horse." Brymmer looked around. "I invite speculation, only hold it till I'm done. Felicia. Kate identified Felicia from her picture. Again, we can eventually confirm that from records. And the tale Felicia told on that lovely afternoon comports with what we know. The rest of what we've got on Felicia means zip. She can either deny she was ever at Starrett's bar, or rig up an alibi, or say she was there, which has nothing at all to do with her killing him later. As for later, we've got the word of an unreliable coke-head who saw her momentarily on the street in the dark and I wouldn't try to sell that as evidence to an infant let alone a D.A.

"Finally, there's Nora. Who's likely in the costume department of the Met. The museum. Again, we can track her from that— and that's somebody's assignment— but again, that's it. We can likely learn the names of the other participants by checking the salon. Or eventually, with luck, their credit card records. But again, that's it. Except for those nice clear fingerprints at Kramer's and the hairs in Tanner's hand, we got nothing but a story."

Brymmer took a quick short hit of his coffee.

"Kate," he said. "I think she was likely playing a game and she was probably showing off. She's a rather plain woman and she'd just lost her job. So there she is, sitting with a lot of attractive women who she figures are well-off. I speculate she figures that the only real trading cards she's got are her brains and her arena of special knowledge. So she starts showing off. She tells them about street cameras and how to avoid them. She tells them how to laser-kill an elevator cam. She tells them what a Crime Scene Unit would be looking for and where they'd take a look. She warns them about fingerprints. She tells them about bleach. And finally,

305

she gives them the brilliant idea about planting the blonde hair. She says she got the gimmick from an episode on the show. So in other words, Kate becomes the bridge to realization. I believe she didn't mean to, but that's what I think it is."

There was silence; each man diving into his own head, asking questions, making links.

"I want to move on to Levy but I'll open up the floor and get your thoughts up till now or any input you want to add."

Again restrained silence.

Jim Reed, from Ritter's group, said, "I want to get it straight then. Whoever murdered Clawson was Andrea's outside man. Or I mean outside woman."

"Or man," Brymmer said.

Matson looked at Reed and said, "No. I don't get it."

"Think about it, Joe." Brymmer studied the man's face. Last night's drinking was written across his nose. This morning's tie stain was scribblings from an egg. Brymmer felt a sudden crude sympathy for the man. He'd never been smart but he was slipping into stupid. Also growing old. And fat. And scared. As Brymmer himself could grow old, fat and scared. And perhaps even dumb. "If Andrea made a personal swap with, say, X, then X killed Clawson. For Andrea. Right? And then Andrea's obliged to kill Y in exchange. For X. Okay?"

"Okay," Matson said. "But in that case, is Andrea's victim one of the dead guys, or somebody not dead?"

"You mean 'yet,'" Brymmer said.

"Yeah. What I meant."

"I believe," Brymmer answered, "he's among the already dead."

"You mean Tanner," Ross said.

"Yep. But I remain wide open to other thoughts."

"No," Kerner said. "It's Tanner."

"Which, I think, makes a segue into Levy. Mister Levy-Laval. Clark? What do you know?"

"Okay so we know that he's one in the same person. His salon's got a website. Picture of Levy there says Guy Laval."

"So I guess it's like a stage name or something," Brymmer said. "How long has he been Laval?"

"Since he started doing hair."

"Which is?"

"About fifteen years ago, I think. He was *George* Laval for a time. He didn't become a Guy until he opened his own shop."

"How long ago?"

Clark took a look at his own notes. "Two years ago July. He's the sole proprietor. Backed the place himself and his credit is down the tubes. That's from public information. Pays his bills on a corporate account signed Laval but his personal bank accounts are still in his own name."

"So's the lease on his apartment," Kerner threw in, "which is why, in the building, they still call him Levy."

"Refresh me," Brymmer said, "on why the lease calls him Levy."

"Easy," Kerner said. "He moved in with his daddy when he chickened out of Dartmouth and exchanged it for beauty school. Daddy, thinking forward, put Georgy on the lease. So when daddy kicked off about a year-and-a-half later, Georgy got to keep the apartment at a steal. Stabilized. He only pays twelve-hundred bucks, he's got six fuckin rooms. Which is reason enough to stay Levy, I suppose."

"Only daddy kicks off and he becomes George

Laval."

"No. He releases his *inner* George Laval. Free at last, free at last."

"Until we nail him," Brymmer said. "What else? We got anything else on Mr. Levy?"

Hamilton, from the team that had worked on McConnell, put a finger in the air. "Yeah. Before he split off and opened his own place, he was employed as a stylist at Alfred of New York. When he left, he stole clients. There's a lot of bad blood."

"Where'd you get that? You talk to Mr. Alfred?" Brymmer said.

"Nope. I just googled. There was gossip in the news. I figured maybe hairdresser guys are like a club and someone else up at Alfred's might tip Levy off there's a cop asking questions."

"Good," Brymmer said. "Because I'm thinking right now that the last thing we do— and I mean very literally, the *last thing*— is to wise Levy up. Before we get to Levy, I want to have a warrant— for his home and for his shop. So I want to hold off on even looking at his records, his appointment book and such. I want him feeling safe. In fact, I wouldn't mind a little leak to the press that we're nowhere on the case."

"All right," Matson said, "I'll buy I'm the designated dummy in the room, but what's cute about Levy? Why's the guy cute?"

"Because," Brymmer said, "there's some buzzing in my head that he looks pretty likely to be Andrea's partner. He's someone, and possibly the *only* someone who she saw between playing the witchy little girl-game and heading out of town for her alibi weekend. Which could mean he killed Clawson. Clawson's the only guy who didn't have sex. In fact, there were no signs of lady there at all except the fucking blonde hairs. Which could come from his salon. Levy's credit was shaky? Makes the link even better. So maybe she offered to pay him for the job. For Andrea, the difference was thirty-eight mil between Clawson alive and Clawson departed."

Brymmer, now beginning to pace around the room, looked at Clark and said, "At least that's a reasonable motive. From there, you can turn it the other way around. What's Tanner to Levy? Okay, to begin with, he's the boy next door. Two doors down the hall. So what's up with that? Were they sometime lovers? Or did Levy make a pass and get told to buzz off? How stable is Levy? I'd like to find out." Brymmer looked at Ross. "Any whichway you can.

"And then there's logistics. Levy gives a party. People are recorded going up to his floor, but nothing says they have to remain in his apartment. Even *be* in his apartment. In fact, the whole party itself could be a cover. Someone slips out, takes care of Tanner's business and slips back in. Or doesn't. I don't know. But I'd speculate the Someone would be Andrea Clawson. The redhead. Who left a little hair in Tanner's hand. And then there's the Formalin. Levy bought the Formalin on January second. Clawson lost his penis on January first."

"Oh," Matson said. "Yeah."

"It's not 'yeah.' I just wrote a movie. I made up a plot. See what happens? I spend a few minutes in Hollywood, I want to write a script. I don't know if it's bullshit. I don't know if the entire bullshit is bullshit and we're up the wrong tree. I work with what we've got and this is what we've got. And we don't have a fucking thing to back it up. So even if it's true, it could simply be a movie. A story in our heads. And the story, even as a story, has holes. So. Okay.— What's the plan," Brymmer said.

He drank some more coffee and knuckled at his jaw. "We got a couple of potentials we could match for DNA. If we had some DNA we could match the stuff *to*. So let's start with Felicia. Stu— you want to get some Felicia DNA?"

"That's depending," Kurtz said, "on the way you want it got."

"Preferably," Brymmer said, "in a way you'll stay alive."

"And if not," Dubisky added, "we can scrape it off your shorts."

Kurtz shot a look at him as Brymmer eyed McAllister. "Brian? Look again at those elevator shots. On the night of that party."

"At Levy's? Oh shit."

"I know. Except this time you're looking for Andrea. Abe? Take a closer look at Levy's credit. Let's see if it's improving." He paused, lit a cigarette and looked around the room. "Let's learn about Nora. Let's look for Woman Five."

Corelli said, "Andrea Clawson's back in town."

"You been reading the *Post* again?"

"Yeah, and I'm putting in expenses for it too."

"Let's watch her, then. I'd like to know her ties, if any, to Felicia Martin. As well as to Levy. I'd also like to grab a little chunk of DNA. Put it up against the hair." He looked around the room again at grim, tired faces. "Look," he said, "at least we've stopped shooting in the dark." He sighed his own weariness. "All right, then. I'm done. So anyone who's got something new to report here, get ready, you're on.—Reggie? Go ahead..."

## 77

At nine, on a scheduled break for dinner, Brymmer and Ross were at the Arizona Zoo. Brymmer, like an actor who's just left the stage, had reverted, Ross thought, to the pre-meeting Brymmer—gone in a moment from commanding presence to stony absence. Settled at a table, they each ordered burgers, fries and a beer, after which Ross immediately launched.

"Okay," Ross said, "I presume the 'fine night' meant you slept with a movie star so let's just skip that and get to what's eating you which has to have something to do with the flight which you said was disgusting and the only thing that happened between last night and now."

"Who says something's eating me?"

"I don't know. Possibly the look in your eyes that says Mess with me, you're dead, or maybe it's the way you took off on Dubisky."

Brymmer shook his head. "Nothing's eating me."

"Right."

"I'm just tired, that's all. But mess with me, you're dead."

The waitress came, setting down the beers on the table.

Brymmer took a sip and then let out an "Aaah."

Ross cocked his head. "So tell me what's *not* bothering you, then."

Brymmer said nothing. Drank. Shrugged. "I had a bad plane seat. Aisle. With my lovelier side facing traffic. About halfway over Kansas, as I'm drifting off to sleep, a four year old kid starts thundering down the aisle screaming 'Mommy, mommy, that man is scary.' This does not happen once, this is back and forth constantly for twenty-some minutes where the kid runs

311

up to me, coming from behind, shrieks, runs away, and during which time, of course, everybody turns to observe the scary man. The mother does nothing. The flight is a cattle car, the stews are all busy about three miles away. Finally, I grab the little brat by the wrist and say 'Listen, this is catching. If you don't stay as far away from me as you can, this could happen to you and you'll be scarier than me.' Little bugger bugs off, screaming all the way. Biddy across the aisle leans over now and hollers, 'That wasn't very nice of you. He's only a child.' I respond to her politely, 'And fuck you too.' She rings for the stewardess. 'That man said something obscene to me,' she says. I say to the stewardess, 'She's got a dirty mind. All I said was Good luck to you. Aside from which—' I flash the shield at her covertly— 'I'm an on-duty cop and does she really want to luck with me?' Stewardess laughs. Even says, 'If I were you, I would've throttled the little brat and I'm sorry I couldn't help you, an old lady was throwing up' and she turns to the biddy and tells her she misheard. Nonetheless, I get the sightseers cruising me for an hour like an epidemic of dysentary has just hit the plane and everybody suddenly needs to take a crap, except once they get to the bathroom they suddenly remember that they didn't need to go. Meanwhile, the biddy is discussing me loudly with the neighboring seats and doing Freud imitations.—That's it," Brymmer said.

"Didn't bother you at all."

"Nope. Not me. Just another little anecdote."

"Well...you're a better man than I am. I dunno. I'd've—"

"What? Just name me any something you'd've done that wouldn't've made you look like a bully or a clown or, to use a rather clumsy metaphor, 'thin-skinned'?"

Ross thought it over and shrugged. "I guess. I guess what I'd've done is pretended to be asleep."

"Bingo."

"And did you? I mean, get some sleep?"

"I was too pissed to sleep. By now, I haven't slept in maybe sixty-two hours."

"I see," Ross said. "Not that I'm in charge of the duty charts or anything but why don't you knock off and go drink yourself to sleep."

"Because," Brymmer said, and couldn't think of a reason. "Yeah," he said, nodding, "that's a decent idea."

The burgers arrived. Brymmer looked at the waitress, pointed at the contents of his plate and said, "Bag it," as though he were talking about criminal evidence.

From the table, Ross watched him as Brymmer got a cab, and wondered how he'd feel if he were in Brymmer's shoes. Or more aptly, in his face. Or even more aptly, *behind* his face. Watching the world watch him. Carrying whatever those scars signified. Once Ross had asked him on a mellow evening, "So how'd that happen?" and Brymmer'd grown tight and said "Don't ever ask," as though it were something that Brymmer was ashamed of or something that had permanently battered his pride. It was pride that held Brymmer together, Ross thought; that, and a natural sense of irony. He didn't understand why the plane thing had reached him when so little else did, but maybe everything did and he just refused to show it. Or maybe it was just because he hadn't had sleep. You could know someone well and even know someone long and never really understand what was ticking in his head. Not unless he told you and Brymmer never did.

313

## 78

"Hi. Welcome home."

"Mmm. Uh-huh. How'd you know I was away?"

"I thought you were a hotshot detective or something. If you are, you could probably tell me how I'd know."

"There are only two ways. The first or the second. Which was it?"

"The first."

"And what was the report?"

She laughed. "You're so good. You realize that you didn't give anything away."

"That's why I'm a hotshot detective," Brymmer said. "Even when I'm plowed."

"She said you were nice. But scary. But nice."

"Scary," Brymmer said. "How scary?"

"Not much."

"Well I meant... scary how?"

"She's scared about having to testify. Or worse."

"Uh-huh."

"And you're not giving anything away."

"At Christmas," he said, "I give to animal shelters and curbside Santas. That's about it."

"I gather that you kept me out of it."

"I did."

"Thank you."

"My pleasure."

"Hmmm. Am I waking you? You sound kind of fuzzy."

"Did I mention I was plowed."

"Oh. I guess. Do you want me to hang up?"

"Not particularly, no. I like the sound of your voice."

"Oh. Okay. I'm not sure what to say."

"Say anything you like. You could talk about the weather."

"Okay. So how was the weather in California?"

"Sunny."

"Good. Did you get a nice tan?"

"I can't get a tan. Sun makes the scars turn uglier and redder."

"You know, they're really not so ugly as you think."

"Oh yes they are."

"You're much too self-conscious, that's all."

"Right. You walk around with raw hamburger meat smeared on your face, people tend to make you get conscious of yourself."

"They look at you."

"That, or else they pointedly don't. You can't imagine how many conversations I have where people talk to my shirt, to my hair, to that fascinating spot just beyond my left shoulder. I happen to look away and their eyes zip furtively over to my face and if I happen to look back, their eyes zip away as though I've caught them in the act of doing something dirty. It doesn't bother me. Occasionally I find it amusing. Mostly it's just tiring."

"And so you withdraw."

"It's a whole lot simpler than an eye-wresting match. Sweet Jesus, I'm a fucking Rorschach, I am. Frightening children. Dangerously beautiful. I'd just, for one fucking day of my fucking life, like to fucking be...uch." He stopped. He'd forgotten where he might have been going. He was suddenly conscious of his own heavy breath; it rasped.

"Be what?"

"I don't know. Just be. Buzz-buzz."

"Ohmydear."

"And don't fucking oh-my-dear me."

"I'm sorry."

"Don't fucking I'm-sorry me either."

"I love you."

"Don't." He mumbled Goodnight and then hung up the phone. And then lay there for a while. Even in a sodden alcoholic haze, he was aware that he'd just been a total asshole.

He called her right back.

"Yes."

"I'm sorry."

"Hey, it's okay."

"I'm not usually...whatever the hell I just was."

"It's really okay."

"No. It's embarrassing. Could you please just forget that we had this conversation?"

"I will if you will."

"I will. I have. I don't even remember what I'm sorry about. I am so fucking plowed."

"Then let yourself sleep."

"Yeah. Good idea."

"Goodnight then."

"Yeah."

## 79

*Saturday April 4th:*

*New York Post, Cardin's Corner:*

### IS BRYMMER'S TASK FORCE
### UP TO THE TASK?

#### by Pete Cardin

It's been over 4 months since the first of the serial "Jackie" killings and according to a source within the PD, the police are absolutely "nowhere at all." Except for a belief that the killer is a blonde, the "Dickless Tracy's," as somebody called them, haven't got a clue...

The Captain said, "Who the fuck ratted this shit?"

"I did," Brymmer said. "I had Corelli do it. He and Cardin are drinking buddies."

"Well His Honor's pissed off."

"Tough," Brymmer said.

"Dickless Tracy's," Parisi said. "Corelli come up with that?"

"No. I think Cardin pulled it out of his own ass."

"Thing is," Parisi said, "I gotta pull some more dicks, in a manner of speaking. Your force is down to thirty? I gotta pull a few more. All your legwork's done anyway."

"Mostly," Brymmer said.

"All you got is this cockamamie swap story, right?"

"Mostly," Brymmer said. "I got some usable evidence at three of the scenes and a lot of circumstantial."

"And a nickel," Parisi said. "Has it occurred to you we might never wrap this at all?"

"Constantly," Brymmer said. "It keeps me awake."

"Good. Then just don't fall asleep on the job."

# 80

*Sunday, April 5th:*

"Hi."

"Well, hi."

"It's Burt."

"Oh gee. As though I wouldn't recognize your voice."

"I just wanted to tell you—and I probably shouldn't but I know you're concerned— that I did find Kate—"

"Oh?"

"—and I kept you out of it."

"Oh... Thanks....Actually..."

"What?"

"Actually, she called me the afternoon you met."

"Oh. Figures. So what did she have to say?"

"She's worried that she might get charged with conspiracy."

"Oh."

"And you still won't tell me if she will."

"What do you mean 'still'?"

Silence; a pause. "Nothing."

"What?"

She sighed. "I am just so bad at playing games. The thing is, we already had this conversation. The night you got back. I called you."

"I'm blank."

"You said you were drunk."

"Was I making any sense?"

"Oh yeah. You strung sentences together like a pro."

"Was I nasty?"

"No."

"Well...you sound...odd. You have company or something?"

"No. I've got a cold. I don't mean to sound odd."

"Hey look, if you think I'm alcoholic—"

"I don't."

"I'm insomniac is all. I get all keyed up and then I can't key down. It's usually— why am I bothering you with this?"

"I don't know. Because we're friends?"

"Ah. Okay. So that's what we are. So listen, friend, your information was very helpful."

"Is it getting you anywhere?"

"Well...put it this way: Don't believe everything you read in the papers.—How about you? What've you been up to?"

"Me? I was covering that bludgeoning in Queens."

"Guy did his wife?"

"With a cleaver. On the street. Queens Boulevard, yet, and in broad daylight. So how's that for crazy?"

"Brilliant. He's gonna plead temporary insanity. Rage defense. Caught her in bed with his brother."

"So why doesn't he take out his rage on the brother?"

"You asking me? Or just being silly out loud."

"And why is that silly?"

"Because how would I know and why would you care? He clocked her with a cleaver. End of report."

"But why only her?"

"He's Serbian, for one thing. Those people have codes. His brother is family. Besides, the way he sees it, it's his wife who betrayed him."

"See? That's an answer."

"No. It's a story. It won't be an answer till he tells you with his mouth and that presumes he's not lying and presumes he even knows. But as long as you're happy..."

"Actually I'm sneezy and you're definitely grouchy."

"If you're talking the Seven Dwarfs, then you have to mean Grumpy. There wasn't any Grouchy."

"Wanna bet?"

"Five bucks."

"Should I look it up now?"

"No. Put your talents to a more constructive use. You want me to explain to you the Serbian mindset? Explain to me Jackie. How does that work?"

"Now it's you being silly."

"I was being Socratic."

She laughed. "You're always interesting to talk to, you know. You say 'clocked with a cleaver.' Then you say 'Socratic.' I suppose it means you're trying to teach me through questions?"

"Actually, I'm teaching myself through questions. I was thinking out loud."

"Well...they're psychotic."

"Yeah. Except the chances of five psychotic women just happening to converge in a beauty parlor waiting room are passingly slim. So it gets us back to relatively usual women. So how does that work?"

"And how would I know?"

"Well, you know Kate."

"But Kate didn't do it. She wouldn't ever do it."

"Okay, then just play. You've been talking to women like Jackie all your life. They get together over drinks in those after-work bars and they talk about the worst bastards in their lives and the lengths of their dicks. You understand women. I understand murder but I only understand it when it's hot or when it's cold or when it's just plain indifferent. But Jackie's something else. The crime is a rage crime, but none of the Jackies are actually enraged. At least not at their victims. So there's cold calculation but a hot bloody crime. So how does that work? I'm not asking for a why, I'm asking for a how. If the Jackies are relatively, functionally normal, how do they pull it off?"

"Well... give me time."

"I'm free for another hour."

"What's happening then?"

"Work. Second tour."

"You work all the time?"

"I'm working right now."

"Oh." A long silence. "Okay. So how's this? Say it's a spy movie. World War Two. Jackie's been working for the French resistance or— what did they used to call the CIA?"

"The OSS."

"Right. She goes to bed with a Nazi colonel and she does the same thing. Okay, so it's grizzly, but she feels very good. She's accomplished something. She doesn't have a reason to have a bad conscience. She's proud of herself. She goes on with her life."

Now Brymmer was silent. He lit a cigarette. "So," he said finally, "you're saying it's a war and that men are the enemy."

"A lot of women think so."

"And what's the war about?"

"I really wouldn't know. I'm a non-combatant. But I think what they want is, they want you to surrender. And instead they get a fight. Offensive maneuvers. Evasive action."

"And taking the penis is a war souvenir."

"I hadn't thought of it like that but, yeah. It's been done. The Viet Cong did it, didn't they?"

"You want to join the squad?"

"No thanks. I prefer my bodies to be warm."

"Listen. You need any orange juice or something?

I could leave it with your doorman."

"Uh-uh. I'm fine."

"Yes. You are. Fine," Brymmer said.

## 81

*Monday, April 6th:*

Alfred of New York was housed in a three-story geometrical building with a lopsided pie wedge cut from the front. Art Deco in design, it sat proudly at the corner of 74th and Madison, looking as it did back in 1931, thanks to the insistence of the New York City Landmarks Preservation Commission.

The entry had a thick, cream-colored carpet patterned with big black Art Deco "A's." A black and white poster of a man and woman, both looking angular, sexless and bored was hung on the wall by the side of a counter with English hairbrushes (200 bucks) and a girl with some short geometrical hair. Her lips were the color of dried blood.

Ross had made a haircut appointment with Alfred— with Alfred Himself— which only took a week on account of a cancellation. He'd previously checked out the Alfred website and knew that he was in for a three-bill tab just for getting a trim but then the New York City taxpayers, who'd ultimately foot the bill, would be getting the benefit of one very spiffy-looking, well-barbered cop. In actual fact, Ross's hair was too shaggy and spilling on his collar so a trim was past due.

He'd given his own name when he'd made the appointment, so he told the girl, "Ross. For Alfred."

She consulted a registry. "You've only booked a cut." Really cool British accent.

"Yeah, that's right."

"I believe you'll need a styling."

"How much is a styling?"

"A styling," she said, "comes to four-sixty-five." She gave him the edge of a slow, raking glance that was meant to imply that if Ross had to ask, then he couldn't afford it and as such he should just stop wasting her bloody time. "Of course," she said, "that includes a wash and a blow."

Ross squinted.

*"Drying,"* she added with a horizontal mouth. "Any follow-up trims, of course, would be less."

"Whatever," Ross said. "Whatever Alfred thinks."

While he waited (a total of twenty-five minutes, also being paid for with taxpayer sweat) he thought about pumping the geometric lady, but decided against it. She did not look chatty and, besides, her telephone was constantly alive, people all over clamoring to take advantage of a $300 haircut with a blow job thrown in for a mere pittance more.

Finally, he was ushered into Alfred's sanctum: black marble counter, black leather chair, a silver-framed mirror with dressing-table lights. Alfred himself was a slim-hipped fifty with carefully teased hair and an animated face. Dressed entirely in black. His working space was shared with a black-clad slim-hipped, but much younger man who was artfully trimming the remaining fringe of hair on the head of some head of a corporation.

As Ross took the seat, Alfred appraised his reflection in the mirror. "You look slightly familiar." He squinted at the image. "Seems to me I've seen you on television recently."

Ross had, in fact, been on television recently. Defending the task force and its work on the case.

"Not recently," Ross said. "But I used to play a cop on *Living on the Edge.* You ever watch that show?"

"In fact." Alfred smiled. "You were...what's the guy's name?"

"Yeah, *that* one," Ross said. "And then, a few years ago, I used to be a customer. I saw, uh, Laval."

"Mmp." Alfred stiffened. "I see. Were you dissatisfied? I mean that you haven't come back in a while?"

"Not exactly," Ross said. "I've been living on the coast. I came back to audition and that's why I'm here. See, this is my problem. They're doing a revival of *Barefoot in the Park* and I'm up for the lead. You know who played the part in the original? Redford. So the thing is, I want to get styled like Redford. Redford then, not now."

"Hmm," Alfred said. "I'm trying to picture...Ah." He moved over to a laptop computer, typed a few clues, and came up with a photo of Robert Redford, circa 1963. "Yes," he said, "yes. You want to keep a little shag and that...thing in the front. All right. Let's go."

Ross closed his eyes as the scissors click-clicked, then he opened them again, getting hair in his eye. "So," he asked casually, "what happened to Laval?"

Alfred exchanged a quick look with his countermate who tittered as he carefully dusted off the neck of the head of the undoubtedly venal corporation.

"Officially— tilt your head back, please— officially, he quit."

The corporate baldie handed several crisp bills to the trimmer-of-his-fringe and duster-of-his-neck and departed from the scene.

"And less than officially?"

"We had to let him go." Ross felt the rumblings of a major Ah-hah! that was about to befall him and would obviate the need for the elaborate fabrications he'd been planning as a wedge.

"How so?" he asked, playing just the right amount of interest.

"Complaints," Alfred said. "Well, one complaint really but one was quite enough. George—" he said, "you did know his real name was George?—got frisky with a customer."

"Frisky," Ross said. "That could mean a lot of things."

"George—" Alfred said, "please turn to your right— George, as he started to get a little older and not quite the red-hot mama of the bars, seemed to compensate by using the workplace as a bar."

"He made a pass at a customer?"

"No, nothing quite so crude as all that. Poor George. The customer in question was married. George has a talent for breaking his own heart. Of course the customer was a hunk." Alfred looked at the countermate who lounged on the counter. "Wouldn't you say so, Kitty?"

"A hunk," Kitty said.

"So they had a little thing. George, when he wanted to, could be quite— how would you describe that, Kitty?"

"Compelling."

"You see? Out of the mouths of babes tumble words like 'compelling.' Well, George could be that. But as far as the *customer* knew, it was just a thing. A little time out of time. Discreet. A few months. A little midsummer madness. Only, George fell in love."

"Poor George," Kitty said. "He could be such a schmuck."

"He started calling the man at home. He declared

his intentions to marry the man too. In his head, George was planning the announcement in the *Times*, the registry at Tiffany's and Bed, Bath and Beyond, and the honeymoon in Hawaii."

"Really, such a schmuck," Kitty added with a smirk.

"All done," Alfred said. "Now look at yourself in the mirror. Is that a *voila* or is that a *voila*?"

Ross looked at himself in the mirror. He saw that he had bangs.

"Very nice," Ross said, hoping he could comb the fucking things back.

"Now Kitty here will wash and then we'll come back and blow."

"Wait a second," Ross said. "How does the story end?"

"Oh, yes. He complained. He said George had been causing him a great deal of trouble when he phoned and hung up which was leading his lovely wife to believe he was fooling around which he didn't believe he was. George was just something in another compartment."

"Or closet," Kitty said.

"By that time of course, he'd stopped seeing George, but George wouldn't let go. He obsessed. That's the word for it, isn't it, Kitty?"

"Deranged," Kitty said.

"Yes, I believe that's the word the man used. He said George had undoubtedly misjudged the whole thing. His marriage, he told me, was the bedrock of his life which, in context, I presumed meant his marriage bed was rocky, but that's another story. He was threatening to sue. *Me*, for heaven's sake. For not reining George in. So of course I let him go. I believe there were two other similar episodes in poor George's life. Now off to the sink with you."

Ross then obediently went to the sink. He had to lean backwards on a black marble bowl while Kitty slimed his head with something viscous and icy that smelled vilely of lavender which Kitty said was also "aromatheraputic." He also told Ross that his actual name was Kitridge. "My last name," he said, "but my first name is really so odiously boring, I tell people to call me Kitty."

"So tell me," Ross said, looking up at the underside of Kitty's smooth chin, "did George find happiness? I mean, did he ever find a more-likely...friend?"

"I wouldn't know," Kitty said. "We have some mutual acquaintances. One of them told me George was ga-ga again. Some muscle-man type. Honestly, George is as luckless as the straights. George falls in love. Most of us, you know— as Madonna once put it— most of us girls just want to have fun."

"Muscle-man, huh."

"I think he works at some gym."

Ross took a breath. "Let's Get Physical," he said.

"Was that a proposition?"

"Sorry," Ross said. "Was that the name of the gym?"

"Yeah. Yeah I think that's the place," Kitty said.

A towel now descended on Ross's wet head and he was sent back to Alfred for the hundred-dollar blow.

---

## 82

It was 3:57 when Brymmer hit the squad room and crossed to his desk which faced towards the arch. Reports had already piled up from first tour or were being typed now. Corelli, as always, moved his lips when he typed. He caught Brymmer watching him and snapped at him, *"What?"* Brymmer mouthed *I love you*, and lit a cigarette before turning to the files.

FORM PD 313-081A
COMPLAINT FOLLOW UP        COMPLAINT: —03065
Homicide, DavidTanner w/m

FILED BY:    Det. A. Dubisky Shield # 4672, MHTF

SUBJECT:    Financial status, George Levy aka Guy Laval

Without Cause for a warrant to check subject's bank, at 1110 hrs on 4/6, accompanied by Det. C. Clark, I went to the offices of Burnham Realty, 1247 Avenue/Americas, owner of the building where Levy rents business space on Madison Avenue.

There, we interviewed Robert L. Markowitz, the managing agent. Markowitz stated that subject (Laval) was behind in his rent, making partial payments since the fall of last year, but had paid up in full on January 12th. The amount was $85,000.

At 1300 hrs. same date, accompanied by Clark, traveled to Buy-Rite Beauty in the Bronx, 1407 Jerome Avenue, a wholesale distributor of products for salons.

There, we interviewed Gladys Cooper-Jones in the accounting dept who told a parallel story. Levy paid up a delinquent account ($1800) on January 12th.

Investigation continues. Case open.

Gotcha, Brymmer thought. He now had a probable cause to get a warrant to inspect Levy's bank. Or to add Levy's personal and business accounts to the items in the warrants he'd eventually get. He wondered how they'd done it. Without Kate's advice about laundering money, had they really had the balls to do a straight-forward deal? Hard money in the bank? And still, he was aware that he was counting fictive chickens; that the eggs could be goose eggs.

Corelli dumped a short printout on his desk. "I *like* you," Corelli said. "It goes no further." He turned and walked away. Brymmer checked the report.

FORM PD 313-081A
COMPLAINT FOLLOW UP          COMPLAINT: ——04829
                             Homicide, Wm McConnell w/m

FILED BY:    Det. Anthony Corelli, Shield # 7654, MHTF

SUBJECT:    Nora Latham, alleged mistress of victim

Various record checks show:
Subject, age 36, b. Moline, IL; SSN 376-26-8894,
Residence: 345 E. 74th St. Manh. 10021, Apt 12L
Employed: Met Museum, Head of Research, Costume Dept.
Records/licenses:
    DMV Lic. #S2021447131. Car: none registered;
    Marriage/ divorce: none registered;
    NYC Substitute Teaching License #660717 (elapsed);
Police records: Victim, gang rape (see file attached).

Brymmer read the attached file. Then he got up and followed Corelli who was putting on his coat and said, "Teacher's license."

"So?" Corelli said. "Two-year license. Elapsed about fifteen years ago. So?"

"So? So her fingerprints didn't elapse. You have to get printed to get a license."

"Oh."

"Oh."

"You want me to—"

329

"Right. Run a match with those nice clear prints from Harri's bed."

"Ah."

"Ah. Also take a look for any parking tickets there. You know what neighborhood, you know what night."

Brymmer stubbed his cigarette and reread the file. Then he made a phone call. Then he made another one. Then he went out.

Sadie O'Grady weighed 180 pounds and stood five-foot-two behind the counter of her bar which at five in the afternoon on Avenue D wasn't doing a lot of business.

"You said on the phone that it's something about Nora Latham," Sadie said. "That was, what now? seventeen years ago, right?"

"Close," Brymmer said.

"So why's it hot now?"

"Her attacker—well, one of her attackers— got sprung. Got pumped out of Auburn and he's back on the streets. According to reports, you were with her that night. Called the cops. Went with her in the ambulance."

"Yeah."

"So I just want to get a few facts on the case. I thought better from you than intruding on Nora.— By the way. Have you been in touch with her at all?"

"Oh no. She moved on. If anything, I'd remind her of— well... of a lot of things she'd like to forget. Hold on," she said. "Will you?"

Brymmer watched as Sadie slid a Miller's to a guy at the other end of the bar. Brymmer pegged her age as being something above seventy and noted that she'd still kept the pretense of red hair and then wondered if she'd once been a flaming beauty.

"So," she said, returning. "Can I get you something to drink?"

"How about a Coke?"

Brymmer watched the guy with the beer light a smoke. Sadie watched him watching the guy light the smoke.

"You're not gonna bust me for that," she said, "are you?"

"How about a Coke and an ashtray?" Brymmer said.

Sadie laughed. "Coming up," and pressed a spigot for the Coke as she handed him a well-used grimy-looking saucer. "So what do you want to know?"

"The story," Brymmer said. "How'd you get to know Nora?"

"She applied for a job. I had a bar then, my husband and me, on the Bowery. The Bowery back then wasn't classy like now. It was half skid row and a quarterways hip. CBGB's was two blocks away. They were into doing punk, so we thought we'd do jazz. New Orleans, you know. Brassy. Loud. For a while, we guessed right. We got the kids coming in, and the jazz fiends who weren't too scared of the nabe. Anyway, Nora was a college kid herself. Working her way."

"Through where?"

"NYU."

"And how would you describe her?"

"Describe her what way?"

"Any way you like."

"Outgoing. Not really pretty. Had style. Used to make her own clothes. Told me she was thinking about leaving NYU and then trying F.I.T. That's the Fashion Institute. Decided that she'd like to be a dress designer maybe."

Brymmer lit a cigarette. Sadie did too.

"Go on," Brymmer said. "So what happened that night?"

"She left with some guy. The one that got jailed."

"Robert Jackson," Brymmer said. "Did she know him?"

"Oh sure. Like for twenty-five minutes? He was cute then, I'll say."

"Did she often leave with guys?"

"Didn't often get the chance. Like I say, she was cheerful but she wasn't any fox."

"Go on."

"You don't mind, I'm gonna come around the front, sit down. I got a bunion. Me, that used to dance until dawn in those shoes like canoes. Pointy in the front. That's what gives you a bunion."

Sadie sat down and shared the ashtray with Brymmer.

"That night..." Brymmer prompted.

"You have to understand the whole era," Sadie said. "Like in *my* day—forgive me for the old fart phrase—but in *my* day I think we were liberated but ladies. We had love affairs, and even when it wasn't exactly love and not quite an affair, we didn't start what we couldn't finish. We didn't cock-tease, to use a good antiquated word. You didn't enter a man's bedroom if you figured later on you'd want to leave it in a huff. You either wanted to or you didn't and if you didn't, you didn't start. And if you started, you didn't count on the kindness of strangers. You accepted that strangers wouldn't always be kind. You did not court trouble.

"The girls like Nora, of Nora's generation, they thought they'd just won the 'woman's right' to have sex—as though nobody'd ever been sexual before— but

332

they didn't know what to do with it. Or where. Or with who. They also felt that nauseating word 'empowered.' Like what was that bigshot who figured he could hold up his hand and stop the tide? They thought they could walk around the dark dirty streets with a skirt up to their navels and a neckline down to their thighs and then hold up a staying hand against a wave of testosterone. Like all those little idiots who'd go to the hotel rooms of rough, semi-literate basketball players in the middle of the night, half stoned for that matter, and think they could say No and then that would be that. It wasn't, I suppose, entirely their fault. They were carefully taught this crapola at college. There were campuses where codes were beginning to turn sex into a game of Simon Says. Where a guy's supposed to ask you a 'May I' with every move. May I kiss you? May I touch the tip of your left breast that you've been shoving in my face? May I also touch the right one? And if the girl says No, then the guy's supposed to stop. Sometimes, I'd have to imagine, it worked. On a college campus. Doesn't work in the world. I'm not saying that any woman, no matter how idiotic, deserves to get raped, but sweet Jesus, they could use the sense God gave to lettuce. The fact is, you're not meant to have it both ways. You can't offer it and then be surprised when it's stolen. Like I said, they felt empowered. But they didn't understand either power or sex."

"So what happened?" Brymmer said.

"She's all over him at the bar and he invites her to his apartment. Which is right down the street. And we're talking the old Bowery. And what lived there back then was, yeah, a bunch of students, but mostly it was crackheads. Winos and the like. She thinks she's in control. She not sure what she wants to do but she thinks she can at any time just say no, stop, enough. But the apartment he takes her to is empty, unfurnished, except it's got a lice-ridden mattress on the floor and there's two other guys. You get the picture, I presume."

"How long did they keep her?"

"All night, half the day. Well that's technically speaking. What they did was, they put her on the mattress on the floor and tied her wrists to the radiator. They left in the morning. Left her there, tied. She could've *died* there for all that anybody knew. The people who lived there, the other apartments, they were junkies and crud. Who knows? They might've also, if they found her, had a turn."

"But she escaped."

"Came crawling to the bar the next day, maybe four in the afternoon. Lucky I was there. Black eye. Broken nose. So the rest is what you know. I called the cops. Stayed with her. They never caught the other two rapists, by the way, except you know that too."

Brymmer nodded. "Uh-huh. And what happened after that?"

"To Nora? For a time, I was like a second mother. She'd come to my bar afternoons and just cry. Never told her own mother. But she dropped out of school. Stopped working at the bar. I think she took a job at some place up in Yonkers where they rescued animals. She was having a breakdown. I mean, who could blame her? A nightmare like that can punch a hole in your life."

"And then what? You know what happened to her then?"

"I guess she straightened out. Got a scoopy new nose that was better than the first one, and I heard from someone else that she went back to school. I think for a while she did some substitute teaching. But by then I didn't see her so that's it for what I know."

Brymmer stubbed his cigarette and knuckled at his jaw. "And what happened to your bar?"

"Oh. I got gentrified out of existence. You know what replaced me? Designer boutique. They sell four-K jackets and three-bill ties. Lucky my husband passed away when he did. If he'd've seen what they were asking for the rent, he would've died."

## 83

*Tuesday, April 7th:*

The bulletin board had acquired a third, and entirely speculative, column.

| Grudgers | Grudgees | Xers |
|---|---|---|
| Andrea Clawson | Richard Clawson | George |
| Kate Marrott | Monty Starrett | Felicia |
| George Levy | David Tanner | Andrea |
| Nora Latham | Bill McConnell | X |
| Felicia Martin | Harri Kramer | Nora ? |
| X ? | (Eric Raven) | (Kate) |

Speculation meant nothing, but nonetheless provided a starting point for Something. If The Story was the truth then except for the lively possibility of copycats, it seemed as though the daisy chain of murders was over. The problem now was proof. It remained Brymmer's strategy to coddle the suspects, to keep them feeling safe till he could find a way to break them— confront them with evidence, make them rat on one another, or whatever it would take.

His focus remained on Andrea and George, though experience told him that of all the known suspects, Nora was the most likely to break. But from here on out he felt time was on his side. He could wait, play games, get his ducks in a row. For the first time in months, he was feeling, if not exactly lucky, not cursed.

So it didn't much surprise him when Corelli informed him that the prints from Harri's bed and the prints from Nora's teaching license made a perfect match. But he still wanted more. The maid, who'd sworn she'd Brasso'd the print-bearing bed posts on the morning before The Night, had a criminal record for shoplifting (twice) and check kiting (once) and could easily be discredited if forced to take the stand. Which could leave Nora claiming that, yes, she'd had a ritual romp on Harri's mattress, but weeks before the crime.

With all that in mind, he pointed Corelli to the Enterprise garage on East 77th, near Nora's apartment.

"So you think," Corelli said, "that she rented a car on the night she killed Harri."

"I think that her apartment is uptown and east and Harri's apartment is downtown and just about as west as you can get. And, considering her mission, she wouldn't want to get there and back by subway or, in fact, *two* subways or a subway and a bus. And she wouldn't chance a cab. Is what I think," Brymmer said. "She didn't get a ticket doesn't mean she didn't drive."

Corelli was nodding as the telephone rang. Brymmer picked it up and got lucky once again.

It was Eric Raven. "I believe I got an urgent message that you called."

"Are you home?" Brymmer said.

336

"Yeah. Just got in. And I really mean just. My bags are on the floor. But the message said to call you 'important, day or night.' So what's going on?"

"Something," Brymmer said, "that isn't for the phone. I'd like to talk to you in person."

"Want to give me an idea? Otherwise, I'll worry that my car was ripped off or I'm wanted for the Brinks robbery or something."

"Actually," Brymmer said, "someone reported you were smiling in Central Park, which is now a misdemeanor." He didn't know why he gave an answer like that but it seemed an appropriate match for Raven's tone and besides, he had a good feeling for a change. "No," he said quickly, "I'm a homicide detective and I think you can help us." He glanced at the clock: 4:27. "When would be good?"

Raven said he'd like to take a shower and unwind and suggested Brymmer might come by at eight o'clock.

Brymmer said, "Fine. Where'm I coming by *to*?"

Raven said, "The same building as my office. Apartment six J. It's the building on the—"

"Yeah. I know," Brymmer said. "I live around the corner. See you later then."

"Fine."


It was Ross who answered the phone after Brymmer had clocked out. A woman was downstairs who was asking for "the sergeant whose name begins with a B and who's working on the Jackie thing."

Ross told the desk guy to send her on up, and prepared himself for yet another meeting with a nut, like the one who'd come Saturday confessing to the crimes.

This one appeared on the surface to be sane. She was well-dressed, fortyish, and very apparently felt out of place. Ross explained that Sergeant Brymmer wasn't here but asked very pleasantly, "How can I help you, Miss...?"

"Mrs.," she said quickly. "Brown. Helen Brown. It's my husband who pretty much insisted that I come." Ross had pulled an empty chair up to his desk and she sat there uncomfortably, fondling the C's on her Chanel leather bag.

Ross helped her out with a softball "Why? Have you got some information?"

"Well, that's the thing. I don't want to waste your time or have you think that I'm crazy..."

"Ma'am," Ross said, "I've seen a whole lot of crazy and I don't think you're it." He could have added "yet," but he obviously didn't. "Just say what's on your mind."

"Well," she said, "we've been in Palm Beach all winter. Or most of the winter. Mid-January on. But I've been reading about, well, about the men being murdered. It's made headlines everywhere." She licked at her lips and then looked around the room, her eye getting captured by the writing on the wall. Staring at the notes about the Grudgers and Grudgees, she seemed literally to freeze. "Good God," she said suddenly. "I think I won't be wasting your time after all."

Ross phoned Brymmer. "We found the sixth woman. She told the same story about the hairdresser meet and identified the photos of Andrea and Felicia as both having been there. She also identified the photograph of Nora that Corelli got from files. And yes, I also showed her a bunch of dummy shots."

"Getting closer," Brymmer told him. "I can almost see land. Knock off, why don't you. Go home. Get some rest."

"Rest and Home don't belong in the same sentence."

"I'm sorry," Brymmer said.

"Yeah. Take care."

Brymmer put the phone back down on the sofa and picked up the ham and cheese sandwich that he'd rested on the brown paper bag. Bing! He had an instant message from Jamie.

*It was Grumpy in the movie made in 1937 but Grouchy in the remake of 1991. Shall we call it a draw?*

Brymmer texted back, *I'm a faster draw than you are. I'll meet you at the target range.*

Jamie texted back, *But I aim for the heart.*

Brymmer, without thinking, typed *Oof! Argh! Splat!*

## 84

The man who opened the door of Apartment 6J was nothing at all like the other five victims. Eric Raven was a short but athletically fit-looking man with nothing but an ear-to-ear fringe of dark hair and a broad open face. He was dressed in a navy blue sweatshirt and jeans, socks but no shoes, a Saint Christopher's medal dangling from his neck. At the door, he said, "You've piqued my curiosity, Sergeant," and gestured, one-handed, towards a room at his left. A landline telephone rang from beyond. Raven rolled his eyes, said, Sorry, and crossed to a table in the hall.

Brymmer heard him saying, "Yes. I am back" and decided that he might as well go into the living room—a room that turned out to have the earmarks of a Wife. A floral patterned sofa (with draperies to match) sat opposite a matched pair of red velvet chairs. Brymmer was drawn to the wall above a fruitwood table at the side that held a few dozen photographic portraits of children. The children were of various colors and sizes, all of them smiling and all showing faces that were cleverly repaired. He was particularly taken by a pretty young woman with a thin line of scarring down the side of her cheek.

He turned at the sound of Raven's footsteps behind him. "Doctors Without Borders?"

"Yeah," Raven said. "It's what I like to think of as what I really do. That and the V.A. The nose jobs and face-lifts support my addiction."

Brymmer said, "And what did you do for that girl?" He pointed at the picture of the pretty young woman.

"Nesta," Raven said. "To put it in simple terms, she had a huge hairy wine-colored blotch that covered her cheek and was likely precancerous as well as just ugly. I removed it and grafted skin."

"Where is she?"

"Bolivia.—Why don't you take a seat so we can talk about murder.— Whose?" Raven said as he settled into a chair.

"Yours," Brymmer said, and then sat on the sofa.

Raven raised his eyebrows —an expression that was neither skeptical nor alarmed. "I assume you're not kidding."

"Safe assumption," Brymmer said. "Let me start with a few questions. If someone— a woman— happened to want you dead, what woman comes to your mind?"

"Leona Gilroy," Raven said.

"Well *that* was pretty fast. Who's Leona Gilroy?"

"A long ago patient. Now it's my turn to ask. Does Leona want me dead?"

"I don't know," Brymmer said. "But somebody sure does. Somebody, in a way, put out a contract."

"On me."

"On you. You want to know how I know, I got it straight from the person who's supposed to have done the job except the person turned it down. The question now is whether a substitute was found. Or will be when your ill-wisher learns it isn't done."

There was silence for a moment. Brymmer rubbed his jaw.

"I think I need a drink now," Raven said, rising. "How about you?"

"Frequently," Brymmer said, "but not at the moment."

Raven crossed to a cabinet and built himself what looked like a generous double bourbon. Brymmer took his coat off. He'd purposely decided to not wear a jacket; to be, on this occasion, a man looking easy in a turtleneck and holster—a reminder, in case a reminder was required, of professional equality. Raven came back, sipping bourbon as he sat, and Brymmer said dryly, "Who's the first runner-up?"

Raven flicked his shoulders and thoughtfully shook his head.

"How about someone in your personal life maybe. Ex-wife. Ex-girlfriend…"

"My wife died a year ago. I haven't had a girlfriend since before we were married. And not many then."

"Okay, not a girlfriend. How about a lay?"

"I regret I'm not much in the lay department either."

"So how about…Jesus, do people still 'date'? How about 'seen.' Anyone you've seen a few times and then dropped?"

341

"Yeah, I suppose. People fix me up. I don't want it, not yet, maybe never. I don't know. But they invite me up to dinner and there just so happens to be a single woman. These are women in their thirties—late thirties, early forties. A lot of them successful. Spent the last twenty years climbing gleefully up the ladder and they just now discover that they want to have a baby and they don't want to die alone. Thing is, they lost the talent or they possibly never had it, of just being...I don't know, I want to say 'women,' but I think I mean... companions. But yeah, so as not to disappoint the good friends who just happened to have her over, I've 'seen' one or two. Like dinner. Or some show. I'm bored. I'm boring. I'm awkward. I'm forty-eight and I don't know how to deal with the small-talk and the bright sophisticated poses. I say to them, insincerely, 'Listen, you're terrific but for me it's too soon.' The too soon part is true. The terrific, not so much. But do I think they want to kill me? No. They don't care. Caring isn't part of it. They just want a someone, or in any case a someone as long as he's got some money."

"My husband, the doctor."

"Some of that too."

"So we're back to Leona and what's Leona's beef."

Raven sipped his drink. "Leona came to me...hell, let me see ... three years ago. May. She's a good-looking woman. She's forty at the time and her husband had just dumped her for somebody much younger and apparently bustier. Leona wants boobs. She wants big—I mean big—silicone boobs. I advise her against it. I don't like to do boobs. I tell her this is not just a one-shot deal, it takes lifelong maintenance. Things can go wrong. I give her a list of the things that go wrong. Take it home, look it over. Discuss it with your doctor,

342

discuss it with your God. You're a grownup woman. You want the kind of man only wants a pair of boobs? Leona comes back to me a couple of weeks later. She still wants the large silicone boobs. I again explain the risks. She signs the release. She gets the operation. She's thrilled with the results. Just what she wanted till she gets the complications and they aren't uncommon. The one Leona gets is called capsular contracture. Her own breast hardens and tightens around the sac. It's painful and not pretty. Not the fault of the implant. Not the fault of the surgeon. It's just the way her body reacts to the intrusion. Now she comes screaming at me, look what you've done. I advise her to take them out and the sooner the better."

Raven took another long pull from his drink, then shook his head slowly.

"Does she listen to me? No. She holds onto them for a while. The situation gets worse. Now she wants them out. So now I say, Leona, you should find another doctor. Someone you'll listen to. Someone you trust. So another guy does it. I know him. He's good. But I also know what happens when you take out a large and troublesome implant if you don't do it fast. Cosmetically, it's lousy, and it was for Leona, but lousier than that, they discovered a tumor. Again, this has nothing to do with the implant except to the extent that it screwed up the pictures at mammogram time. However," Raven said, "she nonetheless sues me for two million bucks."

Brymmer said carefully, "How'd she make out?"

"She lost. Clear and simple. But she didn't stop there. She starts up a website. Calls me a butcher. Calls me a monster, and there's nothing I can do. Freedom of expression. She's entitled to her opinion. Finally, she comes to me— actually she phones me. Fifty-thousand dollars and she'll close down the site. I told her to get lost. Not that it wasn't worth fifty-thousand bucks but I figured once you start with that, it doesn't ever end and then somehow I'd be feeding some cookaboo relationship." Raven paused again and said, "I've got it on a tape."

"Her asking you for money?"

"Yeah. I wasn't sure what to do about it, though. Did I want to report it? Get involved with the law? No. I felt bad. I felt sorry for the woman. She lost her left breast and the other one's deformed. I thought she was tragic. The whole fucking thing. Pitiable. Ironic. No, I just wanted her to leave me alone."

"And did she?"

"Not voluntarily she didn't. But I figured how to fox her. One of my patients is an IT guy and he just kept hacking her until she gave up. Then, for a while, she stalked me," Raven said. "I mean we're talking she's obsessed."

"But it sounds as though she stopped."

"Yeah. Last June. I really thought it was over."

"But she learned about your habits. Where you go. What you do."

"I could put it to you this way. I'm jogging in the park? Oops, there's Leona. I'm at Zabar's for bagels? Three behind me on line. Never talked, just glared. She looked wraithlike and strange. Wearing different color wigs. I figured it's the chemo and she's taunting me with it."

Brymmer said, "Uh-huh." Then he said evenly, "Listen, for a while I'd advise you not to take any sudden invitations from extraneous women. And especially not from pickups at Zabar's or the park."

Raven looked suddenly alarmed and alert. "Good

God!" he said, "you're working on the Jackie thing, aren't you."

Brymmer said nothing. Then he said, "I'd also advise you not to talk about the things we've discussed. Just watch your own ass."

Raven whistled softly. "Well thanks for the tip."

"Yeah. You want to let me have the tape of that call? I'll make a copy and return it."

"I've got one already. In my office. Downstairs. We can get it right now."

"Good." Brymmer nodded. "What else can you tell me?"

"What else do you want to know?"

"Where she lives. What she does."

"Her address is in my files. But she's somewhere up the street." He thumbed out the window to the view of Central Park. "She's in real estate. Or was."

"Describe her."

"Better still, I've got her picture in my files. Technically, of course, I guess you'd have to have a warrant..."

"Technically, of course. But if we went to your office and you happened to leave the room..."

"I believe that could be arranged. You want to drink to that arrangement?"

"A short one," Brymmer said.

When Raven handed him the cut-crystal glass, he noted, Brymmer noted, the scars on Brymmer's hand before returning to his seat where, cooly and openly, he studied Brymmer's face. "You mind if I intrude an off-topic observation?"

Here we go, Brymmer thought. He said nothing, just drank.

Raven tapped his own cheek. "I could fix that if you like."

"No thanks," Brymmer said almost blithely, "I've been fixed."

"I can see that. But whoever did it wasn't...good."

"Tell me." Brymmer laughed. "I should've figured when I saw him trimming pork chops in the window but I didn't pay attention. Anyway, it's all a long time ago and done. And it can't be done again."

"What can't be done again is the crap he did before. Stick a knife into keloids. Did it make matters worse?"

"Matters," Brymmer said. "Yeah, they got worse."

"How long ago was it?"

"What difference does it make?"

"The difference is that now there are other things to do. Short pulse laser. It'll take down the color, it'll smooth out the bumps. It'll never be perfect, it'll simply be better. Hey, I'm not trying to sell you something, Sergeant. I'd consider it a matter of professional courtesy. A straight swap of skills.... No hassle. Just a thought."

"Yeah, well I appreciate the gesture," Brymmer said. "I'll think about it."

"Fine. Let's go down to the office."

"Yeah. Good idea."

## 85

*Late Tuesday night, April 7th*

FORM PD 313-081A
COMPLAINT FOLLOW UP     COMPLAINT: —00549
                        Homicide, Richard Clawson w/m

FILED BY:   Det. Stuart Kurtz, Shield # 3257, MHTF
SUBJECT:    Surveillance, Andrea Clawson,

In sum, it was this:

Andrea Clawson had the townhouse up for sale (for twelve million dollars) and was living in the same Sutton Place apartment she'd repaired to when she'd first stalked out of Richard's life. Andrea's schedule, at least for the two days the task force detectives had accounted for her moves, had consisted of tennis at the Sutton East courts, shopping at the Madison Avenue boutiques, and lunching at the 9th floor restuarant at Barney's. Photographs were taken covertly on the street. The one that was of special interest to Brymmer was the one that was accidentally captured when it happened that Clawson and Felicia Martin arrived dead heat at The Surrey Hotel whose now-trendy bar was a magnet for the people like Clawson and Martin. It was 5:22 so the light was still good as Felicia stepped out of the idling taxi and waved at Andrea, approaching from Park with a Prada shopping bag. The women embraced and then entered the lobby, where Kurtz got a shot of them passing by the six-foot Chuck Close portrait of a dead-eyed Kate Moss as they headed for the bar. Thereafter...

"It gets even better," Kurtz said.

Brymmer looked up. Kurtz stood grinning with some coffee in his hand, peering over Brymmer's shoulder.

"Good. I'm getting eye strain, so talk to me the rest." He tilted his chair back and put up his feet. Kurtz took the visitor's chair by the desk.

"I'm with Hamilton," he said. "Hamilton, luckily, dresses good as you, so we're not sticking out when we settle at the bar. That kind of neighborhood, they don't make police, at least the customers don't, so we have ourselves a drink, eat a bucketful of peanuts, and watch the goings on. Not close enough to listen, just close enough to watch. The ladies start pulling out the lipsticks and the wallets and we know it's time to move. Soon as they're out of there, we get to that table and—"

"The glasses," Brymmer said. "You got the glasses?"

"And the toothpicks from the little bitty hotdogs, and the napkins, just in case."

"Jesus," Brymmer said. "That's enough DNA we could clone them if we want. Where is it?"

"At the lab. Hand delivered."

"Pretty sweet. I'd've liked to see the trick, though, of how you cleared the table."

"Paper bags in our pockets, grab the booty, shove it in. It happened so fast, man, it's almost like a roach. Like you see it but before you know you've seen it, it's away. Woman at the table behind us does a take but she *knows* she didn't see any roaches in the bar."

"So I guess we owe the Surrey for a couple of good glasses."

"Nah. We catch Jackie and I think they owe us."

## 86

*Wednesday, April 8th:*

Brymmer was transcribing the notes from his notebook, trying to word them so as not to, in any way, compromise Raven.

> **Dr. Raven estimates subject Leona Gilroy**
> **is age 43 and recalls that she resides—**

Christ. "Resides." He was sounding like a fucking bureaucrat now. He quickly backed over the hideous "resides" and simply wrote

348

lives on CPW, corner 71st. He also recalled
that she worked for the realtors, Bansel &
Graff, whose website shows offices at 10
Columbus Circle,

Brymmer sat back and examined what he'd typed.
An idea, quite lunatic, arrived in his head. The more
he thought of it, the more he liked it.

He beckoned Corelli. "Pin a tail on this woman."
He handed Corelli a copy of a copy of the photo from
Raven's file: the clever-looking woman with the dark
hair and bangs. "You see these addresses?" He finger-
tapped the screen. "I want to know especially how she
gets to work and then how she gets home. Get Reggie
to go with you. Tomorrow, another team. Let's tail
her for a week."

"Who is she, could I ask?"

Brymmer leaned back and said quietly, "I think
she's McConnell's Jackie."

"Ooo. So we got all six of em now."

Brymmer just shrugged. "Yeah. Could be. So
what've you got about Nora and the car?"

"I got—" Corelli sat on the desk, "that you were
right, which is very hard to take."

"Sir," Brymmer said. "'Hard to take, Sir.'"

"I'll remember that. She rented a dark gray Corolla
at 5:47 on Wednesday, the twenty-fifth, returning it at
8:02 the next morning. She drove it for exactly eight-
point-six miles or about the exact distance of a round
trip journey between her place and Harri's."

"And what about the car?"

"It's already at the lab."

"Good," Brymmer said. "You feeling pretty good?"

"Not good, just better. Feeling good is bad luck."

"You got a point," Brymmer said. "I'll contain my elation."

He stared at his screen again and picked up the phone. When Kate came on the line, he realized, too late, that it was just about 6 in the morning out west. He apologized for waking her, which didn't seem to make her any gladder that he'd called.

"I've got three quick questions," Brymmer said, "that's it. After that's over, you can go back to sleep and pretend it was a dream."

"Like I dream of your calling me?"

"Question," Brymmer said. "You told me there were numbers on the top of those chits. That you all wrote a number so you wouldn't pick your own. What was the number on the chit that said Raven? You remember what it was?"

"Yeah. Thirteen. Kind of easy to remember."

"And what was it written in?"

"In?" Kate yawned at him. "I don't understand."

"In pencil. Pen. Ballpoint. Blood..."

"Oh. In pen. I'd imagine a ballpoint."

"What color ballpoint?"

"Oh. Green."

"And what was the number that you wrote on your own?"

"Seven twenty-seven."

"Like the plane," Brymmer said.

"No. It's a date. July twenty-seventh."

"Ah," Brymmer said. "And the note pads. The little green pads in the salon that you did all the writing on. Where did you find them?"

"On the tables in the waiting room."

"Tables. Plural."

"Yeah, there were a few."

"And they all had the notepads?"

"Gee I don't know. Probably. I think so. People, while they're waiting seem to make a lot of calls so they make a lot of notes. So yeah, I guess so."

"What's the waiting room look like?"

"It's sort of like a patio. White wicker tables, white wicker chairs. A lot of ferns hanging down."

"One final question. Which woman's idea was it to whack off the dicks?"

"And you think after that I'm gonna fall back asleep?"

"I'll sing you a lullabye."

"Thanks but no thanks. I can't say for certain, but I'm pretty sure the gypsy one whose name I don't know."

"The dark hair and bangs."

"Yeah."

"Leona. Does the name ring a bell?"

"No."

"And you're sure you wouldn't like a little Brahams?"

*"What?"*

"Lullabye."

"Listen, you know what would help me fall asleep? To know if you're planning to charge me with something."

"Stupidity, perhaps."

"Is that all?"

"I don't know. But in any case, I'll probably need you as a witness. Or at least your deposition. Can't promise. Don't know. I were you, I'd go to sleep."

She was silent, then sighed. "I suppose 'I don't know' is slightly better than a yes."

"Depends on the question. Sweet dreams, Miss Marrott."

Brymmer looked back at the writing on his screen

and thought about some ways to get a little green pad from a white wicker table with a minimum of fuss.

## 87

When Ross got home with the little green memo pad safely in his pocket ("My wife made some notes and she left them on the table"), a note was on his door.
Billy's with me.
Knock.
Sally
She answered the door wearing tights and a t-shirt, glasses perched up on the top of her head and a pen behind her ear. The apartment smelled of something terrific, with garlic. He looked at her wearily and said, "What now?"
"Come in. Sit down."
Her son looked up from the dining room table where he puzzled through a workbook. Beside him, Sally's laptop had put itself to sleep.
"Billy's in the bedroom."
Ross just nodded.
"Jimmy Lee," Sally said. "Go watch some cartoons now with Billy for a while."
"But mom," he said, "you told me—"
"I know what I told you, but you'll finish later on. Don't grumble at me either and say hello to Steve."
"Hi, Steve," Jimmy said and, gesturing at Sally, did the classic circling-the-finger-by-the-ear.
"Your son thinks you're crazy," Ross said when Jimmy left.
"I told him he couldn't watch cartoons until later.

That he had to do his homework. Thank God they're only up to the times tables now. Once they get into algebra..."

"*What?*" Ross said.

"Why don't you sit down?"

"Is it that kind of story?" Ross sat anyway. Sally sat beside him on the chintz-covered couch.

"She's been wearing the same nightgown, all night, all day, for maybe three days running. So before, she rang the bell. Said she was out of coffee, could she borrow some."

"So?"

"I lied. I said, funny but I'm out of it myself. If you're going to the market, could you get me some too? Honest, Steve, I figured I should get her out of the house, get her out of the damn nightgown. I thought it would do her good."

"Go on," Ross said.

"Well, she left for the market but she hasn't come back."

"How long ago was it?"

"Three hours ago."

"Oh....Well," Ross said, "she's a grownup woman. Three hours doesn't make her a missing person. Maybe she decided, once she was out, to— I dunno—to go to a movie or something. Go shopping uptown. Listen, I wouldn't have a heart attack about it."

Sally shook her head. "It's just that she seems so... fragile. I don't know. I worry. I think she's very deeply depressed."

"You *think*?" Ross said. "Sweet Jesus. It's nineteen-thirty in our house. It's The Great Depression. She won't see a doctor. She won't take a pill. She won't go away with me or even by herself. Her sister's no help. The one lives in Yonkers? The sister is one of those 'God sends us burdens to test our resilience.' That's some lovely God. The only thing to say is that Kathy's resilence has been tested and it flunked and I'm fresh out of answers."

Sally said nothing. Then she said thoughtfully, "I leave it up to you. You'll know when it's time to go look for her or something."

"Hey. She wouldn't take any candy from strangers and if anything had happened, I mean like an accident, someone would've called. So relax." Ross started to rise from the couch. "I'll go collect Billy and—"

"Listen, Steve, why don't you just stay for dinner? It's spaghetti and sausage and I haven't even put the spaghetti on yet so there'd be plenty for everyone..."

"I don't want to trouble you..."

"Geez, I boil an extra handful of pasta. That's really some trouble. Stay. Have a drink."

"I can't tell you how very much I'd like that," Ross said. "Can I help you with anything?"

"Mmm. I suppose you could fix your own drink. Tell you what," Sally said as he followed her into the room full of sausage and peppers, "there's a something you could do. I mean if you wouldn't mind."

"There's *nothing* I wouldn't do," he said, breathing in the aroma of normal living, "in exchange for spaghetti with some sausage and a drink. I'm a wonderfully cheap date."

She looked at him oddly with her head to the side. It was all Ross could do not to reach out and touch her.

She handed him some ice. "Jimmy Lee is developing an affection for the Mets. He doesn't like the Yankees, he says they're 'a buncha snobs,' but the thing is, he suddenly wants to play baseball. You think you could play with him? Some afternoon?"

Ross started grinning and was just about to say how he longed to play baseball when the bell rang beyond.

He and Sally locked eyes, though his and her glances held different interpretations. Sally looked relieved. "That's Kathy," she said.

"I know." Ross sighed and looked longingly at a sausage.

## 88

*Thursday, April 9th:*

Sanders said he'd gotten two reports from the lab. Brymmer would get them but he'd likely want them now.

The dried flecks of blood in Nora's rental car was Harri's, 99% sure. "AB negative," Sanders said flatly. "Only one percent of all caucasians have the type."

"Where'd you find it?" Brymmer said.

"In the tread on the pedals. Little specks in the carpet. In other words, somebody stepped in it, huh?"

"Nice," Brymmer said. "What else we got going?"

"The blood in the tile grout was *not* Monty Starrett's. Not the same type. DNA yet to come."

"And what about the glasses and the stuff from the bar? I'd be looking for a match between the stuff marked Felicia and the blood from Starrett's wall. Also want to match-make with Tanner's red hair and that—"

"Hold it," Sanders said. "Want to hear about the backlog? We're seven weeks behind on the—"

"No," Brymmer said. "I do not want to hear. Just tell me whose ass I have to kick to get action."

"Try 'kiss,'" Sanders said. "You're gonna need to lick brass."

355

Brymmer hung up and called Captain Parisi, suggesting that, if needed, he get hold of the mayor, the commissioner, the president, the almighty God, or the editorial writers of the *New York Times.* "Why?" Parisi said. "Are you closer to anywhere than nowhere, or what?"

"I don't know," Brymmer said. "I got pieces. If the pieces come together, it's a wrap. But I need to know pronto if the pieces come together."

The Captain said carelessly, "I'll see what I can do." Then he said, "You're planning to pull something. What?"

"A rabbit out of a hat."

"Is it kosher?"

"I don't know. Is rabbit meat kosher? I guess if it's blessed by a rabbi, you think?"

"Don't fuck with me, Brymmer. I want to know your plans."

"Captain, I don't even know them myself. They're colliding in my head and they're giving me a headache. I'll have to work it out. But I assure you, I won't make a move without the nod. Not a major move anyway."

"I catch that distinction. I trust you to a point, although not much beyond it. You want to do a high wire act without a net, don't expect to find a net. Even if I know what you're doing. No net. Meanwhile, I'll see what I can do about the lab."

At 4 o'clock, Corelli dumped some pictures on the desk. "Leona," he said.

Brymmer looked her over— in long shot and zoom. In long shot, she was wearing the fur-collared coat. The same coat as Jamie's. The same coat that Carolyn had told him that she'd seen. On the redhead in the elevator.

The redhead riding down from above the 6th floor and very likely from the 9th where McConnell lay dying or, if lucky, lay dead. The zooms showed a lively-looking dark-haired woman; attractive, Brymmer thought, sexy in a promising and taunting kind of way.

"Who replaced you?" Brymmer said.

"Clark and Dubisky."

"And what do we know for now?"

"She walked to her office. She walked down the west side of Central Park West. Left home at exactly—" Corelli checked his notebook—"seven-sixteen. Stayed in the office till a little after noon. She came out, caught a cab and went down to the Village. Want to know the address? Andrea Clawson's. Or Richard's, I should say."

"She's the broker?"

"That's confirmed. She met a guy by the gate. Had the key. Unlocked it. They were there half-an-hour. Came out. Took a cab to a mansion uptown. The guy's Japanese. Chinese. Something. *I* don't know—Asian. Anyway, they look, come out, keep going. I think he saw a hundred-million bucks' worth of house. Anyway, six houses later, we lost em. Went back to her office and waited. She's there. So're Clark and Dubisky. Anyway, I'm typing this up and I'm gone. Okay?"

Brymmer nodded. "Small world though, isn't it."

"What?"

"Her just happening to show Clawson's house."

"Oh yeah. Pure coincidence I'd say, wouldn't you?"

"Well," Brymmer said, "unless our luck is really turning, it might be at that.—Go with God, however. You did a day's work."

Ross, coming in as Corelli walked away, slapped the little green notepad on top of Brymmer's files. "Also got a green-inked ballpoint," Ross said. "They were also

357

on the tables. See? It's got a little green G on the side."

"Classy," Brymmer said as he doodled with the pen.

"It's the endgame, isn't it."

"Maybe," Brymmer said.

Ross phoned Carolyn Klein and Helen Brown and asked them could they come at their convenience to the station, take a look at some photographs. They both said they could.

Brymmer got in touch with Lucinda Hernandez, the parole officer assigned to the rapist Robert Jackson, the only one of Nora's chickenshit attackers who didn't get away. Jackson had been sprung on December 28th and was currently camping on the couch of what she termed as a "pre-prison friend," one Frank Todaro who lived in a walkup on Third and 21st. Todaro, she said, was an employed electrician, a twelve-year resident of that same address, and had no criminal record.

Brymmer, more aware of the practical difference between criminal activity and criminal record, called the 13th Precinct and asked his friend Ritter if anybody down there had heard of Todaro. Ritter just laughed and said, "*Every*body down here has heard of Todaro. We used to get calls from his neighbors once a week. All right, once a month. Domestic violence. The wife— her name's Mary— Mary, little lamb, never chose to press charges. She eventually left him. A year ago, I think.— Why?" Ritter said. "Did he finally beat some-one's brains out or what?"

Brymmer explained about the Jackson connection.

"So your thinking goes how?"

"That Jackson never ratted on his gang-banger buddies. That both of those buddies owe him favors he'd collect."

"Like lending him a sofa? Maybe so," Ritter said.

"But I still don't get it. This is long-ago rape. What's your interest in it?"

"Well...how's justice?" Brymmer said.

"Tell it to your grandma."

"Right," Brymmer laughed. "You could do me a favor. You know what Frank looks like. Get me a head-shot. If you spot Robert Jackson, get me one of him too."

"I suppose," Ritter said. "But I'd like to know your thinking."

"I'm fishing," Brymmer said, "and I'm out for barracuda. I'm thinking how you do it when you're out for a big fish. How you bait em with a little fish. Little fish gets eaten, well it's too fucking bad."

"And you'll tell me about it later."

"Or you'll see it on the news."

Brymmer put the green-ink ballpoint in his drawer and pulled out another one and started to organize the chaos in his head. Two weeks, he thought. If everything actually came together, he could close it in two weeks.

*Friday, April 10th:*

Carolyn Klein, first, and then Helen Brown, second, both clearly identified Leona Gilroy, Helen attesting that Leona had been there on The Fateful Afternoon, and Carolyn, after placing her finger on the photograph to cover Leona's hair, said, "Yeah. I think. Only let me have some scissors." Carolyn then sketched out some artfully done hairdos on a sheet of municipal memo pad paper and cut them to fit the head. Carolyn said Yes to both images of Leona—the one with the long brown hair without the bangs, and the one with the hair that looked surprisingly like Jamie's, except that it was paper white and not red.

359

*Saturday, April 11th:*

After keeping her waiting for a decent ten minutes in the downstairs "reception room," Ross went down the stairway to greet Nora Latham. As promised, Nora Latham was a not-really-pretty not-really blonde, but stylish— her hair parted cleanly down the middle then descending into arcs that brushed softly on her neck. She was dressed in a modest but form-fitting dress— the color of Campbell's tomato soup, he thought— that ended at the knees which revealed some good legs which themselves stood their ground in those dangerously high heels.

"So sorry to have kept you waiting," Ross lied and ushered her up the stairs, past the wide open squad room where the bulletin board was covered with a giant map of the city, and then into the open maw of the interrogation room where he showed her to a seat and thanked her for coming over.

"I suppose," she said softly, "that it's I who should thank you. I— appreciate your effort." She looked around nervously. "I'd like to see them caught."

Ross nodded, sat across from her, hunkering down at the table where a thick plastic binder was conspicuously displayed. "As I told you on the phone," he said, "there isn't any statute of limitations on a rape. If we've batted out this time, we can try, try again. We're as anxious to catch these bastards as you are." He shoved her the binder. "Now you know how this works. We've got pictures of guys here. You look, see if any of the faces ring a bell. Keep in mind something else. It was seventeen years ago. The faces will have aged so you'll have to try using just a bit of imagination. Take your time. Take as long as you want with each shot. There's a buzzer under the table. Buzz me if you think you've found anything you like. You can use these as book-marks." He handed her a clean stack of 3 by 5 cards. "You want coffee or anything?"

She shook her head no, sighed deeply, breathed in as though to steel herself against whatever leapt from the book, and then opened its glossy blue plastic cover.

Ross left the room, closing the door very firmly behind him, and waited in the anteroom, squinting at the monitors, watching her in realtime, though the cameras would preserve every motion, every blink, and the microphones would capture every gasp, every sigh.

She sighed. Chewed her lip. Flipped some pages, then stopped. She stared at the contemporary picture of Robert Jackson and reached for a clean card. Stared at him some more. Placed the card in the book. Good. She was showing she could add on the years and come up with the answer. And even more important, they'd established in her mind the sincerity of the precinct, the legitimacy of her visit. She flipped some more pages, passing impassively over head shots of McConnell and the back-alley pederast "Dippy" Dafoe, and then twelve minutes later, hesitated, squinting at the Blackberry street-shot of Frank Todaro. Her hand reached over and hovered on the card stack. Then it moved away. Then she closed her eyes and put her hand across her mouth. He felt sorry for her, nearly, but it wasn't near enough to stop the grin of excitement. Yes! She left the book wide open, rang the bell.

The way it was left was that Ross would be call-ing her again, maybe soon. Could be any time, he told her. Morning, noon, night, and then they'd want her to come instantly. They might have the guy in the picture for a lineup. They might have a picture of the other, third, guy. Could she do that? Drop everything and come when she was called?

She assured him that she could. She now seemed jubilant. She smiled and shook his hand and then thanked him profusely, "for eveything you do."

*Wednesday, April 15th:*

Surveillance reports: A week in the life of Leona Gilroy. Subject shows consistent weekday habits. Walks to work daily, at or about 7:30 AM, even in hard wind-blown rain; does office work till noon; shows apartments and houses from that time on, returning to her home directly from whatever's her final location by, variously, car service, subway or cab. At least since last Wednesday when surveillance began, spends evenings at home. Lights off at approximately 10 PM nightly. Today was no different (full accounting below)...

*Thursday, April 16th:*

Forensic report: DNA analysis of items #29-0987 to 29-0989 (wine glass, toothpicks, hot dog remnant) submitted as samples from Felicia Martin were shown to match blood samples taken from the tiles at the apartment of homicide victim, Monty Starrett...

Forensic report: DNA analysis of items #29-0990 to 29-0992 (martini glass, cocktail napkin, green olive pits) submitted as samples from Andrea Clawson were shown to match hairs and skin cells found in the hands and under the fingernails of homicide victim, David Tanner...

Forensic report: DNA analysis of item #28-9321 (blood samples scraped from the rental car floor) were shown to match the blood of the homicide victim, Harrison Kramer...

362

Forensic report: DNA analysis of items #29-1201 and 1202 (3 x 5 file cards) submitted as samples from Nora Latham were shown to match skin cells found on the ties used to manacle homicide victim, Harrison Kramer...

*Friday, April 17th:*

Brymmer sat down and prepared some warrants. He didn't submit them, couldn't even complete them. He couldn't even swear, either literally or figuratively, that he'd gotten things right; he just fiddled with the drafts:

IN THE MATTER OF
George Levy aka George Laval aka Guy Laval, w/m, (DOB TK)
New York City, New York

<u>Description of Items to be Seized:</u>

I am requesting any human biological specimens retained by the subject at his place of business, Le Salon de Laval, 8xx Madison Avenue, New York City, NY, 10065, 2nd floor, and his home, 135 East 82nd Street, New York City, New York 10028, # 17J, I am further requesting from the abovementioned Salon all records of appointments and payment receipts as they apply to the afternoon (from 12 PM to closing) on December 31......

IN THE MATTER OF
George Levy aka George Laval aka Guy Laval, w/m, (DOB TK)
New York City, New York

<u>Description of Items to be Seized:</u>

I am requesting all banking information retained by JP Morgan Chase (address TK) as it relates to all accounts of George Levy and of "Guy Laval" DBA Le Salon de Laval. This request is for all records related to these accounts from July 1 of last year to the date of the execution of this warrant, including, but not limited to, debits and credits, electronic or otherwise, along with the details of these transactions, including, but not limited to, the dates, names, addresses, account and routing numbers as shown on all deposited checks; numbers and signatures on all money orders and traveler's checks; copies of all cash deposit slips ; details of direct electronic deposits....

*Saturday, April 18th:*

As Brymmer walked into the Captain's office, Parisi looked up and said, "What? Whatcha got?"

"Something," Brymmer said, and took a chair by the desk. "I want everything, however."

"Start with what you've got."

"Right," Brymmer said. "Forensic evidence on Andrea Clawson, Felicia Martin and Nora Latham."

Parisi blew his nose. "So remind me now," he said, "about who did what to whom."

"Felicia did Starrett, Andrea did Tanner and Nora did Harri."

"And you're solid on it?"

"Yep. I also place Andrea in the elevator at Tanner's. And a couple of witnesses put Felicia at the bar."

"The bar?"

"Starrett's bar. Earlier that night. Got an unreliable witness saw her later near his door."

Parisi thought it over. "Okay," he said carefully. "So what're you still missing?"

"Leona and George and five penises," Brymmer said.

"And what do you plan to do?"

The Captain's office had a long glass wall that looked on the larger of the two squad rooms. Ross, passing by it, saw Brymmer leaning back in the chair beside the desk with his hands in a steeple and the Captain leaning forward with his hands in the air.

Ross cracked a smile. Somewhere in the labyrinth of Brymmer's imagination lay plots of an almost Shakespearean splendor, games within games. "Playing," Brymmer called it, and he played a combination of poker and chess, bluff and maneuver. Like Hamlet, he believed that the play was the thing but, unlike Hamlet, once Brymmer had a plan he'd effect it with dispatch.

If he could sell it to Parisi.

Ross couldn't tell how it was going, either way.

*Monday, April 20th:*

Spring was elusive. The day started sunny, though not very warm, but by late afternoon the skies had turned cloudy, and by night, it was teeming and didn't want to stop. Great slashes of lightning zagged across the sky, followed by the cannon boom of the thunder.

Brymmer, at his window, was considering omens. Tomorrow, if the last little thing fell into place, was his tentative D-Day but D-Day itself had been postponed due to rain. He wondered if the weather was telling him to wait, was counseling caution, was trying to save him from drowning in his own irredeemable chutzpah. He'd knocked off at five since there'd been nothing else to do except wait for the final reports from Dubisky before he set the crazy contraption into motion. And besides, if he was going to wrestle with his doubts, it was better done in private. He moved from the window where the sky went BOOM! at the sound of the intercom buzzer on the wall.

He yelled at the speaker, "Whoever you are, you've got the wrong fucking bell," and Dubisky said, "Burt? F'r chissake, let me up."

Soaked and sneezing, Dubisky cleared the door and announced that he was dying, that he likely had the flu, that he knew he had a fever, he was really burning up, and he'd lost Leona Gilroy.

"I'm glad you've got the order of importance," Brymmer said. "Throw your coat in the bathtub. I'm fixing you a Scotch."

"I'd like tea," Dubisky said. "Tea with lemon and honey."

"What'm I— your mother?"

Brymmer poured a good stiff straight shot of Scotch and gave it to Dubisky who emerged from the bathroom looking drier but flushed.

"You're not drinking?" Dubisky said.

Brymmer shook his head. "Nor am I in the mood to catch your hypochondria so stay on the fucking couch and tell me about Leona."

Dubisky drank some Scotch. "Nice place you got," he said.

"Abe?"

"I came by because I'm three blocks away."

"At Leona's."

"That's true."

"Is Leona at Leona's?"

"That, I don't know."

"Where's Clark?"

"At Leona's."

Brymmer was aware that he now craved a drink, lit a cigarette instead, didn't want it, put it out. "Roll it back to the beginning."

"We tail her from the office. She leaves at five o'clock. Walks over to Broadway to the Lincoln Four theater."

"Movie theater."

"Right."

"Who'd she go with?"

"Herself.—You mind if I take my shoes off or something? My socks are fucking soaked."

"Take your shoes off," Brymmer said. "You want a towel?"

"I'd like a towel."

Brymmer left the room and came back with a towel that he tossed to Dubisky. "Nurse Ratched at your service."

Dubisky dried his feet.

"When you're ready," Brymmer said.

"So the movie she's seeing is in Swedish, f'r chissakes. And it's some kind of rerun. It's *Frannie and Alexander*."

"Fannie," Brymmer said.

"The only *fanny* in question is mine," Dubisky said, "because for five fucking hours me and my hemorrhoids are sitting on my fanny. Do you know what that's *like*?"

"Where was Clark?"

"In the lobby. Well, in the lobby starting three hours in. You ever heard of a movie lasting five hours long?"

"Yeah," Brymmer said. "*Fannie and Alexander.*— Will you fucking go on?"

"So it's over and she goes. And it's raining like—" Dubisky checked the window— "like it's raining. Would you know she gets a cab? The only fucking cab in the world and she gets it. Which leaves Clark and me... I could say high and dry except I mean low and wet. So we shlep to her apartment. Ask the doorman, 'Is she home?' So he says he doesn't know. Someone slipped on the sidewalk. He was busy getting help. So he says, 'Should I ring her?' so we say Never mind. So we stand on the corner, watch her windows from the street. No lights. Does that tell us that she's home and she's in bed? This is now past her bedtime. Or it says she's not home?"

"She went to the movies alone," Brymmer said, "and left alone around when?"

"It was 10:23."

"So we know where she was between, say, 5:30-ish and 10:23."

"Yeah," Dubisky said.

"Put your shoes on."

"Shit. You're gonna throw me out in the rain?"

"I'm gonna lend you an umbrella."

"I will die."

"I will give you a magnificent eulogy. There's a subway. Two blocks."

"About Leona," Dubisky said from the doorway as he left. "I'm really sorry about that."

"How it goes," Brymmer said. "There was nothing you could do."

And there was nothing very much that Clark could do either. "Where are you?" Brymmer asked when he phoned him on his cell.

"In her lobby," Clark said. "I convinced the night doorman that I'm looking for someone else."

"Well, look," Brymmer said. "But go home when you want to go. No reason for all-nighters."

"You sure?"

"What I said."

Brymmer clicked off and checked the time on his phone. 11:41. He made a couple of phone calls. Then he called Ross. Then he sat and thought about what could go wrong and decided that whatever it was that went wrong would be the thing he hadn't thought of.

### 89

*Tuesday, April 21st, 7:43 AM:*

"This is Jamie Rogers, On The Spot News, and the spot this morning—the spot with the ambulance and squad cars around it and the crowd on the sidewalk and the homicide detectives buzzing in and out— is on Central Park West where it looks as though Jackie the Ripper struck again. The action seems centered on a doctor's office right here on the ground floor, but they've told us that we can't show the name on the door... which is opening now. Ah. Sergeant Brymmer. Can you—"

"Good grief, Lucy. Since when do you work mornings?"

"I don't. I got a wake-up call from the station. They said it was a Jackie."

"Why?"

"Why'd they say it? They were monitoring police calls. They said the dispatcher said 'it looks like a Jackie.'"

"The dispatcher. Uh-huh. And it seems the dispatcher dispatched a lot of press. Okay, boys and girls—"

"Sergeant? Glen Thompson, ABC News—"

"Listen. I can say this to all of you at once. I came out to get some air. Actually, some smoke. I have absolutely nothing to say at this time. Thank you for your patience."

"Sergeant? Rona Jarett, Associated Press—"

"Rona...? Nothing means nothing, okay?"

Brymmer walked away to the side of the entrance and leaned against a wall where he lit a cigarette and looked idly at the crowd that had gathered at the curb. A uniformed officer was keeping them in check. Saw-horses blocked off a lane of traffic. Lights on the squad cars swirled against the dark gray mist of the cool early morning in New York. Still looking straight ahead, he saw Jamie, no microphone, coming from the left. He hadn't figured on Jamie.

"Can I have a cigarette?"

"Nope."

"Can I have an answer off the record?"

"Off the record, you still can't have a cigarette. I need you to scram. Okay? Do it now."

She looked at him quizzically. "Is something going down?"

"Well it isn't if you don't— Oh Christ," he said, doing some rapid calculation, "if I don't tell you what, you're gonna watch me and then you're gonna speculate on mike."

"Not if you say you don't want me to, I won't. Just tell me what I'm not supposed to speculate about."

He turned from her, blowing out his smoke towards the crowd. "In a couple of seconds, a Detective Kerner's gonna come through the door and make a non-statement statement. The cameras will be on him and that includes yours. You'll restrict your speculations to whatever Kerner says."

"That's all you want to tell me?"

"That's all I want to tell you. If you happen to watch me with your off-the-record eyes you can speculate at will if you keep it to yourself. Get lost now, pussycat."

*"Pussycat?"*

"Scat."

He waited a few seconds, then beckoned the uniformed officer on the street and asked him to please get the gawkers to disperse. "Tell em this isn't any goddam circus and tell em we need to have access to the curb. Do it now, please."

"Yes, sir."

"Thank you," Brymmer said, and then watched as the officer went about the job, yelling, "All right, people. Show's over. Let's move" and Kerner came suddenly out of Raven's door and the cameras devoured him.

Brymmer counted twenty and slowly walked away, heading down Central Park West to 67th, following the straggling remnants of the crowd. About a yard before the curb, he moved closer to a woman who was confidently striding and softly said, "Leona." She looked up warily. Brymmer flashed his shield. "We'd like to ask a few questions."

She stopped, cocked her head, and then shrugged, saying almost impudently, "Why? I had nothing to do with it."

"Nothing to do with what?"

McAllister and Corelli appeared from the side street.

"With anything," she said.

"Good. Then you won't mind answering some questions."

McAllister and Corelli also showed their shields. She was casing them carefully—Corelli who resembled a young Al Pacino and McAllister who stood about six foot three. She turned back to Brymmer and said to him evenly, "And what if I minded?"

"If you minded," Brymmer said, "I'd be coming to your office with a warrant. Up to you. It would likely be embarrassing, but have it either way."

She hesitated, dark eyes calculating odds.

She's a player, Brymmer thought, and she's ready for a game— a little game of matching wits. He'd encourage her in finding it a game that she could win. "We've got a car," he said, pointing at his car on the side street. He waited.

She accepted the challenge.

Game on.

In the archway of the squadroom, Parisi said to Brymmer, "So what've you got on her?"

"Not a fucking thing."

"What about attempted blackmail? Any good?"

"Technically," Brymmer said, "it wasn't even blackmail. She'd slandered him already so there wasn't any threat."

"So *technically*, then, she isn't in custody."

"Look— you want to wait around for probable cause, I'll be old and you'll be dead."

"You'll be dead if this backfires."

"I'll chance it," Brymmer said.

He moved to the door of the interrogration room, a coffee mug in one hand, and opened it softly, checking out the scene. A television monitor, dead-white and blind, was sitting on a cabinet and facing the table. Leona Gilroy was seated at the table, Corelli on her left, McAllister leaning with his back against the wall. Cool character, he thought as he watched her sitting back, looking clearly half-amused out of nearly black eyes. Whatever had happened to her body didn't show. The black cashmere turtleneck encompassed what appeared to be smooth rounded breasts. A black-and-white soft woolen skirt above the knees showed a fine silky sampling of black-stockinged leg, one foot swinging slightly in a black leather boot. Her hair was drawn back, resting softly on her neck and those eyes of hers peered from under long shiny bangs. You had to go back to find analogies, he thought. She looked like The Temptress in a forties film noir.

"Want some coffee?" Brymmer said as he settled at the table.

She watched him for a moment, then nodded. "Yes I would." She smiled. "Though I know what you're actually after."

"Yeah? What's that?"

"My prints," she said. "You think you can match them to whatever you found in Raven's office. You can't. I wasn't there."

"Milk and sugar?" Brymmer said.

"A little milk."

Brymmer gestured with his head to Corelli. Corelli got up and went over to the door, spoke to someone outside, and then returned to his seat.

Brymmer leaned back and hooked his arm around his chair. "I suppose you can tell us where you were last night. That could clear it up fast."

"At the movies."

"With who?"

"With a hundred other fans of Ingmar Bergman."

"Who's that?" Brymmer said.

"Bergman? He's a Swedish film maker."

"Oh." Brymmer nodded only once. "Can Ingmar and his followers be reached to confirm that?"

She looked at him appraisingly. "You serious?"

He paused. "Why I ask is 'at the movies' is a pretty stale alibi.— What happened after that?"

"After that, I went home."

"Directly?"

"It was raining. Yes. I got a cab."

"And got home about when?"

Leona built a shrug. "However long it takes to get home from the theater. Ten minutes, I'd suppose. So... I don't know. Ten-thirty. Thereabouts."

"And once you got home?"

"I was tired. I went to bed."

It was Clark who came back with the fresh mug of coffee and placed it on the table. Clark said, "Is this enough milk?" She said yes. Clark pulled a chair out and sat, looking blank. "Leona," Brymmer said, "was at the movies last night." Clark said, "The movies." There was silence in the room.

"Arsonists," Corelli said with seeming irrelevance. "Arsonists hang around and watch the firemen, you know?"

Leona looked surprised. "Was there a fire in Raven's office?"

"Killers do the same. Hang around, watch the cops. Why were you watching us this morning, Leona?"

"Try harder, you guys."

"Just answer the question."

"I was on my way to work. I pass by the building every morning on the way. So naturally I stopped when I observed the commotion. Lots of other people stopped."

"But lots of other people didn't want him dead," Brymmer said.

"But then who says that *I* did?"

"Ah," Brymmer said.

Leona sipped coffee and watched him for a while, obviously deciding he was one stupid jerk. She glanced at Corelli, then again looked at Clark. Measuring her enemies. Feeling pretty good.

"So how come I picked you from the crowd?" Brymmer said. "I just happen to pick someone out, say 'Leona'?"

"I imagine he must have had my picture in his files. Or on a dart board," she said.

"And why would he want to throw darts at you, Leona?"

374

"I suppose someone sues you for a few million dollars, kinda tends to turn you off."

"If they win," Brymmer said. "If they lose, what the hell."

"Good point," Corelli said. "But we're not even mentioning the blackmail attempt…"

Brymmer let it hang. She studied him, looking into stony green eyes. "You're fishing now," she said. "You're trying to figure out what I'll believe that you know."

"And you're trying to figure what I *actually* know. We could play twenty questions if you like," Brymmer said. "I'll even let you go first."

"No thanks."

Brymmer shrugged. "How's *Jeopardy*? The answer is fifty thousand bucks. What's the question?"

"I pass."

"You want a lawyer?" Brymmer said. "You can stop and call a lawyer."

Leona shook her head. "No. I think I've paid enough to lawyers in my life. I can handle this myself."

"Just in case," Brymmer said, and then passed her the paper with Miranda rights on it, "you'll want to look it over."

She glanced at it quickly. "That's fine. I understand."

"Good," Brymmer said. "What I know is, you asked him for fifty thousand dollars to stop posting libel."

"The other way around. He offered me fifty thousand dollars if I'd stop."

"Did he pay it?"

"No he didn't."

"Did you stop?"

"Yes I did."

"Why?"

"Because I did, that's all. It was time to move on.

And besides, it wasn't libel."

"Uh-huh. Suppose I told you your attempt was on tape. Your blackmail attempt."

"I'd say you were bluffing since it didn't ever happen. Would you play it for me?"

"No. Not now," Brymmer said. He rose. "I've got a meeting with the Captain right now. I'll be back." He walked out, leaving Clark and Corelli to continue fanning air while McAllister stood like a large and very ominous fly on the wall.

*9:25 AM:*

Brymmer found Ross who was huddling with Kerner. "Act two, scene five starts at—" Brymmer checked the clock— "high noon's looking good. I think Reggie makes the call."

"How goes it?" Kerner said.

"She anticipates. You tease, she moves three squares ahead. Also," Brymmer said, "she's prepared to call a bluff. She'll gamble. She's a liar. She's one of those liars who believes her own lies. Be interesting to see how she angles when she's caught. Meanwhile, we're building up her ego for the fall."

"You hope," Kerner said.

"Hey, look. I didn't say which *one* of us would fall."

*11:07 AM:*

Ross said to Nora, "Thanks for coming by." Today, she wore black. It made her look businesslike but also much paler. "I suppose when Kerner called you, he told you that we had a few pictures you should see."

"Actually," she said as he led her up the stairs, "he didn't say anything. He said he was calling for you and I should come."

"Well, we do," Ross said. "Have pictures you should see." He led her past the tightly closed door of the Green Room and took her to the viewing room, the room right behind it— the room with the monitors that now remained blank. The room had a much smaller table, two chairs, and a camera, newly mounted and angled just so to catch Nora where she'd sit. Ross sat across from her and handed her another of the large plastic binders, reminding her to just take her time with each shot.

He watched her as she leafed through another rogue's gallery of pederasts, murderers, drug pushers, thieves, each page netting nothing. Ross bit his lip. It was coming now. One, two, three more pages, then suddenly the gasp as she hit on the harsh bloody pictures of Harri— Harri with his throat slit and tethered to the bed.

"Yeah, I thought you'd recognize that one," Ross said. "There are more. Keep going."

"What *is* this?" Nora said, so pale he thought she'd faint. "Why... why am I seeing this?"

"I'll help you," Ross said. Moving over behind her, he revealed the next page— a double page spread with a closeup of the crotch and a closup of the face, eyes open, bloody mouth. "See?" he said, "this is where you plucked your souvenir, and this is where—"

She suddenly and violently threw up. All over the table, all over the book.

"Don't worry," Ross said. "We've got copies of the pix." He handed her a handkerchief. She studied it as though it were an alien object— uncertain of its name, let alone of its use. "You might want to wipe off your chin," he said helpfully.

She took it, robotically, and held it in her hand.

"We've got your fingerprints," he said, "where you

377

left them on the bedpost. We've also got Harri Kramer's blood in your car. That's the God's truth, Nora. We can take your confession or, you know, you have rights. You have the right to remain—"

"You fucking trapped me," she said. Not angry. Just stunned.

"Well I'd say you trapped yourself. If it's any consolation, we also got Todaro. That's the guy you identified."

She lifted dull eyes.

*11:28 AM:*

Leona had a fresh cup of coffee, different mug. Corelli and McAllister were gone. Clark was there since she'd apparently chosen him as resident goodguy, the eye to appeal to when everybody else was too stupid, too crude.

Brymmer, who'd come back within the last twenty minutes, was saying, "So you really got obsessed with this guy. The lawsuit. The website. The stalking."

"The *what*? Good God. I never stalked him. That's entirely absurd."

"Well," Clark said gently, "his brother says you did. And that Eric said if anything should happen, like what happened, the police should check you out."

"That's paranoid," she said. "And besides, it's just hearsay."

Brymmer looked at Clark and then slowly shook his head. "You believe that? She's also a lawyer," Brymmer said. "No, what I'm getting at," he said to Leona, "is you wanted your revenge. Almost biblically— right? An eye for an eye? A dick for a boob? Look," he said, "I really understand the way you'd feel. You're disfigured. And ugly. And it won't go away. You look at other

378

women, the women on the street, and you know you're not like them. You'll never be like them, you'll never be the same or like everybody else. It's humiliating, isn't it. Shameful. You hide it but you always know it's there. You hate to look in mirrors. You hate to look down when you're taking off your clothes. Because it's ugly and it's you, and you can't get away from it. A guy looks you over and you're already thinking, What happens when he sees me? Can I bear his disgust? You wanted a guy who'd go after pretty boobs and then—"

"Stop it! Just fucking stop it!" she said.

He shrugged. "I'm just saying why you'd want some revenge. Not only against Raven but maybe all the other guys who've throw you out of bed."

Her breathing came rapidly; she tried to slow it down. Took a long deep breath. "What I want," she said, "has nothing to do with what I did. Or in this case, didn't. And I didn't kill Raven."

Brymmer met her eyes. "Where were you, Leona, on the Wednesday afternoon of December thirty-first?"

It stopped her, but again she was calculating quickly. "I...I was getting my hair done, I think."

"You think?"

"I know."

"Good. You remember where the hairdo took place?"

"Yes. Guy Laval's."

"And you also remember a discussion you were part of?"

"It was just a discussion."

"Yeah?— I got six corpses say it wasn't."

"I repeat. I did not kill Eric Raven."

"Uh-huh. You told somebody else to do it, though. And when your contract was welshed on, you did the job yourself."

"What contract?" she said. "It was just a conversation. You haven't got anything to—"

"No?" Brymmer said. He slapped down a sealed plastic pouch on the table with a folded piece of pale green paper facing out and the number 13 written clearly, in a green-ink ballpoint, on the top.

Her mouth came open but nothing came out. She looked quickly up at Clark who was examining his nails.

"This is bullshit," she said. "It doesn't mean anything."

"This bullshit," Brymmer said, "has two sets of prints. The first set belongs to the woman you gave it to. The second set, I'd bet any money, would be yours. You want to bet on it, Leona? We'll check it with the prints you just left on that cup."

Leona grabbed the coffee cup and threw it at the wall where it shattered with a nice loud satisfying *smash!*

"Feel better?" Brymmer said. "Not that we couldn't take the prints off the shards but I'm talking about the first cup. The one you used before. It's already at the lab."

She wheeled on him. "Which still proves nothing whatsover. I did not kill Raven and it won't match any damn prints you might have found."

"Not even in McConnell's hotel room?" Brymmer said.

He'd seen that expression. He'd seen it on a man he'd once kicked in the balls and on a killer he'd confronted with the bloody broomstick that he'd rammed up his mother.

"We've got— how many witnesses?" Brymmer said to Clark.

"Three," Clark said.

"Three who can place you in the bar with McConnell and another in the elevator down from his floor."

"You couldn't possibly."

"No? Brown coat. Fur collar. Your face is still your face no matter how you do your hair." He signalled to Clark. "You want to show her something else?"

Clark rose silently and crossed to the monitor that sat against the wall— the monitor connected to the room behind The Room where Ross engaged Nora. Nora looking grim. No sound, just the picture as Nora moved her mouth.

"Look familiar?" Brymmer said. "That's the one you killed McConnell for. She told Detective Ross there she saw you draw his name. She recognized the number that she'd written on the top. She'll take you down with her, Leona. "

"She's lying."

"Uh-huh. Then how did your fingerprints get on his doorknob?"

"I didn't touch his doorknob. I was wearing—" She stopped.

"Gloves," Brymmer added, trying to be helpful. Then he said softly, "You have the right to remain silent. Anything you say can and will be used against you. You remember that part? Because before you shut up and decide to call a lawyer, let me tell you how it goes. You give us a little help and we try to return the favor. Bring it down a notch from Murder One to Murder Two. Who knows? You get lucky, you'll be out just in time to get social security. Medicare. Nice fat cushy old age."

"Then, too, we wouldn't charge you with Raven," Clark said. He looked across at Brymmer. "We could do that, couldn't we?"

Brymmer nodded yes. Clark killed the picture of Nora on the wall.

*11:39 AM:*

"Let me show you something, Nora." Ross brought a couple of the monitors to life. No sound, just picture, as Leona moved her mouth. "You see that woman? That woman's just telling us what happened New Year's Eve. New Year's Eve afternoon. In some beauty shop, she said. She says she wasn't part of it—"

"She was," Nora said.

"You'll identify her?"

"Yes."

"And you'll tell us, in your very own words, what went down? How the planning session went?"

"Yes."

"Because she already told us you were there. She identified your picture."

"Bitch," Nora said.

"Well...that's the trouble with conspiracies, you know. Two or more people get involved in a murder plot and someone rats you out. That's just the way it goes."

*11:43 AM:*

"You hungry?" Brymmer said. "We could get you a sandwich or a pizza, if you like."

"So you can brag that 'the condemned woman ate heartily,'? No thank you," Leona said.

"Well, see, if we didn't at least offer you a sandwich, you could call it brutality. You think we've been brutal?"

"I think you're a bunch of creeps."

"Just as long as you haven't got an ice pick," Brymmer said, "you can think whatever you want." He took another pull of his ninth cup of coffee, then scratched his itching jaw. "So what did you do with his penis,

382

Leona? That's your ticket to happy days. Women, I'm told, often live to be ninety. So you tell us, you can buy yourself thirty free years."

"I'm stuck," she said, "aren't I."

"It seems so," Brymmer said.

"I sent it to Guy Laval."

"Sent it?"

"By messenger."

"Jesus. *You sent McConnell's penis by messenger?*"

"Yes."

"To where?"

"To the address of his salon."

"And why'd you do that?"

"It was part of the agreement."

"And when was that agreed?"

"After Andrea came out. I mean from getting her hair cut. She said that it would prove that we'd really done the job."

"And how do you know that she was Andrea?" Brymmer said.

"Her picture was in the papers."

"Did she say Guy would keep it?"

"No. She didn't say."

Brymmer said to Clark, "Finish up here, okay?"

*1:18 PM:*

After looking at the warrant, Ramirez, the superintendant, let Brymmer and Ross into Levy's apartment, telling them to "just slam it good when you go." Now they stood restlessly in George's living room, examining the photographs of Audrey Hepburn and Marilyn Monroe.

Ross said, "You know she said she sent it to his office..."

383

Brymmer said, "A private collection like that—"

"A collection of privates," Ross interrupted.

"—you wouldn't just keep where anyone could find it. It's here," Brymmer said, and looked around vaguely and wondered where to start.

Ross said musingly, "If I were a penis, where would I be...?"

Brymmer looked across at him. "If you were a penis, you'd be standing with your head up a—"

"No," Ross said. "I mean the game we played as kids. Like, say, when you were seven and you couldn't find whatever it was you couldn't find, didn't your mother say to you, 'Now Burtie, before you go running around in circles sit quietly and think: If I were nerf ball, where would I be?'"

"No," Brymmer said.

"So if I were a penis awash in formaldehyde, where would I be?"

"In a jar," Brymmer said. "In a place where the cleaning lady wouldn't ever find me."

"In a closet," Ross said. "Or a cabinet."

"With a lock."

"So take the first bedroom and I'll take the second."

Brymmer was prowling through the innards of a closet when Ross called, "C'mere," and Brymmer found him leaning on the edge of a door frame and beckoning with a finger. They entered together. Brymmer looked around. It was one of those serious, elderly rooms, all gloom and mahogany. A massive table desk with green leather inlay bore a standing brass plaque that read *Cyrus Levy*, a remnant, perhaps, from some downtown office where Cyrus Levy must have been a big deal. Behind it, a cushioned green leather chair and across from it, a wallful of obviously custom-made mahogany book shelves, two of which were closed off with cabinet doors that stood along the length of their three upper shelves.

"Locked." Ross pointed at the empty brass key-holes.

Brymmer went immediately over to the desk and opened the top drawer.

"Key," Brymmer said, holding the thing up. It was fancy and brass—a skeleton key with a green silk tassle.

"Oo-kay," Ross said. "So which do you want first? The right one or the left?"

"What difference does it make? Whichever we pick first, it'll be in the second. If it is," Brymmer said.

"I feel lucky, don't you?"

Brymmer shot him a look and then opened the left cabinet.

Ross expelled a quick loudly audible whoosh.

Five large Mason jars were sitting in a row, each with a nice neat caligraphic label. *Clawson...Starrett...*

They stood for a moment in hard-eyed reverence.

"Well," Brymmer said.

"Well well," Ross agreed. "Peter Piper— I'd say— picked a peck of pickled peckers."

"You would," Brymmer said.

"What?"

"Say that."

He pulled out his cell phone and called for a wagon from the Crime Scene Unit.

*Report filed at 4:21 PM:*

FORM PD 313-081A
COMPLAINT FOLLOW UP    COMPLAINT: —00549
                                Homicide, Richard Clawson w/m

FILED BY:    Det. Reginald Kerner, Shield # 5329, MHTF

SUBJECT:    Bank info, George Levy, aka Guy Laval

At about 1300 hours, April 21, I presented a warrant to
the Chase Bank (1257 Lexington Ave, NYC 10128) to ex-
amine the records of above named subject, learning that
on Jan.11, this year, he received a direct electronic deposit from the United States Treasury in the notable sum of
$200,000.

I was able to ascertain that this deposit represented a (non-
taxable) "return of principal" on a 10-year Treasury Note.

On further warrant, by tracing the CUSIP number of the
note, I determined it was purchased and held to maturity
(Jan 11) in the name, and in the personal Treasury account,
of Richard Clawson. I was further informed that the interest and principal from unrenewed T-notes are automati-
cally deposited in the bank accounts of owners.

A further inquiry led me to understand that such treasury
accounts (Treasury Direct) can be managed online wherein, if proper passwords and codes are provided, the owner can change the instructions as to where such deposits
should be sent.

Alert readers may reach their own interesting conclusions.

Case open. Investigation continues.


*5:32PM:*

The green and white "patio" at Levy's salon was still
occupied by half a dozen put-together women, calmly
reading magazines or talking on their phones.

386

The receptionist/ cashier looked up with disapproval as Brymmer, saying nothing, and Ross, saying "Hi," strode past her objections and straight to the cutting room where Guy stood posing with a visionary look as he held high the strand of a slim brunette's hair and, with scissors in his right hand, said to her "I think we should—"

"Put down the scissors," Brymmer said flatly.

Guy Laval watched him through the filter of the mirror. Brymmer watched Guy. The woman turned around. Ross said, "Lady, you would likely like to leave." The woman looked from Ross to Brymmer to Ross and decided that she'd like to, though she wasn't sure why.

George Levy turned around.

"Now put down the scissors," Brymmer repeated. "Move away from the table."

George was deciding on an attitude to take, but he put down the scissors; he even moved away. He opened his mouth and said, "What—"

"Oh c'mon, George," Ross said impatiently. "I'm sure you know what," and Brymmer, approaching with the handcuffs dangling, said, "Now, George Levy or Guy Laval or whatever the fuck you call yourself, you're under arrest for the murder of Richard Clawson."

*5:37 PM:*

Corelli said to Felicia, "You're under arrest for the murder of Monty Starrett."

*5:41PM:*

Clark said to Andrea, "You're under arrest for the murder of David Tanner."

*7:26 PM:*

Brymmer phoned Raven and told him he was once again officially alive.

*8:37 PM:*

Parisi said to Brymmer, "Everybody booked?"

Brymmer just nodded.

"You realize how goddam lucky you are?"

Brymmer just nodded.

"You realize you didn't have a thing on Leona till you punked her into saying where the evidence was? She could've signed a confession, she could laugh it out of court."

"Uh-huh," Brymmer said.

"What I *mind*," Parisi said, "is that you're not even smug."

"I'm just tired," Brymmer said. "Tomorrow I'll be smug."

"Tomorrow's your RDO, am I right?"

"Three days," Brymmer said. "I've got three days off."

"Except for tomorrow. Press conference. Two PM sharp. City Hall. Wear your bar mitzvah suit and carry your tap shoes. To dance around questions. You follow what I mean?"

Brymmer just nodded.

*9:20 PM:*

Ross said to Brymmer, "You want to have a drink? Celebrate?"

Brymmer said, "No. I want to sleep."

# 90

*Wednesday, April 22nd:*

Ross didn't have to attend the damn conference. He wasn't, like Brymmer, forced to be present, though Brymmer, he knew (and he knew Brymmer knew) was required to be present to protect the brass ass. If the press had a problem, it was Brymmer who was slated now to serve as the lightning rod, the target for the heat-seeking missiles to seek. Ross had attended out of wry curiosity, standing at the back of the crowded auditorium to see how it was played.

The way it was played was, the Mayor took the credit. He acknowledged the Commissioner, who mentioned the Commander, who generously gave the nod to "the superlative detectives" who'd "worked day and night to finally put an end to the city's long nightmare." These included, not even in alphabetical order, Matson, Ritter and Poll, who'd originally caught the first three murders in the run and were therefore responsible for closing those cases, and "of course Sergeant Brymmer."

Brymmer, at that point, was looking out vaguely at the gathering of reporters and Ross saw him wink with a very slight smile that disappeared without a trace. Ross looked around in the direction of the wink where he spotted Jamie Rogers— like how could you miss her? that flaming red hair— and observed she was smiling like she knew it was for her, and Ross wished her well, wished both of them well, though he wondered if Brymmer had the heart or the guts or the sense to follow through.

The Mayor took the mike again, announcing there was time for a very few questions and called on a slavering fan from the *Times*. But the man from the

*Times* aimed his question at Brymmer: "Exactly what happened on Central Park West?"

"Nothing," Brymmer said.

"The story was, a Dr. Raven had been killed."

"Whose story?" Brymmer said. "Not mine or the department's."

"Then what were you doing there? Setting up the press?"

"The *press*?" Brymmer said. "It seems to me the press was setting up itself. You saw a few cop cars, an ambulance, some tape and went leaping to conclusions. Didn't you?"

"I'd like to ask a follow-up question."

"Go ahead," Brymmer said.

"Was anybody killed or was it some kind of sting?"

"I'd say you should've asked that at the time," Brymmer said. "What's the old saying? 'Death, where is thy sting?' I guess you should've contemplated, 'Sting, where is thy death?' There wasn't any death."

"Does that mean it was a sting?"

"We got a tip," Brymmer said. "Someone anonymously called nine-one-one. Someone at the scene went overboard. I really couldn't tell you any more. It's under investigation."

"Then why didn't anybody tell us that before?"

"You mean me," Brymmer said. "Because I never answer questions that haven't been asked and I sometimes never answer any questions that have. Not when I think they're gonna jeopardize a case. And that's the end of this subject.—Anybody else?"

Ross watched the Mayor who wasn't very pleased that Brymmer'd taken over. He also watched Parisi who looked as though he'd just dodged a battery of fire since Parisi had given his permission for the op and Brymmer had deflected it. Skillfully, in fact.

Ronan from the *News* wanted eagerly to know if Andrea Clawson hadn't really murdered Richard but had murdered someone else.

Brymmer shook his head. "What Andrea did or else didn't," Brymmer said, "is up to a jury. We filed our complaint; the D.A. has arraigned her. I assume if you're asking that, the record has been sealed. And I think further questions should go back to the Mayor."

Brymmer turned abruptly and faded from the mike which the Mayor grabbed hungrily and blah blah blah.

Ross had left quietly and headed off for home.

Brymmer took a shower. Long. Hot. Letting the water beat down on his shoulders, forcing the tension in his muscles to relent. Afterwards, he grabbed for a terry cloth robe, went into the bedroom and plucked a CD from the shelf above the dresser, Pablo Casals playing Brandenburg Concertos, and shoved it in the Mac. Then he drew the blinds against the afternoon sunshine and settled on the bed. No whiskey, no pills. He was boarding the sleep train completely on his own, heading for a needed vacation in oblivion. The music consoled him, presenting once again that illusion of order, the necessary myth that the heart of things would hold, that questions had answers, that stories had ends, when he knew all along that reality was entropy—the tendency of structures to devolve into utterly meaningless chaos, that the phone could start ringing, that a corpse without a head could be discovered in a trunk, that the rotting remains of a six-week-old baby could be waiting in a dumpster....

---

The telephone rang. He woke like a diver hitting surface too fast, head roaring, heart pounding. The night table clock told him twenty after six. AM or PM? He picked up the telephone and mumbled something at it.

A woman's voice was saying to him, "Sergeant? You don't know me but my name's Sally Davis..." (PM, he saw) "and I live across the hall from your partner. Steve?"

"What happened?" Brymmer said. He was now sitting up.

There was silence; a quick sharp intake of breath. "I just think it would be good you got over here fast. Don't call him, just come."

"Twenty minutes," Brymmer said.

The woman who was standing in the second floor corridor when Brymmer arrived looked competent, shaken and calmly terrified which wasn't, Brymmer thought, a contradiction in terms. She conveyed the impression that something monumentally bad was going down but she was strong enough to meet it.

"What?" Brymmer said.

"He was right outside playing baseball with my son. Jimmy said Kathy had been watching from the window. She was cheering them on. Smiling, Jimmy said."

"And?"

Sally Davis looked up, shook her head. "Go in," she said, pointing off at Ross's apartment. "The door isn't locked."

Brymmer opened it slowly. From somewhere in the distance, he could hear Ross singing. Softly. Oddly. Slightly off key.

"God rest ye, merry gentlemen..."

He moved through the foyer.

"Let nothing ye dismay.
Remember Christ, our sa-a-vior..."

He got to the living room and took it in at once. Ross in a sweatshirt and jeans on the sofa, a cigarette smoking by itself in his hand and a piece of green note paper crumpled in the other. Billy, in his chair, was shot once in the head; Kathy, in the heart. She was lying on the floor with the Glock in her hand.

Ross said quietly, "I did this, you know. You think Christ will save me?"

Brymmer sat next to him. "Jesus loves a sinner," Brymmer said. "So I'm told."

"I was right downstairs. Right below the window. On the lawn," Ross said. "She was watching us a while. Then she pulled down the blinds. I wasn't paying attention. She did it pretty fast. Bang-bang. I ran. They were dead when I arrived."

Brymmer took the cigarette out of Ross's hand and stubbed it out in an ashtray.

"I just didn't pay enough attention," Ross said. "She was killing herself slowly and I didn't pay attention. All the pointers were there. Everything. Psychology One-oh-one."

"And what could you have done?"

"I don't know. But something."

"Have her committed? That's tough in New York. She wouldn't go voluntarily. You'd've had to arrest her."

"Okay. Then I should've."

"That's easier said."

"I am—" Ross lamented, "a selfish son of a bitch."

"True," Brymmer said. "But it's hard to pull back and be entirely objective when you're in it to your neck.

And it's hard to take action when you're stuck with reacting. You get caught up in moments."

"I imagine that's profound."

"It's bullshit," Brymmer said. "Anything that anybody says now is bullshit. And that includes you." He gestured at the paper that was still in Ross's hand. "Would you want to let me see it?"

"I was planning to eat it. I'm serious. That way I'd have it inside me. I'd digest it. Little bits of it would scatter in my cells. Here. I think the line would be 'Read it and weep.'"

Under the inscription, "Le Salon de Laval," Kathy had written, *I did this for you. I couldn't give you a son but I can give you a life.*

"Would you believe it?" Ross said, and the tears were coming now. "I brought the fucking pad home from George's salon. It had a death germ on it."

Brymmer said nothing; just let Ross cry, not watching him, giving him the present of privacy. Some of Billy's brains had been spattered on his chair. Kathy's eyes were wide open.

Brymmer said, "You're sleeping on my sofa tonight."

Ross shook his head. "No. Staying here."

"Bad move," Brymmer said.

"No. This is right. I need to listen to the ghosts. I need to be close to them. Really. I'll be fine."

"Where's your gun?"

"Are you blind?"

"The other one."

"You think I'm gonna shoot myself?"

"No. Not really. On the other hand, I'd rather be wrong about you-would than wrong about you-wouldn't."

"In the closet. On a shelf. In a locker."

394

"Okay."

Sally Davis made a tentative appearance from the hall. "I don't want to interrupt but is there something I can do?"

"Yeah," Brymmer said. "Get Steve the hell out of here. Give him what he needs. Enough whiskey to drown in or a bed to lie down in or a wall to beat his head on, but get him the hell out. Steve, that's an order. And I swear, I have to cuff you to Sally, I'll do it."

Sally walked up to him and held out her hand. Ross said, "I'm capable of standing by myself." He rose, but then stumbled. Sally took his arm.

Brymmer waited till they left. Then he sat for a moment. Then he phoned it in.

## 91

*Thursday, April 23rd:*

*New York Post, page 1:*

# JACKIE CASE CRACKED!
## BEAUTY SHOP SWAP
## ENDS IN ARRESTS

*New York Daily News, page 1:*

## FIVE ARRESTED IN "JACKIE" KILLINGS
### SOCIALITE, MODEL AMONG ALLEGED PERPS

*New York Newsday, page 1:*

## POLICE ROUND UP "JACKIE" SUSPECTS
### "NIGHTMARE OVER," MAYOR SAYS

*New York Times, page 17:*

### A.C.L.U TO PROBE POLICE PLOYS
#### ASKS IF ENDS JUSTIFY MEANS

"How are you?"

"Alive," Ross said. "I suppose I should thank you but I'm not sure I will."

"Ah, but some morning, on observing the God-given glories of the sunrise and the fragrance of the dew…"

Ross laughed. He was red-eyed and hunched in Brymmer's wing chair; his hand on the coffee cup was not very steady. "Can you do me another favor?"

"Probably," Brymmer said. He was bathrobed and barefoot and sprawling on the couch.

"I need to get a long leave of absence."

"How long?"

"Six months?"

Brymmer nodded. "Okay. What's the plan?"

"Oklahoma."

"Sounds radical enough. I'll bite. What's the plan in Oklahoma?"

"I grew up there."

"I know."

"Got an uncle's got a farm that can always use a hand and I thought I'd just maybe like to do that for a while. Feed pigs. Bale hay. Eat fat. See stars. I could even go to church, see what Jesus has to say. What I need," Ross said, "is a vacation in America. The actual America. The one I grew up in. I need a little head-time away from this godforsaken soul-sucking hole so I can see what I want to do. So that's what I want to do. Figure out what I want to do. Does that make a little sense?"

Brymmer nodded. "Just never let go of your apartment. You quit that apartment and you're never coming back. Not unless you want to be a hedge fund manager, sell coke, be a pimp. You should try to sublet it."

"Yeah. Sally said she'd take care of that for me. I want to leave now."

"So," Brymmer said.

"So," Ross said. "Funeral's tomorrow."

"Don't worry. I'll be there."

"They're expecting it to rain."

"Does it matter?" Brymmer said.

———

"Burt?"

"I've been wanting to call you, you know? I've just—"

"I know. I got the story on the feed. Oh Burt, I'm so sorry."

"Yeah. Well."

"Is there something I can do?"

"No. He's with a friend."

"What I meant was, for you."

"Oh. Me. Well then. You owe me a dinner, I suppose, or the other way around except I can't tell you when. I've got the funeral tomorrow. And I just made a pitch for vacation after that. I've got a couple of weeks."

"So where are you going?"

"Shit. I don't know. You want to come with me?"

"Yes."

"Okay. But we'll have dinner first. I'll call you."

"Good."

"Listen...."

"...What?"

"Nothing. Forget it."

"Never mind. I know."

"What?"

"You love me."

"More than you know."

"Good."

"I'll call you when I get back from Steve's."

"Listen..."

"What?"

"Take care of yourself, will you?"

"Yes. And you."